"No character was ever thrown into such strange relief as Gilliatt… here, indeed, the true position of man in the universe."
—Robert Louis Stevenson

*T**HE TOILERS OF THE SEA* tells the fairytale-esque story of Gilliatt, an outcast fisherman who must rescue an engine from a wrecked steamship. If successful, he will win the hand of the shipowner's beautiful daughter, Déruchette. He will brave the harsh rocks, the freezing waves, and even the grasp of a sea monster to prove his worth.

A richly detailed study of early nineteenth-century Guernsey, *The Toilers of the Sea* is the oft-forgotten novel that completes a trilogy with Hugo's famed *The Hunchback of Notre Dame* and *Les Misérables.* It is a tribute to the drama of nature and the insignificance of man against it, to solitude in exile, and the light we choose to carry in the darkness.

Victor Hugo (1802-1885) was born in Besançon, France on February 26, 1802. Originally on track to become a lawyer, he instead became France's revered Romantic poet, novelist, and dramatist. He is the author of *The Hunchback of Notre Dame* and *Les Misérables*, among countless others. For fifteen years, Hugo lived on the island of Guernsey in political exile following the 1851 coup d'état by Napoleon III. There he wrote *The Toilers of the Sea*, published in 1866. When Hugo died in 1885, he was given a national funeral and burial in Paris' Pantheon.

William Moy Thomas (1828–1910) was an English journalist, literary editor, translator, and author of *When the Snow Falls* (1859), *Pictures in a Mirror* (1861), and *A Guild Clerk's Tale* (1895) among others.

In conversation with

Andrew Chater is a broadcaster, storyteller and cultural explorer. The winner of six BAFTA awards for his history programming in the UK, he now lectures in History and Literature at the University of Southern California, Los Angeles, where he leads students on a series of classes exploring regional cultures through the medium of classic and contemporary fiction, a format he calls "bookpacking" (www.bookpackers.com).

Maya Weeks is a geographer, writer, and artist from rural California working on feminist environmental justice. A first-generation college student, she holds her B.A. in Language Studies (Spanish) from the University of California in Santa Cruz and her M.F.A. in Creative Writing (Poetry) from Mills College. She earned her Ph.D. in Geography at the University of California in Davis, where she wrote her dissertation on marine pollution, gender, and feminist political economy using qualitative and creative methods. Recent poetry has been published in *Space on Space* and recent nonfiction has been published in *Zócalo Public Square*. A record, Tethers, is out on Full Spectrum Records. She has exhibited at Vague Research Studios and performed at Historical Materialism. She is the author of a poetry chapbook, *How to Be on the Outside of Every Inside/How to Be Inside Every Outside* (these signals press, 2016). Residencies include Konstepidemin, The Arctic Circle, Mustarinda, Norton Island, and more. Maya lives and works on unceded Chumash land.

Dear Reader,

Smith & Taylor Classics seeks to uncover forgotten works, unearth gems, and unite contemporary voices in conversation. We hope to capture the first thrill of discovery and the urgent quest to forge community around an author who has left behind something unexpectedly resonant even to this day.

At the end of this volume, you will find a conversation between readers brought together by the very book you now hold in your hand. You may engage with it however you wish—before you begin, after you've finished, or anytime in-between. Consider us a part of your new favorite book club.

Sincerely,
The Editors

Allison Miriam Smith & Brandon Taylor

Smith & Taylor Classics

Twilight Sleep
The Odd Women
The Country of the Pointed Firs
The Toilers of the Sea

The Toilers of the Sea

Victor Hugo

✷

Translated by W. Moy Thomas

SMITH & TAYLOR CLASSICS

A SMITH & TAYLOR BOOK

©2024 Smith & Taylor Classics
Conversation ©2024 Andrew Chater and Maya Weeks

Originally published in English by Sampson Low, Son, & Marston, 1866
Now in the public domain.

Learn more at www.unnamedpress.com.

LCCN: 2024944786
Paperback ISBN-13: 9781961884281
eBook ISBN-13: 9781961884298

Published in North America by Unnamed Press
Printed by Sheridan in the United States of America

Cover design and typeset by Jaya Nicely
Set in Adobe Caslon Pro and Bembo Std

Edited by Allison Miriam Smith & Brandon Taylor
Editorial Assistance and Publicity by Cassidy Kuhle
Copyedited by Nancy Tan
Published by Chris Heiser
Distributed by Publishers Group West

Photograph, *Victor Hugo on the Rock of the Exiles*, Guernsey circa 1853

Smith & Taylor Classics
An Imprint of Unnamed Press
First Edition

Contents

I DEDICATE THIS BOOK
TO THE
ROCK OF HOSPITALITY AND LIBERTY
TO THAT PORTION OF OLD NORMAN GROUND
INHABITED BY
THE NOBLE LITTLE NATION OF THE SEA
TO THE ISLAND OF GUERNSEY
SEVERE YET KIND, MY PRESENT ASYLUM
PERHAPS MY TOMB.

PREFACE

Religion, Society, and Nature! these are the three struggles of man. They constitute at the same time his three needs. He has need of a faith; hence the temple. He must create; hence the city. He must live; hence the plough and the ship. But these three solutions comprise three perpetual conflicts. The mysterious difficulty of life results from all three. Man strives with obstacles under the form of superstition, under the form of prejudice, and under the form of the elements. A triple ἀναγκη weighs upon us. There is the fatality of dogmas, the oppression of human laws, the inexorability of nature. In *Notre Dame de Paris* the author denounced the first; in the *Misérables* he exemplified the second; in this book he indicates the third. With these three fatalities mingles that inward fatality—the supreme ἀναγκη, the human heart.

HAUTEVILLE HOUSE,
March, 1866.

The Toilers of the Sea

Part I

Sieur Clubin

Book I
The History of a Bad Reputation

*

I
A WORD WRITTEN ON A WHITE PAGE

CHRISTMAS DAY in the year 182— was somewhat remarkable in the island of Guernsey. Snow fell on that day. In the Channel Islands a frosty winter is uncommon, and a fall of snow is an event.

On that Christmas morning, the road which skirts the seashore from St. Peter's Port to the Vale was clothed in white. From midnight till the break of day the snow had been falling. Towards nine o'clock, a little after the rising of the wintry sun, as it was too early yet for the Church of England folks to go to St. Sampson's, or for the Wesleyans to repair to Eldad Chapel, the road was almost deserted. Throughout that portion of the highway which separates the first from the second tower, only three foot-passengers could be seen. These were a child, a man, and a woman. Walking at a distance from each other, these wayfarers had no visible connection. The child, a boy of about eight years old, had stopped, and was looking curiously at the wintry scene. The man walked behind the woman, at a distance of about a hundred paces. Like her he was coming from the direction of the church of St. Sampson. The appearance of the man, who was still young, was something between that of a workman and a sailor. He wore his working-day clothes—a kind of Guernsey shirt of coarse brown stuff, and trousers partly concealed by tarpaulin leggings—a costume which seemed to indicate that, notwithstanding the holy day, he was going to no place of worship. His heavy shoes of rough leather, with their soles covered with large nails, left upon the snow, as he walked, a print more like that of a prison lock than the foot of a man. The woman, on the contrary, was evidently dressed for church. She wore a large mantle of black silk, wadded, under which she had coquettishly adjusted a dress of Irish poplin, trimmed alternately with white and pink; but for her red stockings, she might have been taken for a Parisian. She walked on with a light and free step, so little suggestive of the burden of life that it might easily be seen that she was young. Her movements possessed that subtle grace which indicates the most delicate of all transitions—that soft intermingling, as it were, of two twilights—the passage from the condition of a child to that of womanhood. The man seemed to take no heed of her.

Suddenly, near a group of oaks at the corner of a field, and at the spot called the Basses Maisons, she turned, and the movement seemed to attract the attention of the man. She stopped, seemed to reflect a moment, then stooped, and the man fancied that he could discern that she was tracing with her finger some letters in the snow. Then she rose again, went on her way at a quicker pace, turned once more, this time smiling, and disappeared to the left of the roadway, by the footpath under the hedges which leads to the Ivy Castle. When she had turned for the second time, the man had recognised her as Déruchette, a charming girl of that neighbourhood.

The man felt no need of quickening his pace; and some minutes later he found himself near the group of oaks. Already he had ceased to think of the vanished Déruchette; and if, at that moment, a porpoise had appeared above the water, or a robin had caught his eye in the hedges, it is probable that he would have passed on his way. But it happened that his eyes were fixed upon the ground; his gaze fell mechanically upon the spot where the girl had stopped. Two little footprints were there plainly visible; and beside them he read this word, evidently written by her in the snow—

"GILLIATT."

It was his own name.

He lingered for awhile motionless, looking at the letters, the little footprints, and the snow; and then walked on, evidently in a thoughtful mood.

II
THE BÛ DE LA RUE

GILLIATT LIVED IN the parish of St. Sampson. He was not liked by his neighbours; and there were reasons for that fact.

To begin with, he lived in a queer kind of "haunted" dwelling. In the islands of Jersey and Guernsey, sometimes in the country, but often in streets with many inhabitants, you will come upon a house the entrance to which is completely barricaded. Holly bushes obstruct the doorway, hideous boards, with nails, conceal the windows below; while the casements of the upper stories are neither closed nor open: for all the window-frames are barred, but the glass is broken. If there is a little yard, grass grows between its stones; and the parapet of its wall is crumbling away. If there is a garden, it is choked with nettles, brambles, and hemlock, and strange insects abound in it. The chimneys are cracked, the roof is falling in; so much as can be seen from without of the rooms presents a dismantled appearance. The woodwork is rotten; the stone mildewed. The paper of the walls has dropped away and hangs loose, until it presents a history of the bygone fashions of paper-hangings—the scrawling patterns of the time of the Empire, the crescent-shaped draperies of the Directory, the balustrades and pillars of the days of Louis XVI. The thick draperies of cobwebs, filled with flies, indicate the quiet reign long enjoyed by innumerable spiders. Sometimes a broken jug may be noticed on a shelf. Such houses are considered to be haunted. Satan is popularly believed to visit them by night. Houses are like the human beings who inhabit them. They become to their former selves what the corpse is to the living body. A superstitious belief among the people is sufficient to reduce them to this state of death. Then their aspect is terrible. These ghostly houses are common in the Channel Islands.

The rural and maritime populations are easily moved with notions of the active agency of the powers of evil. Among the Channel Isles, and on the neighbouring coast of France, the ideas of the people on this subject are deeply rooted. In their view, Beelzebub has his ministers in all parts of the earth. It is certain that Belphegor is the ambassador from the infernal regions in France, Hutgin in Italy, Belial in Turkey, Thamuz in Spain, Martinet in Switzerland, and Mammon in England. Satan is an Emperor just like any other: a sort of Satan Cæsar. His establishment is well organised. Dagon is grand almoner, Succor Benoth chief of the Eunuchs; Asmodeus, banker at the gaming-table; Kobal, manager of the theatre, and Verdelet, grand-master of the ceremonies. Nybbas is the court-fool; Wierus, a savant, a good strygologue, and a man of much learning in demonology, calls Nybbas the great parodist.

The Norman fishermen, who frequent the Channel, have many precautions to take at sea, by reason of the illusions with which Satan environs them. It has long been an article of popular faith, that Saint Maclou inhabited the great square rock called Ortach, in the sea between Aurigny and the Casquets; and many old sailors used to declare that they had often seen him there, seated and reading in a book. Accordingly the sailors, as they passed, were in the habit of kneeling many times before the Ortach rock, until the day when the fable was destroyed, and the truth took its place. For it has been discovered, and is now well established, that the lonely inhabitant of the rock is not a saint, but a devil. This evil spirit, whose name is Jochmus, had the impudence to pass himself off, for many centuries, as Saint Maclou. Even the Church herself is not proof against snares of this kind. The demons Raguhel, Oribel, and Tobiel, were regarded as saints until the year 745; when Pope Zachary, having at length exposed them, turned them out of saintly company. This sort of weeding of the saintly calendar is certainly very useful; but it can only be practised by very accomplished judges of devils and their ways.

The old inhabitants of these parts relate—though all this refers to bygone times—that the Catholic population of the Norman Archipelago was once, though quite involuntarily, even in more intimate correspondence with the powers of darkness than the Huguenots themselves. How this happened, however, we do not pretend to say; but it is certain that the people suffered considerable annoyance from this cause. It appears that Satan had taken a fancy to the Catholics, and sought their company a good deal; a circumstance which has given rise to the belief that the devil is more Catholic than Protestant. One of his most insufferable familiarities consisted in paying nocturnal visits to married Catholics in bed, just at the moment when the husband had fallen fast asleep, and the wife had begun to doze; a fruitful source of domestic trouble. Patouillet was of opinion that a faithful biography of Voltaire ought not to be without some allusion to this practice of the evil one. The truth of all this is perfectly well known, and described in the forms of excommunication in the rubric *de erroribus nocturnis et de semine diabolorum*. The practice was raging particularly at St. Helier's towards the end of the last century, probably as a punishment for the Revolution; for the evil consequences of revolutionary excesses are incalculable. However this may have been, it is certain that this possibility of a visit from the demon at night, when it is impossible to see distinctly, or even in slumber, caused much embarrassment among orthodox dames. The idea of giving to the world a Voltaire was by no means a pleasant one. One of these, in some anxiety, consulted her confessor on this extremely difficult subject, and the best mode for timely discovery of the cheat. The confessor replied, "In order to be sure that it is your husband by your side, and not a demon, place your hand upon his head. If you find horns, you may be sure there is something wrong." But this test was far from satisfactory to the worthy dame.

Gilliatt's house had been haunted, but it was no longer in that condition; it was for that reason, however, only regarded with more suspicion. No one learned in demonology can be unaware of the fact that, when a sorcerer has installed himself in a haunted dwelling, the devil considers the house sufficiently occupied, and is polite enough to abstain from visiting there, unless called in, like the doctor, on some special occasion.

This house was known by the name of the Bû de la Rue. It was situated at the extremity of a little promontory, rather of rock than of land, forming a small harbourage apart in the creek of Houmet Paradis. The water at this spot is deep. The house stood quite alone upon the point, almost separated from the island, and with just sufficient ground about it for a small garden, which was sometimes inundated by the high tides. Between the port of St. Sampson and the creek of Houmet Paradis, rises a steep hill, surmounted by the block of towers covered with ivy, and known as Vale Castle, or the Château de l'Archange; so that, at St. Sampson, the Bû de la Rue was shut out from sight.

Nothing is commoner than sorcerers in Guernsey. They exercise their profession in certain parishes, in profound indifference to the enlightenment of the nineteenth century. Some of their practices are downright criminal. They set gold boiling, they gather herbs at midnight, they cast sinister looks upon the people's cattle. When the people consult them they send for bottles containing "water of the sick," and they are heard to mutter mysteriously, "the water has a sad look." In March, 1857, one of them discovered, in water of this kind, seven demons. They are universally feared. Another only lately bewitched a baker "as well as his oven." Another had the diabolical wickedness to wafer and seal up envelopes "containing nothing inside."

Another went so far as to have on a shelf three bottles labelled "B." These monstrous facts are well authenticated. Some of these sorcerers are obliging, and for two or three guineas will take on themselves the complaint from which you are suffering. Then they are seen to roll upon their beds, and to groan with pain; and while they are in these agonies the believer exclaims, "There! I am well again." Others cure all kinds of diseases, by merely tying a handkerchief round the patient's loins, a remedy so simple that it is astonishing that no one had yet thought of it. In the last century, the Cour Royale of Guernsey bound such folks upon a heap of fagots and burnt them alive. In these days it condemns them to eight weeks' imprisonment; four weeks on bread and water, and the remainder of the term in solitary confinement. *Amant alterna catenæ.*

The last instance of burning sorcerers in Guernsey took place in 1747. The city authorities devoted one of its squares, the Carrefour du Bordage, to that ceremony. Between 1565 and 1700, eleven sorcerers thus suffered at this spot. As a rule the criminals made confession of their guilt. Torture was used to assist their confession. The Carrefour du Bordage has indeed rendered many other services to society and religion. It was here that heretics were brought to the stake. Under Queen Mary, among other Huguenots burnt here, were a mother and two daughters. The name of this mother was Perrotine Massy. One of the daughters was *enceinte*, and was delivered of a child even in the midst of the flames. As the old chronicle expresses it, "*Son ventre éclata.*" The new-born infant rolled out of the fiery furnace. A man named House took it in his arms; but Helier Gosselin the bailli, like a good Catholic as he was, sternly commanded the child to be cast again into the fire.

III
FOR YOUR WIFE: WHEN YOU MARRY

WE MUST return to Gilliatt.

The country people told how, towards the close of the great Revolution, a woman, bringing with her a little child, came to live in Guernsey. She

was English, or perhaps French. She had a name which the Guernsey pronunciation and the country folks' bad spelling had finally converted into
"Gilliatt." She lived alone with the child, which, according to some, was a
nephew; according to others, a son or grandson; according to others, again,
a strange child whom she was protecting. She had some means; enough to
struggle on in a poor way. She had purchased a small plot of ground at La
Sergentée, and another at La Roque Crespel, near Rocquaine. The house of
the Bû de la Rue was haunted at this period. For more than thirty years no
one had inhabited it. It was falling into ruins. The garden, so often invaded
by the sea, could produce nothing. Besides noises and lights seen there at
night-time, the house had this mysterious peculiarity: any one who should
leave there in the evening, upon the mantelpiece, a ball of worsted, a few
needles, and a plate filled with soup, would assuredly find, in the morning,
the soup consumed, the plate empty, and a pair of mittens ready knitted.
The house, demon included, was offered for sale for a few pounds sterling.
The stranger woman became the purchaser, evidently tempted by the devil,
or by the advantageous bargain.

She did more than purchase the house; she took up her abode there
with the child; and from that moment peace reigned within its walls. The
Bû de la Rue has found a fit tenant, said the country people. The haunting
ceased. There was no longer any light seen there, save that of the tallow
candle of the new comer. "Witch's candle is as good as devil's torch." The
proverb satisfied the gossips of the neighbourhood.

The woman cultivated some acres of land which belonged to her. She
had a good cow, of the sort which produces yellow butter. She gathered her
white beans, cauliflowers, and "Golden drop" potatoes. She sold, like other
people, her parsnips by the tonneau, her onions by the hundred, and her
beans by the denerel. She did not go herself to market, but disposed of her
crops through the agency of Guilbert Falliot, at the sign of the Abreveurs of
St. Sampson. The register of Falliot bears evidence that Falliot sold for her,
on one occasion, as much as twelve bushels of rare early potatoes.

The house had been meanly repaired; but sufficiently to make it habitable. It was only in very bad weather that the rain-drops found their way
through the ceilings of the rooms. The interior consisted of a ground-floor
suite of rooms, and a granary overhead. The ground-floor was divided into

three rooms; two for sleeping, and one for meals. A ladder connected it with
the granary above. The woman attended to the kitchen and taught the child
to read. She did not go to church or chapel, which, all things considered, led
to the conclusion that she must be French not to go to a place of worship.
The circumstance was grave. In short, the new comers were a puzzle to the
neighbourhood.

That the woman was French seemed probable. Volcanoes cast forth
stones, and revolutions men, so families are removed to distant places;
human beings come to pass their lives far from their native homes; groups
of relatives and friends disperse and decay; strange people fall, as it were,
from the clouds—some in Germany, some in England, some in America.
The people of the country view them with surprise and curiosity. Whence
come these strange faces? Yonder mountain, smoking with revolutionary
fires, casts them out. These barren aërolites, these famished and ruined people, these footballs of destiny, are known as refugees, émigrés, adventurers.
If they sojourn among strangers, they are tolerated; if they depart, there
is a feeling of relief. Sometimes these wanderers are harmless, inoffensive
people, strangers—at least, as regards the women—to the events which have
led to their exile, objects of persecution, helpless and astonished at their
fate. They take root again somewhere as they can. They have done no harm
to any one, and scarcely comprehend the destiny that has befallen them.
So thus I have seen a poor tuft of grass uprooted and carried away by the
explosion of a mine. No great explosion was ever followed by more of such
strays than the first French Revolution.

The strange woman whom the Guernsey folks called "Gilliatt" was,
possibly, one of these human strays.

The woman grew older; the child became a youth. They lived alone and
avoided by all; but they were sufficient for each other. *Louve et louveteau se
pourlèchent.* This was another of the generous proverbs which the neighbourhood applied to them. Meanwhile, the youth grew to manhood; and
then, as the old and withered bark falls from the tree, the mother died.
She left to her son the little field of Sergentée, the small property called
La Roque Crespel, and the house known as the Bû de la Rue; with the
addition, as the official inventory said, of "one hundred guineas in gold in
the *pid d'une cauche*," that is to say, in the foot of a stocking. The house was

already sufficiently furnished with two oaken chests, two beds, six chairs and a table, besides necessary household utensils. Upon a shelf were some books, and in the corner a trunk, by no means of a mysterious character, which had to be opened for the inventory. This trunk was of drab leather, ornamented with brass nails and little stars of white metal, and it contained a bride's outfit, new and complete, of beautiful Dunkirk linen—chemises and petticoats, and some silk dresses—with a paper on which was written, in the handwriting of the deceased,—

"For your wife: when you marry."

The loss of his mother was a terrible blow for the young man. His disposition had always been unsociable; he became now moody and sullen. The solitude around him was complete. Hitherto it had been mere isolation; now his life was a blank. While we have only one companion, life is endurable; left alone, it seems as if it is impossible to struggle on, and we fall back in the race, which is the first sign of despair. As time rolls on, however, we discover that duty is a series of compromises; we contemplate life, regard its end, and submit; but it is a submission which makes the heart bleed.

Gilliatt was young; and his wound healed with time. At that age sorrows cannot be lasting. His sadness, disappearing by slow degrees, seemed to mingle itself with the scenes around him, to draw him more and more towards the face of nature, and further and further from the need of social converse; and, finally, to assimilate his spirit more completely to the solitude in which he lived.

IV
AN UNPOPULAR MAN

GILLIATT, as we have said, was not popular in the parish. Nothing could be more natural than that antipathy among his neighbours. The reasons for it were abundant. To begin with, as we have already explained, there was the strange house he lived in; then there was his mysterious origin. Who could that woman have been? and what was the meaning of this child? Country people do not like mysteries, when they relate to strange sojourners among them. Then his clothes were the clothes of a workman, while he had, although certainly not rich, sufficient to live without labour. Then there was his garden, which he succeeded in cultivating, and from which he produced crops of potatoes, in spite of the stormy equinoxes; and then there were the big books which he kept upon a shelf, and read from time to time.

More reasons: why did he live that solitary life? The Bû de la Rue was a kind of lazaretto, in which Gilliatt was kept in a sort of moral quarantine. This, in the popular judgment, made it quite simple that people should be astonished at his isolation, and should hold him responsible for the solitude which society had made around his home.

He never went to chapel. He often went out at night-time. He held converse with sorcerers. He had been seen, on one occasion, sitting on the grass with an expression of astonishment on his features. He haunted the druidical stones of the Ancresse, and the fairy caverns which are scattered about in that part. It was generally believed that he had been seen politely saluting the Roque qui Chante, or Crowing Rock. He bought all birds which people brought to him, and having bought them, set them at liberty. He was civil to the worthy folks in the streets of St. Sampson, but willingly turned out of his way to avoid them if he could. He often went out on fishing expeditions, and always returned with fish. He trimmed his garden on Sundays. He had a bagpipe which he had bought from one of the Highland soldiers who are sometimes in Guernsey, and on which he played occasionally at twilight, on the rocks by the seashore. He had been seen to make strange gestures, like those of one sowing seeds. What kind of treatment could be expected for a man like that?

As regards the books left by the deceased woman, which he was in the habit of reading, the neighbours were particularly suspicious. The Reverend Jaquemin Hérode, rector of St. Sampson, when he visited the house at the time of the woman's funeral, had read on the backs of these books the titles *Rosier's Dictionary*, *Candide*, by Voltaire, *Advice to the People on Health*, by Tissot. A French noble, an émigré, who had retired to St. Sampson, remarked that this Tissot, "must have been the Tissot who carried the head of the Princess de Lamballe upon a pike."

The Reverend gentleman had also remarked upon one of these books, the highly fantastic and terribly significant title, *De Rhubarbaro*.

In justice to Gilliatt, however, it must be added that this volume being in Latin—a language which it is doubtful if he understood—the young man had possibly never read it.

But it is just those books which a man possesses, but does not read, which constitute the most suspicious evidence against him. The Spanish Inquisition have deliberated on that point, and have come to a conclusion which places the matter beyond further doubt.

The book in question, however, was no other than the treatise of Doctor Tilingius upon the rhubarb plant, published in Germany in 1679.

It was by no means certain that Gilliatt did not prepare philters and unholy decoctions. He was undoubtedly in possession of certain phials.

Why did he walk abroad at evening, and sometimes even at midnight, on the cliffs? Evidently to hold converse with the evil spirits who, by night, frequent the seashores, enveloped in smoke.

On one occasion he had aided a witch at Torteval to clean her chaise: this was an old woman named Moutonne Gahy.

When a census was taken in the island, in answer to a question about his calling, he replied, "Fisherman; when there are fish to catch." Imagine yourself in the place of Gilliatt's neighbours, and admit that there is something unpleasant in answers like this.

Poverty and wealth are comparative terms. Gilliatt had some fields and a house, his own property; compared with those who had nothing, he was not poor. One day, to test this, and perhaps, also as a step towards a correspondence—for there are base women who would marry a demon for the sake of riches—a young girl of the neighbourhood said to Gilliatt, "When are you going to take a wife, neighbour?" He answered, "I will take a wife when the Roque qui Chante takes a husband."

This Roque qui Chante is a great stone, standing in a field near Mons. Lemézurier de Fry's. It is a stone of a highly suspicious character. No one knows what deeds are done around it. At times you may hear there a cock crowing, when no cock is near—an extremely disagreeable circumstance. Then it is commonly asserted that this stone was originally placed in the field by the elfin people known as *Sarregousets*, who are the same as the *Sins*.

At night, when it thunders, if you should happen to see men flying in the lurid light of the clouds, or on the rolling waves of the air, these are no other than the Sarregousets. A woman who lives at the Grand Mielles knows them well. One evening, when some Sarregousets happened to be assembled at a crossroad, this woman cried out to a man with a cart, who did not know which route to take, "Ask them your way. They are civil folks, and always ready to direct a stranger." There can be little doubt that this woman was a sorceress.

The learned and judicious King James I. had women of this kind boiled, and then tasting the water of the cauldron, was able to say from its flavour, "That was a sorceress;" or "That was not one."

It is to be regretted that the kings of these latter days no longer possess a talent which placed in so strong a light the utility of monarchical institutions.

It was not without substantial grounds that Gilliatt lived in this odour of sorcery. One midnight, during a storm, Gilliatt being at sea alone in a bark, on the coast by La Sommeilleuse, he was heard to ask—

"Is there a passage sufficient for me?"

And a voice cried from the heights above:

"Passage enough: steer boldly."

To whom could he have been speaking, if not to those who replied to him? This seems something like evidence.

Another time, one stormy evening, when it was so dark that nothing could be distinguished, Gilliatt was near the Catiau Roque—a double row of rocks where witches, goats, and other diabolical creatures assemble and dance on Fridays—and here, it is firmly believed, that the voice of Gilliatt was heard mingling in the following terrible conversation:—

"How is Vesin Brovard?" (This was a mason who had fallen from the roof of a house.)

"He is getting better."

"Ver dia! he fell from a greater height than that of yonder peak. It is delightful to think that he was not dashed to pieces."

"Our folks had a fine time for the seaweed gathering last week."

"Ay, finer than to-day."

"I believe you. There will be little fish at the market to-day."

"It blows too hard."

"They can't lower their nets."

"How is Catherine?"

"She is charming."

Catherine was evidently the name of a Sarregouset.

According to all appearance, Gilliatt had business on hand at night: at least none doubted it.

Sometimes he was seen with a pitcher in his hand, pouring water on the ground. Now water, cast upon the ground, is known to make a shape like that of devils.

On the road to St. Sampson, opposite the Martello tower, number 1, stand three stones, arranged in the form of steps. Upon the platform of those stones, now empty, stood anciently a cross, or perhaps a gallows. These stones are full of evil influences.

Staid and worthy people, and perfectly credible witnesses, testified to having seen Gilliatt at this spot conversing with a toad. Now there are no toads at Guernsey. The share of Guernsey in the reptiles of the Channel Isles consisting exclusively of the snakes. It is Jersey that has all the toads. This toad, then, must have swum from the neighbouring island, in order to hold converse with Gilliatt. The converse was of a friendly kind.

These facts were clearly established; and the proof is that the three stones are there to this day. Those who doubt it may go and see them; and at a little distance, there is also a house on which the passer-by may read this inscription:—

"DEALER IN CATTLE, ALIVE AND DEAD, OLD CORDAGE, IRON, BONES, AND TOBACCO FOR CHEWING, PROMPT PAYMENT FOR GOODS, AND EVERY ATTENTION GIVEN TO ORDERS."

A man must be sceptical indeed to contest the existence of those stones, and of the house in question. Now both these circumstances were injurious to the reputation of Gilliatt.

Only the most ignorant are unaware of the fact that the greatest danger of the coasts of the Channel Islands is the King of the Auxcriniers. No inhabitant of the seas is more redoubtable. Whoever has seen him is certain to be wrecked between one St. Michel and the other. He is little, being in fact a dwarf; and is deaf, in his quality of king. He knows the names of all those who have been drowned in the seas, and the spots where they lie. He has a profound knowledge of that great graveyard which stretches far and wide beneath the waters of the ocean. A head, massive in the lower part and narrow in the forehead; a squat and corpulent figure; a skull, covered with warty excrescences; long legs, long arms, fins for feet, claws for hands, and a sea-green countenance; such are the chief characteristics of this king of the waves. His claws have palms like hands; his fins human nails. Imagine a spectral fish with the face of a human being. No power could check his career unless he could be exorcised, or mayhap, fished up from the sea. Meanwhile he continues his sinister operations. Nothing is more unpleasant than an interview with this monster: amid the rolling waves and breakers, or in the thick of the mist, the sailor perceives, sometimes, a strange creature with a beetle brow, wide nostrils, flattened ears, an enormous mouth, gap-toothed jaws, peaked eyebrows, and great grinning eyes. When the lightning is livid, he appears red; when it is purple, he looks wan. He has a stiff spreading beard, running with water, and overlapping a sort of pelerine, ornamented with fourteen shells, seven before and seven behind. These shells are curious to those who are learned in conchology. The King of the Auxcriniers is only seen in stormy seas. He is the terrible harbinger of the tempest. His hideous form traces itself in the fog, in the squall, in the tempest of rain. His breast is hideous. A coat of scales covers his sides like a vest. He rises above the waves which fly before the wind, twisting and curling like thin shavings of wood beneath the carpenter's plane. Then his entire form issues out of the foam, and if there should happen to be in the horizon any vessels in distress, pale in the twilight, or his face lighted up with a sinister smile, he dances terrible and uncouth to behold. It is an evil omen indeed to meet him on a voyage.

At the period when the people of St. Sampson were particularly excited on the subject of Gilliatt, the last persons who had seen the King of the Auxcriniers declared that his pelerine was now ornamented with only thirteen shells. Thirteen! He was only the more dangerous. But what had become of the fourteenth? Had he given it to some one? No one would say positively; and folks confined themselves to conjecture. But it was an undoubted fact that a certain Mons. Lupin Mabier, of Godaines, a man of property, paying a good sum to the land tax, was ready to depose on oath, that he had once seen in the hands of Gilliatt a very remarkable kind of shell.

It was not uncommon to hear dialogues like the following among the country people:—

"I have a fine bull here, neighbour, what do you say?"

"Very fine, neighbour?"

"It is a fact, tho' 'tis I who say it; he is better though for tallow than for meat."

"Ver dia!"

"Are you sure that Gilliatt hasn't cast his eye upon it?"

Gilliatt would stop sometimes beside a field where some labourers were assembled, or near gardens in which gardeners were engaged, and would perhaps hear these mysterious words:

"When the *mors du diable* flourishes, reap the winter rye."

(The *mors du diable* is the scabwort plant.)

"The ash tree is coming out in leaf. There will be no more frost."

"Summer solstice, thistle in flower."

"If it rain not in June, the wheat will turn white. Look out for mildew."

"When the wild cherry appears, beware of the full moon."

"If the weather on the sixth day of the new moon is like that of the fourth, or like that of the fifth day, it will be the same nine times out of twelve, in the first case, and eleven times out of twelve in the second, during the whole month."

"Keep your eye on neighbours who go to law with you. Beware of malicious influences. A pig which has had warm milk given to it will die. A cow which has had its teeth rubbed with leeks will eat no more."

"Spawning time with the smelts; beware of fevers."

"When frogs begin to appear, sow your melons."

"When the liverwort flowers, sow your barley."

"When the limes are in bloom, mow the meadows."

"When the elm-tree flowers, open the hot-bed frames."

"When tobacco fields are in blossom, close your greenhouses."

And, fearful to relate, these occult precepts were not without truth. Those who put faith in them could vouch for the fact.

One night, in the month of June, when Gilliatt was playing upon his bagpipe, upon the sand-hills on the shore of the Demie de Fontenelle, it had happened that the mackerel fishing had failed.

One evening, at low water, it came to pass that a cart filled with seaweed for manure overturned on the beach, in front of Gilliatt's house. It is most probable that he was afraid of being brought before the magistrates, for he took considerable trouble in helping to raise the cart, and he filled it again himself.

A little neglected child of the neighbourhood being troubled with vermin, he had gone himself to St. Peter's Port, and had returned with an ointment, with which he rubbed the child's head. Thus Gilliatt had removed the pest from the poor child, which was an evidence that Gilliatt himself had originally given it; for everybody knows that there is a certain charm for giving vermin to people.

Gilliatt was suspected of looking into wells—a dangerous practice with those who have an evil eye; and, in fact, at Arculons, near St. Peter's Port, the water of a well became unwholesome. The good woman to whom this well belonged said to Gilliatt:

"Look here, at this water;" and she showed him a glassful. Gilliatt acknowledged it.

"The water is thick," he said; "that is true."

The good woman, who dreaded him in her heart, said, "Make it sweet again for me."

Gilliatt asked her some questions: whether she had a stable? whether the stable had a drain? whether the gutter of the drain did not pass near the well? The good woman replied "Yes." Gilliatt went into the stable; worked at the drain; turned the gutter in another direction; and the water became pure again. People in the country round might think what they pleased. A well does not become foul one moment and sweet the next without good cause; the bottom of the affair was involved in obscurity; and, in short, it was difficult to escape the conclusion that Gilliatt himself had bewitched the water.

On one occasion, when he went to Jersey, it was remarked that he had taken a lodging in the street called the Rue des Alleurs. Now the word *alleurs* signifies spirits from the other world.

In villages it is the custom to gather together all these little hints and indications of a man's career; and when they are gathered together, the total constitutes his reputation among the inhabitants.

It happened that Gilliatt was once caught with blood issuing from his nose. The circumstances appeared grave. The master of a barque who had sailed almost entirely round the world, affirmed that among the Tongusians all sorcerers were subject to bleeding at the nose. In fact, when you see a man in those parts bleeding at the nose, you know at once what is in the wind. Moderate reasoners, however, remarked that the characteristics of sorcerers among the Tongusians may possibly not apply in the same degree to the sorcerers of Guernsey.

In the environs of one of the St. Michels, he had been seen to stop in a close belonging to the Huriaux, skirting the highway from the Videclins. He whistled in the field, and a moment afterwards a crow alighted there; a moment later, a magpie. The fact was attested by a worthy man who has since been appointed to the office of Douzenier of the Douzaine, as those are called who are authorised to make a new survey and register of the fief of the king.

At Hamel, in the Vingtaine of L'Epine, there lived some old women who were positive of having heard one morning a number of swallows distinctly calling "Gilliatt."

Add to all this that he was of a malicious temper.

One day, a poor man was beating an ass. The ass was obstinate. The poor man gave him a few kicks in the belly with his wooden shoe, and the ass fell. Gilliatt ran to raise the unlucky beast, but he was dead. Upon this Gilliatt administered to the poor man a sound thrashing.

Another day, Gilliatt seeing a boy come down from a tree with a brood of little birds, newly hatched and unfledged, he took the brood away from the boy, and carried his malevolence so far as even to take them back and replace them in the tree.

Some passers-by took up the boy's complaint; but Gilliatt made no reply, except to point to the old birds, who were hovering and crying plaintively over the tree, as they looked for their nest. He had a weakness for birds—another sign by which the people recognise a magician.

Children take a pleasure in robbing the nests of birds along the cliff. They bring home quantities of yellow, blue, and green eggs, with which they make rosaries for mantelpiece ornaments. As the cliffs are peaked, they sometimes slip and are killed. Nothing is prettier than shutters decorated with sea-birds' eggs. Gilliatt's mischievous ingenuity had no end. He would climb, at the peril of his own life, into the steep places of the sea rocks, and hang up bundles of hay, old hats, and all kinds of scarecrows, to deter the birds from building there, and, as a consequence, to prevent the children from visiting those spots.

These are some of the reasons why Gilliatt was disliked throughout the country. Perhaps nothing less could have been expected.

V

MORE SUSPICIOUS FACTS ABOUT GILLIATT

PUBLIC OPINION was not yet quite settled with regard to Gilliatt.

In general he was regarded as a *Marcou*: some went so far as to believe him to be a *Cambion*. A cambion is the child of a woman begotten by a devil.

When a woman bears to her husband seven male children consecutively, the seventh is a marcou. But the series must not be broken by the birth of any female child.

The marcou has a natural fleur-de-lys imprinted upon some part of his body; for which reason he has the power of curing scrofula, exactly the same as the King of France. Marcous are found in all parts of France, but particularly in the Orléanais. Every village of Gâtinais has its marcou. It is sufficient for the cure of the sick that the marcou should breathe upon their wounds, or let them touch his fleur-de-lys. The night of Good Friday is particularly favourable to these ceremonies. Ten years ago there lived, at Ormes in Gâtinais, one of these creatures who was nicknamed the Beau Marcou, and consulted by all the country of Beauce. He was a cooper, named Foulon, who kept a horse and vehicle. To put a stop to his miracles, it was found necessary to call in the assistance of the gendarmes. His fleur-de-lys was on the left breast; other marcous have it in different parts.

There are marcous at Jersey, Auvigny, and at Guernsey. This fact is doubtless in some way connected with the rights possessed by France over Normandy: or why the fleur-de-lys?

There are also, in the Channel Islands, people afflicted with scrofula; which of course necessitates a due supply of these marcous.

Some people, who happened to be present one day when Gilliatt was bathing in the sea, had fancied that they could perceive upon him a fleur-de-lys. Interrogated on that subject he made no reply, but merely burst into laughter. For he laughed sometimes like other men. From that time, however, no one ever saw him bathe: he bathed thenceforth only in perilous and solitary places; probably by moonlight: a thing in itself somewhat suspicious.

Those who obstinately regarded him as a cambion, or son of the devil, were evidently in error. They ought to have known that cambions scarcely exist out of Germany. But The Vale and St. Sampson were, fifty years ago, places remarkable for the ignorance of their inhabitants.

To fancy that a resident of the island of Guernsey could be the son of a devil was evidently absurd.

Gilliatt, for the very reason that he caused disquietude among the people, was sought for and consulted. The peasants came in fear, to talk to him of their diseases. That fear itself had in it something of faith in his powers; for in the country, the more the doctor is suspected of magic, the more certain is the cure. Gilliatt had certain remedies of his own, which he had inherited from the deceased woman. He communicated them to all who had need of them, and would never receive money for them. He cured whitlows with applications of herbs. A liquor in one of his phials allayed fever. The chemist of St. Sampson, or *pharmacien*, as they would call him in France, thought that this was probably a decoction of Jesuits' bark. The more generous among his censors admitted that Gilliatt was not so bad a demon in his dealings with the sick, so far as regarded his ordinary remedies. But in his character of a marcou, he would do nothing. If persons afflicted with scrofula came to him to ask to touch the fleur-de-lys on his skin, he made no other answer than that of shutting the door in their faces. He persistently refused to perform any miracles—a ridiculous position for a sorcerer. No one is bound to be a sorcerer; but when a man is one, he ought not to shirk the duties of his position.

One or two exceptions might be found to this almost universal antipathy. Sieur Landoys, of the Clos-Landés, was clerk and registrar of St. Peter's Port, custodian of the documents, and keeper of the register of births, marriages, and deaths. This Landoys was vain of his descent from Peter Landoys, treasurer of the province of Brittany, who was hanged in 1485.

One day, when Sieur Landoys was bathing in the sea, he ventured to swim out too far, and was on the point of drowning: Gilliatt plunged into the water, narrowly escaping drowning himself, and succeeded in saving him. From that day Landoys never spoke an evil word of Gilliatt. To those who expressed surprise at this change, he replied, "Why should I detest a man who never did me any harm, and who has rendered me a service?" The parish clerk and registrar even came at last to feel a sort of friendship for Gilliatt. This public functionary was a man without prejudices. He had no faith in sorcerers. He laughed at people who went in fear of ghostly visitors. As for him, he had a boat in which he amused himself by making fishing excursions in his leisure hours; but he had never seen anything extraordinary, unless it was on one occasion —a woman clothed in white, who rose about the waters in the light of the moon—and even of this circumstance he was not quite sure. Moutonne Gahy, the old witch of Torteval, had given him a little bag to be worn under the cravat, as a protection against evil spirits: he ridiculed the bag, and knew not what it contained, though, to be sure, he carried it about him, feeling more security with this charm hanging on his neck.

Some courageous persons, emboldened by the example of Landoys, ventured to cite, in Gilliatt's favour, certain extenuating circumstances; a few signs of good qualities, as his sobriety, his abstinence from spirits and tobacco; and sometimes they went so far as to pass this elegant eulogium upon him: "He neither smokes, drinks, chews tobacco, or takes snuff."

Sobriety, however, can only count as a virtue when there are other virtues to support it.

The ban of public opinion lay heavily upon Gilliatt.

In any case, as a marcou, Gilliatt had it in his power to render great services. On a certain Good Friday, at midnight, a day and an hour propitious to this kind of cure, all the scrofulous people of the island, either by sudden inspiration, or by concerted action, presented themselves in a crowd at the Bû de la Rue, and with pitiable sores and imploring gestures, called on Gilliatt to make them clean. But he refused; and herein the people found another proof of his malevolence.

VI
THE DUTCH SLOOP

SUCH WAS THE character of Gilliatt.

The young women considered him ugly.

Ugly he was not. He might, perhaps, have been called handsome. There was something in his profile of rude but antique grace. In repose it had some resemblance to that of a sculptured Dacian on the Trajan column. His ears were small, delicate, without lobes, and of an admirable form for hearing. Between his eyes he had that proud vertical line which indicates in a man boldness and perseverance. The corners of his mouth were depressed, giving a slight expression of bitterness. His forehead had a calm and noble roundness. The clear pupils of his eyes possessed a steadfast look, although troubled a little with that involuntary movement of the eyelids which fishermen contract from the glitter of the waves. His laugh was boyish and pleasing. No ivory could be of a finer white than his teeth; but exposure to the sun had made him swarthy as a moor. The ocean, the tempest, and the darkness cannot be braved with impunity. At thirty he looked already like a man of forty-five. He wore the sombre mask of the wind and the sea.

The people had nicknamed him "Malicious Gilliatt."

There is an Indian fable to the effect that one day the god Brahma inquired of the Spirit of Power, "Who is stronger than thee?" and the spirit replied "Cunning." A Chinese proverb says, "What could not the lion do, if he was the monkey also?" Gilliatt was neither the lion nor the monkey; but his actions gave some evidence of the truth of the Chinese proverb, and of the Hindoo fable. Although only of ordinary height and strength, he was enabled, so inventive and powerful was his dexterity, to lift burdens that might have taxed a giant, and to accomplish feats which would have done credit to an athlete.

He had in him something of the power of the gymnast. He used, with equal address, his left hand and his right.

He never carried a gun; but was often seen with his net. He spared the birds, but not the fish. Ill-luck to these dumb creatures! He was an excellent swimmer.

Solitude either develops the mental powers, or renders men dull and vicious. Gilliatt sometimes presented himself under both these aspects. At times, when his features wore that air of strange surprise already mentioned, he might have been taken for a man of mental powers scarcely superior to the savage. At other moments an indescribable air of penetration lighted up his face. Ancient Chaldea possessed some men of this stamp. At certain times the dullness of the shepherd mind became transparent, and revealed the inspired sage.

After all, he was but a poor man; uninstructed, save to the extent of reading and writing. It is probable that the condition of his mind was at that limit which separates the dreamer from the thinker. The thinker wills, the dreamer is a passive instrument. Solitude sinks deeply into pure natures, and modifies them in a certain degree. They become, unconsciously, penetrated with a kind of sacred awe. The shadow in which the mind of Gilliatt constantly dwelt was composed in almost equal degrees of two elements, both obscure, but very different. Within himself all was ignorance and weakness; without, infinity and mysterious power.

By dint of frequent climbing on the rocks, of escalading the rugged cliffs, of going to and fro among the islands in all weathers, of navigating any sort of craft which came to hand, of venturing night and day in difficult channels, he had become, without taking count of his other advantages, and merely in following his fancy and pleasure, a seaman of extraordinary skill.

He was a born pilot. The true pilot is the man who navigates the bed of the ocean even more than its surface. The waves of the sea are an external problem, continually modified by the submarine conditions of the waters in which the vessel is making her way. To see Gilliatt guiding his craft among the reefs and shallows of the Norman Archipelago, one might have fancied that he carried in his head a plan of the bottom of the sea. He was familiar with it all, and feared nothing.

He was better acquainted with the buoys in the channels than the cormorants who make them their resting-places. The almost imperceptible differences which distinguish the four upright buoys of the Creux, Alligande, the Trémies, and the Sardrette, were perfectly visible and clear to him, even in misty weather. He hesitated neither at the oval, apple-headed buoy of Anfré, nor at the triple iron point of the Rousse, nor at the white ball of the Corbette, nor at the black ball of Longue Pierre; and there was no fear of his confounding the cross of Goubeau with the sword planted in earth at La Platte, nor the hammer-shaped buoy of the Barbées with the curled-tail buoy of the Moulinet.

His rare skill in seamanship showed itself in a striking manner one day at Guernsey, on the occasion of one of those sea tournaments which are called regattas. The feat to be performed was to navigate alone a boat with four sails from St. Sampson to the Isle of Herm, at one league distance, and to bring the boat back from Herm to St. Sampson. To manage, without assistance, a boat with four sails, is a feat which every fisherman is equal to, and the difficulty seemed little; but there was a condition which rendered it far from simple. The boat, to begin with, was one of those large and heavy sloops of bygone times which the sailors of the last century knew by the name of "Dutch Belly Boats." This ancient style of flat, pot-bellied craft, carrying on the larboard and starboard sides, in compensation for the want of a keel, two wings, which lowered themselves, sometimes the one, sometimes the other, according to the wind, may occasionally be met with still at sea. In the second place, there was the return from Herm, a journey which was rendered more difficult by a heavy ballasting of stones. The conditions were to go empty, but to return loaded. The sloop was the prize of the contest. It was dedicated beforehand to the winner. This "Dutch Belly Boat" had been employed as a pilot-boat. The pilot who had rigged and worked it for twenty years was the most robust of all the sailors of the channel. When he died no one had been found capable of managing the sloop; and it was, in consequence, determined to make it the prize of the regatta. The sloop, though not decked, had some sea qualities, and was a tempting prize for a skilful sailor. Her mast was somewhat forward, which increased the motive-power of her sails; besides having the advantage of not being in the way of her pilot. It was a strong-built vessel, heavy, but roomy, and taking the open sea well; in fact, a good, serviceable craft. There was eager anxiety for the prize; the task was a rough one, but the reward of success was worth having. Seven or eight fishermen, among the most vigorous of the island, presented themselves. One by one they essayed; but not one could succeed in reaching Herm. The last one who tried his skill was known for having crossed, in a rowing-boat, the terrible narrow sea between Sark and

Brecq-Hou. Sweating with his exertions, he brought back the sloop, and said, "It is impossible." Gilliatt then entered the bark, seized first of all the oar, then the mainsail, and pushed out to sea. Then, without either making fast the boom, which would have been imprudent, or letting it go, which kept the sail under his direction, and leaving the boom to move with the wind without drifting, he held the tiller with his left hand. In three quarters of an hour he was at Herm. Three hours later, although a strong breeze had sprung up and was blowing across the roads, the sloop, guided by Gilliatt, returned to St. Sampson with its load of stones. He had, with an extravagant display of his resources, even added to the cargo the little bronze cannon at Herm, which the people were in the habit of firing off on the 5th of November, by way of rejoicing over the death of Guy Fawkes.

Guy Fawkes, by the way, has been dead two hundred and sixty years; a remarkably long period of rejoicing.

Gilliatt, thus burdened and encumbered, although he had the Guy Fawkes'-day cannon in the boat and the south wind in his sails, steered, or rather brought back, the heavy craft to St. Sampson.

Seeing which, Mess Lethierry exclaimed, "There's a bold sailor for you!"

And he held out his hand to Gilliatt.

We shall have occasion to speak again of Mess Lethierry.

The sloop was awarded to Gilliatt.

This adventure detracted nothing from his evil reputation.

Several persons declared that the feat was not at all astonishing, for that Gilliatt had concealed in the boat a branch of wild medlar. But this could not be proved.

From that day forward, Gilliatt navigated no boat except the old sloop. In this heavy craft he went on his fishing avocation. He kept it at anchor in the excellent little shelter which he had all to himself, under the very wall of his house of the Bû de la Rue. At nightfall, he cast his nets over his shoulder, traversed his little garden, climbed over the parapet of dry stones, stepped lightly from rock to rock, and jumping into the sloop, pushed out to sea.

He brought home heavy takes of fish; but people said that his medlar branch was always hanging up in the boat. No one had ever seen this branch, but every one believed in its existence.

When he had more fish than he wanted, he did not sell it, but gave it away.

The poor people took his gift, but were little grateful, for they knew the secret of his medlar branch. Such devices cannot be permitted. It is unlawful to trick the sea out of its treasures.

He was a fisherman; but he was something more. He had, by instinct, or for amusement, acquired a knowledge of three or four trades. He was a carpenter, worker in iron, wheelwright, boat-caulker, and, to some extent, an engineer. No one could mend a broken wheel better than he could. He manufactured, in a fashion of his own, all the things which fishermen use. In a corner of the Bû de la Rue he had a small forge and an anvil; and the sloop having but one anchor, he had succeeded, without help, in making another. The anchor was excellent. The ring had the necessary strength; and Gilliatt, though entirely uninstructed in this branch of the smith's art, had found the exact dimensions of the stock for preventing the over-balancing of the fluke ends.

He had patiently replaced all the nails in the planks by rivets; which rendered rust in the holes impossible.

In this way he had much improved the sea-going qualities of the sloop. He employed it sometimes when he took a fancy to spend a month or two in some solitary islet, like Chousey or the Casquets. People said, "Ay! ay! Gilliatt is away;" but this was a circumstance which nobody regretted.

VII
A FIT TENANT FOR A HAUNTED HOUSE

GILLIATT WAS a man of dreams, hence his daring, hence also his timidity. He had ideas on many things which were peculiarly his own.

There was in his character, perhaps, something of the visionary and the transcendentalist. Hallucinations may haunt the poor peasant like Martin, no less than the king like Henry IV. There are times when the unknown reveals itself in a mysterious way to the spirit of man. A sudden rent in the veil of darkness will make manifest things hitherto unseen, and then close again upon the mysteries within. Such visions have occasionally the power to effect a transfiguration in those whom they visit. They convert a poor camel-driver into a Mahomet; a peasant girl tending her goats into a Joan of Arc. Solitude generates a certain amount of sublime exaltation. It is like the smoke arising from the burning bush. A mysterious lucidity of mind results, which converts the student into a seer, and the poet into a prophet: herein we find a key to the mysteries of Horeb, Kedron, Ombos; to the intoxication of Castilian laurels, the revelations of the month Busion. Hence, too, we have Peleia at Dodona, Phemonoe at Delphos, Trophonius in Lebadea, Ezekiel on the Chebar, and Jerome in the Thetais.

More frequently this visionary state overwhelms and stupefies its victim. There is such a thing as a divine besottedness. The Hindoo fakir bears about with him the burden of his vision, as the Cretin his goître. Luther holding converse with devils in his garret at Wittenburg; Pascal shutting out the view of the infernal regions with the screen of his cabinet; the African Obi conversing with the white-faced god Bossum; are each and all the same phenomenon, diversely interpreted by the minds in which they manifest themselves, according to their capacity and power. Luther and Pascal were grand, and are grand still; the Obi is simply a poor half-witted creature.

Gilliatt was neither so exalted nor so low. He was a dreamer: nothing more.

Nature presented itself to him under a somewhat strange aspect.

Just as he had often found in the perfectly limpid water of the sea strange creatures of considerable size and of various shapes, of the Medusa genus, which out of the water bore a resemblance to soft crystal, and which, cast again into the sea, became lost to sight in that medium by reason of their identity in transparency and colour, so he imagined that other transparencies, similar to these almost invisible denizens of the ocean, might probably inhabit the air around us. The birds are scarcely inhabitants of the air, but rather amphibious creatures passing much of their lives upon the earth. Gilliatt could not believe the air a mere desert. He used to say, "Since the water is filled with life, why not the atmosphere?" Creatures colourless and transparent like the air would escape from our observation. What proof have we that there are no such creatures? Analogy indicates that the liquid fields of air must have their swimming habitants, even as the waters of the deep. These aerial fish would, of course, be diaphanous; a provision of their wise Creator for our sakes as well as their own. Allowing the light to pass through their forms, casting no shadow, having no defined outline, they would necessarily remain unknown to us, and beyond the grasp of human sense. Gilliatt indulged the wild fancy that if it were possible to exhaust the earth of its atmosphere, or if we could fish the air as we fish the depths of the sea, we should discover the existence of a multitude of strange animals. And then, he would add in his reverie, many things would be made clear.

Reverie, which is thought in its nebulous state, borders closely upon the land of sleep, by which it is bounded as by a natural frontier. The discovery of a new world, in the form of an atmosphere filled with transparent creatures, would be the beginning of a knowledge of the vast unknown. But beyond opens up the illimitable domain of the possible, teeming with yet other beings, and characterised by other phenomena. All this would be nothing supernatural, but merely the occult continuation of the infinite variety of creation. In the midst of that laborious idleness, which was the chief feature in his existence, Gilliatt was singularly observant. He even carried his observations into the domain of sleep. Sleep has a close relation with the possible, which we call also the *invraisemblable*. The world of sleep has an existence of its own. Night-time, regarded as a separate sphere of creation, is a universe in itself. The material nature of man, upon which philosophers tell us that a column of air forty-five miles in height continually presses, is wearied out at night, sinks into lassitude, lies down, and finds repose. The eyes of the flesh are closed; but in that drooping head, less inactive than is supposed, other eyes are opened. The unknown reveals itself. The shadowy existences of the invisible world become more akin to man; whether it be that there is a real communication, or whether things far off in the unfathomable abyss are mysteriously brought nearer, it seems as if the impalpable creatures inhabiting space come then to contemplate our natures, curious to comprehend the denizens of the earth. Some phantom creation ascends or descends to walk beside us in the dim twilight: some existence altogether different from our own, composed partly of human consciousness, partly of something else, quits his fellows and returns again, after presenting himself for a moment to our inward sight; and the sleeper, not wholly slumbering, nor yet entirely conscious, beholds around him strange manifestations of life—pale spectres, terrible or smiling, dismal phantoms, uncouth masks, unknown faces, hydra-headed monsters, undefined shapes, reflections of moonlight where there is no moon, vague fragments of monstrous forms. All these things which come and go in the troubled atmosphere of sleep, and to which men give the name of dreams, are, in truth, only realities invisible to those who walk about the daylight world. The dream-world is the Aquarium of Night.

So, at least, thought Gilliatt.

VIII
THE GILD-HOLM-'UR SEAT

THE CURIOUS VISITOR, in these days, would seek in vain in the little bay of Houmet for the house in which Gilliatt lived, or for his garden, or the creek in which he sheltered the Dutch sloop. The Bû de la Rue no longer exists. Even the little peninsula on which his house stood has vanished, levelled by the pickaxe of the quarryman, and carried away, cart-load by cart-load, by dealers in rock and granite. It must be sought now in the churches, the palaces, and the quays of a great city. All that ridge of rocks has been long ago conveyed to London.

These long lines of broken cliffs in the sea, with their frequent gaps and crevices, are like miniature chains of mountains. They strike the eye with the impression which a giant may be supposed to have in contemplating the Cordilleras. In the language of the country they are called "Banques." These banques vary considerably in form. Some resemble a long spine, of which each rock forms one of the vertebræ; others are like the backbone of a fish; while some bear an odd resemblance to a crocodile in the act of drinking.

At the extremity of the ridge on which the Bû de la Rue was situate, was a large rock, which the fishing people of Houmet called the "Beast's Horn." This rock, a sort of pyramid, resembled, though less in height, the "Pinnacle" of Jersey. At high water the sea divided it from the ridge, and the Horn stood alone; at low water it was approached by an isthmus of rocks.

The remarkable feature of this "Beast's Horn" was a sort of natural seat on the side next the sea, hollowed out by the water, and polished by the rains. The seat, however, was a treacherous one. The stranger was insensibly attracted to it by "the beauty of the prospect," as the Guernsey folks said. Something detained him there in spite of himself, for there is a charm in a wide view. The seat seemed to offer itself for his convenience; it formed a sort of niche in the peaked *façade* of the rock. To climb up to it was easy, for the sea, which had fashioned it out of its rocky base, had also cast beneath it, at convenient distances, a kind of natural stairs composed of flat stones. The perilous abyss is full of these snares; beware, therefore, of its proffered aids. The spot was tempting: the stranger mounted and sat down. There he found himself at his ease; for his seat he had the granite rounded and hollowed out by the foam; for supports, two rocky elbows which seemed made expressly for him; against his back, the high vertical wall of rock which he looked up to and admired, without thinking of the impossibility of scaling it. Nothing could be more simple than to fall into reverie in that convenient resting-place. All around spread the wide sea; far off the ships were seen passing to and fro. It was possible to follow a sail with the eye, till it sank in the horizon beyond the Casquets. The stranger was entranced: he looked around, enjoying the beauty of the scene, and the light touch of wind and wave. There is a sort of bat found at Cayenne, which has the power of fanning people to sleep in the shade with a gentle beating of its dusky wings. Like this strange creature the wind wanders about, alternately ravaging or lulling into security. So the stranger would continue contemplating the sea, listening for a movement in the air, and yielding himself up to dreamy indolence. When the eyes are satiated with light and beauty, it is a luxury to close them for awhile. Suddenly the loiterer would arouse; but it was too late. The sea had crept up step by step; the waters surrounded the rock; the stranger had been lured on to his death.

A terrible rock was this in a rising sea.

The tide gathers at first insensibly, then with violence; when it touches the rocks a sudden wrath seems to possess it, and it foams. Swimming is difficult in the breakers: excellent swimmers have been lost at the Horn of the Bû de la Rue.

In certain places, and at certain periods, the aspect of the sea is dangerous—fatal; as at times is the glance of a woman.

Very old inhabitants of Guernsey used to call this niche, fashioned in the rock by the waves, "Gild-Holm-'Ur" seat, or Kidormur; a Celtic word, say some authorities, which those who understand Celtic cannot interpret, and which all who understand French can—"*Qui-dort-meurt:*"* such is the country folks' translation.

The reader may choose between the translation, *Qui-dort-meurt*, and that given in 1819, I believe in *The Armorican*, by M. Athenas. According to this learned Celtic scholar, Gild-Holm-'Ur signifies "The resting-place of birds."

There is, at Aurigny, another seat of this kind, called the Monk's Chair, so well sculptured by the waves, and with steps of rock so conveniently placed, that it might be said that the sea politely sets a footstool for those who rest there.

In the open sea, at high water, the Gild-Holm-'Ur was no longer visible; the water covered it entirely.

The Gild-Holm-'Ur was a neighbour of the Bû de la Rue. Gilliatt knew it well, and often seated himself there. Was it his meditating place? No. We have already said he did not meditate, but dream. The sea, however, never entrapped him there.

*HE WHO SLEEPS MUST DIE.

Book II
Mess Lethierry

❈

I
A TROUBLED LIFE, BUT A QUIET CONSCIENCE

MESS LETHIERRY, a conspicuous man in St. Sampson, was a redoubtable sailor. He had voyaged a great deal. He had been a cabin-boy, seaman, top-mast-man, second mate, mate, pilot, and captain. He was at this period a ship-owner. There was not a man to compare with him for general knowledge of the sea. He was brave in putting off to ships in distress. In foul weather he would take his way along the beach, scanning the horizon. "What have we yonder?" he would say; "some craft in trouble?" Whether it were an interloping Weymouth fisherman, a cutter from Aurigny, a bisquine from Courseulle, the yacht of some nobleman, an English craft or a French one—poor or rich, mattered little. He jumped into a boat, called together two or three strong fellows, or did without them, as the case might be, pushed out to sea, rose and sank, and rose again on rolling waves, plunged into the storm, and encountered the danger face to face. Then afar off, amid the rain and lightning, and drenched with water, he was sometimes seen upright in his boat like a lion with a foaming mane. Often he would pass whole days in danger amidst the waves, the hail, and the wind, making his way to the sides of foundering vessels during the tempest, and rescuing men and merchandise. At night, after feats like these, he would return home, and pass his time in knitting stockings.

For fifty years he led this kind of life—from ten years of age to sixty—so long did he feel himself still young. At sixty, he began to discover that he could no longer lift with one hand the great anvil at the forge of Varclin. This anvil weighed three hundredweight. At length rheumatic pains compelled him to be a prisoner; he was forced to give up his old struggle with the sea, to pass from the heroic into the patriarchal stage, to sink into the condition of a harmless, worthy old fellow.

Happily his rheumatism attacks happened at the period when he had secured a comfortable competency. These two consequences of labour are natural companions. At the moment when men become rich, how often comes paralysis—the sorrowful crowning of a laborious life!

Old and weary men say among themselves, "Let us rest and enjoy life."

The population of islands like Guernsey is composed of men who have passed their lives in going about their little fields or in sailing round the world. These are the two classes of the labouring people; the labourers on the land, and the toilers of the sea. Mess Lethierry was of the latter class; he had had a life of hard work. He had been upon the continent; was for some time a ship carpenter at Rochefort, and afterwards at Cette. We have just spoken of sailing round the world; he had made the circuit of all France, getting work as a journeyman carpenter; and had been employed at the great salt works of Franche-Comte. Though a humble man, he had led a life of adventure. In France he had learned to read, to think, to have a will of his own. He had had a hand in many things, and in all he had done had kept a character for probity. At bottom, however, he was simply a sailor. The water was his element; he used to say that he lived with the fish when really at home. In short, his whole existence, except two or three years, had been devoted to the ocean. Flung into the water, as he said, he had navigated the great oceans both of the Atlantic and the Pacific, but he preferred the Channel. He used to exclaim enthusiastically, "That is the sea for a rough time of it!" He was born at sea, and at sea would have preferred to end his days. After sailing several times round the world, and seeing most countries, he had returned to Guernsey, and never permanently left the island again. Henceforth his great voyages were to Granville and St. Malo.

Mess Lethierry was a Guernsey man—that peculiar amalgamation of Frenchman and Norman, or rather English. He had within himself this quadruple extraction, merged and almost lost in that far wider country, the ocean. Throughout his life and wheresoever he went, he had preserved the habits of a Norman fisherman.

All this, however, did not prevent his looking now and then into some old book; of taking pleasure in reading, in knowing the names of philosophers and poets, and in talking a little now and then in all languages.

II
A CERTAIN PREDILECTION

GILLIATT was a child of Nature. Mess Lethierry was the same.

Lethierry's uncultivated nature, however, was not without certain refinements.

He was fastidious upon the subject of women's hands. In his early years, while still a lad, passing from the stage of cabin-boy to that of sailor, he had heard the Admiral de Suffren say, "There goes a pretty girl; but what horrible great red hands." An observation from an admiral on any subject is a command, a law, an authority far above that of an oracle. The exclamation of Admiral de Suffren had rendered Lethierry fastidious and exacting in the matter of small and white hands. His own hand, a large club fist of the colour of mahogany, was like a mallet or a pair of pincers for a friendly grasp, and, tightly closed, would almost break a paving-stone.

He had never married; he had either no inclination for matrimony, or had never found a suitable match. That, perhaps, was due to his being a stickler for hands like those of a duchess. Such hands are, indeed, somewhat rare among the fishermen's daughters at Portbail.

It was whispered, however, that at Rochefort, on the Charente, he had, once upon a time, made the acquaintance of a certain grisette, realising his ideal. She was a pretty girl with graceful hands; but she was a vixen, and had also a habit of scratching. Woe betide any one who attacked her! yet her nails, though capable at a pinch of being turned into claws, were of a cleanliness which left nothing to be desired. It was these peculiarly bewitching nails which had first enchanted and then disturbed the peace of Lethierry, who, fearing that he might one day become no longer master of his mistress, had decided not to conduct that young lady to the nuptial altar.

Another time he met at Aurigny a country girl who pleased him. He thought of marriage, when one of the inhabitants of the place said to him, "I congratulate you; you will have for your wife a good fuel maker." Lethierry asked the meaning of this. It appeared that the country people at Aurigny have a certain custom of collecting manure from their cow-houses, which they throw against a wall, where it is left to dry and fall to the ground.

Cakes of dried manure of this kind are used for fuel, and are called *coipiaux*. A country girl of Aurigny has no chance of getting a husband if she is not a good fuel maker; but the young lady's especial talent only inspired disgust in Lethierry.

Besides, he had in his love matters a kind of rough country folks' philosophy, a sailor-like sort of habit of mind. Always smitten but never enslaved, he boasted of having been in his youth easily conquered by a petticoat, or rather a *cotillon*; for what is now-a-days called a crinoline, was in his time called a *cotillon*; a term which, in his use of it, signifies both something more and something less than a wife.

These rude seafaring men of the Norman Archipelago, have a certain amount of shrewdness. Almost all can read and write. On Sundays, little cabin-boys may be seen in those parts, seated upon a coil of ropes, reading, with book in hand. From all time these Norman sailors have had a peculiar satirical vein, and have been famous for clever sayings. It was one of these men, the bold pilot Quéripel, who said to Montgomery, when he sought refuge in Jersey after the unfortunate accident in killing Henry II. at a tournament, with a blow of his lance, "*Tête folle a cassé tête vide.*" Another one, Touzeau, a sea-captain at St. Brélade, was the author of that philosophical pun, erroneously attributed to Camus, "*Après la mort, les papes deviennent papillons, et les sires deviennent cirons.*"

III
THE OLD SEA LANGUAGE

THE MARINERS of the Channel are the true ancient Gauls. The islands, which in these days become rapidly more and more English—preserved for many ages their old French character. The peasant in Sark speaks the language of Louis XIV. Forty years ago, the old classical nautical language was to be found in the mouths of the sailors of Jersey and Aurigny. When amongst them, it was possible to imagine oneself carried back to the sea life of the seventeenth century. From that speaking trumpet which terrified Admiral Hidde, a philologist might have learnt the ancient technicalities of manœuvring and giving orders at sea, in the very words which were roared out to his sailors by Jean Bart. The old French maritime vocabulary is now almost entirely changed, but was still in use in Jersey in 1820. A ship that was a good plyer was *bon boulinier*; one that carried a weather-helm in spite of her foresails and rudder was *un vaisseau ardent*; to get under way was *prendre aire*; to lie to in a storm, *capeyer*; to make fast running rigging was *faire dormant*; to get to windward, *faire chapelle*; to keep the cable tight, *faire teste*; to be out of trim, *être en pantenne*; to keep the sails full, *porter plain*. These expressions have fallen out of use. To-day we say *louvoyer* for to beat to windward, they said *leauvoyer*; for *naviguer*, sail, they said *naviger*; for *virer vent devant*, to tack, *donner vent devant*; for *aller de l'avant*, to make headway, *tailler de l'avant*; for *tirez d'accord*, haul together, *halez d'accord*; for *dérapez*, to weigh anchor, *deplantez*; for *embraquez*, to haul tight, *abraquez*; for *taquets*, cleats, *bittons*; for *burins*, toggles, *tappes*; for *balancine*, fore-lift, main-lift, etc., *valancine*; for *tribord*, starboard, *stribord*; for *les hommes de quart à bâbord*, men of the larboard watch, *les basbourdis*. Tourville wrote to Hocquincourt: *nous avons singlét* (sailed), for *cinglé*. Instead of *la rafale*, squall, *le raffal*; instead of *bossoir*, cat-head, *boussoir*; instead of *drosse*, truss, *drousse*; instead of *loffer*, to luff, *faire une olofée*; instead of *elonger*, to lay alongside, *alonger*; instead of *forte brise*, stiff breeze, *survent*; instead of *jouail*, stock of an anchor, *jas*; instead of *soute*, store-room, *fosse*.

Such, at the beginning of this century, was the maritime dialect of the Channel Islands. Ango would have been startled had he heard the speech of a Jersey pilot. Whilst everywhere else the sails *faseyaient* (shivered), in these islands they *barbeyaient*. A *saute de vent*, sudden shift of wind, was a *folle-vente*. The old methods of mooring known as *la valture* and *la portugaise* were alone used, and such commands as *jour-et-chaque!* and *bosse et vilte!* might still be heard. While a sailor of Granville was already employing the word *clan* for sheave-hold, one of St. Aubin or of St. Sampson still stuck to his *canal de pouliot*. What was called *bout d'alonge* (upper fultock) at St. Malo, was *oreille d'âne* at St. Helier. Mess Lethierry, as did the Duke de Vibonne, called the sheer of the decks *la tonture*, and the caulker's chisel *la patarasse*.

It was with this uncouth sea dialect in his mouth that Duquesne beat De Ruyter, that Duguay Trouin defeated Wasnaer, and that Tourville, in 1681, poured a broadside into the first galley which bombarded Algiers. It is now a dead language. The idiom of the sea is altogether different. Duperré would not be able to understand Suffren.

The language of French naval signals is not less transformed; there is a long distance between the four pennants, red, white, yellow, and blue, of Labourdonnaye, and the eighteen flags of these days, which, hoisted two and two, three and three, or four and four, furnish, for distant communication, sixty-six thousand combinations, are never deficient, and, so to speak, foresee the unforeseen.

IV
ONE IS VULNERABLE WHERE ONE LOVES

MESS LETHIERRY'S heart and hand were always ready—a large heart and a large hand. His failing was that admirable one, self-confidence. He had a certain fashion of his own of undertaking to do a thing. It was a solemn fashion. He said, "I give my word of honour to do it, with God's help." That said, he went through with his duty. He put his faith in God—nothing more. His rare churchgoing was merely formal. At sea he was superstitious.

Nevertheless, the storm had never yet arisen which could daunt him. One reason of this was his impatience of opposition. He could tolerate it neither from the ocean nor anything else. He meant to have his way; so much the worse for the sea if it thwarted him. It might try, if it would, but Mess Lethierry would not give in. A refractory wave could no more stop him than an angry neighbour. What he had said was said; what he planned out was done. He bent neither before an objection nor before the tempest. The word "no" had no existence for him, whether it was in the mouth of a man or in the angry muttering of a thunder-cloud. In the teeth of all he went on in his way. He would take no refusals. Hence his obstinacy in life, and his intrepidity on the ocean.

He seasoned his simple meal of fish soup for himself, knowing the quantities of pepper, salt, and herbs which it required, and was as well pleased with the cooking as with the meal. To complete the sketch of Lethierry's peculiarities, the reader must conjure a being to whom the putting on of a surtout would amount to a transfiguration; whom a landsman's greatcoat would convert into a strange animal; one who, standing with his locks blown about by the wind, might have represented old Jean Bart, but who, in the landsman's round hat, would have looked an idiot; awkward in cities, wild and redoubtable at sea; a man with broad shoulders, fit for a porter; one who indulged in no oaths, was rarely in anger, whose voice had a soft accent, which became like thunder in a speaking-trumpet; a peasant who had read something of the philosophy of Diderot and D'Alembert; a Guernsey man who had seen the great Revolution; a learned ignoramus, free from bigotry, but indulging in visions, with more faith in the White Lady than in the Holy Virgin; possessing the strength of Polyphemus, the perseverance of Columbus, with a little of the bull in his nature, and a little of the child. Add to these physical and mental peculiarities a somewhat flat nose, large cheeks, a set of teeth still perfect, a face filled with wrinkles, and which seemed to have been buffeted by the waves and subjected to the beating of the winds of forty years, a brow in which the storm and tempest were plainly written—an incarnation of a rock in the open sea. Add to this, too, a good-tempered smile always ready to light up his weather-beaten countenance, and you have before you Mess Lethierry.

Mess Lethierry had two special objects of affection only. Their names were Durande and Déruchette.

Book III
Durande and Déruchette

※

I
PRATTLE AND SMOKE

THE HUMAN BODY might well be regarded as a mere simulacrum; but it envelopes our reality, it darkens our light, and broadens the shadow in which we live. The soul is the reality of our existence. Strictly speaking, the human visage is a mask. The true man is that which exists under what is called man. If that being, which thus exists sheltered and secreted behind that illusion which we call the flesh, could be approached, more than one strange revelation would be made. The vulgar error is to mistake the outward husk for the living spirit. Yonder maiden, for example, if we could see her as she really is, might she not figure as some bird of the air?

A bird transmuted into a young maiden, what could be more exquisite? Picture it in your own home, and call it Déruchette. Delicious creature! One might be almost tempted to say, "Good-morning, Mademoiselle Goldfinch." The wings are invisible, but the chirping may still be heard. Sometimes, too, she pipes a clear, loud song. In her childlike prattle, the creature is, perhaps, inferior; but in her song, how superior to humanity! When womanhood dawns, this angel flies away; but sometimes returns, bringing back a little one to a mother. Meanwhile, she who is one day to be a mother is for a long while a child; the girl becomes a maiden, fresh and joyous as the lark. Noting her movements, we feel as if it was good of her not to fly away. The dear familiar companion moves at her own sweet will about the house; flits from branch to branch, or rather from room to room; goes to and fro; approaches and retires; plumes her wings, or rather combs her hair, and makes all kinds of gentle noises—murmurings of unspeakable delight to certain ears. She asks a question, and is answered; is asked something in return, and chirps a reply. It is delightful to chat with her when tired of serious talk; for this creature carries with her something of her skyey element. She is, as it were, a thread of gold interwoven with your sombre thoughts; you feel almost grateful to her for her kindness in not making herself invisible, when it would be so easy for her to be even impalpable; for the beautiful is a necessary of life. There is, in this world, no function more important than that of being charming. The forest-glade would be incomplete without the humming-bird. To shed joy around, to radiate happiness, to cast light upon dark days, to be the golden thread of our destiny, and the very spirit of grace and harmony, is not this to render a service? Does not beauty confer a benefit upon us, even by the simple fact of being beautiful? Here and there we meet with one who possesses that fairy-like power of enchanting all about her; sometimes she is ignorant herself of this magical influence, which is, however, for that reason, only the more perfect. Her presence lights up the home; her approach is like a cheerful warmth; she passes by; and we are content; she stays awhile, and we are happy. To behold her is to live: she is the Aurora with a human face. She has no need to do more than simply to be: she makes an Eden of the house; Paradise breathes from her; and she communicates this delight to all, without taking any greater trouble than that of existing beside them. Is it not a thing divine to have a smile which, none know how, has the power to lighten the weight of that enormous chain which all the living, in common, drag behind them? Déruchette possessed this smile: we may even say that this smile was Déruchette herself. There is one thing which has more resemblance to ourselves than even our face, and that is our expression: but there is yet another thing which more resembles us than this, and that is our smile. Déruchette smiling was simply Déruchette.

There is something peculiarly attractive in the Jersey and Guernsey race. The women, particularly the young, are remarkable for a pure and exquisite beauty. Their complexion is a combination of the Saxon fairness, with the proverbial ruddiness of the Norman people—rosy cheeks and blue eyes; but the eyes want brilliancy. The English training dulls them. Their liquid glances will be irresistible whenever the secret is found of giving them that depth which is the glory of the Parisienne. Happily Englishwomen are not yet quite transformed into the Parisian type. Déruchette was not a Parisian; yet she was certainly not a Guernesiaise. Lethierry had brought her up to be neat and delicate and pretty; and so she was.

Déruchette had, at times, an air of bewitching langour, and a certain mischief in the eye, which were altogether involuntary. She scarcely knew, perhaps, the meaning of the word love, and yet not unwillingly ensnared those about her in the toils. But all this in her was innocent. She never thought of marrying.

Déruchette had the prettiest little hands in the world, and little feet to match them. Sweetness and goodness reigned throughout her person; her family and fortune were her uncle Mess Lethierry; her occupation was only to live her daily life; her accomplishments were the knowledge of a few songs; her intellectual gifts were summed up in her simple innocence; she had the graceful repose of the West Indian woman, mingled at times with giddiness and vivacity, with the teasing playfulness of a child, yet with a dash of melancholy. Her dress was somewhat rustic, and like that peculiar to her country—elegant, though not in accordance with the fashions of great cities; for she wore flowers in her bonnet all the year round. Add to all this an open brow, a neck supple and graceful, chestnut hair, a fair skin slightly freckled with exposure to the sun, a mouth somewhat large, but well-defined, and visited from time to time by a dangerous smile. This was Déruchette.

Sometimes in the evening, a little after sunset, at the moment when the dusk of the sky mingles with the dusk of the sea, and twilight invests the waves with a mysterious awe, the people beheld, entering the harbour of St. Sampson, upon the dark rolling waters, a strange, undefined thing, a monstrous form which puffed and blew; a horrid machine which roared like a wild beast, and smoked like a volcano; a species of Hydra foaming among the breakers, and leaving behind it a dense cloud, as it rushed on towards the town with a frightful beating of its fins, and a throat belching forth flame. This was Durande.

II
THE OLD STORY OF UTOPIA

A STEAMBOAT WAS a prodigious novelty in the waters of the Channel in 182-. The whole coast of Normandy was long strangely excited by it.

Now-a-days, ten or a dozen steam vessels, crossing and recrossing within the bounds of the horizon, scarcely attract a glance from loiterers on the shore. At the most, some persons, whose interest or business it is to note such things, will observe the indications in their smoke of whether they burn Welsh or Newcastle coal. They pass, and that is all. "Welcome," if coming home; "a pleasant passage," if outward bound.

Folks were less calm on the subject of these wonderful inventions in the first quarter of the present century; and the new and strange machines, and their long lines of smoke regarded with no good-will by the Channel Islanders. In that Puritanical Archipelago, where the Queen of England has been censured for violating the Scriptures* by using chloroform during her accouchments, the first steam-vessel which made its appearance received the name of the "Devil Boat." In the eyes of these worthy fishermen, once Catholics, now Calvinists, but always bigots, it seemed to be a portion of the infernal regions which had been somehow set afloat. A local preacher selected for his discourse the question of "Whether man has the right to make fire and water work together when God had divided them."** This beast, composed of iron and fire, did it not resemble Leviathan? Was it not an attempt to bring chaos again into the universe? This is not the only occasion on which the progress of civilisation has been stigmatised as a return to chaos.

"A mad notion—a gross delusion—an absurdity!" Such was the verdict of the Academy of Sciences when consulted by Napoleon on the subject of steamboats, early in the present century. The poor fishermen of St. Sampson may be excused for not being, in scientific matters, any wiser than the mathematicians of Paris; and in religious matters, a little island like Guernsey is not bound to be more enlightened than a great continent like America. In the year 1807, when the first steamboat of Fulton, commanded by Livingston, furnished with one of Watt's engines, sent from England, and manœuvred, besides her ordinary crew, by two Frenchmen only, André Michaux and another, made her first voyage from New York to Albany, it happened that she set sail on the 17th of August. The Methodists took up this important fact, and in numberless chapels, preachers were heard calling down a malediction on the machine, and declaring that this number 17 was no other than the total of the ten horns and seven heads of the beast of the Apocalypse. In America, they invoked against the steamboats the beast from

the book of Revelation; in Europe, the reptile of the book of Genesis. This
was the simple difference.

The savants had rejected steamboats as impossible; the priests had anath-
ematised them as impious. Science had condemned, and religion consigned
them to perdition. Fulton was a new incarnation of Lucifer. The simple
people on the coasts and in the villages were confirmed in their prejudice
by the uneasiness which they felt at the outlandish sight. The religious view
of steamboats may be summed up as follows: Water and fire were divorced
at the creation. This divorce was enjoined by God himself. Man has no right
to join what his Maker has put asunder; to reunite what he has disunited.
The peasants' view was simply, "I don't like the look of this thing."

No one but Mess Lethierry, perhaps, could have been found at that early
period daring enough to dream of such an enterprise as the establishment
of a steam-vessel between Guernsey and St. Malo. He, alone, as an independent thinker, was capable of conceiving such an idea, or, as a hardy mariner,
of carrying it out. The French part of his nature, probably, conceived the
idea; the English part supplied the energy to put it in execution.

How and when this was, we are about to inform the reader.

*GENESIS, CHAP. III. V. 16.

**GENESIS, CHAP. I. V. 4.

III
RANTAINE

ABOUT FORTY YEARS before the period of the commencement of
our narrative, there stood in the suburbs of Paris, near the city wall, between
the Fosse-aux-Loups and the Tombe-Issoire, a house of doubtful reputation. It was a lonely, ruinous building, evidently a place for dark deeds on
an occasion. Here lived, with his wife and child, a species of town bandit;
a man who had been clerk to an attorney practising at the Châtelet—he
figured somewhat later at the Assize Court; the name of this family was
Rantaine. On a mahogany chest of drawers in the old house were two china

cups, ornamented with flowers, on one of which appeared, in gilt letters, the words, "A souvenir of friendship;" on the other, "A token of esteem." The child lived in an atmosphere of vice in this miserable home. The father and mother having belonged to the lower middle class, the boy had learnt to read, and they brought it up in a fashion. The mother, pale and almost in rags, gave "instruction," as she called it, mechanically, to the little one, heard it spell a few words to her, and interrupted the lesson to accompany her husband on some criminal expedition, or to earn the wages of prostitution. Meanwhile, the book remained open on the table as she had left it, and the boy sat beside it, meditating in his way.

The father and mother, detected one day in one of their criminal enterprises, suddenly vanished into that obscurity in which the penal laws envelop convicted malefactors. The child, too, disappeared.

Lethierry, in his wanderings about the world, stumbled, one day, on an adventurer like himself; helped him out of some scrape; rendered him a kindly service, and was apparently repaid with gratitude. He took a fancy to the stranger, picked him up, and brought him to Guernsey, where, finding him intelligent in learning the duties of a sailor aboard a coasting vessel, he made him a companion. This stranger was the little Rantaine, now grown up to manhood.

Rantaine, like Lethierry, had a bull neck, a large and powerful breadth of shoulders for carrying burdens, and loins like those of the Farnese Hercules. Lethierry and he had a remarkable similarity of appearance: Rantaine was the taller. People who saw their forms behind as they were walking side by side along the port, exclaimed, "There are two brothers." On looking them in the face the effect was different: all that was open in the countenance of Lethierry was reserved and cautious in that of Rantaine. Rantaine was an expert swordsman, played on the harmonica, could snuff a candle at twenty paces with a pistol-ball, could strike a tremendous blow with the fist, recite verses from Voltaire's *Henriade*, and interpret dreams; he knew by heart *Les Tombeaux de Saint Denis*, by Treneuil. He talked sometimes of having had relations with the Sultan of Calicut, "whom the Portuguese call the Zamorin." If any one had seen the little memorandum-book which he carried about with him, he would have found notes and jottings of this kind: "At Lyons in a fissure of the wall of one of the cells in the prison of St. Joseph, a file." He spoke always with a grave deliberation; he called himself the son of a Chevalier de Saint Louis. His linen was of a miscellaneous kind, and marked with different initials. Nobody was ever more tender than he was on the point of honour; he fought and killed his man. The mother of a pretty actress could not have an eye more watchful for an insult.

He might have stood for the personification of subtlety under an outer garb of enormous strength.

It was the power of his fist, applied one day at a fair, upon a *cabeza de moro*, which had originally taken the fancy of Lethierry. No one in Guernsey knew anything of his adventures. They were of a chequered kind. If the great theatre of destiny had a special wardrobe, Rantaine ought to have taken the dress of harlequin. He had lived, and had seen the world. He had run through the gamut of possible trades and qualities; had been a cook at Madagascar, trainer of birds at Honolulu, a religious journalist at the Galapagos Islands, a poet at Oomrawuttee, a freeman at Haiti. In this latter character he had delivered at Grand Goave a funeral oration, of which the local journals have preserved this fragment: "Farewell, then, noble spirit. In the azure vault of the heavens, where thou wingest now thy flight, thou wilt, no doubt, rejoin the good Abbé Leander Crameau, of Little Goave. Tell him that, thanks to ten years of glorious efforts, thou hast completed the church of the *Ansa-à-Veau*. Adieu! transcendent genius, model mason!" His freemason's mask did not prevent him, as we see, wearing a little of the Roman Catholic. The former won to his side the men of progress, and the latter the men of order. He declared himself a white of pure caste, and hated the negroes; though, for all that, he would certainly have been an admirer of the Emperor Soulouque. In 1815, at Bordeaux, the glow of his royalist enthusiasm broke forth in the shape of a huge white feather in his cap. His life had been a series of eclipses—of appearances, disappearances, and reappearances. He was a sort of revolving light upon the coasts of scampdom. He knew a little Turkish: instead of "guillotined," would say "*néboïssé*." He had been a slave in Tripoli, in the house of a Thaleb, and had learnt Turkish by dint of blows with a stick. His employment had been to stand at evenings at the doors of the mosque, there to read aloud to the faithful the Koran inscribed upon slips of wood, or pieces of camel leather. It is not improbable that he was a renegade.

He was capable of everything, and something worse.

He had a trick of laughing loud and knitting his brows at the same time. He used to say, "In politics, I esteem only men inaccessible to influences;" or, "I am for decency and good morals;" or, "The pyramid must be replaced upon its base." His manner was rather cheerful and cordial than otherwise. The expression of his mouth contradicted the sense of his words. His nostrils had an odd way of distending themselves. In the corners of his eyes he had a little network of wrinkles, in which all sorts of dark thoughts seemed to meet together. It was here alone that the secret of his physiognomy could be thoroughly studied. His flat foot was a vulture's claw. His skull was low at the top and large about the temples. His ill-shapen ear, bristled with hair, seemed to say, "Beware of speaking to the animal in this cave."

One fine day, in Guernsey, Rantaine was suddenly missing.

Lethierry's partner had absconded, leaving the treasury of their partnership empty.

In this treasury there was some money of Rantaine's, no doubt, but there were also fifty thousand francs belonging to Lethierry.

By forty years of industry and probity as a coaster and ship carpenter, Lethierry had saved one hundred thousand francs. Rantaine robbed him of half the sum.

Half ruined, Lethierry did not lose heart, but began at once to think how to repair his misfortune. A stout heart may be ruined in fortune, but not in spirit. It was just about that time that people began to talk of the new kind of boat to be moved by steam-engines. Lethierry conceived the idea of trying Fulton's invention, so much disputed about; and by one of these fire-boats to connect the Channel Islands with the French coast. He staked his all upon this idea; he devoted to it the wreck of his savings. Accordingly, six months after Rantaine's flight, the astonished people of St. Sampson beheld, issuing from the port, a vessel discharging huge volumes of smoke, and looking like a ship a-fire at sea. This was the first steam-vessel to navigate the Channel.

This vessel, to which the people in their dislike and contempt for novelty immediately gave the nickname of "Lethierry's Galley," was announced as intended to maintain a constant communication between Guernsey and St. Malo.

IV

CONTINUATION OF THE STORY OF UTOPIA

IT MAY be well imagined that the new enterprise did not prosper much at first. The owners of cutters passing between the Island of Guernsey and the French coast were loud in their outcries. They denounced this attack upon the Holy Scriptures and their monopoly. The chapels began to fulminate against it. One reverend gentleman, named Elihu, stigmatised the new steam-vessel as an "atheistical construction," and the sailing-boat was declared the only orthodox craft. The people saw the horns of the devil among the beasts which the fireship carried to and fro. This storm of protest continued a considerable time. At last, however, it began to be perceived that these animals arrived less tired and sold better, their meat being superior; that the sea risk was less also for passengers; that this mode of travelling was less expensive, shorter, and more sure; that they started at a fixed time, and arrived at a fixed time; that consignments of fish travelling faster arrived fresher, and that it was now possible to find a sale in the French markets for the surplus of great takes of fish so common in Guernsey. The butter, too, from the far-famed Guernsey cows, made the passage quicker in the "Devil Boat" than in the old sailing vessels, and lost nothing of its good quality, insomuch that Dinan, in Brittany, began to become a customer for it, as well as St. Brieuc and Rennes. In short, thanks to what they called "Lethierry's Galley," the people enjoyed safe travelling, regular communication, prompt and easy passages to and fro, an increase of circulation, an extension of markets and of commerce, and, finally, it was felt that it was necessary to patronise this "Devil Boat," which flew in the face of the Holy Scriptures, and brought wealth to the island. Some daring spirits even went so far as to express a positive satisfaction at it. Sieur Landoys, the registrar, bestowed his approval upon the vessel—an undoubted piece of impartiality on his part, as he did not like Lethierry. For, first of all, Lethierry was entitled to the dignity of "Mess," while Landoys was merely "Sieur Landoys." Then, although registrar of St. Peter's Port, Landoys was a parishioner of St. Sampson. Now, there was not in the entire parish another man besides them devoid of prejudices. It seemed little enough, therefore, to indulge themselves with a detestation of each other. Two of a trade, says the proverb, rarely agree.

Sieur Landoys, however, had the honesty to support the steamboat. Others followed Landoys. By little and little, these facts multiplied. The growth of opinion is like the rising tide. Time and the continued and increasing success of the venture, with the evidence of real service rendered and the improvement in the general welfare, gradually converted the people; and the day at length arrived when, with the exception of a few wiseacres, every one admired "Lethierry's Galley."

It would probably win less admiration now-a-days. This steamboat of forty years since would doubtless provoke a smile among our modern boat-builders; for this marvel was ill-shaped; this prodigy was clumsy and infirm.

The distance between our grand Atlantic steam-vessels of the present day and the boats with wheel-paddles which Denis Papin floated on the Fulda in 1707, is not greater than that between a three-decker, like the *Montebello*, 200 feet long, having a mainyard of 115 feet, carrying a weight of 3000 tons, 1100 men, 120 guns, 10,000 cannon-balls, and 160 packages of canister, belching forth at every broadside, when in action, 3300 pounds of iron, and spreading to the wind, when it moves, 5600 square mètres of canvas, and the old Danish galley of the second century, discovered, full of stone hatchets, and bows and clubs, in the mud of the seashore, at Wester-Satrup, and preserved at the Hotel de Ville at Flensburg.

Exactly one hundred years—from 1707 to 1807—separate the first paddle-boat of Papin from the first steamboat of Fulton. "Lethierry's Galley" was assuredly a great improvement upon those two rough sketches; but it was itself only a sketch. For all that, it was a masterpiece in its way. Every scientific discovery in embryo presents that double aspect—a monster in the fœtus, a marvel in the germ.

V
THE DEVIL BOAT

"LETHIERRY'S GALLEY" was not masted with a view to sailing well; a fact which was not a defect; it is, indeed, one of the laws of naval construction.

Besides, her motive power being steam, her sails were only accessory. A paddle steamboat, moreover, is almost insensible to sails. The new steam-vessel
was too short, round, and thick-set. She had too much bow, and too great
a breadth of quarter. The daring of inventors had not yet reached the point
of making a steam-vessel light; Lethierry's boat had some of the defects of
Gilliatt's Dutch sloop. She pitched very little, but she rolled a good deal. Her
paddle-boxes were too high. She had too much beam for her length. The
massive machinery encumbered her, and to make her capable of carrying a
heavy cargo, her constructors had raised her bulwarks to an unusual height,
giving to the vessel the defects of old seventy-fours, a bastard model which
would have to be cut down to render them really seaworthy, or fit to go
into action. Being short, she ought to have been able to veer quickly—the
time employed in a manœuvre of that kind being in proportion to the
length of the vessel—but her weight deprived her of the advantage of her
shortness. Her midship-frame was too broad, a fact which retarded her; the
resistance of the sea being proportioned to the largest section below the
water-line, and to the square of the speed. Her prow was vertical, which
would not be regarded as a fault at the present day, but at that period this
portion of the construction was invariably sloped at an angle of forty-five
degrees. All the curving lines of the hull agreed well together, but it was
not long enough for oblique sailing, or for lying parallel with the water
displaced, which should always be thrown off laterally. In rough weather
she drew too much water, sometimes fore, sometimes aft, which showed
that her centre of gravity was not rightly adjusted. Owing to the weight
of the engine, the cargo shifted, so that the centre of gravity was often aft
of the mainmast, and then steam power had to be resorted to, for at such
times the mainsail had to be furled as it only made the vessel fall off. If close
to the wind, very careful manœuvring was required. The rudder was the
old-fashioned bar-rudder, not the wheeled one of the present time. Two
skiffs, a species of *you-yous*, were suspended to the davits. The vessel had
four anchors; the sheet-anchor, the second or working anchor, and two
bower-anchors. These four anchors, slung by chains, were moved, according
to the occasion, by the great capstan of the poop, or by the small capstan at
the prow. At that period the pump windlass had not superseded the intermitting efforts of the old handspike. Having only two bower-anchors, one

on the starboard and the other on the larboard side, the vessel could not move conveniently in certain winds, though she could aid herself at such times with the second anchor. Her buoys were normal, and so constructed that they carried the weight of the buoy-ropes without dipping. The launch was of a useful size, of service in all cases of need, and able to raise the main anchor. A novelty about her was that she was rigged with chains, which in no way detracted, however, from the mobility of the running rigging, or from the firmness of the standing rigging. The masts, yards, etc., although not of first-rate quality, were not in any way amiss, and the rigging at the mast-head was not very noticeable. The ribs were solid, but coarse, less delicacy of wood being required for steam than for sail. Her speed was six knots an hour. When lying-to she rode well. Take her as she was, "Lethierry's Galley" was a good sea boat; but people felt, that in moments of danger from reefs or waterspouts, she would be hardly manageable. Unhappily her build made her roll about on the waves, with a perpetual creaking like that of a new shoe.

She was, above all, a merchandise boat, and, like all ships built more for commerce than for fighting, was constructed exclusively with a view to stowage. She carried few passengers. The transport of cattle rendered stowage difficult and very peculiar. Vessels carried bullocks at that time in the hold, which was a complication of the difficulty. At the present day they are stowed on the fore-deck. The paddle-boxes of Lethierry's "Devil Boat" were painted white, the hull, down to the water-line, red, and all the rest of the vessel black, according to the somewhat ugly fashion of this century. When empty she drew seven feet of water, and when laden fourteen.

With regard to the engine, it was of considerable power. To speak exactly, its power was equal to that of one horse to every three tons burden, which is almost equal to that of a tugboat. The paddles were well placed, a little in advance of the centre of gravity of the vessel. The maximum pressure of the engine was equal to two atmospheres. It consumed a great deal of coal, although it was constructed on the condensation and expansion principles. It had no fly-wheel on account of the instability of the point of support, but this was then, as now, compensated for by two cranks at the extremities of the revolving shaft, so arranged that one was always at right angles when the other was at dead-point. The whole rested on a single sheet of cast-iron, so that even in case of any serious damage, no shock of the waves could upset its equilibrium, and even if the hull were injured the engine would remain intact. To render it stronger still, the connecting-rod had been placed near the steam-cylinders, so that the centre of oscillation of the working-beam was transferred from the middle to the end. Since then oscillating cylinders have been invented which do away with the necessity of connecting-rods, but in those days the placing of the connecting-rod near the cylinder was thought a triumph of engineering. The boiler was in sections and provided with a salt-water pump. The wheels were very large, which lessened the loss of power; the smoke-stack was lofty, which increased the draught. On the other hand, the size of the wheels exposed them to the force of the waves, and the height of the smoke-stack to the violence of the wind. Wooden paddle-floats, iron clamps, bosses of cast-iron—such were the wheels, which, well constructed, could, strange though it may seem, be taken to pieces. Three floats were always under water. The speed of the centre of the floats only exceeded by a sixth the speed of the vessel itself; this was the chief defect of the wheels. Moreover, the cranks were too long, and the slide-valve caused too much friction in the admission of steam into the cylinder. For that period the engine seemed, and indeed was, admirable. It had been constructed in France, at the works at Bercy. Mess Lethierry had roughly sketched it: the engineer who had constructed it in accordance with his diagram was dead, so that the engine was unique, and probably could not have been replaced. The designer still lived, but the constructor was no more.

The engine had cost forty thousand francs.

Lethierry had himself constructed the "Devil Boat" upon the great covered stocks by the side of the first tower between St. Peter's Port and St. Sampson. He had been to Brême to buy the wood. All his skill as a shipwright was exhausted in its construction; his ingenuity might be seen in the planks, the seams of which were straight and even, and covered with sarangousti, an Indian mastic, better than resin. The sheathing was well beaten. To remedy the roundness of the hull, Lethierry had fitted out a boom at the bowsprit, which allowed him to add a false spritsail to the regular one. On the day of the launch, he cried aloud, "At last I am afloat!" The vessel was successful, in fact, as the reader has already learnt.

Either by chance or design she had been launched on the 14th of July, the anniversary of the taking of the Bastille. On that day, mounted upon the bridge between the two paddle-boxes, looked Lethierry upon the sea, and exclaimed, "It is your turn now! The Parisians took the Bastille, now science takes the sea."

Lethierry's boat made the voyage from Guernsey to St. Malo once a week. She started on the Tuesday morning, and returned on the Friday evening, in time for the Saturday market. She was a stronger craft than any of the largest coasting sloops in all the Archipelago, and her capacity being in proportion to her dimensions, one of her voyages was equal to four voyages of an ordinary boat in the same trade; hence they were very profitable. The reputation of a vessel depends on its stowage, and Lethierry was an admirable stower of cargo. When he was no longer able to work himself, he trained up a sailor to undertake this duty. At the end of two years, the steamboat brought in a clear seven hundred and fifty pounds sterling a year, or eighteen thousand francs. The pound sterling of Guernsey is worth twenty-four francs only, that of England twenty-five, and that of Jersey twenty-six. These differences are less unimportant than they seem: the banks, at all events, know how to turn them to advantage.

VI
LETHIERRY'S EXALTATION

THE "DEVIL BOAT" prospered. Mess Lethierry began to look forward to the time when he should be called "Monsieur." At Guernsey, people do not become "Monsieurs" at one bound. Between the plain man and the gentleman, there is quite a scale to climb. To begin with, we have the simple name, plain "Peter," let us suppose; the second step is "Neighbour Peter;" the third, "Father Peter;" the fourth, "Sieur Peter;" the fifth, "Mess Peter;" and then we reach the summit in "Monsieur Peter."

This scale ascending thus from the ground is carried to still greater heights. All the upper classes of England join on and continue it. Here are the various steps, becoming more and more glorious. Above the Monsieur, or "Mr.," there is the "Esquire;" above the squire, the knight; above the knight, still rising, we have the baronet, the Scotch laird, the baron, the viscount, the earl (called count in France, and jarl in Norway); the marquis, the duke, the prince of the blood royal, and the king: so, by degrees, we ascend from the people to the middle class, from the middle class to the baronetage, from the baronetage to the peerage, from the peerage to royalty.

Thanks to his successful ingenuity, thanks to steam, and his engines, and the "Devil Boat," Mess Lethierry was fast becoming an important personage. When building his vessel he had been compelled to borrow money. He had become indebted at Brême, he had become indebted at St. Malo; but every year he diminished his obligations.

He had, moreover, purchased on credit, at the very entrance to the port of St. Sampson, a pretty stone-built house, entirely new, situate between the sea and a garden. On the corner of this house was inscribed the name of the "Bravées." Its front formed a part of the wall of the port itself, and it was remarkable for a double row of windows: on the north, alongside a little enclosure filled with flowers, and on the south commanding a view of the ocean. It had thus two *façades*, one open to the tempest and the sea, the other looking into a garden filled with roses.

These two frontages seemed made for the two inmates of the house— Mess Lethierry and Déruchette.

The "Bravées" was popular at St. Sampson, for Mess Lethierry had at length become a popular man. This popularity was due partly to his good nature, his devotedness, and his courage; partly to the number of lives he had saved; and a great deal to his success, and to the fact that he had awarded to St. Sampson the honour of being the port of the departure and arrival of the new steamboat. Having made the discovery that the "Devil Boat" was decidedly a success, St. Peter's, the capital, desired to obtain it for that port, but Lethierry held fast to St. Sampson. It was his native town. "It was there that I was first pitched into the water," he used to say; hence his great local popularity. His position as a small landed proprietor paying land-tax, made him, what they call in Guernsey, an *unhabitant*. He was chosen douzenier. The poor sailor had mounted five out of six steps of the Guernsey social scale; he had attained the dignity of "Mess"; he was rapidly approaching the Monsieur; and who could predict whether he might not even rise higher than that? who could say that they might not one day find in the almanack of Guernsey, under the heading of "Nobility and Gentry," the astonishing and superb inscription,—*Lethierry, Esq.*?

But Mess Lethierry had nothing of vanity in his nature, or he had no sense of it; or if he had, disdained it: to know that he was useful was his greatest pleasure; to be popular touched him less than being necessary; he had, as we have already said, only two objects of delight, and consequently only two ambitions: the Durande and Déruchette.

However this may have been, he had embarked in the lottery of the sea, and had gained the chief prize.

This chief prize was the Durande steaming away in all her pride.

VII
THE SAME GODFATHER AND THE SAME PATRON SAINT

HAVING CREATED HIS steamboat, Lethierry had christened it: he had called it Durande—"La Durande." We will speak of her henceforth by no other name; we will claim the liberty, also, in spite of typographical usage, of not italicising this name Durande; conforming in this to the notion of Mess Lethierry, in whose eyes La Durande was almost a living person.

Durande and Déruchette are the same name. Déruchette is the diminutive.

This diminutive is very common in France.

In the country the names of saints are endowed with all these diminutives as well as all their augmentatives. One might suppose there were several persons when there is, in fact, only one. This system of patrons and patronesses under different names is by no means rare. Lise, Lisette, Lisa, Elisa, Isabelle, Lisbeth, Betsy, all these are simply Elizabeth. It is probable that Mahout, Maclou, Malo, and Magloire are the same saint: this, however, we do not vouch for.

Saint Durande is a saint of l'Angoumois, and of the Charente; whether she is an orthodox member of the calendar is a question for the Bollandists: orthodox or not, she has been made the patron saint of numerous chapels.

It was while Lethierry was a young sailor at Rochefort that he had made the acquaintance of this saint, probably in the person of some pretty Charantaise, perhaps in that of the grisette with the white nails. The saint had remained sufficiently in his memory for him to give the name to the two things which he loved most—Durande to the steamboat, Déruchette to the girl.

Of one he was the father, of the other the uncle.

Déruchette was the daughter of a brother who had died: she was an orphan child: he had adopted her, and had taken the place both of father and mother.

Déruchette was not only his niece, she was his godchild; he had held her in his arms at the baptismal font; it was he who had chosen her patron saint, Durande, and her Christian name, Déruchette.

Déruchette, as we have said, was born at St. Peter's Port. Her name was inscribed at its date on the register of the parish.

As long as the niece was a child, and the uncle poor, nobody took heed of her appellation of Déruchette; but when the little girl became a miss, and the sailor a gentleman, the name of Déruchette shocked the feelings of Guernsey society. The uncouthness of the sound astonished every one. Folks asked Mess Lethierry "why Déruchette?" He answered, "It is a very good name in its way." Several attempts were made to get him to obtain a change in the baptismal name, but he would be no party to them. One day, a fine lady of the upper circle of society in St. Sampson, the wife of a rich retired ironfounder, said to Mess Lethierry, "In future, I shall call your daughter Nancy."

"If names of country towns are in fashion," said he, "why not Lons le Saulnier?" The fine lady did not yield her point, and on the morrow said, "We are determined not to have it Déruchette; I have found for your daughter a pretty name—*Marianne*." "A very pretty name, indeed," replied Mess Lethierry, "composed of two words which signify—a husband and an ass."* He held fast to Déruchette.

It would be a mistake to infer from Lethierry's pun that he had no wish to see his niece married. He desired to see her married, certainly; but in his own way: he intended her to have a husband after his own heart, one who would work hard, and whose wife would have little to do. He liked rough hands in a man, and delicate ones in a woman. To prevent Déruchette spoiling her pretty hands he had always brought her up like a young lady; he had provided her with a music-master, a piano, a little library, and a few needles and threads in a pretty work-basket. She was, indeed, more often reading than stitching; more often playing than reading. This was as Mess Lethierry wished it. To be charming was all that he expected of her. He had reared the young girl like a flower. Whoever has studied the character of sailors will understand this: rude and hard in their nature, they have an odd partiality for grace and delicacy. To realise the idea of the uncle, the niece ought to have been rich; so indeed felt Mess Lethierry. His steamboat voyaged for this end. The mission of Durande was to provide a marriage portion for Déruchette.

*A PLAY UPON THE FRENCH WORDS, *MARI* AND *ÂNE*.

VIII
"BONNIE DUNDEE"

DÉRUCHETTE occupied the prettiest room at the Bravées. It had two windows, was furnished with various articles made of fine-grained mahogany, had a bed with four curtains, green and white, and looked out upon the garden, and beyond it towards the high hill, on which stands the Vale Castle. Gilliatt's house, the Bû de la Rue, was on the other side of this hill.

Déruchette had her music and piano in this chamber; she accompanied herself on the instrument when singing the melody which she preferred—the melancholy Scottish air of "Bonnie Dundee." The very spirit of night breathes in this melody; but her voice was full of the freshness of dawn. The contrast was quaint and pleasing; people said, "Miss Déruchette is at her piano."

The passers-by at the foot of the hill stopped sometimes before the wall of the garden of the Bravées to listen to that sweet voice and plaintive song.

Déruchette was the very embodiment of joy as she went to and fro in the house. She brought with her a perpetual spring. She was beautiful, but more pretty than beautiful; and still more graceful than pretty. She reminded the good old pilots, friends of Mess Lethierry, of that princess in the song which the soldiers and sailors sing, who was so beautiful:

"Qu'elle passait pour telle dans le regiment."

Mess Lethierry used to say, "She has a head of hair like a ship's cable."

From her infancy she had been remarkable for beauty. The learned in such matters had grave doubts about her nose, but the little one having probably determined to be pretty, had finally satisfied their requirements. She grew to girlhood without any serious loss of beauty; her nose became neither too long nor too short; and when grown up, her critics admitted her to be charming.

She never addressed her uncle otherwise than as father.

Lethierry allowed her to soil her fingers a little in gardening, and even in some kind of household duties: she watered her beds of pink holly-hocks, purple foxgloves, perennial phloxes, and scarlet herb bennets. She took good advantage of the climate of Guernsey, so favourable to flowers. She had, like many other persons there, aloes in the open ground, and, what is more difficult, she succeeded in cultivating the Nepaulese cinquefoil. Her little kitchen-garden was scientifically arranged; she was able to produce from it several kinds of rare vegetables. She sowed Dutch cauliflower and Brussels cabbages, which she thinned out in July, turnips for August, endive for September, short parsnip for the autumn, and rampions for winter. Mess Lethierry did not interfere with her in this, so long as she did not handle the spade and rake too much, or meddle with the coarser kinds of garden labour. He had provided her with two servants, one named Grace, and the other Douce, which are favourite names in Guernsey. Grace and Douce did the hard work of the house and garden, and they had the right to have red hands.

With regard to Mess Lethierry, his room was a little retreat with a view over the harbour, and communicating with the great lower room of the ground floor, on which was situated the door of the house, near which the various staircases met.

His room was furnished with his hammock, his chronometer, and his pipe: there were also a table and a chair. The ceiling had been whitewashed, as well as the four walls. A fine marine map, bearing the inscription *W. Faden*,

5 Charing Cross, Geographer to His Majesty, and representing the Channel Islands, was nailed up at the side of the door, and on the left, stretched out and fastened with other nails, appeared one of those large cotton handkerchiefs on which are printed, in colours, the signals of all countries in the world, having at the four corners the standards of France, Russia, Spain, and the United States, and in the centre the union-jack of England.

Douce and Grace were two faithful creatures within certain limits. Douce was good-natured enough, and Grace was probably good-looking. Douce was unmarried, and had secretly "a gallant." In the Channel Islands the word is common, as indeed is the fact itself. The two girl's regarded as servants had something of the Creole in their character, a sort of slowness in their movements, not out of keeping with the Norman spirit pervading the relations of servant and master in the Channel Islands. Grace, coquettish and good-looking, was always scanning the future with a nervous anxiety. This arose from the fact of her not only having, like Douce, "a gallant," but also, as the scandal-loving averred, a sailor husband, whose return one day was a thing she dreaded. This, however, does not concern us. In a household less austere and less innocent, Douce would have continued to be the servant, but Grace would have become the *soubrette.* The dangerous talents of Grace were lost upon a young mistress so pure and good as Déruchette. For the rest, the intrigues of Douce and Grace were cautiously concealed. Mess Lethierry knew nothing of such matters, and no token of them had ever reached Déruchette.

The lower room of the ground floor, a hall with a large fireplace and surrounded with benches and tables, had served in the last century as a meeting-place for a conventicle of French Protestant refugees. The sole ornament of the bare stone wall was a sheet of parchment, set in a frame of black wood, on which were represented some of the charitable deeds of the great Bossuet, Bishop of Meaux. Some poor diocesans of this famous orator, surnamed the "Eagle," persecuted by him at the time of the Revocation of the Edict of Nantes, and driven to take shelter at Guernsey, had hung this picture on the wall to preserve the remembrance of those facts. The spectator who had the patience to decipher a rude handwriting in faded ink might have learnt the following facts, which are but little known:—"29th October, 1685, Monsieur the Bishop of Meaux, appeals to the king to destroy the temples of Morcef and Nanteuil"—"2nd April, 1686, Arrest of Cochard, father and son, for their religious opinions, at the request of Monsieur the Bishop of Meaux. Released: the Cochards having recanted."—"28th October, 1699, Monsieur the Bishop of Meaux sent to Mde. Pontchartrain a petition of remonstrance, pointing out that it will be necessary to place the young ladies named Chalandes and de Neuville, who are of the reformed religion, in the House of the 'New Catholics' at Paris."—"7th July, 1703, the king's order executed as requested by Monsieur the Bishop of Meaux, for shutting up in an asylum Baudouin and his wife, two bad Catholics of Fublaines."

At the end of the hall, near the door of Mess Lethierry's room, was a little corner with a wooden partition, which had been the Huguenot's sanctum, and had become, thanks to its row of rails and a small hole to pass paper or money through, the steamboat office; that is to say, the office of the Durande, kept by Mess Lethierry in person. Upon the old oaken reading-desk, where once rested the Holy Bible, lay a great ledger with its alternate pages headed Dr. and Cr.

IX
THE MAN WHO DISCOVERED RANTAINE'S CHARACTER

AS LONG as Mess Lethierry had been able to do duty, he had commanded the Durande, and had had no other pilot or captain but himself; but a time had come, as we have said, when he had been compelled to find a successor. He had chosen for that purpose Sieur Clubin, of Torteval, a taciturn man. Sieur Clubin had a character upon the coast for strict probity. He became the *alter ego*, the double, of Mess Lethierry.

Sieur Clubin, although he had rather the look of a notary than of a sailor, was a mariner of rare skill. He had all the talents which are required to meet dangers of every kind. He was a skilful stower, a safe man aloft, an able and careful boatswain, a powerful steersman, an experienced pilot, and a bold captain. He was prudent, and he carried his prudence sometimes to the point of daring, which is a great quality at sea. His natural apprehensiveness of danger was tempered by a strong instinct of what was possible in an emergency. He was one of those mariners who will face risks to a point perfectly well known to themselves, and who generally manage to come successfully out of every peril. Every certainty which a man can command, dealing with so fickle an element as the sea, he possessed. Sieur Clubin, moreover, was a renowned swimmer; he was one of that race of men broken into the buffeting of the waves, who can remain as long as they please in the water—who can start from the Havre-des-Pas at Jersey, double the Colettes, swim round the Hermitage and Castle Elizabeth, and return in two hours to the point from which they started. He came from Torteval, where he had the reputation of often having swum across the passage so much dreaded, from the Hanway rocks to the point of Pleinmont.

One circumstance which had recommended Sieur Clubin to Mess Lethierry more than any other, was his having judged correctly the character of Rantaine. He had pointed out to Lethierry the dishonesty of the man, and had said "Rantaine will rob you." His prediction was verified. More than once—in matters, it is true, not very important—Mess Lethierry had put his ever-scrupulous honesty to the proof; and he freely communicated with him on the subject of his affairs. Mess Lethierry used to say, "A good conscience expects to be treated with perfect confidence."

X
LONG YARNS

MESS LETHIERRY, for the sake of his own ease, always wore his seafaring clothes, and preferred his tarpaulin overcoat to his pilot jacket. Déruchette felt vexed, occasionally, about this peculiarity. Nothing is prettier than a pouting beauty. She laughed and scolded. "My dear father," she would say, "what a smell of pitch!" and she would give him a gentle tap upon his broad shoulders.

This good old seaman had gathered from his voyages many wonderful stories. He had seen at Madagascar birds' feathers, three of which sufficed to make a roof of a house. He had seen in India, field sorrel, the stalks of which were nine inches high. In New Holland he had seen troops of turkeys and geese led about and guarded by a bird, like a flock by a shepherd's dog; this bird was called the Agami. He had visited elephants' cemeteries. In Africa, he had encountered gorillas, a terrible species of man-monkey. He knew the ways of all the ape tribe, from the wild dog-faced monkey, which he called the Macaco-bravo, to the howling monkey or *Macaco-barbado*. In Chili, he had seen a pouched monkey move the compassion of the huntsman by showing its little one. He had seen in California a hollow trunk of a tree fall to the ground, so vast that a man on horseback could ride one hundred paces inside. In Morocco, he had seen the Mozabites and the Bisskris fighting with matraks and bars of iron—the Bisskris, because they had been called *kelbs*, which means dogs; and the Mozabites, because they had been treated as *khamsi*, which means people of the fifth sect. He had seen in China the pirate Chanh-thong-quan-larh-Quoi cut to pieces for having assassinated the Ap of a village. At Thu-dan-mot, he had seen a lion carry off an old woman in the open market-place. He was present at the arrival of the Great Serpent brought from Canton to Saigon to celebrate in the pagoda of Cho-len the fête of Quan-nam, the goddess of navigators. He had beheld the great Quan-Sû among the Moi. At Rio de Janeiro, he had seen the Brazilian ladies in the evening put little balls of gauze into their hair, each containing a beautiful kind of firefly; and the whole forming a head-dress of little twinkling lights. He had combated in Paraguay with swarms of enormous ants and spiders, big and downy as an infant's head, and compassing with their long legs a third of a yard, and attacking men by pricking them with their bristles, which enter the skin as sharp as arrows, and raise painful blisters. On the river Arinos, a tributary of the Tocantins, in the virgin forests to the north of Diamantina, he had determined the existence of the famous bat-shaped people, the Murcilagos, or men who are born with white hair and red eyes, who live in the shady solitudes of the woods, sleep by day, awake by night, and fish and hunt in the dark, seeing better then than by the light of the moon. He told how, near Beyrout, once in an encampment of an expedition of which he formed part, a rain gauge belonging to one of the party happened to be stolen from a tent. A wizard, wearing two or three strips of leather only, and looking like a man having nothing on but his braces, thereupon rang a bell at the end of a horn so violently, that a hyena finally answered the summons by bringing back the missing instrument. The hyena was, in fact, the thief. These veritable histories bore a strong resemblance to fictions; but they amused Déruchette.

The *poupée* or "doll" of the Durande, as the people of the Channel Islands call the figure-head of a ship, was the connecting link between the vessel and Lethierry's niece. In the Norman Islands the figure-head of a ship, a roughly-carved wooden statue, is called the Poupée. Hence the local saying, meaning to sail, "*être entre poupe et poupée.*"

The *poupée* of the Durande was particularly dear to Mess Lethierry. He had instructed the carver to make it resemble Déruchette. It looked like a rude attempt to cut out a face with a hatchet; or like a clumsy log trying hard to look like a girl.

This unshapely block produced a great effect upon Mess Lethierry's imagination. He looked upon it with an almost superstitious admiration. His faith in it was complete. He was able to trace in it an excellent resemblance to Déruchette. Thus the dogma resembles the truth, and the idol the deity.

Mess Lethierry had two grand fête days in every week; one was Tuesday, the other Friday. His first delight consisted in seeing the Durande weigh anchor; his second in seeing her enter the port again. He leaned upon his elbows at the window contemplating his work, and was happy.

On Fridays, the presence of Mess Lethierry at his window was a signal. When people passing the Bravées saw him lighting his pipe, they said, "Ay! the steamboat is in sight." One kind of smoke was the herald of the other.

The Durande, when she entered the port, made her cable fast to a huge iron ring under Mess Lethierry's window, and fixed in the basement of the house. On those nights Lethierry slept soundly in his hammock, with a soothing consciousness of the presence of Déruchette asleep in her room near him, and of the Durande moored opposite.

The moorings of the Durande were close to the great bell of the port. A little strip of quay passed thence before the door of the Bravées.

The quay, the Bravées and its house, the garden, the alleys bordered with edges, and the greater part even of the surrounding houses, no longer exist. The demand for Guernsey granite has invaded these too. The whole of this part of the town is now occupied by stone-cutters' yards.

XI
MATRIMONIAL PROSPECTS

DÉRUCHETTE WAS approaching womanhood, and was still unmarried.

Mess Lethierry in bringing her up to have white hands had also rendered her somewhat fastidious. A training of that kind has its disadvantages; but Lethierry was himself still more fastidious. He would have liked to have provided at the same time for both his idols; to have found in the guide and companion of the one a commander for the other. What is a husband but the pilot on the voyage of matrimony? Why not then the same conductor for the vessel and for the girl? The affairs of a household have their tides, their ebbs and flows, and he who knows how to steer a bark, ought to know how to guide a woman's destiny, subject as both are to the influences of the moon and the wind. Sieur Clubin being only fifteen years younger than Lethierry, would necessarily be only a provisional master for the Durande. It would be necessary to find a young captain, a permanent master, a true successor of the founder, inventor, and creator of the first channel steamboat. A captain for the Durande who should come up to his ideal, would have been, already, almost a son-in-law in Lethierry's eyes. Why not make him son-in-law in a double sense? The idea pleased him. The husband *in posse* of Déruchette haunted his dreams. His ideal was a powerful seaman, tanned and browned by weather, a sea athlete. This, however, was not exactly the ideal of Déruchette. Her dreams, if dreams they could even be called, were of a more ethereal character.

The uncle and the niece were at all events agreed in not being in haste to seek a solution of these problems. When Déruchette began to be regarded as a probable heiress, a crowd of suitors had presented themselves. Attentions under these circumstances are not generally worth much. Mess Lethierry felt this. He would grumble out the old French proverb, "*A maiden of gold, a suitor of brass.*" He politely showed the fortune-seekers to the door. He was content to wait, and so was Déruchette.

It was, perhaps, a singular fact, that he had little inclination for the local aristocracy. In that respect Mess Lethierry showed himself not entirely English. It will hardly be believed that he even refused for Déruchette a

Ganduel of Jersey, and a Bugnet Nicolin of Sark. People were bold enough to affirm, although we doubt if this were possible, that he had even declined the proposals of a member of the family of Edou, which is evidently descended from "Edou-ard" (Anglicè Edward) the Confessor.

XII
AN ANOMALY IN THE CHARACTER OF LETHIERRY

MESS LETHIERRY had a failing, and a serious one. He detested a priest; though not as an individual, but as an institution. Reading one day—for he used to read—in a work of Voltaire—for he would even read Voltaire—the remark, that priests "have something cat-like in their nature," he laid down the book and was heard to mutter, "Then, I suppose, I have something dog-like in mine."

It must be remembered that the priests—Lutheran and Calvinist, as well as Catholic—had vigorously combated the new "Devil Boat," and had persecuted its inventor. To be a sort of revolutionist in the art of navigation, to introduce a spirit of progress in the Norman Archipelago, to disturb the peace of the poor little island of Guernsey with a new invention, was in their eyes, as we have not concealed from the reader, an abominable and most condemnable rashness. Nor had they omitted to condemn it pretty loudly. It must not be forgotten that we are now speaking of the Guernsey clergy of a bygone generation, very different from that of the present time, who in almost all the local places of worship display a laudable sympathy with progress. They had embarrassed Lethierry in a hundred ways; every sort of resisting force which can be found in sermons and discourses had been employed against him. Detested by the churchmen, he naturally came to detest them in his turn. Their hatred was the extenuating circumstance to be taken into account in judging of his.

But it must be confessed that his dislike for priests was, in some degree, in his very nature. It was hardly necessary for them to hate him in order to inspire him with aversion. As he said, he moved among them like the dog among cats. He had an antipathy to them, not only in idea, but in what is more difficult to analyse, his instincts. He felt their secret claws, and showed his teeth; sometimes, it must be confessed, a little at random and out of season. It is a mistake to make no distinctions: a dislike in the mass is a prejudice. The good Savoyard curé would have found no favour in his eyes. It is not certain that a worthy priest was even a possible thing in Lethierry's mind. His philosophy was carried so far that his good sense sometimes abandoned him. There is such a thing as the intolerance of tolerants, as well as the violence of moderates. But Lethierry was at bottom too good-natured to be a thorough hater. He did not attack so much as avoid. He kept the church people at a distance. He suffered evil at their hands; but he confined himself to not wishing them any good. The shade of difference, in fact, between his aversion and theirs, lay in the fact that they bore animosity, while he had only a strong antipathy. Small as is the island of Guernsey, it has, unfortunately, plenty of room for differences of religion; there, to take the broad distinction, is the Catholic faith and the Protestant faith; every form of worship has its temple or chapel. In Germany, at Heidelberg, for example, people are not so particular; they divide a church in two, one half for St. Peter, the other half for Calvin, and between the two is a partition to prevent religious variances terminating in fisticuffs. The shares are equal; the Catholics have three altars, the Huguenots three altars. As the services are at the same hours, one bell summonses both denominations to prayers; it rings, in fact, both for God and for Satan, according as each pleases to regard it. Nothing can be more simple.

The phlegmatic character of the Germans favours, I suppose, this peculiar arrangement, but in Guernsey every religion has its own domicile; there is the orthodox parish and the heretic parish; the individual may choose. "Neither one nor the other" was the choice of Mess Lethierry.

This sailor, workman, philosopher, and parvenu trader, though a simple man in appearance, was by no means simple at bottom. He had his opinions and his prejudices. On the subject of the priests he was immovable; he would have entered the lists with Montlosier.

Occasionally he indulged in rather disrespectful jokes upon this subject. He had certain odd expressions thereupon peculiar to himself, but significant enough. Going to confession he called "combing one's conscience." The little learning that he had—a certain amount of reading picked up here and there between the squalls at sea—did not prevent his making blunders in spelling. He made also mistakes in pronunciation, some of which, however, gave a double sense to his words, which might have been suspected of a sly intention. After peace had been brought about by Waterloo between the France of Louis XVIII. and the England of Wellington, Mess Lethierry was heard to say, "Bour mont a été le traître d'union entre les deux camps." On one occasion he wrote *pape ôté* for *papauté*. We do not think these puns were intentional.

Though he was a strong anti-papist, that circumstance was far from conciliating the Anglicans. He was no more liked by the Protestant rectors than by the Catholic curés. The enunciation of the greatest dogmas did not prevent his anti-theological temper bursting forth. Accident, for example, having once brought him to hear a sermon on eternal punishment, by the Reverend Jaquemin Hérode—a magnificent discourse, filled from one end to the other with sacred texts, proving the everlasting pains, the tortures, the torments, the perditions, the inexorable chastisements, the burnings without end, the inextinguishable maledictions, the wrath of the Almighty, the celestial fury, the divine vengeance, and other incontestable realities—he was heard to say as he was going out in the midst of the faithful flock, "You see, I have an odd notion of my own on this matter; I imagine God as a merciful being."

This leaven of atheism was doubtless due to his sojourn in France.

Although a Guernsey man of pure extraction, he was called in the island "the Frenchman;" but chiefly on account of his "improper" manner of speaking. He did not indeed conceal the truth from himself. He was impregnated with ideas subversive of established institutions. His obstinacy in constructing the "Devil Boat" had proved that. He used to say, "I was suckled by the '89"—a bad sort of nurse. These were not his only indiscretions. In France "to preserve appearances," in England "to be respectable," is the chief condition of a quiet life. To be respectable implies a multitude of little observances, from the strict keeping of Sunday down to the careful tying of a cravat. "To act so that nobody may point at you;" this is the terrible social law. To be pointed at with the finger is almost the same thing as an anathematisation. Little towns, always hotbeds of gossip, are remarkable for that isolating malignancy, which is like the tremendous malediction of the

Church seen through the wrong end of the telescope. The bravest are afraid
of this ordeal. They are ready to confront the storm, the fire of cannon,
but they shrink at the glance of "Mrs. Grundy." Mess Lethierry was more
obstinate than logical; but under pressure even his obstinacy would bend.
He put—to use another of his phrases, eminently suggestive of latent compromises, not always pleasant to avow—"a little water in his wine." He kept
aloof from the clergy, but he did not absolutely close his door against them.
On official occasions, and at the customary epochs of pastoral visits, he received with sufficiently good grace both the Lutheran rector and the Papist
chaplain. He had even, though at distant intervals, accompanied Déruchette
to the Anglican parish church, to which Déruchette herself, as we have said,
only went on the four great festivals of the year.

On the whole, these little concessions, which always cost him a pang,
irritated him; and far from inclining him towards the Church people, only
increased his inward disinclination to them. He compensated himself by
more raillery. His nature, in general so devoid of bitterness, had no unchar-
itable side except this. To alter him, however, was impossible.

In fact, this was in his very temperament, and was beyond his own power
to control.

Every sort of priest or clergyman was distasteful to him. He had a little
of the old revolutionary want of reverence. He did not distinguish between
one form of worship and another. He did not do justice to that great step
in the progress of ideas, the denial of the real presence. His shortsightedness in these matters even prevented his perceiving any essential difference
between a minister and an abbé. A reverend doctor and a reverend father
were pretty nearly the same to him. He used to say, "Wesley is not more
to my taste than Loyola." When he saw a reverend pastor walking with his
wife, he would turn to look at them, and mutter, "a married priest," in a
tone which brought out all the absurdity which those words had in the
ears of Frenchmen at that time. He used to relate how, on his last voyage to
England, he had seen the "Bishopess" of London. His dislike for marriages
of that sort amounted almost to disgust. "Gown and gown do not mate
well," he would say. The sacerdotal function was to him in the nature of
a distinct sex. It would have been natural to him to have said, "Neither a
man nor a woman, only a priest;" and he had the bad taste to apply to the

Anglican and the Roman Catholic clergy the same disdainful epithets. He confounded the two cassocks in the same phraseology. He did not take the trouble to vary in favour of Catholics or Lutherans, or whatever they might be, the figures of speech common among military men of that period. He would say to Déruchette, "Marry whom you please, provided you do not marry a parson."

XIII
THOUGHTLESSNESS ADDS A GRACE TO BEAUTY

A WORD ONCE SAID, Mess Lethierry remembered it: a word once said, Déruchette soon forgot it. Here was another difference between the uncle and the niece.

Brought up in the peculiar way already described, Déruchette was little accustomed to responsibility. There is a latent danger in an education not sufficiently serious, which cannot be too much insisted on. It is perhaps unwise to endeavour to make a child happy too soon.

So long as she was happy, Déruchette thought all was well. She knew, too, that it was always a pleasure to her uncle to see her pleased. The religious sentiment in her nature was satisfied with going to the parish church four times in the year. We have seen her in her Christmas-day toilet. Of life, she was entirely ignorant. She had a disposition which one day might lead her to love passionately. Meanwhile she was contented.

She sang by fits and starts, chatted by fits and starts, enjoyed the hour as it passed, fulfilled some little duty, and was gone again, and was delightful in all. Add to all this the English sort of liberty which she enjoyed. In England the very infants go alone, girls are their own mistresses, and adolescence is almost wholly unrestrained. Such are the differences of manners. Later, how many of these free maidens become female slaves? I use the word in its least odious sense; I mean that they are free in the development of their nature, but slaves to duty.

Déruchette awoke every morning with little thought of her actions of the day before. It would have troubled her a good deal to have had to give an account of how she had spent her time the previous week. All this, however, did not prevent her having certain hours of strange disquietude; times when some dark cloud seemed to pass over the brightness of her joy. Those azure depths are subject to such shadows! But clouds like these soon passed away. She quickly shook off such moods with a cheerful laugh, knowing neither why she had been sad, nor why she had regained her serenity. She was always at play. As a child, she would take delight in teasing the passers-by. She played practical jokes upon the boys. If the fiend himself had passed that way, she would hardly have spared him some ingenious trick. She was pretty and innocent; and she could abuse the immunity accorded to such qualities. She was ready with a smile, as a cat with a stroke of her claws. So much the worse for the victim of her scratches. She thought no more of them. Yesterday had no existence for her. She lived in the fullness of to-day. Such it is to have too much happiness fall to one's lot! With Déruchette impressions vanished like the melted snow.

Book IV
The Bagpipe

✱

I
STREAKS OF FIRE ON THE HORIZON

GILLIATT HAD NEVER spoken to Déruchette; he knew her from having seen her at a distance, as men know the morning star.

At the period when Déruchette had met Gilliatt on the road leading from St. Peter's Port to Vale, and had surprised him by tracing his name in the snow, she was just sixteen years of age. Only the evening before Mess Lethierry had said to her, "Come, no more childish tricks; you are a great girl."

That word "Gilliatt," written by the young maiden, had sunk into an unfathomed depth.

What were women to Gilliatt? He could not have answered that question himself. When he met one he generally inspired her with something of the timidity which he felt himself. He never spoke to a woman except from urgent necessity. He had never played the part of a "gallant" to any one of the country girls. When he found himself alone on the road, and perceived a woman coming towards him, he would climb over a fence, or bury himself in some copse: he even avoided old women. Once in his life he had seen a Parisian lady. A *Parisienne* on the wing was a strange event in Guernsey at that distant epoch; and Gilliatt had heard this gentle lady relate her little troubles in these words: "I am very much annoyed; I have got some spots of rain upon my bonnet. Pale buff is a shocking colour for rain." Having found, some time afterwards, between the leaves of a book, an old engraving, representing "a lady of the Chaussée d'Antin" in full dress, he had stuck it against the wall at home as a souvenir of this remarkable apparition.

On that Christmas morning when he had met Déruchette, and when she had written his name and disappeared laughing, he returned home, scarcely conscious of why he had gone out. That night he slept little; he was dreaming of a thousand things: that it would be well to cultivate black radishes in the garden; that he had not seen the boat from Sark pass by; had anything happened to it? Then he remembered that he had seen the white stonecrop in flower, a rare thing at that season. He had never known exactly who was the woman who had reared him, and he made up his mind that she must have been his mother, and thought of her with redoubled tenderness. He called to mind the lady's clothing in the old leathern trunk. He thought that the Reverend Jaquemin Hérode would probably one day or other be appointed dean of St. Peter's Port and surrogate of the bishop, and that the rectory of St. Sampson would become vacant. Next, he remembered that the morrow of Christmas would be the twenty-seventh day of the moon, and that consequently high water would be at twenty-one minutes past three, the half-ebb at a quarter past seven, low water at thirty-three minutes past nine, and half flood at thirty-nine minutes past twelve. He recalled, in the most trifling details, the costume of the Highlander who had sold him the bagpipe; his bonnet with a thistle ornament, his claymore, his close-fitting short jacket, his philabeg ornamented with a pocket, and his snuff-horn, his pin set with a Scottish stone, his two girdles, his sash and belts, his sword, cutlass, dirk, and skene-dhu—his black-sheathed knife, with its black handle ornamented with two cairngorms—and the bare knees of the soldier; his socks, gaiters, and buckled shoes. This highly-equipped figure became a spectre in his imagination, which pursued him with a sense of feverishness as he sunk into oblivion. When he awoke it was full daylight, and his first thought was of Déruchette.

The next night he slept more soundly, but he was dreaming again of the Scottish soldier. In the midst of his sleep he remembered that the after-Christmas sittings of the Chief Law Court would commence on the 21st of January. He dreamed also about the Reverend Jaquemin Hérode. He thought of Déruchette, and seemed to be in violent anger with her. He wished he had been a child again to throw stones at her windows. Then he thought that if he were a child again he should have his mother by his side, and he began to sob.

Gilliatt had a project at this time of going to pass three months at Chousey, or at the Miriquiers; but he did not go.

He walked no more along the road to St. Peter's Port.

He had an odd fancy that his name of "Gilliatt" had remained there traced upon the ground, and that the passers-by stopped to read it.

II
THE UNKNOWN UNFOLDS ITSELF BY DEGREES

ON THE OTHER HAND, Gilliatt had the satisfaction of seeing the Bravées every day. By some accident he was continually passing that way. His business seemed always to lead him by the path which passed under the wall of Déruchette's garden.

One morning, as he was walking along this path, he heard a market-woman who was returning from the Bravées, say to another: "Mess Lethierry is fond of sea-kale."

He dug in his garden of the Bû de la Rue a trench for sea-kale. The sea-kale is a vegetable which has a flavour like asparagus.

The wall of the garden of the Bravées was very low; it would have been easy to scale it. The idea of scaling it would have appeared, to him, terrible. But there was nothing to hinder his hearing, as any one else might, the voices of persons talking as he passed, in the rooms or in the garden. He did not listen, but he heard them. Once he could distinguish the voices of the two servants, Grace and Douce, disputing. It was a sound which belonged to the house, and their quarrel remained in his ears like a remembrance of music.

On another occasion, he distinguished a voice which was different, and which seemed to him to be the voice of Déruchette. He quickened his pace, and was soon out of hearing.

The words uttered by that voice, however, remained fixed in his memory. He repeated them at every instant. They were, "Will you please give me the little broom?"

By degrees he became bolder. He had the daring to stay awhile. One day it happened that Déruchette was singing at her piano, altogether invisible from without, although her window was open. The air was that of "Bonnie Dundee." He grew pale, but he screwed his courage to the point of listening.

Springtide came. One day Gilliatt enjoyed a beatific vision. The heavens were opened, and there, before his eyes, appeared Déruchette, watering lettuces in her little garden.

Soon afterwards he look to doing more than merely listening there. He watched her habits, observed her hours, and waited to catch a glimpse of her.

In all this he was very careful not to be seen.

The year advanced; the time came when the trellises were heavy with roses, and haunted by the butterflies. By little and little, he had come to conceal himself for hours behind her wall, motionless and silent, seen by no one, and holding his breath as Déruchette passed in and out of her garden. Men grow accustomed to poison by degrees.

From his hiding-place he could often hear the sound of Déruchette conversing with Mess Lethierry under a thick arch of leaves, in a spot where there was a garden-seat. The words came distinctly to his ears.

What a change had come over him! He had even descended to watch and listen. Alas! there is something of the character of a spy in every human heart.

There was another garden-seat, visible to him, and nearer. Déruchette would sit there sometimes.

From the flowers that he had observed her gathering he had guessed her taste in the matter of perfumes. The scent of the bindweed was her favourite, then the pink, then the honeysuckle, then the jasmine. The rose stood only fifth in the scale. She looked at the lilies, but did not smell them.

Gilliatt figured her in his imagination from this choice of odours. With each perfume he associated some perfection.

The very idea of speaking to Déruchette would have made his hair stand on end. A poor old rag-picker, whose wandering brought her, from time to time, into the little road leading under the inclosure of the Bravées, had occasionally remarked Gilliatt's assiduity beside the wall, and his devotion for this retired spot. Did she connect the presence of a man before this wall with the possibility of a woman behind it? Did she perceive that vague, invisible thread? Was she, in her decrepit mendicancy, still youthful enough to remember something of the old happier days? And could she, in this dark night and winter of her wretched life, still recognise the dawn? We know not: but it appears that, on one occasion, passing near Gilliatt at his post, she brought to bear upon him something as like a smile as she was still capable of, and muttered between her teeth, "It is getting warmer."

Gilliatt heard the words, and was struck by them. "It warms one," he muttered, with an inward note of interrogation. "It is getting warmer." What did the old woman mean?

He repeated the phrase mechanically all day, but he could not guess its meaning.

III
THE AIR "BONNIE DUNDEE" FINDS AN ECHO ON THE HILL

IT WAS in a spot behind the enclosure of the garden of the Bravées, at an angle of the wall, half concealed with holly and ivy, and covered with nettles, wild mallow, and large white mullen growing between the blocks of stone, that he passed the greater part of that summer. He watched there, lost in deep thought. The lizards grew accustomed to his presence, and basked in the sun among the same stones. The summer was bright and full of dreamy indolence: overhead the light clouds came and went. Gilliatt sat upon the grass. The air was full of the songs of birds. He held his two hands up to his forehead, sometimes trying to recollect himself: "Why should she write my name in the snow?" From a distance the sea breeze came up in gentle breaths, at intervals the horn of the quarrymen sounded abruptly, warning the passers-by to take shelter, as they shattered some mass with gunpowder. The Port of St. Sampson was not visible from this place, but he could see the tips of masts above the trees. The sea-gulls flew wide and afar. Gilliatt had heard his mother say that women could love men; that such things happened sometimes. He remembered it; and said within himself, "Who knows, may not Déruchette love me?" Then a feeling of sadness would come upon him; he would say, "She, too, thinks of me in her turn. It is well." He remembered that Déruchette was rich, and that he was poor: and then the new boat appeared to him an execrable invention. He could never remember what day of the month it was. He would stare listlessly at the great bees, with their yellow bodies and their short wings, as they entered with a buzzing noise into the holes in the wall.

One evening Déruchette went in-doors to retire to bed. She approached her window to close it. The night was dark. Suddenly, something caught her ear, and she listened. Somewhere in the darkness there was a sound of music. It was some one, perhaps, on the hill-side, or at the foot of the towers of Vale Castle, or, perhaps, further still, playing an air upon some instrument. Déruchette recognised her favourite melody, "Bonnie Dundee," played upon the bagpipe. She thought little of it.

From that night the music might be heard again from time to time at the same hours, particularly when the nights were very dark.

Déruchette was not much pleased with all this.

IV

"A serenade by night may please a lady fair,
But of uncle and guardian let the troubadour beware."
Unpublished Comedy

FOUR YEARS passed away.

Déruchette was approaching her twenty-first year, and was still unmarried. Some writer has said that a fixed idea is a sort of gimlet; every year gives it another turn. To pull out the first year is like plucking out the hair by the roots; in the second year, like tearing the skin; in the third, like breaking the bones; and in the fourth, like removing the very brain itself.

Gilliatt had arrived at this fourth stage.

He had never yet spoken a word to Déruchette. He lived and dreamed near that delightful vision. This was all.

It happened one day that, finding himself by chance at St. Sampson, he had seen Déruchette talking with Mess Lethierry at the door of the Bravées, which opens upon the roadway of the port. Gilliatt ventured to approach very near. He fancied that at the very moment of his passing she had smiled. There was nothing impossible in that.

Déruchette still heard, from time to time, the sound of the bagpipe.

Mess Lethierry had also heard this bagpipe. By degrees he had come to remark this persevering musician under Déruchette's window. A tender strain, too; all the more suspicious. A nocturnal gallant was a thing not to his taste. His wish was to marry Déruchette in his own time, when she was willing and he was willing, purely and simply, without any romance, or music, or anything of that sort. Irritated at it, he had at last kept a watch, and he fancied that he had detected Gilliatt. He passed his fingers through his beard—a sign of anger—and grumbled out, "What has that fellow got to pipe about? He is in love with Déruchette, that is clear. You waste your time, young man. Any one who wants Déruchette must come to me, and not loiter about playing the flute."

An event of importance, long foreseen, occurred soon afterwards. It was announced that the Reverend Jaquemin Hérode was appointed surrogate of the Bishop of Winchester, dean of the island, and rector of St. Peter's Port, and that he would leave St. Sampson for St. Peter's immediately after his successor should be installed.

It could not be long to the arrival of the new rector. He was a gentleman of Norman extraction, Monsieur Ebenezer Caudray.

Some facts were known about the new rector, which the benevolent and malevolent interpreted in a contrary sense. He was known to be young and poor, but his youth was tempered with much learning, and his poverty by good expectations. In the dialect specially invented for the subject of riches and inheritances, death goes by the name of "expectations." He was the nephew and heir of the aged and opulent dean of St. Asaph. At the death of this old gentleman he would be a rich man. M. Caudray had distinguished relations. He was almost entitled to the quality of "Honourable." As regarded his doctrine, people judged differently. He was an Anglican, but, according to the expression of Bishop Tillotson, a "libertine"—that is, in reality, one who was very severe. He repudiated all pharisaism. He was a friend rather of the Presbytery than the Episcopacy. He dreamed of the Primitive Church of the days when even Adam had the right to choose his Eve, and when Frumentinus, Bishop of Hierapolis, carried off a young maiden to make her his wife, and said to her parents, "Her will is such, and such is mine. You are no longer her mother, and you are no longer her father. I am the Bishop of Hierapolis, and this is my wife. Her father is in heaven." If the common belief could be trusted, M. Caudray subordinated the text, "Honour thy father and thy mother," to that other text, in his eyes of higher significance, "The woman is the flesh of the man. She shall leave her father and mother to follow her husband." This tendency, however, to circumscribe the parental authority and to favour religiously every mode of forming the conjugal tie, is peculiar to all Protestantism, particularly in England, and singularly so in America.

V

A DESERVED SUCCESS HAS ALWAYS ITS DETRACTORS

AT THIS PERIOD the affairs of Mess Lethierry were in this position:— The Durande had well fulfilled all his expectations. He had paid his debts, repaired his misfortunes, discharged his obligations at Brême, met his acceptances at St. Malo. He had paid off the mortgage upon his house at the Bravées, and had bought up all the little local rent charges upon the property. He was also the proprietor of a great productive capital. This was the Durande herself. The net revenue from the boat was about a thousand pounds sterling per annum, and the traffic was constantly increasing. Strictly speaking, the Durande constituted his entire fortune. She was also the fortune of the island. The carriage of cattle being one of the most profitable portions of her trade, he had been obliged, in order to facilitate the stowage, and the embarking and disembarking of animals, to do away with the luggage-boxes and the two boats. It was, perhaps, imprudent. The Durande had but one boat—namely, her long-boat; but this was an excellent one.

Ten years had elapsed since Rantaine's robbery.

This prosperity of the Durande had its weak point. It inspired no confidence. People regarded it as a risk. Lethierry's good fortune was looked upon as exceptional. He was considered to have gained by a lucky rashness. Some one in the Isle of Wight who had imitated him had not succeeded. The enterprise had ruined the shareholders. The engines, in fact, were badly constructed. But people shook their heads. Innovations have always to contend with the difficulty that few wish them well. The least false step compromises them.

One of the commercial oracles of the Channel Islands, a certain banker from Paris, named Jauge, being consulted upon a steamboat speculation, was reported to have turned his back, with the remark, "An investment is it you propose to me? Exactly; an investment in smoke."

On the other hand, the sailing vessels had no difficulty in finding capitalists to take shares in a venture. Capital, in fact, was obstinately in favour of sails, and as obstinately against boilers and paddle-wheels. At Guernsey, the Durande was indeed a fact, but steam was not yet an established principle. Such is the fanatical spirit of conservatism in opposition to progress. They said of Lethierry, "It is all very well; but he could not do it a second time." Far from encouraging, his example inspired timidity. Nobody would have dared to risk another Durande.

VI
THE SLOOP "CASHMERE" SAVES
A SHIPWRECKED CREW

THE EQUINOCTIAL GALES begin early in the Channel. The sea there is narrow, and the winds disturb it easily. The westerly gales begin from the month of February, and the waves are beaten about from every quarter. Navigation becomes an anxious matter. The people on the coasts look to the signal-post, and begin to watch for vessels in distress. The sea is then like a cut-throat in ambush for his victim. An invisible trumpet sounds the alarm of war with the elements, furious blasts spring up from the horizon, and a terrible wind soon begins to blow. The dark night whistles and howls. In the depth of the clouds the black tempest distends its cheeks, and the storm arises.

The wind is one danger; the fogs are another.

Fogs have from all time been the terror of mariners. In certain fogs microscopic prisms of ice are found in suspension, to which Mariotte attributes halos, mock suns, and paraselenes. Storm-fogs are of a composite character;

various gases of unequal specific gravity combine with the vapour of water, and arrange themselves, layer over layer, in an order which divides the dense mist into zones. Below ranges the iodine; above the iodine is the sulphur; above the sulphur the brome; above the brome the phosphorus. This, in a certain manner, and making allowance for electric and magnetic tension, explains several phenomena, as the St. Elmo's Fire of Columbus and Magellan, the flying stars moving about the ships, of which Seneca speaks; the two flames, Castor and Pollux, mentioned by Plutarch; the Roman legion, whose spears appeared to Cæsar to take fire; the peak of the Chateau of Duino in Friuli which the sentinel made to sparkle by touching it with his lance; and perhaps even those fulgurations from the earth which the ancients called Satan's terrestrial lightnings. At the equator, an immense mist seems permanently to encircle the globe. It is known as the cloud-ring. The function of the cloud-ring is to temper the heat of the tropics, as that of the Gulf-stream is to mitigate the coldness of the Pole. Under the cloud-ring fogs are fatal. These are what are called *horse latitudes*. It was here that navigators of bygone ages were accustomed to cast their horses into the sea to lighten the ship in stormy weather, and to economise the fresh water when becalmed. Columbus said, "*Nube abaxo ex muerte,*" death lurks in the low cloud. The Etruscans, who bear the same relation to meteorology which the Chaldeans did to astronomy, had two high priests—the high priest of the thunder, and the high priest of the clouds. The "fulgurators" observed the lightning, and the weather sages watched the mists. The college of Priest-Augurs was consulted by the Syrians, the Phœnicians, the Pelasgi, and all the primitive navigators of the ancient *Mare Internum*. The origin of tempests was, from that time forward, partially understood. It is intimately connected with the generation of fogs, and is, properly speaking, the same phenomenon. There exist upon the ocean three regions of fogs, one equatorial and two polar. The mariners give them but one name, the *pitch-pot*.

In all latitudes, and particularly in the Channel, the equinoctial fogs are dangerous. They shed a sudden darkness over the sea. One of the perils of fogs, even when not very dense, arises from their preventing the mariners perceiving the change of the bed of the sea by the variations of the colour of the water. The result is a dangerous concealment of the approach of sands and breakers. The vessel steers towards the shoals without receiving any warning. Frequently the fogs leave a ship no resource except to lie-to, or to cast anchor. There are as many shipwrecks from the fogs as from the winds.

After a very violent squall succeeding one of these foggy days, the mail-boat *Cashmere* arrived safely from England. It entered at St. Peter's Port as the first gleam of day appeared upon the sea, and at the very moment when the cannon of Castle Cornet announced the break of day. The sky had cleared: the sloop *Cashmere* was anxiously expected, as she was to bring the new rector of St. Sampson.

A little after the arrival of the sloop, a rumour ran through the town that she had been hailed during the night at sea by a long-boat containing a shipwrecked crew.

VII

HOW AN IDLER HAD THE GOOD FORTUNE TO BE SEEN BY A FISHERMAN

ON THAT very night, at the moment when the wind abated, Gilliatt had gone out with his nets, without, however, taking his famous old Dutch boat too far from the coast.

As he was returning with the rising tide, towards two o'clock in the afternoon, the sun was shining brightly, and he passed before the Beast's Horn to reach the little bay of the Bû de la Rue. At that moment he fancied that he saw, in the projection of the "Gild-Holm-'Ur" seat a shadow, which was not that of the rock. He steered his vessel nearer, and was able to perceive a man sitting in the "Gild-Holm-'Ur." The sea was already very high, the rock encircled by the waves, and escape entirely cut off. Gilliatt made signs to the man. The stranger remained motionless. Gilliatt drew nearer; the man was asleep.

He was attired in black. "He looks like a priest," thought Gilliatt. He approached still nearer, and could distinguish the face of a young man.

The features were unknown to him.

The rock, happily, was peaked; there was a good depth. Gilliatt wore off, and succeeded in skirting the rocky wall. The tide raised the bark so high that Gilliatt, by standing upon the gunwale of the sloop, could touch the man's feet. He raised himself upon the planking, and stretched out his hands. If he had fallen at that moment, it is doubtful if he would have risen again on the water; the waves were rolling in between the boat and the rock, and destruction would have been inevitable. He pulled the foot of the sleeping man. "Ho! there. What are you doing in this place?"

The man aroused, and muttered—

"I was looking about."

He was now completely awake, and continued—

"I have just arrived in this part. I came this way on a pleasure trip. I have passed the night on the sea: the view from here seemed beautiful. I was weary, and fell asleep."

"Ten minutes later, and you would have been drowned."

"Ha!"

"Jump into my bark."

Gilliatt kept the bark fast with his foot, clutched the rock with one hand, and stretched out the other to the stranger in black, who sprang quickly into the boat. He was a fine young man.

Gilliatt seized the tiller, and in two minutes his boat entered the bay of the Bû de la Rue.

The young man wore a round hat and a white cravat; and his long black frock-coat was buttoned up to the neck. He had fair hair, which he wore *en couronne*. He had a somewhat feminine cast of features, a clear eye, a grave manner.

Meanwhile the boat had touched the ground. Gilliatt passed the cable through the mooring-ring, then turned and perceived the young man holding out a sovereign in a very white hand.

Gilliatt moved the hand gently away.

There was a pause. The young man was the first to break the silence.

"You have saved me from death."

"Perhaps," replied Gilliatt.

The moorings were made fast, and they went ashore.

The stranger continued—

"I owe you my life, sir."

"No matter."

This reply from Gilliatt was again followed by a pause.

"Do you belong to this parish?"

"No," replied Gilliatt.

"To what parish, then?"

Gilliatt lifted up his right hand, pointed to the sky, and said—

"To that yonder."

The young man bowed, and left him.

After walking a few paces, the stranger stopped, felt in his pocket, drew out a book, and returning towards Gilliatt, offered it to him.

"Permit me to make you a present of this."

Gilliatt took the volume.

It was a Bible.

An instant after, Gilliatt, leaning upon the parapet, was following the young man with his eyes as he turned the angle of the path which led to St. Sampson.

By little and little he lowered his gaze, forgot all about the stranger—knew no more whether the "Gild-Holm-'Ur" existed. Everything disappeared before him in the bottomless depth of a reverie.

There was one abyss which swallowed up all his thought. This was Déruchette.

A voice calling him, aroused him from this dream.

"Ho there, Gilliatt!"

He recognised the voice and looked up.

"What is the matter, Sieur Landoys?"

It was, in fact, Sieur Landoys, who was passing along the road about one hundred paces from the Bû de la Rue in his phaeton, drawn by one little horse. He had stopped to hail Gilliatt, but he seemed hurried.

"There is news, Gilliatt."

"Where is that?"

"At the Bravées."

"What is it?"

"I am too far off to tell you the story."

Gilliatt shuddered.

"Is Miss Déruchette going to be married?"

"No; but she had better look out for a husband."

"What do you mean?"

"Go up to the house, and you will learn."

And Sieur Landoys whipped on his horse.

Book V
The Revolver

❈

I

CONVERSATIONS AT THE JEAN AUBERGE

SIEUR CLUBIN was a man who bided his time. He was short in stature, and his complexion was yellow. He had the strength of a bull. His sea life had not tanned his skin; his flesh had a sallow hue; it was the colour of a wax candle, of which his eyes, too, had something of the steady light. His memory was peculiarly retentive. With him, to have seen a man once, was to have him like a note in a note-book. His quiet glance took possession of you. The pupil of his eye received the impression of a face, and kept it like a portrait. The face might grow old, but Sieur Clubin never lost it; it was impossible to cheat that tenacious memory. Sieur Clubin was curt in speech, grave in manner, bold in action. No gestures were ever indulged in by him. An air of candour won everybody to him at first; many people thought him artless. He had a wrinkle in the corner of his eye, astonishingly expressive of simplicity. As we have said, no abler mariner existed; no one like him for reefing a sail, for keeping a vessel's head to the wind, or the sails well set. Never did reputation for religion and integrity stand higher than his. To have suspected him would have been to bring yourself under suspicion. He was on terms of intimacy with Monsieur Rébuchet, a money-changer at St. Malo, who lived in the Rue St. Vincent, next door to the armourer's; and Monsieur Rébuchet would say, "I would leave my shop in Clubin's hands."

Sieur Clubin was a widower; his wife, like himself, had enjoyed a high reputation for probity. She had died with a fame for incorruptible virtue. If the bailli had whispered gallant things in her ear, she would have impeached him before the king. If a saint had made love to her, she would have told it to the priest. This couple, Sieur and Dame Clubin, had realised in Torteval the ideal of the English epithet "respectable." Dame Clubin's reputation was as the snowy whiteness of the swan; Sieur Clubin's like that of ermine itself—a spot would have been fatal to him. He could hardly have picked up a pin without making inquiries for the owner. He would send round the town-crier about a box of matches. One day he went into a wine-shop at St. Servan, and said to the man who kept it, "Three years ago I breakfasted here; you made a mistake in the bill;" and he returned the man thirteen sous. He was the very personification of probity, with a certain compression of the lips indicative of watchfulness.

He seemed, indeed, always on the watch—for what? For rogues probably.

Every Tuesday he commanded the Durande on her passage from Guernsey to St. Malo. He arrived at St. Malo on the Tuesday evening, stayed two days there to discharge and take in a new cargo, and started again for Guernsey on Friday morning.

There was at that period, at St. Malo, a little tavern near the harbour, which was called the "Jean Auberge."

The construction of the modern quays swept away this house. At this period, the sea came up as far as the St. Vincent and Dinan gates. St. Merlan and St. Servan communicated with each other by covered carts and other vehicles, which passed to and fro among vessels lying high and dry, avoiding the buoys, the anchors, and cables, and running the risk now and then of smashing their leathern hoods against the lowered yards, or the end of a jib-boom. Between the tides, the coachmen drove their horses over those sands, where, six hours afterwards, the winds would be beating the rolling waves. The four-and-twenty carrying dogs of St. Malo, who tore to pieces a naval officer in 1770, were accustomed to prowl about this beach. This excess of zeal on their part led to the destruction of the pack. Their nocturnal barkings are no longer heard between the little and the great Talard.

Sieur Clubin was accustomed to stay at the Jean Auberge. The French office of the Durande was held there.

The custom-house officers and coast-guardmen came to take their meals and to drink at the Jean Auberge. They had their separate tables. The custom-house officers of Binic found it convenient for the service to meet there with their brother officers of St. Malo.

Captains of vessels came there also; but they ate at another table.

Sieur Clubin sat sometimes at one, sometimes at the other table, but preferred the table of the custom-house men to that of the sea captains. He was always welcome at either.

The tables were well served. There were strange drinks especially provided for foreign sailors. A dandy sailor from Bilboa could have been supplied there with a *helada*. People drank stout there, as at Greenwich; or brown *gueuse*, as at Antwerp.

Masters of vessels who came from long voyages and privateersmen sometimes appeared at the captains' table, where they exchanged news. "How are sugars? That commission is only for small lots.—The brown kinds, however, are going off. Three thousand bags of East India, and five hundred hogsheads of Sagua.—Take my word, the opposition will end by defeating Villèle.—What about indigo? Only seven serons of Guatemala changed hands.—The *Nanino-Julia* is in the roads; a pretty three-master from Brittany.—The two cities of La Plata are at loggerheads again.— When Monte Video gets fat, Buenos Ayres grows lean.—It has been found necessary to transfer the cargo of the *Regina-Cœli*, which has been con-demned at Callao.—Cocoas go off briskly.—Caraque bags are quoted at one hundred and thirty-four, and Trinidad's at seventy-three.—It appears that at the review in the Champ de Mars, the people cried, 'Down with the ministers!'—The raw salt Saladeros hides are selling—ox-hides at sixty francs, and cows' at forty-eight.—Have they passed the Balkan?—What is Diebitsch about?—Aniseed is in demand at San Francisco. Plagniol olive oil is quiet.—Gruyère cheese, in bulk, is thirty-two francs the quintal.—Well, is Leon XII. dead?" etc., etc.

All these things were talked about and commented on aloud. At the table of the custom-house and coast-guard officers they spoke in a lower key.

Matters of police and revenue on the coast and in the ports require, in fact, a little more privacy, and a little less clearness in the conversation.

The sea-captains' table was presided over by an old captain of a large vessel, M. Gertrais-Gaboureau. M. Gertrais-Gaboureau could hardly be regarded as a man; he was rather a living barometer. His long life at sea had given him a surprising power of prognosticating the state of the weather. He seemed to issue a decree for the weather to-morrow. He sounded the winds, and felt the pulse, as it were, of the tides. He might be imagined

requesting the clouds to show their tongue—that is to say, their forked
lightnings. He was the physician of the wave, the breeze, and the squall. The
ocean was his patient. He had travelled round the world like a doctor going
his visits, examining every kind of climate in its good and bad condition.
He was profoundly versed in the pathology of the seasons. Sometimes
he would be heard delivering himself in this fashion—"The barometer descended in 1796 to three degrees below tempest point." He was a sailor
from real love of the sea. He hated England as much as he liked the ocean.
He had carefully studied English seamanship, and considered himself to
have discovered its weak point. He would explain how the *Sovereign* of 1637
differed from the *Royal William* of 1670, and from the *Victory* of 1775. He
compared their build as to their forecastles and quarter-decks. He looked
back with regret to the towers upon the deck, and the funnel-shaped
tops of the *Great Harry* of 1514—probably regarding them from the point
of view of convenient lodging-places for French cannon-balls. In his
eyes, nations only existed for their naval institutions. He indulged in some
odd figures of speech on this subject. He considered the term "The Trinity
House" as sufficiently indicating England. The "Northern Commissioners"
were in like manner synonymous in his mind with Scotland; the "Ballast Board," with Ireland. He was full of nautical information. He was, in
himself, a marine alphabet and almanack, a tariff and low-water mark, all
combined. He knew by heart all the lighthouse dues—particularly those of
the English coast—one penny per ton for passing before this; one farthing
before that. He would tell you that the Small Rock Light which once used
to burn two hundred gallons of oil, now consumes fifteen hundred. Once,
aboard ship, he was attacked by a dangerous disease, and was believed to
be dying. The crew assembled round his hammock, and in the midst of his
groans and agony he addressed the chief carpenter with the words, "You
had better make a mortise in each side of the main caps, and put in a bit of
iron to help pass the top ropes through." His habit of command had given
to his countenance an expression of authority.

It was rare that the subjects of conversation at the captains' table and at
that of the custom-house men were the same. This, however, did happen to
be the case in the first days of that month of February to which the course
of this history has now brought us. The three-master *Tamaulipas*, Captain

Zuela, arrived from Chili, and bound thither again, was the theme of discussion at both tables.

At the captains' table they were talking of her cargo; and at that of the custom-house people, of certain circumstances connected with her recent proceedings.

Captain Zuela, of Copiapo, was partly a Chilian and partly a Columbian. He had taken a part in the War of Independence in a true independent fashion, adhering sometimes to Bolivar, sometimes to Morillo, according as he had found it to his interest. He had enriched himself by serving all causes. No man in the world could have been more Bourbonist, more Bonapartist, more absolutist, more liberal, more atheistical, or more devoutly catholic. He belonged to that great and renowned party which may be called the Lucrative party. From time to time he made his appearance in France on commercial voyages; and if report spoke truly, he willingly gave a passage to fugitives of any kind—bankrupts or political refugees, it was all the same to him, provided they could pay. His mode of taking them aboard was simple. The fugitive waited upon a lonely point of the coast, and at the moment of setting sail, Zuela would detach a small boat to fetch him. On his last voyage he had assisted in this way an outlaw and fugitive from justice, named Berton; and on this occasion he was suspected of being about to aid the flight of the men implicated in the affair of the Bidassoa. The police were informed, and had their eye upon him.

This period was an epoch of flights and escapes. The Restoration in France was a reactionary movement. Revolutions are fruitful of voluntary exile; and restorations of wholesale banishments. During the first seven or eight years which followed the return of the Bourbons, panic was universal—in finance, in industry, in commerce, men felt the ground tremble beneath them. Bankruptcies were numerous in the commercial world; in the political, there was a general rush to escape. Lavalette had taken flight, Lefebvre Desnouettes had taken flight, Delon had taken flight. Special tribunals were again in fashion—*plus* Treetaillon. People instinctively shunned the Pont de Saumur, the Esplanade de la Réole, the wall of the Observatoire in Paris, the tower of Taurias d'Avignon—dismal landmarks in history where the period of reaction has left its sign-spots, on which the marks of that blood-stained hand are still visible. In London the Thistlewood affair, with its ramifications in France: in Paris the Trogoff trial, with its ramifications in Belgium, Switzerland, and Italy, had increased the motives for anxiety and flight, and given an impetus to that mysterious rout which left so many gaps in the social system of that day. To find a place of safety, this was the general care. To be implicated was to be ruined. The spirit of the military tribunals had survived their institution. Sentences were matters of favour. People fled to Texas, to the Rocky Mountains, to Peru, to Mexico. The men of the Loire, traitors then, but now regarded as patriots, had founded the *Champ d'Asile*. Béranger in one of his songs says—

> "Barbarians! we are Frenchmen born;
> Pity us, glorious, yet forlorn."

Self-banishment was the only resource left. Nothing, perhaps, seems simpler than flight, but that monosyllable has a terrible significance. Every obstacle is in the way of the man who slips away. Taking to flight necessitates disguise. Persons of importance—even illustrious characters—were reduced to these expedients, only fit for malefactors. Their independent habits rendered it difficult for them to escape through the meshes of authority. A rogue who violates the conditions of his ticket-of-leave comports himself before the police as innocently as a saint; but imagine innocence constrained to act a part; virtue disguising its voice; a glorious reputation hiding under a mask. Yonder passer-by is a man of well-earned celebrity; he is in quest of a false passport. The equivocal proceedings of one absconding from the reach of the law is no proof that he is not a hero. Ephemeral but characteristic features of the time of which our so-called regular history takes no note, but which the true painter of the age will bring out into relief. Under cover of these flights and concealments of honest men, genuine rogues, less watched and suspected, managed often to get clear off. A scoundrel, who found it convenient to disappear, would take advantage of the general pell-mell, tack himself on to the political refugees, and, thanks to his greater skill in the art, would contrive to appear in that dim twilight more honest even than his honest neighbours. Nothing looks more awkward and confused sometimes than honesty unjustly condemned. It is out of its element, and is almost sure to commit itself.

It is a curious fact, that this voluntary expatriation, particularly with honest folks, appeared to lead to every strange turn of fortune. The modicum of civilisation which a scamp brought with him from London or Paris became, perhaps, a valuable stock in trade in some primitive country, ingratiated him with the people, and enabled him to strike into new paths. There is nothing impossible in a man's escaping thus from the laws, to reappear elsewhere as a dignitary among the priesthood. There was something phantasmagorial in these sudden disappearances; and more than one such flight has led to events like the marvels of a dream. An escapade of this kind, indeed, seemed to end naturally in the wild and wonderful; as when some broken bankrupt suddenly decamps to turn up again twenty years later as Grand Vizier to the Mogul, or as a king in Tasmania.

Rendering assistance to these fugitives was an established trade, and, looking to the abundance of business of that kind, was a highly profitable one. It was generally carried on as a supplementary branch of certain recognised kinds of commerce. A person, for instance, desiring to escape to England, applied to the smugglers; one who desired to get to America, had recourse to sea-captains like Zuela.

II

CLUBIN OBSERVES SOMEONE

ZUELA CAME sometimes to take refreshment at the Jean Auberge. Clubin knew him by sight.

For that matter Clubin was not proud. He did not disdain even to know scamps by sight. He went so far sometimes as to cultivate even a closer acquaintance with them; giving his hand in the open street, or saying good-day to them. He talked English with the smugglers, and jabbered Spanish with the *contrebandistas*. On this subject he had at command a number of apologetic phrases. "Good," he said, "can be extracted out of the knowledge of evil. The gamekeeper may find advantage in knowing the poacher. The good pilot may sound the depths of a pirate, who is only a sort of hidden rock. I test the quality of a scoundrel as a doctor will test a poison." There was no answering a battery of proverbs like this. Everybody gave Clubin credit for his shrewdness. People praised him for not indulging in a ridiculous delicacy. Who, then, should dare to speak scandal of him on this point? Everything he did was evidently "for the good of the service." With him, all was straightforward. Nothing could stain his good fame. Crystal might more easily become sullied. This general confidence in him was the natural reward of a long life of integrity, the crowning advantage of a settled reputation. Whatever Clubin might do, or appear to do, was sure to be interpreted favourably. He had attained almost to a state of impeccability. Over and above this, "he is very wary," people said: and from a situation which in others would have given rise to suspicion, his integrity would extricate itself, with a still greater halo of reputation for ability. This reputation for ability mingled harmoniously with his fame for perfect simplicity of character. Great simplicity and great talents in conjunction are not uncommon. The compound constitutes one of the varieties of the virtuous man, and one of the most valuable. Sieur Clubin was one of those men who might be found in intimate conversation with a sharper or a thief, without suffering any diminution of respect in the minds of their neighbours.

The *Tamaulipas* had completed her loading. She was ready for sea, and was preparing to sail very shortly.

One Tuesday evening the Durande arrived at St. Malo while it was still broad daylight. Sieur Clubin, standing upon the bridge of the vessel, and superintending the manœuvres necessary for getting her into port, perceived upon the sandy beach near the Petit-Bey, two men, who were conversing between the rocks, in a solitary spot. He observed them with his sea-glass, and recognised one of the men. It was Captain Zuela. He seemed to recognise the other also.

This other was a person of high stature, a little grey. He wore the broad-brimmed hat and the sober clothing of the Society of Friends. He was probably a Quaker. He lowered his gaze with an air of extreme diffidence.

On arriving at the Jean Auberge, Sieur Clubin learnt that the *Tamaulipas* was preparing to sail in about ten days.

It has since become known that he obtained information on some other points.

That night he entered the gunsmith's shop in the St. Vincent Street, and said to the master:

"Do you know what a revolver is?"

"Yes," replied the gunsmith. "It is an American weapon."

"It is a pistol with which a man can carry on a conversation."

"Exactly: an instrument which comprises in itself both the question and the answer."

"And the rejoinder too."

"Precisely, Monsieur Clubin. A rotatory clump of barrels."

"I shall want five or six balls."

The gunmaker twisted the corner of his lip, and made that peculiar noise with which, when accompanied by a toss of the head, Frenchmen express admiration.

"The weapon is a good one, Monsieur Clubin."

"I want a revolver with six barrels."

"I have not one."

"What! and you a gunmaker!"

"I do not keep such articles yet. You see, it is a new thing. It is only just coming into vogue. French makers, as yet, confine themselves to the simple pistol."

"Nonsense."

"It has not yet become an article of commerce."

"Nonsense, I say."

"I have excellent pistols."

"I want a revolver."

"I agree that it is more useful. Stop, Monsieur Clubin!"

"What?"

"I believe I know where there is one at this moment in St. Malo; to be had a bargain."

"A revolver?"

"Yes."

"For sale?"

"Yes."

"Where is that?"

"I believe I know; or I can find out."

"When can you give me an answer?"

"A bargain; but of good quality."

"When shall I return?"

"If I procure you a revolver, remember, it will be a good one."

"When will you give me an answer?"

"After your next voyage."

"Do not mention that it is for me," said Clubin.

III
CLUBIN CARRIES AWAY SOMETHING AND BRINGS BACK NOTHING

SIEUR CLUBIN completed the loading of the Durande, embarked a number of cattle and some passengers, and left St. Malo for Guernsey, as usual, on the Friday morning.

On that same Friday, when the vessel had gained the open, which permits the captain to absent himself a moment from the place of command, Clubin entered his cabin, shut himself in, took a travelling bag which he kept there, put into one of its compartments some biscuit, some boxes of preserves, a few pounds of chocolate in sticks, a chronometer, and a sea telescope, and passed through the handles a cord, ready prepared to sling it if necessary. Then he descended into the hold, went into the compartment where the cables are kept, and was seen to come up again with one of those knotted ropes heavy with pieces of metal, which are used for ship caulkers at sea and by robbers ashore. Cords of this kind are useful in climbing.

Having arrived at Guernsey, Clubin repaired to Torteval. He took with him the travelling bag and the knotted cord, but did not bring them back again.

Let us repeat once for all, the Guernsey which we are describing is that ancient Guernsey which no longer exists, and of which it would be impossible to find a parallel now anywhere except in the country. There it is still flourishing, but in the towns it has passed away. The same remarks apply to Jersey. St. Helier's is as civilised as Dieppe, St. Peter's Port as L'Orient. Thanks to the progress of civilisation, thanks to the admirably enterprising spirit of that brave island people, everything has been changed during the last forty years in the Norman Archipelago. Where there was darkness there is now light. With these premises let us proceed.

At that period, then, which is already so far removed from us as to have become historical, smuggling was carried on very extensively in the Channel. The smuggling vessels abounded, particularly on the western coast of Guernsey. People of that peculiarly clever kind who know, even in the smallest details, what went on half a century ago, will even cite you the names of these suspicious craft, which were almost always Austrians or Guiposeans. It is certain that a week scarcely ever passed without one or two being seen either in Saint's Bay or at Pleinmont. Their coming and going had almost the character of a regular service. A cavern in the cliffs at Sark was called then, and is still called, the "Shops" ("Les Boutiques"), from its being the place where these smugglers made their bargains with the purchasers of their merchandise. This sort of traffic had in the Channel a dialect of its own, a vocabulary of contraband technicalities now forgotten, and which was to the Spanish what the "Levantine" is to the Italian.

On many parts of the English coast smuggling had a secret but cordial understanding with legitimate and open commerce. It had access to the house of more than one great financier, by the back-stairs it is true; and its influence extended itself mysteriously through all the commercial world, and the intricate ramifications of manufacturing industry. Merchant on one side, smuggler on the other; such was the key to the secret of many great fortunes. Séguin affirmed it of Bourgain, Bourgain of Séguin. We do not vouch for their accusations; it is possible that they were calumniating each other. However this may have been, it is certain that the contraband trade, though hunted down by the law, was flourishing enough in certain financial circles. It had relations with "the very best society." Thus the brigand Mandrin, in other days, found himself occasionally *tête-à-tête* with the Count of Charolais; for this underhand trade often contrived to put on a very respectable appearance; kept a house of its own with an irreproachable exterior.

All this necessitated a host of manœuvres and connivances, which required impenetrable secrecy. A contrabandist was entrusted with a good many things, and knew how to keep them secret. An inviolable confidence was the condition of his existence. The first quality, in fact, in a smuggler was strict honour in his own circle. No discreetness, no smuggling. Fraud has its secrets like the priest's confessional.

These secrets were indeed, as a rule, faithfully kept. The contrabandist swore to betray nothing, and he kept his word; nobody was more trustworthy than the genuine smuggler. The Judge Alcade of Oyarzun captured a smuggler one day, and put him to torture to compel him to disclose the name of the capitalist who secretly supported him. The smuggler refused to tell. The capitalist in question was the Judge Alcade himself. Of these two accomplices, the judge and the smuggler, the one had been compelled, in order to appear in the eyes of the world to fulfil the law, to put the other to the torture, which the other had patiently borne for the sake of his oath.

The two most famous smugglers who haunted Pleinmont at that period were Blasco and Blasquito. They were *Tocayos*. This was a sort of Spanish or Catholic relationship which consisted in having the same patron saint in heaven; a thing, it will be admitted, not less worthy of consideration than having the same father upon earth.

When a person was initiated into the furtive ways of the contraband business, nothing was more easy, or, from a certain point of view, more troublesome. It was sufficient to have no fear of dark nights, to repair to Pleinmont, and to consult the oracle located there.

IV

PLEINMONT

PLEINMONT, near Torteval, is one of the three corners of the island of Guernsey. At the extremity of the cape there rises a high turfy hill, which looks over the sea.

The height is a lonely place. All the more lonely from there being one solitary house there.

This house adds a sense of terror to that of solitude.

It is popularly believed to be haunted.

Haunted or not, its aspect is singular.

Built of granite, and rising only one story high, it stands in the midst of the grassy solitude. It is in a perfectly good condition as far as exterior is concerned; the walls are thick and the roof is sound. Not a stone is wanting in the sides, not a tile upon the roof. A brick-built chimney-stack forms the angle of the roof. The building turns its back to the sea, being on that side merely a blank wall. On examining this wall, however, attentively, the visitor perceives a little window bricked up. The two gables have three dormer windows, one fronting the east, the others fronting the west, but both are bricked up in like manner. The front, which looks inland, has alone a door and windows. This door, too, is walled in, as are also the two windows of the ground-floor. On the first floor—and this is the feature which is most striking as you approach—there are two open windows; but these are even more suspicious than the blind windows. Their open squares look dark even in broad day, for they have no panes of glass, or even window-frames. They open simply upon the dusk within. They strike the imagination like hollow eye-sockets in a human face. Inside all is deserted. Through the gaping casements you may mark the ruin within. No panellings, no woodwork; all bare stone. It is like a windowed sepulchre, giving liberty to the spectres to look out upon the daylight world. The rains sap the foundations on the seaward side. A few nettles, shaken by the breeze, flourish in the lower part of the walls. Far around the horizon there is no other human habitation. The house is a void; the abode of silence: but if you place your ear against the wall and listen, you may distinguish a confused noise now and then, like the flutter of wings. Over the walled door, upon the stone which forms its architrave, are sculptured these letters, "ELM-PBILG," with the date "1780."

The dark shadow of night and the mournful light of the moon find entrance there.

The sea completely surrounds the house. Its situation is magnificent; but for that reason its aspect is more sinister. The beauty of the spot becomes a puzzle. Why does not a human family take up its abode here? The place is beautiful, the house well-built. Whence this neglect? To these questions, obvious to the reason, succeed others, suggested by the reverie which the place inspires. Why is this cultivatable garden uncultivated? No master for it; and the bricked-up doorway? What has happened to the place? Why is it shunned by men? What business is done here? If none, why is there no one here? Is it only when all the rest of the world are asleep that some one in this spot is awake? Dark squalls, wild winds, birds of prey, strange creatures, unknown forms, present themselves to the mind, and connect themselves somehow with this deserted house. For what class of wayfarers can this be the hostelry? You imagine to yourself whirlwinds of rain and hail beating in at the open casements, and wandering through the rooms. Tempests have left their vague traces upon the interior walls. The chambers, though walled and covered in, are visited by the hurricanes. Has the house been the scene of some great crime? You may almost fancy that this spectral dwelling, given up to solitude and darkness, might be heard calling aloud for succour. Does it remain silent? Do voices indeed issue from it? What business has it on hand in this lonely place? The mystery of the dark hours rests securely here. Its aspect is disquieting at noonday; what must it be at midnight? The dreamer asks himself—for dreams have their coherence—what this house may be between the dusk of evening and the twilight of approaching dawn? Has the vast supernatural world some relation with this deserted height, which sometimes compels it to arrest its movements here, and to descend and to become visible? Do the scattered elements of the spirit world whirl around it? Does the impalpable take form and substance here? Insoluble riddles! A holy awe is in the very stones; that dim twilight has surely relations with the infinite Unknown. When the sun has gone down, the song of the birds will be hushed, the goatherd behind the hills will go homeward with his goats; reptiles, taking courage from the gathering darkness, will creep through the fissures of rocks; the stars will begin to appear, night will come, but yonder two blank casements will still be staring at the sky. They open to welcome spirits and apparitions; for it is by the names of apparitions, ghosts, phantom faces vaguely distinct, masks in the lurid light, mysterious movements of minds, and shadows, that the popular faith, at once ignorant and profound, translates the sombre relations of this dwelling with the world of darkness.

The house is "haunted;" the popular phrase comprises everything.

Credulous minds have their explanation; common-sense thinkers have theirs also. "Nothing is more simple," say the latter, "than the history of the house. It is an old observatory of the time of the revolutionary wars and the days of smuggling. It was built for such objects. The wars being ended, the house was abandoned; but it was not pulled down, as it might one day again become useful. The door and windows have been walled to prevent people entering, or doing injury to the interior. The walls of the windows, on the three sides which face the sea, have been bricked up against the winds of the south and south-west. That is all."

The ignorant and the credulous, however, are not satisfied. In the first place, the house was not built at the period of the wars of the Revolution. It bears the date "1780," which was anterior to the Revolution. In the next place it was not built for an observatory. It bears the letters "ELM-PBILG," which are the double monogram of two families, and which indicate, according to usage, that the house was built for the use of a newly-married couple. Then it has certainly been inhabited: why then should it be abandoned? If the door and windows were bricked up to prevent people entering the house only, why were two windows left open? Why are there no shutters, no window-frames, no glass? Why were the walls bricked in on one side if not on the other? The wind is prevented from entering from the south; but why is it allowed to enter from the north?

The credulous are wrong, no doubt; but it is clear that the common-sense thinkers have not discovered the key to the mystery. The problem remains still unsolved.

It is certain that the house is generally believed to have been more useful than inconvenient to the smugglers.

The growth of superstitious terror tends to deprive facts of their true proportions. Without doubt, many of the nocturnal phenomena which have, by little and little, secured to the building the reputation of being haunted, might be explained by obscure and furtive visits, by brief sojourns of sailors near the spot, and sometimes by the precaution, sometimes by the daring, of men engaged in certain suspicious occupations concealing themselves for their dark purposes, or allowing themselves to be seen in order to inspire dread.

At this period, already a remote one, many daring deeds were possible. The police—particularly in small places—was by no means as efficient as in these days.

Add to this, that if the house was really, as was said, a resort of the smugglers, their meetings there must, up to a certain point, have been safe from interruptions precisely because the house was dreaded by the superstitious people of the country. Its ghostly reputation prevented its being visited for other reasons. People do not generally apply to the police, or officers of customs, on the subject of spectres. The superstitious rely on making the sign of the cross; not on magistrates and indictments. There is always a tacit connivance, involuntary it may be, but not the less real, between the objects which inspire fear and their victims. The terror-stricken feel a sort of culpability in having encountered their terrors; they imagine themselves to have unveiled a secret; and they have an inward fear, unknown even to themselves, of aggravating their guilt, and exciting the anger of the apparitions. All this makes them discreet. And over and above this reason, the very instinct of the credulous is silence; dread is akin to dumbness; the terrified speak little; horror seems always to whisper, "Hush!"

It must be remembered that this was a period when the Guernsey peasants believed that the Mystery of the Holy Manger is repeated by oxen and asses every year on a fixed day; a period when no one would have dared to enter a stable at night for fear of coming upon the animals on their knees.

If the local legends and stories of the people can be credited, the popular superstition went so far as to fasten to the walls of the house at Pleinmont things of which the traces are still visible—rats without feet, bats without wings, and bodies of other dead animals. Here, too, were seen toads crushed between the pages of a Bible, bunches of yellow lupins, and other strange offerings, placed there by imprudent passers-by at night, who, having fancied that they had seen something, hoped by these small sacrifices to obtain pardon, and to appease the ill-humours of were-wolves and evil spirits. In all times, believers of this kind have flourished; some even in very high places. Cæsar consulted Saganius, and Napoleon Mademoiselle Lenormand. There are a kind of consciences so tender, that they must seek indulgences even from Beelzebub. "May God do, and Satan not undo," was one of the prayers of Charles the Fifth. They come to persuade themselves that they may commit sins even against the Evil One; and one of their cherished objects was, to be irreproachable even in the eyes of Satan. We find here an explanation of those adorations sometimes paid to infernal spirits. It is only one more species of fanaticism. Sins against the devil certainly exist in certain morbid imaginations. The fancy that they have violated the laws of the lower regions torments certain eccentric casuists; they are haunted with scruples even about offending the demons. A belief in the efficacy of devotions to the spirits of the Brocken or Armuyr, a notion of having committed sins against hell, visionary penances for imaginary crimes, avowals of the truth to the spirit of falsehood, self-accusation before the origin of all evil, and confessions in an inverted sense—are all realities, or things at least which have existed. The annals of criminal procedure against witchcraft and magic prove this in every page. Human folly unhappily extends even thus far: when terror seizes upon a man he does not stop easily. He dreams of imaginary faults, imaginary purifications, and clears out his conscience with the old witches' broom.

Be this as it may, if the house at Pleinmont had its secrets, it kept them to itself; except by some rare chance, no one went there to see. It was left entirely alone. Few people, indeed, like to run the risk of an encounter with the other world.

Owing to the terror which it inspired, and which kept at a distance all who could observe or bear testimony on the subject, it had always been easy to obtain an entrance there at night by means of a rope ladder, or even by the use of the first ladder coming to hand in one of the neighbouring fields. A consignment of goods or provisions left there might await in perfect safety the time and opportunity for a furtive embarkation. Tradition relates that forty years ago a fugitive—for political offences as some affirm, for commercial as others say—remained for some time concealed in the haunted house at Pleinmont; whence he finally succeeded in embarking in a fishing-boat for England. From England a passage is easily obtained to America.

Tradition also avers that provisions deposited in this house remain there untouched, Lucifer and the smugglers having an interest in inducing who-ever places them there to return.

From the summit of the house, there is a view to the south of the Hanway Rocks, at about a mile from the shore.

These rocks are famous. They have been guilty of all the evil deeds of which rocks are capable. They are the most ruthless destroyers of the sea. They lie in a treacherous ambush for vessels in the night. They have con-tributed to the enlargement of the cemeteries at Torteval and Rocquaine.

A lighthouse was erected upon these rocks in 1862. At the present day, the Hanways light the way for the vessels which they once lured to destruc-tion; the destroyer in ambush now bears a lighted torch in his hand; and mariners seek in the horizon, as a protector and a guide, the rock which they used to fly as a pitiless enemy. It gives confidence by night in that vast space where it was so long a terror—like a robber converted into a gendarme.

There are three Hanways: the Great Hanway, the Little Hanway, and the Mauve. It is upon the Little Hanway that the red light is placed at the present time.

This reef of rocks forms part of a group of peaks, some beneath the sea, some rising out of it. It towers above them all; like a fortress, it has advanced works: on the side of the open sea, a chain of thirteen rocks; on the north, two breakers—the High Fourquiés, the Needles, and a sandbank called the Hérouée. On the south, three rocks—the Cat Rock, the Percée, and the Herpin Rock; then two banks—the South Bank and the Muet: besides which, there is, on the side opposite Pleinmont, the Tas de Pois d'Aval.

To swim across the channel from the Hanways to Pleinmont is difficult, but not impossible. We have already said that this was one of the achievements of Clubin. The expert swimmer who knows this channel can find two resting-places, the Round Rock, and further on, a little out of the course, to the left, the Red Rock.

V
THE BIRDS'-NESTERS

IT WAS NEAR the period of that Saturday which was passed by Sieur Clubin at Torteval that a curious incident occurred, which was little heard of at the time, and which did not generally transpire till a long time afterwards. For many things, as we have already observed, remain undivulged, simply by reason of the terror which they have caused in those who have witnessed them.

In the night-time between Saturday and Sunday—we are exact in the matter of the date, and we believe it to be correct—three boys climbed up the hill at Pleinmont. The boys returned to the village: they came from the seashore. They were what are called, in the corrupt French of that part, "déniquoiseaux," or birds'-nesters. Wherever there are cliffs and cleft-rocks overhanging the sea, the young birds'-nesters abound. The reader will re-

member that Gilliatt interfered in this matter for the sake of the birds as well
as for the sake of the children.

The "déniquoiseaux" are a sort of sea-urchins, and are not a very timid
species.

The night was very dark. Dense masses of cloud obscured the zenith.
Three o'clock had sounded in the steeple of Torteval which is round and
pointed like a magician's hat.

Why did the boys return so late? Nothing more simple. They had been
searching for sea-gulls' nests in the Tas de Pois d'Aval. The season having
been very mild, the pairing of the birds had begun very early. The children
watching the fluttering of the male and female about their nests, and excited
by the pursuit, had forgotten the time. The waters had crept up around
them; they had no time to regain the little bay in which they had moored
their boat, and they were compelled to wait upon one of the peaks of the
Tas de Pois for the ebb of the tide. Hence their late return. Mothers wait
on such occasions in feverish anxiety for the return of their children, and
when they find them safe, give vent to their joy in the shape of anger, and
relieve their tears by dealing them a sound drubbing. The boys accordingly
hastened their steps, but in fear and trembling. Their haste was of that sort
which is glad of an excuse for stopping, and which is not inconsistent with
a reluctance to reach their destination; for they had before them the prospect of warm embraces, to be followed with an inevitable thrashing.

One only of the boys had nothing of this to fear. He was an orphan: a
French boy, without father or mother, and perfectly content just then with
his motherless condition; for nobody taking any interest in him, his back
was safe from the dreaded blows. The two others were natives of Guernsey,
and belonged to the parish of Torteval.

Having climbed the grassy hill, the three birds'-nesters reached the
tableland on which was situate the haunted house.

They began by being in fear, which is the proper frame of mind of every
passer-by; and particularly of every child at that hour and in that place.

They had a strong desire to take to their heels as fast as possible, and a
strong desire, also, to stay and look.

They did stop.

They looked towards the solitary building.

It was all dark and terrible.

It stood in the midst of the solitary plain—an obscure block, a hideous but symmetrical excrescence; a high square mass with right-angled corners, like an immense altar in the darkness.

The first thought of the boys was to run: the second was to draw nearer. They had never seen this house before. There is such a thing as a desire to be frightened arising from curiosity. They had a little French boy with them, which emboldened them to approach.

It is well known that the French have no fear.

Besides, it is reassuring to have company in danger; to be frightened in the company of two others is encouraging.

And then they were a sort of hunters accustomed to peril. They were children; they were used to search, to rummage, to spy out hidden things. They were in the habit of peeping into holes; why not into this hole? Hunting is exciting. Looking into birds' nests perhaps gives an itch for looking a little into a nest of ghosts. A rummage in the dark regions. Why not?

From prey to prey, says the proverb, we come to the devil. After the birds, the demons. The boys were on the way to learn the secret of those terrors of which their parents had told them. To be on the track of hobgoblin tales—nothing could be more attractive. To have long stories to tell like the good housewives. The notion was tempting.

All this mixture of ideas, in their state of half-confusion, half-instinct, in the minds of the Guernsey birds'-nesters, finally screwed their courage to the point. They approached the house.

The little fellow who served them as a sort of moral support in the adventure was certainly worthy of their confidence. He was a bold boy— an apprentice to a ship-caulker; one of those children who have already become men. He slept on a little straw in a shed in the ship-caulker's yard, getting his own living, having red hair, and a loud voice; climbing easily up walls and trees, not encumbered with prejudices in the matter of property in the apples within his reach; a lad who had worked in the repairing dock for vessels of war—a child of chance, a happy orphan, born in France, no one knew exactly where; ready to give a centime to a beggar; a mischievous fellow, but a good one at heart; one who had talked to Parisians. At this time he was earning a shilling a day by caulking the fishermen's boats under repair at the Pêqueries. When he felt inclined he gave himself a holiday, and went birds'-nesting. Such was the little French boy.

The solitude of the place impressed them with a strange feeling of dread. They felt the threatening aspect of the silent house. It was wild and savage. The naked and deserted plateau terminated in a precipice at a short distance from its steep incline. The sea below was quiet. There was no wind. Not a blade of grass stirred.

The birds'-nesters advanced by slow steps, the French boy at their head, and looking towards the house.

One of them, afterwards relating the story, or as much of it as had remained in his head, added, "It did not speak."

They came nearer, holding their breath, as one might approach a savage animal.

They had climbed the hill at the side of the house which descended to seaward towards a little isthmus of rocks almost inaccessible. Thus they had come pretty near to the building; but they saw only the southern side, which was all walled up. They did not dare to approach by the other side, where the terrible windows were.

They grew bolder, however; the caulker's apprentice whispered, "Let's veer to larboard. That's the handsome side. Let's have a look at the black windows."

The little band accordingly "veered to larboard," and came round to the other side of the house.

The two windows were lighted up.

The boys took to their heels.

When they had got to some distance, the French boy, however, returned. "Hillo!" said he, "the lights have vanished."

The light at the windows had, indeed, disappeared. The outline of the building was seen as sharply defined as if stamped out with a punch against the livid sky.

Their fear was not abated, but their curiosity had increased. The birds'-nesters approached.

Suddenly the light reappeared at both windows at the same moment.

The two young urchins from Torteval took to their heels and vanished. The daring French boy did not advance, but he kept his ground.

He remained motionless, confronting the house and watching it.

The light disappeared, and appeared again once more. Nothing could be more horrible. The reflection made a vague streak of light upon the grass, wet with the night dew. All of a moment the light cast upon the walls of the house two huge dark profiles, and the shadows of enormous heads.

The house, however, being without ceilings, and having nothing left but its four walls and roof, one window could not be lighted without the other.

Perceiving that the caulker's apprentice kept his ground, the other birds'-nesters returned, step by step, and one after the other, trembling and curious. The caulker's apprentice whispered to them, "There are ghosts in the house. I have seen the nose of one." The two Torteval boys got behind their companion, standing tiptoe against his shoulder; and thus sheltered, and taking him for their shield, felt bolder and watched also.

The house on its part seemed also to be watching them. There it stood in the midst of that vast darkness and silence, with its two glaring eyes. These were its upper windows. The light vanished, reappeared, and vanished again, in the fashion of these unearthly illuminations. These sinister inter-missions had, probably, some connection with the opening and shutting of the infernal regions. The air-hole of a sepulchre has thus been seen to produce effects like those from a dark lantern.

Suddenly a dark form, like that of a human being, ascended to one of the windows, as if from without, and plunged into the interior of the house.

To enter by the window is the custom with spirits.

The light was for a moment more brilliant, then went out, and appeared no more. The house became dark. The noises resembled voices. This is always the case. When there was anything to be seen it is silent. When all became invisible again, noises were heard.

There is a silence peculiar to night-time at sea. The repose of darkness is deeper on the water than on the land. When there is neither wind nor wave in that wild expanse, over which, in ordinary time, even the flight of eagles makes no sound, the movement of a fly could be heard. This sepul-chral quiet gave a dismal relief to the noises which issued from the house.

"Let us look," said the French boy.

And he made a step towards the house.

The others were so frightened that they resolved to follow him. They did not dare even to run away alone.

Just as they had passed a heap of fagots, which for some mysterious reason seemed to inspire them with a little courage in that solitude, a white owl flew towards them from a bush. The owls have a suspicious sort of flight, a sidelong skim which is suggestive of mischief afloat. The bird passed near the boys, fixing upon them its round eyes, bright amidst the darkness.

A shudder ran through the group behind the French boy.

He looked up at the owl and said:

"Too late, my bird; I *will* look."

And he advanced.

The crackling sound made by his thick-nailed boots among the furze bushes did not prevent his hearing the noise in the house, which rose and fell with the continuousness and the calm accent of a dialogue.

A moment afterwards the boy added:

"Besides, it is only fools who believe in spirits."

Insolence in the face of danger rallies the cowardly, and inspirits them to go on.

The two Torteval lads resumed their march, quickening their steps behind the caulker's apprentice.

The haunted house seemed to them to grow larger before their eyes. This optical illusion of fear is founded in reality. The house did indeed grow larger, for they were coming nearer to it.

Meanwhile the voices in the house took a tone more and more distinct. The children listened. The ear, too, has its power of exaggerating. It was different to a murmur, more than a whispering, less than an uproar. Now and then one or two words, clearly articulated, could be caught. These words, impossible to be understood, sounded strangely. The boys stopped and listened; then went forward again.

"It's the ghosts talking," said the caulker's apprentice; "but I don't believe in ghosts."

The Torteval boys were sorely tempted to shrink behind the heap of fagots, but they had already left it far behind; and their friend the caulker continued to advance towards the house. They trembled at remaining with him; but they dared not leave him.

Step by step, and perplexed, they followed. The caulker's apprentice turned towards them and said—

"You know it isn't true. There are no such things."

The house grew taller and taller. The voices became more and more distinct. They drew nearer.

And now they could perceive within the house something like a muffled light. It was a faint glimmer, like one of those effects produced by dark lanterns, already referred to, and which are common at the midnight meetings of witches.

When they were close to the house they halted.

One of the two Torteval boys ventured on an observation:

"It isn't spirits: it is ladies dressed in white."

"What's that hanging from the window?" asked the other.

"It looks like a rope."

"It's a snake."

"It is only a hangman's rope," said the French boy, authoritatively. "That's what they use. Only I don't believe in them."

And in three bounds, rather than steps, he found himself against the wall of the building.

The two others, trembling, imitated him, and came pressing against him, one on his right side, the other on his left. The boys applied their ears to the wall. The sounds continued.

The following was the conversation of the phantoms:—

"Asi, entendido esta?"

"Entendido."

"Dicho?"

"Dicho."

"Aqui esperara un hombre, y podra marcharse en Inglaterra con Blasquito."

"Pagando?"

"So that is understood?"

"Perfectly."

"As is arranged?"

"As is arranged."

"A man will wait here, and can accompany Blasquito to England."

"Paying the expense?"

"Pagando."

"Blasquito tomara al hombre en su barca."

"Sin buscar para conocer a su pais?"

"No nos toca."

"Ni a su nombre del hombre?"

"No se pide el nombre, pero se pesa la bolsa."

"Bien: esperara el hombre en esa casa."

"Tenga que comer."

"Tendra."

"Onde?"

"En este saco que he llevado."

"Muy bien."

"Puedo dexar el saco aqui?"

"Los contrabandistas no son ladrones."

"Y vosotros, cuando marchais?"

"Mañana por la mañana. Si su hombre de usted parado podria venir con nosotros."

"Parado no esta."

"Hacienda suya."

"Cuantos dias esperara alli?"

"Paying the expense."

"Blasquito will take the man in his bark."

"Without seeking to know what country he belongs to?"

"That is no business of ours."

"Without asking his name?"

"We do not ask for names; we only feel the weight of the purse."

"Good: the man shall wait in this house."

"He must have provisions."

"He will be furnished with them."

"How?"

"From this bag which I have brought."

"Very good."

"Can I leave this bag here?"

"Smugglers are not robbers."

"And when do you go?"

"To-morrow morning. If your man was ready he could come with us."

"He is not prepared."

"That is his affair."

"How many days will he have to wait in this house?"

"Dos, tres, quatro dias; menos o mas."

"Es cierto que el Blasquito vendra?"

"Cierto."

"En est Plainmont?"

"En est Plainmont."

"A qual semana?"

"La que viene."

"A qual dia?"

"Viernes, o sabado, o domingo."

"No peuede faltar?"

"Es mi tocayo."

"Por qualquiera tiempo viene?"

"Qualquiera. No tieme. Soy el Blasco, es el Blasquito."

"Asi, no puede faltar de venir en Guernesey?"

"Vengo a un mes, y viene al otro mes."

"Entiendo."

"A cuentar del otro sabado, desde hoy en ocho, no se parasan cinco dias sin que venga el Blasquito."

"Pero un muy malo mar?"

"Egurraldia gaiztoa."

"Two, three, or four days; more or less."

"Is it certain that Blasquito will come?"

"Certain."

"Here to Pleinmont?"

"To Pleinmont."

"When?"

"Next week."

"What day?"

"Friday, Saturday, or Sunday."

"May he not fail?"

"He is my Tocayo."

"Will he come in any weather?"

"At any time. He has no fear. My name is Blasco, his Blasquito."

"So he cannot fail to come to Guernsey?"

"I come one month—he the other."

"I understand."

"Counting from Saturday last, one week from to-day, five days cannot elapse without bringing Blasquito."

"But if there is much sea?"

"Bad weather?"

"Si."

"No vendria el Blasquito tan pronto, pero vendria."

"Donde vendra?"

"De Vilvao."

"Onde ira?"

"En Portland."

"Bien."

"O en Tor Bay."

"Mejor."

"Su humbre de usted puede estarse quieto."

"No traidor sera, el Blasquito?"

"Los cobardes son traidores. Somos valientes. El mar es la iglesia del invierno. La traicion es la iglesia del infierno."

"No se entiende a lo que dicemos?"

"Escuchar a nosotros y mirar a nosotros es imposible. La espanta hace alli el desierto."

"Lo sè."

"Quien se atravesaria a escuchar?"

"Es verdad."

"Y escucharian que no entiendrian. Hablamos a una lengua fiera y nuestra que no se conoce. Despues que la sabeis, eries con nosotros."

"Yes."

"Blasquito will not come so quickly, but he will come."

"Whence will he come?"

"From Bilbao."

"Where will he be going?"

"To Portland."

"Good."

"Or to Torbay."

"Better still."

"Your man may rest easy."

"Blasquito will betray nothing?"

"Cowards are the only traitors. We are men of courage. The sea is the church of winter. Treason is the church of hell."

"No one hears what we say?"

"It is impossible to be seen or overheard. The people's fear of this spot makes it deserted."

"I know it."

"Who is there who would dare to listen here?"

"True."

"Besides, if they listened, none would understand. We speak a wild language of our own, which nobody knows hereabouts. As you know it, you are one of us."

"Soy viendo para componer las haciendas con ustedes."

"Bueno."

"Y allora me voy."

"Mucho."

"Digame usted, hombre. Si el pasagero quiere que el Blasquito le lleven en unguna otra parte que Portland o Tor Bay?"

"Tenga onces."

"El Blasquito hara lo que querra el hombre?"

"El Blasquito hace lo que quieren las onces."

"Es menester mucho tiempo para ir en Tor Bay?"

"Como quiere el viento."

"Ocho horas?"

"Menos, o mas."

"El Blasquito obedecera al pasagero?"

"Si le obedece el mar al Blasquito."

"Bien pagado sera."

"El oro es el oro. El viento es el viento."

"Mucho."

"I came only to make these arrangements with you."

"Very good."

"I must now take my leave."

"Be it so."

"Tell me; suppose the passenger should wish Blasquito to take him anywhere else than to Portland or Torbay?"

"Let him bring some gold coins."

"Will Blasquito consult the stranger's convenience?"

"Blasquito will do whatever the gold coins command."

"Does it take long to go to Torbay?"

"That is as it pleases the winds."

"Eight hours?"

"More or less."

"Will Blasquito obey the passenger?"

"If the sea will obey Blasquito."

"He will be well rewarded."

"Gold is gold; and the sea is the sea."

"That is true."

"El hombre hace lo que puede con el oro. Dios con el viento hace lo que quiere."

"Aqui sera viernes el que desea marcharse con Blasquito."

"Pues."

"A qual momento llega Blasquito."

"A la noche. A la noche se llega, a la noche se marcha. Tenemos una muger quien se llama el mar, y una quien se llama la noche."

"La muger puede faltar, la hermana no."

"Todo dicho esta. Abour, hombres."

"Buenas tardes. Un golpe de aquardiente?"

"Gracias."

"Es mejor que xarope."

"Tengo vuestra palabra."

"Mi nombre es Pundonor."

"Sea usted con Dios."

"Ereis gentleman, y soy caballero."

"Man with his gold does what he can. Heaven with its winds does what it will."

"The man who is to accompany Blasquito will be here on Friday."

"Good."

"At what hour will Blasquito appear?"

"In the night. We arrive by night; and sail by night. We have a wife who is called the sea, and a sister called night. The wife betrays sometimes; but the sister never."

"All is settled, then. Good-night, my men."

"Good-night. A drop of brandy first?"

"Thank you."

"That is better than a syrup."

"I have your word."

"My name is Point-of-Honour."

"Adieu."

"You are a gentleman: I am a caballero."

It was clear that only devils could talk in this way. The children did not listen long. This time they took to flight in earnest; the French boy, convinced at last, running even quicker than the others.

On the Tuesday following this Saturday, Sieur Clubin returned to St. Malo, bringing back the Durande.

The *Tamaulipas* was still at anchor in the roads.

Sieur Clubin, between the whiffs of his pipe, said to the landlord of the Jean Auberge:

"Well; and when does the *Tamaulipas* get under way?"

"The day after to-morrow—Thursday," replied the landlord.

On that evening, Clubin supped at the coast-guard officers' table; and, contrary to his habit, went out after his supper. The consequence of his absence was, that he could not attend to the office of the Durande, and thus lost a little in the matter of freights. This fact was remarked in a man ordinarily punctual.

It appeared that he had chatted a few moments with his friend the money-changer.

He returned two hours after Noguette had sounded the Curfew bell. The Brazilian bell sounds at ten o'clock. It was therefore midnight.

VI

THE JACRESSADE

FORTY YEARS AGO, St. Malo possessed an alley known by the name of the "Ruelle Coutanchez." This alley no longer exists, having been removed for the improvements of the town.

It was a double row of houses, leaning one towards the other, and leaving between them just room enough for a narrow rivulet, which was called the street. By stretching the legs, it was possible to walk on both sides of the stream, touching with head or elbows, as you went, the houses either on the right or the left. These old relics of mediæval Normandy have almost a human interest. Tumbledown houses and sorcerers always go together. Their leaning stories, their overhanging walls, their bowed penthouses, and their old thick-set irons, seem like lips, chin, nose, and eyebrows. The garret window is the blind eye. The walls are the wrinkled and blotchy cheeks. The opposite houses lay their foreheads together as if they were plotting some malicious deed. All those words of ancient villany—like cut-throat, "slit-weazand," and the like—are closely connected with architecture of this kind.

One of these houses in the alley—the largest and the most famous, or notorious—was known by the name of the Jacressade.

The Jacressade was a lodging-house for people who do not lodge. In all towns, and particularly in sea-ports, there is always found beneath the

lowest stratum of society a sort of residuum: vagabonds who are more than
a match for justice; rovers after adventures; chemists of the swindling order,
who are always dropping their lives into the melting-pot; people in rags of
every shape, and in every style of wearing them; withered fruits of roguery;
bankrupt existences; consciences that have filed their schedule; men who
have failed in the house-breaking trade (for the great masters of burglary
move in a higher sphere); workmen and workwomen in the trade of wickedness; oddities, male and female; men in coats out at elbows; scoundrels
reduced to indigence; rogues who have missed the wages of roguery; men
who have been hit in the social duel; harpies who have no longer any prey;
petty larceners; *queux* in the double and unhappy meaning of that word.
Such are the constituents of that living mass. Human nature is here reduced
to something bestial. It is the refuse of the social state, heaped up in an
obscure corner, where from time to time descends that dreaded broom
which is known by the name of police. In St. Malo, the Jacressade was the
name of this corner.

It is not in dens of this sort that we find the high-class criminals—
the robbers, forgers, and other great products of ignorance and poverty.
If murder is represented here, it is generally in the person of some coarse
drunkard; in the matter of robbery, the company rarely rise higher than the
mere sharper. The vagrant is there; but not the highwayman. It would not,
however, be safe to trust this distinction. This last stage of vagabondage may
have its extremes of scoundrelism. It was on an occasion, when casting their
nets into the Epi-scié—which was in Paris what the Jacressade was in St.
Malo—that the police captured the notorious Lacenaire.

These lurking-places refuse nobody. To fall in the social scale has a tendency to bring men to one level. Sometimes honesty in tatters found itself
there. Virtue and probity have been known before now to be brought to
strange passes. We must not judge always by appearances, even in the palace
or at the galleys. Public respect, as well as universal reprobation, requires
testing. Surprising results sometimes spring from this principle. An angel
may be discovered in the stews; a pearl in the dunghill. Such sad and dazzling
discoveries are not altogether unknown.

The Jacressade was rather a courtyard than a house; and more of a well
than a courtyard. It had no stories looking on the street. Its façade was simply

a high wall, with a low gateway. You raised the latch, pushed the gate, and were at once in the courtyard.

In the midst of this yard might be perceived a round hole, encircled with a margin of stones, and even with the ground. The yard was small, the well large. A broken pavement surrounded it.

The courtyard was square, and built on three sides only. On the side of the street was only the wall; facing you as you entered the gateway stood the house, the two wings of which formed the sides to right and left.

Any one entering there after nightfall, at his own risk and peril, would have heard a confused murmur of voices; and, if there had been moonlight or starlight enough to give shape to the obscure forms before his eyes, this is what he would have seen.

The courtyard: the well. Around the courtyard, in front of the gate, a lean-to or shed, in a sort of horse-shoe form, but with square corners; a rotten gallery, with a roof of joists supported by stone pillars at unequal distances. In the centre, the well; around the well, upon a litter of straw, a kind of circular chaplet, formed of the soles of boots and shoes; some trodden down at heel, some showing the toes of the wearers, some the naked heels. The feet of men, women, and children, all asleep.

Beyond these feet, the eye might have distinguished, in the shadow of the shed, bodies, drooping heads, forms stretched out lazily, bundles of rags of both sexes, a promiscuous assemblage, a strange and revolting mass of life. The accommodation of this sleeping chamber was open to all, at the rate of two sous a week. On a stormy night the rain fell upon the feet, the whirling snow settled on the bodies of those wretched sleepers.

Who were these people? The unknown. They came there at night, and departed in the morning. Creatures of this kind form part of the social fabric. Some stole in during the darkness, and paid nothing. The greater part had scarcely eaten during the day. All kinds of vice and baseness, every sort of moral infection, every species of distress were there. The same sleep settled down upon all in this bed of filth. The dreams of all these companions in misery went on side by side. A dismal meeting-place, where misery and weakness, half-sobered debauchery, weariness from long walking to and fro, with evil thoughts, in quest of bread, pallor with closed eyelids, remorse, envy, lay mingled and festering in the same miasma, with faces that had the look of death, and dishevelled hair mixed with the filth and sweepings of the streets. Such was the putrid heap of life fermenting in this dismal spot. An unlucky turn of the wheel of fortune, a ship arrived on the day before, a discharge from prison, a dark night, or some other chance, had cast them here, to find a miserable shelter. Every day brought some new accumulation of such misery. Let him enter who would, sleep who could, speak who dared; for it was a place of whispers. The new comers hastened to bury themselves in the mass, or tried to seek oblivion in sleep, since there was none in the darkness of the place. They snatched what little of themselves they could from the jaws of death. They closed their eyes in that confusion of horrors which every day renewed. They were the embodiment of misery, thrown off from society, as the scum is from the sea.

It was not every one who could even get a share of the straw. More than one figure was stretched out naked upon the flags. They lay down worn out with weariness, and awoke paralysed. The well, without lid or parapet, and thirty feet in depth, gaped open night and day. Rain fell around it; filth accumulated about, and the gutters of the yard ran down and filtered through its sides. The pail for drawing the water stood by the side. Those who were thirsty drank there; some, disgusted with life, drowned themselves in it—slipped from their slumber in the filthy shed into that profounder sleep. In the year 1819, the body of a boy, of fourteen years old, was taken up out of this well.

To be safe in this house, it was necessary to be of the "right sort." The uninitiated were regarded with suspicion.

Did these miserable wretches, then, know each other? No; yet they scented out the genuine guest of the Jacressade.

The mistress of the house was a young and rather pretty woman, wearing a cap trimmed with ribbons. She washed herself now and then with water from the well. She had a wooden leg.

At break of day, the courtyard became empty. Its inmates dispersed.

An old cock and some other fowls were kept in the courtyard, where they raked among the filth of the place all day long. A long horizontal beam, supported by posts, traversed the yard—a gibbet-shaped erection, not out of keeping with the associations of the place. Sometimes on the morrow of a rainy-day, a silk dress, mudded and wet, would be seen hanging out to dry upon this beam. It belonged to the woman with the wooden leg.

Over the shed, and like it, surrounding the yard, was a story, and above this story a loft. A rotten wooden ladder, passing through a hole in the roof of the shed, conducted to this story; and up this ladder the woman would climb, sometimes staggering while its crazy rounds creaked beneath her.

The occasional lodgers, whether by the week or the night, slept in the courtyard; the regular inmates lived in the house.

Windows without a pane of glass, door-frames with no door, fireplaces without stoves; such were the chief features of the interior. You might pass from one room to the other, indifferently, by a long square aperture which had been the door, or by a triangular hole between the joists of the partitions. The fallen plaster of the ceiling lay about the floor. It was difficult to say how the old house still stood erect. The high winds indeed shook it. The lodgers ascended as they could by the worn and slippery steps of the ladder. Everything was open to the air. The wintry atmosphere was absorbed into the house, like water into a sponge. The multitude of spiders seemed alone to guarantee the place against falling to pieces immediately. There was no sign of furniture. Two or three paillasses were in the corner, their ticking torn in parts, and showing more dust than straw within. Here and there were a water-pot and an earthen pipkin. A close, disagreeable odour haunted the rooms.

The windows looked out upon the square yard. The scene was like the interior of a scavenger's cart. The things, not to speak of the human beings, which lay rusting, mouldering, and putrefying there, were indescribable. The fragments seemed to fraternise together. Some fell from the walls, others from the living tenants of the place. The débris were sown with their tatters.

Besides the floating population which bivouacked nightly in the square yard, the Jacressade had three permanent lodgers—a charcoal man, a rag-picker, and a "gold-maker." The charcoal man and the rag-picker occupied two of the paillasses of the first story; the "gold-maker," a chemist, lodged in the loft, which was called, no one knew why, the garret. Nobody knew where the woman slept. The "gold-maker" was a poet in a small way. He inhabited a room in the roof, under the tiles—a chamber with a narrow window, and a large stone fireplace forming a gulf, in which the wind howled at will. The garret window having no frame, he had nailed across it a piece of iron sheathing, part of the wreck of a ship. This sheathing left little room for the entrance of light and much for the entrance of cold. The charcoal-man paid rent from time to time in the shape of a sack of charcoal; the rag-picker paid with a bowl of grain for the fowls every week; the "gold-maker" did not pay at all. Meanwhile the latter consumed the very house itself for fuel. He had pulled down the little woodwork which remained; and every now and then he took from the wall or the roof a lath or some scantling, to heat his crucible. Upon the partition, above the rag-picker's mattress, might have been seen two columns of figures, marked in chalk by the rag-picker himself from week to week—a column of threes, and a column of fives—according as the bowl of grain had cost him three liards or five centimes. The gold-pot of the "chemist" was an old fragment of a bomb-shell, promoted by him to the dignity of a crucible, in which he mixed his ingredients. The transmutation of metals absorbed all his thoughts. He was determined before he died to revenge himself by breaking the windows of orthodox science with the real philosopher's stone. His furnace consumed a good deal of wood. The hand-rail of the stairs had disappeared. The house was slowly burning away. The landlady said to him, "You will leave us nothing but the shell." He mollified her by addressing her in verses.

Such was the Jacressade.

A boy of twelve, or, perhaps, sixteen—for he was like a dwarf, with a large wen upon his neck, and always carrying a broom in his hand—was the domestic of the place.

The habitués entered by the gateway of the courtyard; the public entered by the shop.

In the high wall, facing the street, and to the right of the entrance to the courtyard, was a square opening, serving at once as a door and a window. This was the shop. The square opening had a shutter and a frame—the only shutter in all the house which had hinges and bolts. Behind this square aperture, which was open to the street, was a little room, a compartment obtained by curtailing the sleeping shed in the courtyard. Over the door, passers-by read the inscription in charcoal, "Curiosities sold here." On three boards, forming the shop front, were several china pots without ears, a Chinese parasol made of goldbeater's skin, and ornamented with figures, torn here and there, and impossible to open or shut; fragments of iron, and shapeless pieces of old pottery, and dilapidated hats and bonnets, three or four shells, some packets of old bone and metal buttons, a tobacco-box with a portrait of Marie-Antoinette, and a dog's-eared volume of Boisbertrand's *Algebra*. Such was the stock of the shop; this assortment completed the "curiosities." The shop communicated by a back door with the yard in which was the well. It was furnished with a table and a stool. The woman with a wooden leg presided at the counter.

VII
NOCTURNAL BUYERS AND MYSTERIOUS SELLERS

CLUBIN HAD BEEN absent from the Jean Auberge all the evening of Tuesday. On the Wednesday night he was absent again.

In the dusk of that evening, two strangers penetrated into the mazes of the Ruelle Coutanchez. They stopped in front of the Jacressade. One of them knocked at the window; the door of the shop opened, and they entered. The woman with the wooden leg met them with the smile which she reserved for respectable citizens. There was a candle on the table.

The strangers were, in fact, respectable citizens. The one who had knocked said, "Good-day, mistress. I have come for that affair."

The woman with the wooden leg smiled again, and went out by the back-door leading to the courtyard, and where the well was. A moment afterwards the back-door was opened again, and a man stood in the doorway. He wore a cap and a blouse. It was easy to see the shape of something under his blouse. He had bits of old straw in his clothes, and looked as if he had just been aroused from sleep.

He advanced and exchanged glances with the strangers. The man in the blouse looked puzzled, but cunning; he said—

"You are the gunsmith?"

The one who had tapped at the window replied—

"Yes; you are the man from Paris?"

"Known as Redskin. Yes."

"Show me the thing."

The man took from under his blouse a weapon extremely rare at that period in Europe. It was a revolver.

The weapon was new and bright. The two strangers examined it. The one who seemed to know the house, and whom the man in the blouse had called "the gunsmith," tried the mechanism. He passed the weapon to the other, who appeared less at home there, and kept his back turned to the light.

The gunsmith continued—

"How much?"

The man in the blouse replied—

"I have just brought it from America. Some people bring monkeys, parrots, and other animals, as if the French people were savages. For myself I brought this. It is a useful invention."

"How much?" inquired the gunsmith again.

"It is a pistol which turns and turns."

"How much?"

"Bang! the first fire. Bang! the second fire. Bang! the third fire. What a hailstorm of bullets! That will do some execution."

"The price?"

"There are six barrels."

"Well, well, what do you want for it?"

"Six barrels; that is six Louis."

"Will you take five?"

"Impossible. One Louis a ball. That is the price."

"Come, let us do business together. Be reasonable."

"I have named a fair price. Examine the weapon, Mr. Gunsmith."

"I have examined it."

"The barrel twists and turns like Talleyrand himself. The weapon ought to be mentioned in the *Dictionary of Weathercocks*. It is a gem."

"I have looked at it."

"The barrels are of Spanish make."

"I see they are."

"They are twisted. This is how this twisting is done. They empty into a forge the basket of a collector of old iron. They fill it full of these old scraps, with old nails, and broken horseshoes swept out of farriers' shops."

"And old sickle-blades."

"I was going to say so, Mr. Gunsmith. They apply to all this rubbish a good sweating heat, and this makes a magnificent material for gun-barrels."

"Yes; but it may have cracks, flaws, or crosses."

"True; but they remedy the crosses by little twists, and avoid the risk of doublings by beating hard. They bring their mass of iron under the great hammer; give it two more good sweating heats. If the iron has been heated too much, they re-temper it with dull heats, and lighter hammers. And then they take out their stuff and roll it well; and with this iron they manufacture you a weapon like this."

"You are in the trade, I suppose?"

"I am of all trades."

"The barrels are pale-coloured."

"That's the beauty of them, Mr. Gunsmith. The tint is obtained with antimony."

"It is settled, then, that we give you five Louis?"

"Allow me to observe that I had the honour of saying six."

The gunsmith lowered his voice.

"Hark you, master. Take advantage of the opportunity. Get rid of this thing. A weapon of this kind is of no use to a man like you. It will make you remarked."

"It is very true," said the Parisian. "It is rather conspicuous. It is more suited to a gentleman."

"Will you take five Louis?"

"No, six; one for every shot."

"Come, six Napoleons."

"I will have six Louis."

"You are not a Bonapartist, then. You prefer a Louis to a Napoleon."

The Parisian nicknamed "Redskin" smiled.

"A Napoleon is greater," said he, "but a Louis is worth more."

"Six Napoleons."

"Six Louis. It makes a difference to me of four-and-twenty francs."

"The bargain is off in that case."

"Good: I keep the toy."

"Keep it."

"Beating me down! a good idea! It shall never be said that I got rid like that of a wonderful specimen of ingenuity."

"Good-night, then."

"It marks a whole stage in the progress of making pistols, which the Chesapeake Indians call Nortay-u-Hah."

"Five Louis, ready money. Why, it is a handful of gold."

"'Nortay-u-Hah,' that signifies 'short gun.' A good many people don't know that."

"Will you take five Louis, and just a bit of silver?"

"I said six, master."

The man who kept his back to the candle, and who had not yet spoken, was spending his time during the dialogue in turning and testing the mechanism of the pistol. He approached the armourer's ear and whispered—

"Is it a good weapon?"

"Excellent."

"I will give the six Louis."

Five minutes afterwards, while the Parisian nicknamed "Redskin" was depositing the six Louis which he had just received in a secret slit under the breast of his blouse, the armourer and his companion carrying the revolver in his trousers pocket, stepped out into the straggling street.

VIII

A "CANNON" OFF THE RED BALL AND THE BLACK

ON THE MORROW, which was a Thursday, a tragic circumstance occurred at a short distance from St. Malo, near the peak of the "Décollé," a spot where the cliff is high and the sea deep.

A line of rocks in the form of the top of a lance, and connecting themselves with the land by a narrow isthmus, stretch out there into the water, ending abruptly with a large peak-shaped breaker. Nothing is commoner in the architecture of the sea. In attempting to reach the plateau of the peaked rock from the shore, it was necessary to follow an inclined plane, the ascent of which was here and there somewhat steep.

It was upon a plateau of this kind, towards four o'clock in the afternoon, that a man was standing, enveloped in a large military cape, and armed; a fact easy to be perceived from certain straight and angular folds in his mantle. The summit on which this man was resting was a rather extensive platform, dotted with large masses of rock, like enormous paving-stones, leaving between them narrow passages. This platform, on which a kind of thick, short grass grew here and there, came to an end on the sea side in an open space, leading to a perpendicular escarpment. The escarpment, rising about sixty feet above the level of the sea, seemed cut down by the aid of a plumb-line. Its left angle, however, was broken away, and formed one of those natural staircases common to granite cliffs worn by the sea, the steps of which are somewhat inconvenient, requiring sometimes the strides of a giant or the leaps of an acrobat. These stages of rock descended perpendicularly to the sea, where they were lost. It was a break-neck place. However, in case of absolute necessity, a man might succeed in embarking there, under the very wall of the cliff.

A breeze was sweeping the sea. The man wrapped in his cape and standing firm, with his left hand grasping his right shoulder, closed one eye, and applied the other to a telescope. He seemed absorbed in anxious scrutiny. He had approached the edge of the escarpment, and stood there motionless, his gaze immovably fixed on the horizon. The tide was high; the waves were beating below against the foot of the cliffs.

The object which the stranger was observing was a vessel in the offing, and which was manœuvring in a strange manner. The vessel, which had hardly left the port of St. Malo an hour, had stopped behind the Banquetiers. It had not cast anchor, perhaps because the bottom would only have permitted it to bear to leeward on the edge of the cable, and because the ship would have strained on her anchor under the cutwater. Her captain had contented himself with lying-to.

The stranger, who was a coast-guardman, as was apparent from his uniform cape, watched all the movements of the three-master, and seemed to note them mentally. The vessel was lying-to, a little off the wind, which was indicated by the backing of the small topsail, and the bellying of the main-topsail. She had squared the mizen, and set the topmast as close as possible, and in such a manner as to work the sails against each other, and to make little way either on or off shore. Her captain evidently did not care to expose his vessel much to the wind, for he had only braced up the small mizen-topsail. In this way, coming crossway on, he did not drift at the utmost more than half a league an hour.

It was still broad daylight, particularly on the open sea, and on the heights of the cliff. The shores below were becoming dark.

The coast-guardman, still engaged in his duty, and carefully scanning the offing, had not thought of observing the rocks at his side and at his feet. He turned his back towards the difficult sort of causeway which formed the communication between his resting-place and the shore. He did not, therefore, remark that something was moving in that direction. Behind a fragment of rock, among the steps of that causeway, something like the figure of a man had been concealed, according to all appearances, since the arrival of the coast-guardman. From time to time a head issued from the shadow behind the rock; looked up and watched the watcher. The head, surmounted by a wide-brimmed American hat, was that of the Quaker-looking man, who, ten days before, was talking among the stones of the Petit-Bey to Captain Zuela.

Suddenly, the curiosity of the coast-guardman seemed to be still more strongly awakened. He polished the glass of his telescope quickly with his sleeve, and brought it to bear closely upon the three-master.

A little black spot seemed to detach itself from her side.

The black spot, looking like a small insect upon the water, was a boat.

The boat seemed to be making for the shore. It was manned by several sailors, who were pulling vigorously.

She pulled crosswise by little and little, and appeared to be approaching the Pointe du Décollé.

The gaze of the coast-guardman seemed to have reached its most intense point. No movement of the boat escaped it. He had approached nearer still to the verge of the rock.

At that instant a man of large stature appeared on one of the rocks behind him. It was the Quaker. The officer did not see him.

The man paused an instant, his arms at his sides, but with his fists doubled; and with the eye of a hunter, watching for his prey, he observed the back of the officer.

Four steps only separated them. He put one foot forward, then stopped; took a second step, and stopped again. He made no movement except the act of walking; all the rest of his body was motionless as a statue. His foot fell upon the tufts of grass without noise. He made a third step, and paused again. He was almost within reach of the coast-guard, who stood there still motionless with his telescope. The man brought his two closed fists to a level with his collar-bone, then struck out his arms sharply, and his two fists, as if thrown from a sling, struck the coast-guardman on the two shoulders. The shock was decisive. The coast-guardman had not the time to utter a cry. He fell head first from the height of the rock into the sea. His boots appeared in the air about the time occupied by a flash of lightning. It was like the fall of a stone in the sea, which instantly closed over him.

Two or three circles widened out upon the dark water.

Nothing remained but the telescope, which had dropped from the hands of the man, and lay upon the turf.

The Quaker leaned over the edge of the escarpment a moment, watched the circles vanishing on the water, waited a few minutes, and then rose again, singing in a low voice:

> "The captain of police is dead,
> Through having lost his life."

He knelt down a second time. Nothing reappeared. Only at the spot where the officer had been engulfed, he observed on the surface of the water a sort of dark spot, which became diffused with the gentle lapping of the waves. It seemed probable that the coast-guardman had fractured his skull against some rock under water, and that his blood caused the spot in the foam. The Quaker, while considering the meaning of this spot, began to sing again:

> "Not very long before he died,
> The luckless man was still alive."

He did not finish his song.

He heard an extremely soft voice behind him, which said:

"Is that you, Rantaine? Good-day. You have just killed a man!"

He turned. About fifteen paces behind him, in one of the passages between the rocks, stood a little man holding a revolver in his hand.

The Quaker answered:

"As you see. Good-day, Sieur Clubin."

The little man started.

"You know me?"

"You knew me very well," replied Rantaine.

Meanwhile they could hear a sound of oars on the sea. It was the approach of the boat which the officer had observed.

Sieur Clubin said in a low tone, as if speaking to himself:

"It was done quickly."

"What can I do to oblige you?" asked Rantaine.

"Oh, a trifling matter! It is very nearly ten years since I saw you. You must have been doing well. How are you?"

"Well enough," answered Rantaine. "How are you?"

"Very well," replied Clubin.

Rantaine advanced a step towards Clubin.

A little sharp click caught his ear. It was Sieur Clubin who was cocking his revolver.

"Rantaine, there are about fifteen paces between us. It is a nice distance. Remain where you are."

"Very well," said Rantaine. "What do you want with me?"

"I! Oh, I have come to have a chat with you."

Rantaine did not offer to move again. Sieur Clubin continued:

"You assassinated a coast-guardman just now."

Rantaine lifted the flap of his hat, and replied:

"You have already done me the honour to mention it."

"Exactly; but in terms less precise. I said a man: I say now, a coast-guard-man. The man wore the number 619. He was the father of a family; leaves a wife and five children."

"That is no doubt correct," said Rantaine.

There was a momentary pause.

"They are picked men—those coast-guard people," continued Clubin; "almost all old sailors."

"I have remarked," said Rantaine, "that people generally do leave a wife and five children."

Sieur Clubin continued:

"Guess how much this revolver cost me?"

"It is a pretty tool," said Rantaine.

"What do you guess it at?"

"I should guess it at a good deal."

"It cost me one hundred and forty-four francs."

"You must have bought that," said Rantaine, "at the shop in the Ruelle Coutanchez."

Clubin continued:

"He did not cry out. The fall stopped his voice, no doubt."

"Sieur Clubin, there will be a breeze to-night."

"I am the only one in the secret."

"Do you still stay at the Jean Auberge?"

"Yes: you are not badly served there."

"I remember getting some excellent sour-krout there."

"You must be exceedingly strong, Rantaine. What shoulders you have! I should be sorry to get a tap from you. I, on the other hand, when I came into the world, looked so spare and sickly, that they despaired of rearing me."

"They succeeded though, which was lucky."

"Yes: I still stay at the Jean Auberge."

"Do you know, Sieur Clubin, how I recognised you? It was from your having recognised me. I said to myself, there is nobody like Sieur Clubin for that."

And he advanced a step.

"Stand back where you were, Rantaine."

Rantaine fell back, and said to himself:

"A fellow becomes like a child before one of those weapons."

Sieur Clubin continued:

"The position of affairs is this: we have on our right, in the direction of St. Enogat, at about three hundred paces from here, another coast-guard-man—his number is 618—who is still alive; and on our left, in the direction of St. Lunaire—a customs station. That makes seven armed men who could be here, if necessary, in five minutes. The rock would be surrounded; the

way hither guarded. Impossible to elude them. There is a corpse at the foot
of this rock."

Rantaine took a side-way glance at the revolver.

"As you say, Rantaine, it is a pretty tool. Perhaps it is only loaded with
powder; but what does that matter? A report would be enough to bring an
armed force—and I have six barrels here."

The measured sound of the oars became very distinct. The boat was
not far off.

The tall man regarded the little man curiously. Sieur Clubin spoke in a
voice more and more soft and subdued.

"Rantaine, the men in the boat which is coming, knowing what you
did here just now, would lend a hand and help to arrest you. You are to pay
Captain Zuela ten thousand francs for your passage. You would have made
a better bargain, by the way, with the smugglers of Pleinmont; but they
would only have taken you to England; and besides, you cannot risk going
to Guernsey, where they have the pleasure of knowing you. To return, then,
to the position of affairs—if I fire, you are arrested. You are to pay Zuela for
your passage ten thousand francs. You have already paid him five thousand
in advance. Zuela would keep the five thousand and be gone. These are the
facts. Rantaine, you have managed your masquerading very well. That hat—
that queer coat—and those gaiters make a wonderful change. You forgot
the spectacles; but did right to let your whiskers grow."

Rantaine smiled spasmodically. Clubin continued:

"Rantaine, you have on a pair of American breeches, with a double fob.
In one side you keep your watch. Take care of it."

"Thank you, Sieur Clubin."

"In the other is a little box made of wrought iron, which opens and
shuts with a spring. It is an old sailor's tobacco-box. Take it out of your
pocket, and throw it over to me."

"Why, this is robbery."

"You are at liberty to call the coast-guardman."

And Clubin fixed his eye on Rantaine.

"Stay, Mess Clubin," said Rantaine, making a slight forward movement,
and holding out his open hand.

The title "Mess" was a delicate flattery.

"Stay where you are, Rantaine."

"Mess Clubin, let us come to terms. I offer you half."

Clubin crossed his arms, still showing the barrels of his revolver.

"Rantaine, what do you take me for? I am an honest man."

And he added after a pause:

"I must have the whole."

Rantaine muttered between his teeth, "This fellow's of a stern sort."

The eye of Clubin lighted up, his voice became clear and sharp as steel. He cried:

"I see that you are labouring under a mistake. Robbery is your name, not mine. My name is Restitution. Hark you, Rantaine. Ten years ago you left Guernsey one night, taking with you the cash-box of a certain partnership concern, containing fifty thousand francs which belonged to you, but forgetting to leave behind you fifty thousand francs which were the property of another. Those fifty thousand francs, the money of your partner, the excellent and worthy Mess Lethierry, make at present, at compound interest, calculated for ten years, eighty thousand six hundred and sixty-six francs. You went into a money-changer's yesterday. I'll give you his name—Rébuchet, in St. Vincent Street. You counted out to him seventy-six thousand francs in French bank-notes; in exchange for which he gave you three notes of the Bank of England for one thousand pounds sterling each, plus the exchange. You put these bank-notes in the iron tobacco-box, and the iron tobacco-box into your double fob on the right-hand side. On the part of Mess Lethierry, I shall be content with that. I start to-morrow for Guernsey, and intend to hand it to him. Rantaine, the three-master lying-to out yonder is the *Tamaulipas*. You have had your luggage put aboard there with the other things belonging to the crew. You want to leave France. You have your reasons. You are going to Arequipa. The boat is coming to fetch you. You are awaiting it. It is at hand. You can hear it. It depends on me whether you go or stay. No more words. Fling me the tobacco-box."

Rantaine dipped his hand in the fob, drew out a little box, and threw it to Clubin. It was the iron tobacco-box. It fell and rolled at Clubin's feet.

Clubin knelt without lowering his gaze; felt about for the box with his left hand, keeping all the while his eyes and the six barrels of the revolver fixed upon Rantaine.

Then he cried:

"Turn your back, my friend."

Rantaine turned his back.

Sieur Clubin put the revolver under one arm, and touched the spring of the tobacco-box. The lid flew open.

It contained four bank-notes; three of a thousand pounds, and one of ten pounds.

He folded up the three bank-notes of a thousand pounds each, replaced them in the iron tobacco-box, shut the lid again, and put it in his pocket.

Then he picked up a stone, wrapped it in the ten-pound note, and said:

"You may turn round again."

Rantaine turned.

Sieur Clubin continued:

"I told you I would be contented with three thousand pounds. Here, I return you ten pounds."

And he threw to Rantaine the note enfolding the stone.

Rantaine, with a movement of his foot, sent the bank-note and the stone into the sea.

"As you please," said Clubin. "You must be rich. I am satisfied."

The noise of oars, which had been continually drawing nearer during the dialogue, ceased. They knew by this that the boat had arrived at the base of the cliff.

"Your vehicle waits below. You can go, Rantaine."

Rantaine advanced towards the steps of stones, and rapidly disappeared.

Clubin moved cautiously towards the edge of the escarpment, and watched him descending.

The boat had stopped near the last stage of the rocks, at the very spot where the coast-guardman had fallen.

Still observing Rantaine stepping from stone to stone, Clubin muttered:

"A good number 619. He thought himself alone. Rantaine thought there were only two there. I alone knew that there were three."

He perceived at his feet the telescope which had dropped from the hands of the coast-guardman.

The sound of oars was heard again. Rantaine had stepped into the boat, and the rowers had pushed out to sea.

When Rantaine was safely in the boat, and the cliff was beginning to recede from his eyes, he arose again abruptly. His features were convulsed with rage; he clenched his fist and cried:

"Ha! he is the devil himself; a villain!"

A few seconds later, Clubin, from the top of the rock, while bringing his telescope to bear upon the boat, heard distinctly the following words articulated by a loud voice, and mingling with the noise of the sea:

"Sieur Clubin, you are an honest man; but you will not be offended if I write to Lethierry to acquaint him with this matter; and we have here in the boat a sailor from Guernsey, who is one of the crew of the *Tamaulipas*; his name is Ahier-Tostevin, and he will return to St. Malo on Zuela's next voyage, to bear testimony to the fact of my having returned to you, on Mess Lethierry's account, the sum of three thousand pounds sterling."

It was Rantaine's voice.

Clubin rarely did things by halves. Motionless as the coast-guardman had been, and in the exact same place, his eye still at the telescope, he did not lose sight of the boat for one moment. He saw it growing less amidst the waves; watched it disappear and reappear, and approach the vessel, which was lying-to; finally he recognised the tall figure of Rantaine on the deck of the *Tamaulipas*.

When the boat was raised, and slung again to the davits, the *Tamaulipas* was in motion once more. The land-breeze was fresh, and she spread all her sails. Clubin's glass continued fixed upon her outline growing more and more indistinct; until half an hour later, when the *Tamaulipas* had become only a dark shape upon the horizon, growing smaller and smaller against the pale twilight in the sky.

IX

USEFUL INFORMATION FOR PERSONS WHO EXPECT OR FEAR THE ARRIVAL OF LETTERS FROM BEYOND SEA

ON THAT EVENING, Sieur Clubin returned late.

One of the causes of his delay was, that before going to his inn, he had paid a visit to the Dinan gate of the town, a place where there were several wine-shops. In one of these wine-shops, where he was not known, he had bought a bottle of brandy, which he placed in the pocket of his overcoat, as if he desired to conceal it. Then, as the Durande was to start on the following morning, he had taken a turn aboard to satisfy himself that everything was in order.

When Sieur Clubin returned to the Jean Auberge, there was no one left in the lower room except the old sea-captain, M. Gertrais-Gaboureau, who was drinking a jug of ale and smoking his pipe.

M. Gertrais-Gaboureau saluted Sieur Clubin between a whiff and a draught of ale.

"How d'ye do, Captain Clubin?"

"Good evening, Captain Gertrais."

"Well, the *Tamaulipas* is gone."

"Ah!" said Clubin, "I did not observe."

Captain Gertrais-Gaboureau expectorated, and said:

"Zuela has decamped."

"When was that?"

"This evening."

"Where is he gone?"

"To the devil."

"No doubt; but where is that?"

"To Arequipa."

"I knew nothing of it," said Clubin.

He added:

"I am going to bed."

He lighted his candle, walked towards the door, and returned.

"Have you ever been at Arequipa, Captain?"

"Yes; some years ago."

"Where do they touch on that voyage?"

"A little everywhere; but the *Tamaulipas* will touch nowhere."

M. Gertrais-Gaboureau emptied his pipe upon the corner of a plate and continued:

"You know the lugger called the *Trojan Horse*, and that fine three-master, the *Trentemouzin*, which are gone to Cardiff? I was against their sailing on account of the weather. They have returned in a fine state. The lugger was laden with turpentine; she sprang a leak, and in working the pumps they pumped up with the water all her cargo. As to the three-master, she has suffered most above water. Her cutwater, her headrail, the stock of her larboard anchor are broken. Her standing jibboom is gone clean by the cap. As for the jib-shrouds and bobstays, go and see what they look like. The mizenmast is not injured, but has had a severe shock. All the iron of the bowsprit has given way; and it is an extraordinary fact that, though the bowsprit itself is not scratched, it is completely stripped. The larboard-bow of the vessel is stove in a good three feet square. This is what comes of not taking advice."

Clubin had placed the candle on the table, and had begun to readjust a row of pins which he kept in the collar of his overcoat. He continued:

"Didn't you say, Captain, that the *Tamaulipas* would not touch anywhere?"

"Yes; she goes direct to Chili."

"In that case, she can send no news of herself on the voyage."

"I beg your pardon, Captain Clubin. In the first place, she can send any letters by vessels she may meet sailing for Europe."

"That is true."

"Then there is the ocean letter-box."

"What do you mean by the ocean letter-box?"

"Don't you know what that is, Captain Clubin?"

"No."

"When you pass the straits of Magellan——"

"Well."

"Snow all round you; always bad weather; ugly down-easters, and bad seas."

"Well."

"When you have doubled Cape Monmouth——"

"Well, what next?"

"Then you double Cape Valentine."

"And then?"

"Why, then you double Cape Isidore."

"And afterwards?"

"You double Point Anne."

"Good. But what is it you call the ocean letter-box?"

"We are coming to that. Mountains on the right, mountains on the left. Penguins and stormy petrels all about. A terrible place. Ah! by Jove, what a howling and what cracks you get there! The hurricane wants no help. That's the place for holding on to the sheer-rails; for reefing topsails. That's where you take in the mainsail, and fly the jibsail; or take in the jibsail and try the stormjib. Gusts upon gusts! And then, sometimes four, five, or six days of scudding under bare poles. Often only a rag of canvas left. What a dance! Squalls enough to make a three-master skip like a flea. I saw once a cabin-boy hanging on to the jibboom of an English brig, the *True Blue*, knocked, jibboom and all, to ten thousand nothings. Fellows are swept into the air there like butterflies. I saw the second mate of the *Revenue*, a pretty schooner, knocked from under the forecross-tree, and killed dead. I have had my sheer-rails smashed, and come out with all my sails in ribbons. Frigates of fifty guns make water like wicker baskets. And the damnable coast! Nothing can be imagined more dangerous. Rocks all jagged-edged. You come, by and by, to Port Famine. There it's worse and worse. The worst seas I ever saw in my life. The devil's own latitudes. All of a sudden you spy the words, painted in red, 'Post Office.'"

"What do you mean, Captain Gertrais?"

"I mean, Captain Clubin, that immediately after doubling Point Anne you see, on a rock, a hundred feet high, a great post with a barrel suspended to the top. This barrel is the letter-box. The English sailors must needs go and write up there 'Post Office.' What had they to do with it? It is the ocean post-office. It isn't the property of that worthy gentleman, the King of England. The box is common to all. It belongs to every flag. *Post Office!* there's a crack-jaw word for you. It produces an effect on me as if the devil had suddenly offered me a cup of tea. I will tell you now how the postal arrangements are carried out. Every vessel which passes sends to the post a boat with despatches. A vessel coming from the Atlantic, for instance, sends there its letters for Europe; and a ship coming from the Pacific, its letters for New Zealand or California. The officer in command of the boat puts his packet into the barrel, and takes away any packet he finds there. You take charge of these letters, and the ship which comes after you takes charge of yours. As ships are always going to and fro, the continent whence you come is that to which I am going. I carry your letters; you carry mine. The barrel is made fast to the post with a chain. And it rains, snows and hails! A pretty sea. The imps of Satan fly about on every side. The *Tamaulipas* will pass there. The barrel has a good lid with a hinge, but no padlock. You see, a fellow can write to his friends this way. The letters come safely."

"It is very curious," muttered Clubin thoughtfully.

Captain Gertrais-Gaboureau returned to his bottle of ale.

"If that vagabond Zuela should write (continued Clubin aside), the scoundrel puts his scrawl into the barrel at Magellan, and in four months I have his letter."

"Well, Captain Clubin, do you start to-morrow?"

Clubin, absorbed in a sort of somnambulism, did not notice the question; and Captain Gertrais repeated it.

Clubin woke up.

"Of course, Captain Gertrais. It is my day. I must start to-morrow morning."

"If it was my case, I shouldn't, Captain Clubin. The hair of the dog's coat feels damp. For two nights past, the sea-birds have been flying wildly round the lanthorn of the lighthouse. A bad sign. I have a storm-glass, too, which gives me a warning. The moon is at her second quarter; it is the maximum of humidity. I noticed to-day some pimpernels with their leaves shut, and a field of clover with its stalks all stiff. The worms come out of the ground to-day; the flies sting; the bees keep close to their hives; the sparrows chatter together. You can hear the sound of bells from far off. I heard to-night the Angelus at St. Lunaire. And then the sun set angry. There will be a good fog to-morrow, mark my words. I don't advise you to put to sea. I dread the fog a good deal more than a hurricane. It's a nasty neighbour that."

Book VI
The Drunken Steersman and the Sober Captain

❋

I
THE DOUVRES

AT ABOUT five leagues out, in the open sea, to the south of Guernsey, opposite Pleinmont Point, and between the Channel Islands and St. Malo, there is a group of rocks, called the Douvres. The spot is dangerous.

This term Douvres, applied to rocks and cliffs, is very common. There is, for example, near the *Côtes du Nord*, a Douvre, on which a lighthouse is now being constructed, a dangerous reef; but one which must not be confounded with the rock above referred to.

The nearest point on the French coast to the Douvres is Cape Bréhat. The Douvres are a little further from the coast of France than from the nearest of the Channel Islands. The distance from Jersey may be pretty nearly measured by the extreme length of Jersey. If the island of Jersey could be turned round upon Corbière, as upon a hinge, St. Catherine's Point would almost touch the Douvres, at a distance of more than four leagues.

In these civilised regions the wildest rocks are rarely desert places. Smugglers are met with at Hagot, custom-house men at Binic, Celts at Bréhat, oyster-dredgers at Cancale, rabbit-shooters at Césambre or Cæsar's Island, crab-gatherers at Brecqhou, trawlers at the Minquiers, dredgers at Ecréhou, but no one is ever seen upon the Douvres.

The sea birds alone make their home there.

No spot in the ocean is more dreaded. The Casquets, where it is said the *Blanche Nef* was lost; the Bank of Calvados; the Needles in the Isle of Wight; the Ronesse, which makes the coast of Beaulieu so dangerous; the sunken reefs at Préel, which block the entrance to Merquel, and which necessitates the red-painted beacon in twenty fathoms of water, the treacherous approaches to Etables and Plouha; the two granite Druids to the south of Guernsey, the Old Anderlo and the Little Anderlo, the Corbière, the Hanways, the Isle of Ras, associated with terror in the proverb:

"*Si jamais tu passes le Ras,*

Si tu ne meurs, tu trembleras."

the Mortes-Femmes, the Déroute between Guernsey and Jersey, the Hardent between the Minquiers and Chousey, the Mauvais Cheval between Bouley Bay and Barneville, have not so evil a reputation. It would be preferable to have to encounter all these dangers, one after the other, than the Douvres once.

In all that perilous sea of the Channel, which is the Egean of the West, the Douvres have no equal in their terrors, except the Paternoster between Guernsey and Sark.

From the Paternoster, however, it is possible to give a signal—a ship in distress there may obtain succour. To the north rises Dicard or D'Icare Point, and to the south Grosnez. From the Douvres you can see nothing.

Its associations are the storm, the cloud, the wild sea, the desolate waste, the uninhabited coast. The blocks of granite are hideous and enormous—everywhere perpendicular wall—the severe inhospitality of the abyss.

It is in the open sea; the water about is very deep. A rock completely isolated like the Douvres attracts and shelters creatures which shun the haunts of men. It is a sort of vast submarine cave of fossil coral branches—a drowned labyrinth. There, at a depth to which divers would find it difficult to descend, are caverns, haunts, and dusky mazes, where monstrous creatures multiply and destroy each other. Huge crabs devour fish and are devoured in their turn. Hideous shapes of living things, not created to be seen by human eyes, wander in this twilight. Vague forms of antennæ, tentacles, fins, open jaws, scales, and claws, float about there, quivering, growing larger, or decomposing and perishing in the gloom, while horrible swarms of swimming things prowl about seeking their prey.

To gaze into the depths of the sea is, in the imagination, like beholding the vast unknown, and from its most terrible point of view. The submarine gulf is analogous to the realm of night and dreams. There also is sleep, unconsciousness, or at least apparent unconsciousness, of creation. There, in the awful silence and darkness, the rude first forms of life, phantom-like, demoniacal, pursue their horrible instincts.

Forty years ago, two rocks of singular form signalled the Douvres from afar to passers on the ocean. They were two vertical points, sharp and curved—their summits almost touching each other. They looked like the two tusks of an elephant rising out of the sea; but they were tusks, high as tall towers, of an elephant huge as a mountain. These two natural towers, rising out of the obscure home of marine monsters, only left a narrow passage between them, where the waves rushed through. This passage, tortuous and full of angles, resembled a straggling street between high walls. The two twin rocks are called the Douvres. There was the Great Douvre and the Little Douvre; one was sixty feet high, the other forty. The ebb and flow of the tide had at last worn away part of the base of the towers, and a violent equinoctial gale on the 26th of October, 1859, overthrew one of them. The smaller one, which still remains, is worn and tottering.

One of the most singular of the Douvres is a rock known as "The Man." This still exists. Some fisherman in the last century visiting this spot found on the height of the rock a human body. By its side were a number of empty sea-shells. A sailor escaped from shipwreck had found a refuge there; had lived some time upon rock limpets, and had died. Hence its name of "The Man."

The solitudes of the sea are peculiarly dismal. The things which pass there seem to have no relation to the human race; their objects are unknown. Such is the isolation of the Douvres. All around, as far as eye can reach, spreads the vast and restless sea.

II
AN UNEXPECTED FLASK OF BRANDY

ON THE FRIDAY morning, the day after the departure of the *Tamaulipas*, the Durande started again for Guernsey.

She left St. Malo at nine o'clock. The weather was fine; no haze. Old Captain Gertrais-Gaboureau was evidently in his dotage.

Sieur Clubin's numerous occupations had decidedly been unfavourable to the collection of freight for the Durande. He had only taken aboard some packages of Parisian articles for the fancy shops of St. Peter's Port; three cases for the Guernsey hospital, one containing yellow soap and long candles, and the other French shoe leather for soles, and choice Cordovan skins. He brought back from his last cargo a case of crushed sugar and three chests of congou tea, which the French custom-house would not permit to pass. He had embarked very few cattle; some bullocks only. These bullocks were in the hold loosely tethered.

There were six passengers aboard; a Guernsey man, two inhabitants of St. Malo, dealers in cattle: a "tourist,"—a phrase already in vogue at this period—a Parisian citizen, probably travelling on commercial affairs, and an American, engaged in distributing Bibles.

Without reckoning Clubin, the crew of the Durande amounted to seven men; a helmsman, a stoker, a ship's carpenter, and a cook—serving as sailors in case of need—two engineers, and a cabin boy. One of the two engineers was also a practical mechanic. This man, a bold and intelligent Dutch negro, who had originally escaped from the sugar plantations of Surinam, was named Imbrancam. The negro, Imbrancam, understood and attended admirably to the engine. In the early days of the "Devil Boat," his black face, appearing now and then at the top of the engine-room stairs, had contributed not a little to sustain its diabolical reputation.

The helmsman, a native of Guernsey, but of a family originally from Cotentin, bore the name of Tangrouille. The Tangrouilles were an old noble family.

This was strictly true. The Channel Islands are like England, an aristocratic region. Castes exist there still. The castes have their peculiar ideas, which are, in fact, their protection. These notions of caste are everywhere similar; in Hindostan, as in Germany, nobility is won by the sword; lost by soiling the hands with labour: but preserved by idleness. To do nothing, is to live nobly; whoever abstains from work is honoured. A trade is fatal. In France, in old times, there was no exception to this rule, except in the case of glass manufacturers. Emptying bottles being then one of the glories of gentlemen, making them was probably, for that reason, not considered dishonourable. In the Channel archipelago, as in Great Britain, he who would remain noble must contrive to be rich. A working man cannot possibly be a gentleman. If he has ever been one, he is so no longer. Yonder

sailor, perhaps, descends from the Knights Bannerets, but is nothing but
a sailor. Thirty years ago, a real Gorges, who would have had rights over
the Seigniory of Gorges, confiscated by Philip Augustus, gathered seaweed,
naked-footed, in the sea. A Carteret is a waggoner in Sark. There are at
Jersey a draper, and at Guernsey a shoemaker, named Gruchy, who claim
to be Grouchys, and cousins of the Marshal of Waterloo. The old registers
of the Bishopric of Coutances make mention of a Seigniory of Tangroville, evidently from Tancarville on the lower Seine, which is identical
with Montmorency. In the fifteenth century, Johan de Héroudeville, archer
and *étoffe* of the Sire de Tangroville, bore behind him "*son corset et ses autres
harnois.*" In May, 1371, at Pontorson, at the review of Bertrand du Guesclin,
Monsieur de Tangroville rendered his homage as Knight Bachelor. In the
Norman islands, if a noble falls into poverty, he is soon eliminated from
the order. A mere change of pronunciation is enough. Tangroville becomes
Tangrouille: and the thing is done.

This had been the fate of the helmsman of the Durande.

At the Bordagé of St. Peter's Port, there is a dealer in old iron named
Ingrouille, who is probably an Ingroville. Under Lewis le Gros the Ingro-
villes possessed three parishes in the district of Valognes. A certain Abbé
Trigan has written an Ecclesiastical History of Normandy. This chronicler
Trigan was the curé of the Seigniory of Digoville. The Sire of Digoville, if
he had sunk to a lower grade, would have been called Digouille.

Tangrouille, this probable Tancarville, and possible Montmorency, had
an ancient noble quality, but a grave failing for a steersman; he got drunk
occasionally.

Sieur Clubin had obstinately determined to retain him. He answered
for his conduct to Mess Lethierry.

Tangrouille the helmsman never left the vessel; he slept aboard.

On the eve of their departure, when Sieur Clubin came at a late hour to
inspect the vessel, the steersman was in his hammock asleep.

In the night Tangrouille awoke. It was his nightly habit. Every drunkard
who is not his own master has his secret hiding-place. Tangrouille had his,
which he called his store. The secret store of Tangrouille was in the hold.
He had placed it there to put others off the scent. He thought it certain
that his hiding-place was known only to himself. Captain Clubin, being a

sober man himself, was strict. The little rum or gin which the helmsman could conceal from the vigilant eyes of the captain, he kept in reserve in this mysterious corner of the hold, and nearly every night he had a stolen interview with the contents of this store. The surveillance was rigorous, the orgie was a poor one, and Tangrouille's nightly excesses were generally confined to two or three furtive draughts. Sometimes it happened that the store was empty. This night Tangrouille had found there an unexpected bottle of brandy. His joy was great; but his astonishment greater. From what cloud had it fallen? He could not remember when or how he had ever brought it into the ship. He soon, however, consumed the whole of it; partly from motives of prudence, and partly from a fear that the brandy might be discovered and seized. The bottle he threw overboard. In the morning, when he took the helm, Tangrouille exhibited a slight oscillation of the body.

He steered, however, pretty nearly as usual.

With regard to Clubin, he had gone, as the reader knows, to sleep at the Jean Auberge.

Clubin always wore, under his shirt, a leathern travelling belt, in which he kept a reserve of twenty guineas; he took this belt off only at night. Inside the belt was his name "Clubin," written by himself on the rough leather, with thick lithographer's ink, which is indelible.

On rising, just before his departure, he put into this girdle the iron box containing the seventy-five thousand francs in bank-notes; then, as he was accustomed to do, he buckled the belt round his body.

III
CONVERSATIONS INTERRUPTED

THE DURANDE started pleasantly. The passengers, as soon as their bags and portmanteaus were installed upon and under the benches, took that customary survey of the vessel which seems indispensable under the circumstances. Two of the passengers—the tourist and the Parisian—had never seen a steam-vessel before, and from the moment the paddles began to revolve, they stood admiring the foam. Then they looked with wonderment at the smoke. Then they examined one by one, and almost piece by piece upon the upper and lower deck, all those naval appliances such as rings, grapnels, hooks and bolts, which, with their nice precision and adaptation, form a kind of colossal *bijouterie*—a sort of iron jewellery, fantastically gilded with rust by the weather. They walked round the little signal gun upon the upper deck. "Chained up like a sporting dog," observed the tourist. "And covered with a waterproof coat to prevent its taking cold," added the Parisian. As they left the land further behind, they indulged in the customary observations upon the view of St. Malo. One passenger laid down the axiom that the approach to a place by sea is always deceptive; and that at a league from the shore, for example, nothing could more resemble Ostend than Dunkirk. He completed his series of remarks on Dunkirk by the observation that one of its two floating lights painted red was called *Ruytingen*, and the other *Mardyck*.

St. Malo, meanwhile, grew smaller in the distance, and finally disappeared from view.

The aspect of the sea was a vast calm. The furrow left in the water by the vessel was a long double line edged with foam, and stretching straight behind them as far as the eye could see.

A straight line drawn from St. Malo in France to Exeter in England would touch the island of Guernsey. The straight line at sea is not always the one chosen. Steam-vessels, however, have, to a certain extent, a power of following the direct course denied to sailing ships.

The wind in co-operation with the sea is a combination of forces. A ship is a combination of appliances. Forces are machines of infinite power. Machines are forces of limited power. That struggle which we call navigation is between these two organisations, the one inexhaustible, the other intelligent.

Mind, directing the mechanism, forms the counterbalance to the infinite power of the opposing forces. But the opposing forces, too, have their organisation. The elements are conscious of where they go, and what they are about. No force is merely blind. It is the function of man to keep watch upon these natural agents, and to discover their laws.

While these laws are still in great part undiscovered, the struggle continues, and in this struggle navigation, by the help of steam, is a perpetual victory won by human skill every hour of the day, and upon every point of the sea. The admirable feature in steam navigation is, that it disciplines the very ship herself. It diminishes her obedience to the winds, and increases her docility to man.

The Durande had never worked better at sea than on that day. She made her way marvellously.

Towards eleven o'clock, a fresh breeze blowing from the nor'-nor'-west, the Durande was off the Minquiers, under little steam, keeping her head to the west, on the starboard tack, and close up to the wind. The weather was still fine and clear. The trawlers, however, were making for shore.

By little and little, as if each one was anxious to get into port, the sea became clear of the boats.

It could not be said that the Durande was keeping quite her usual course. The crew gave no thought to such matters. The confidence in the captain was absolute; yet, perhaps through the fault of the helmsman, there was a slight deviation. The Durande appeared to be making rather towards Jersey than Guernsey. A little after eleven the captain rectified the vessel's course, and put her head fair for Guernsey. It was only a little time lost, but in short days time lost has its inconveniences. It was a February day, but the sun shone brightly.

Tangrouille, in his half-intoxicated state, had not a very sure arm, nor a very firm footing. The result was, that the helmsman lurched pretty often, which also retarded progress.

The wind had almost entirely fallen.

The Guernsey passenger, who had a telescope in his hand, brought it to bear from time to time upon a little cloud of grey mist, lightly moved by the wind, in the extreme western horizon. It resembled a fleecy down sprinkled with dust.

Captain Clubin wore his ordinary austere, Puritan-like expression of countenance. He appeared to redouble his attention.

All was peaceful and almost joyous on board the Durande. The passengers chatted. It is possible to judge of the state of the sea in a passage with the eyes closed, by noting the *tremolo* of the conversation about you. The full freedom of mind among the passengers answers to the perfect tranquillity of the waters.

It is impossible, for example, that a conversation like the following could take place otherwise than on a very calm sea.

"Observe that pretty green and red fly."

"It has lost itself out at sea, and is resting on the ship."

"Flies do not soon get tired."

"No doubt; they are light; the wind carries them."

"An ounce of flies was once weighed, and afterwards counted; and it was found to comprise no less than six thousand two hundred and sixty-eight."

The Guernsey passenger with the telescope had approached the St. Malo cattle dealers; and their talk was something in this vein:

"The Aubrac bull has a round and thick buttock, short legs, and a yellowish hide. He is slow at work by reason of the shortness of his legs."

"In that matter the Salers beats the Aubrac."

"I have seen, sir, two beautiful bulls in my life. The first has the legs low, the breast thick, the rump full, the haunches large, a good length of neck to the udder, withers of good height, the skin easy to strip. The second had all the signs of good fattening, a thick-set back, neck and shoulders strong, coat white and brown, rump sinking."

"That's the Cotentin race."

"Yes; with a slight cross with the Angus or Suffolk bull."

"You may believe it if you please, sir, but I assure you in the south they hold shows of donkeys."

"Shows of donkeys?"

"Of donkeys, on my honour. And the ugliest are the most admired."

"Ha! it is the same as with the mule shows. The ugly ones are considered best."

"Exactly. Take also the Poitevin mares; large belly, thick legs."

"The best mule known is a sort of barrel upon four posts."

"Beauty in beasts is a different thing from beauty in men."

"And particularly in women."

"That is true."

"As for me, I like a woman to be pretty."

"I am more particular about her being well dressed."

"Yes; neat, clean, and well set off."

"Looking just new. A pretty girl ought always to appear as if she had just been turned out by a jeweller."

"To return to my bulls; I saw these two sold at the market at Thouars."

"The market at Thouars; I know it very well. The Bonneaus of La Rochelle, and the Babas corn merchants at Marans, I don't know whether you have heard of them attending that market."

The tourist and the Parisian were conversing with the American of the Bibles.

"Sir," said the tourist, "I will tell you the tonnage of the civilised world. France 716,000 tons; Germany 1,000,000; the United States, 5,000,000; England, 5,500,000; add the small vessels. Total 12,904,000 tons, carried in 145,000 vessels scattered over the waters of the globe."

The American interrupted:

"It is the United States, sir, which have 5,500,000."

"I agree," said the tourist. "You are an American?"

"Yes, sir."

"I agree again."

There was a pause. The American missionary was considering whether this was a case for the offer of a Bible.

"Is it true, sir," asked the tourist, "that you have a passion for nicknames in America, so complete, that you confer them upon all your celebrated men, and that you call your famous Missouri banker, Thomas Benton, 'Old Lingot'?"

"Yes; just as we call Zachary Taylor 'Old Zach.'"

"And General Harrison, 'Old Tip;' am I right? and General Jackson, 'Old Hickory?'"

"Because Jackson is hard as hickory wood; and because Harrison beat the redskins at *Tippecanoe.*"

"It is an odd fashion that of yours."

"It is our custom. We call Van Buren 'The Little Wizard;' Seward, who introduced the small bank-notes, 'Little Billy;' and Douglas, the democrat senator from Illinois, who is four feet high and very eloquent, 'The Little Giant.' You may go from Texas to the State of Maine without hearing the name of Mr. Cass. They say the 'Great Michiganer.' Nor the name of Clay; they say 'The miller's boy with the scar.' Clay is the son of a miller."

"I should prefer to say 'Clay' or 'Cass,'" said the Parisian. "It's shorter."

"Then you would be out of the fashion. We call Corwin, who is the Secretary of the Treasury, 'The Waggoner-boy;' Daniel Webster, 'Black Dan.' As to Winfield Scott, as his first thought after beating the English at Chippeway, was to sit down to dine, we call him 'Quick—a basin of soup.'"

The small white mist perceived in the distance had become larger. It filled now a segment of fifteen degrees above the horizon. It was like a cloud loitering along the water for want of wind to stir it. The breeze had almost entirely died away. The sea was glassy. Although it was not yet noon, the sun was becoming pale. It lighted but seemed to give no warmth.

"I fancy," said the tourist, "that we shall have a change of weather."

"Probably rain," said the Parisian.

"Or fog," said the American.

"In Italy," remarked the tourist, "Molfetta is the place where there falls the least rain; and Tolmezzo, where there falls the most."

At noon, according to the usage of the Channel Islands, the bell sounded for dinner. Those dined who desired. Some passengers had brought with them provisions, and were eating merrily on the after-deck. Clubin did not eat.

While this eating was going on, the conversations continued.

The Guernsey man, having probably a scent for Bibles, approached the American. The latter said to him:

"You know this sea?"

"Very well; I belong to this part."

"And I, too," said one of the St. Malo men.

The native of Guernsey followed with a bow and continued:

"We are fortunately well out at sea now; I should not have liked a fog when we were off the Minquiers."

The American said to the St. Malo man:

"Islanders are more at home on the sea than the folks of the coast."

"True; we coast people are only half dipped in salt water."

"What are the Minquiers?" asked the American.

The St. Malo man replied:

"They are an ugly reef of rocks."

"There are also the Grelets," said the Guernsey man.

"Parbleu!" ejaculated the other.

"And the Chouas," added the Guernsey man.

The inhabitant of St. Malo laughed.

"As for that," said he, "there are the Savages also."

"And the Monks," observed the Guernsey man.

"And the Duck," cried the St. Maloite.

"Sir," remarked the inhabitant of Guernsey, "you have an answer for everything."

The tourist interposed with a question:

"Have we to pass all that legion of rocks?"

"No; we have left it to the sou'-south-east. It is behind us."

And the Guernsey passenger continued:

"Big and little rocks together, the Grelets have fifty-seven peaks."

"And the Minquiers forty-eight," said the other.

The dialogue was now confined to the St. Malo and the Guernsey passenger.

"It strikes me, Monsieur St. Malo, that there are three rocks which you have not included."

"I mentioned all."

"From the Derée to the Maître Ile."

"And Les Maisons?"

"Yes; seven rocks in the midst of the Minquiers."

"I see you know the very stones."

"If I didn't know the stones, I should not be an inhabitant of St. Malo."

"It is amusing to hear French people's reasonings."

The St. Malo man bowed in his turn, and said:

"The Savages are three rocks."

"And the Monks two."

"And the Duck one."

"*The* Duck; this is only one, of course."

"No: for *the* Suarde consists of four rocks."

"What do you mean by the Suarde?" asked the inhabitant of Guernsey.

"We call the Suarde what you call the Chouas."

"It is a queer passage, that between the Chouas and the Duck."

"It is impassable except for the birds."

"And the fish."

"Scarcely: in bad weather they give themselves hard knocks against the walls."

"There is sand near the Minquiers?"

"Around the Maisons."

"There are eight rocks visible from Jersey."

"Visible from the strand of Azette; that's correct: but not eight; only seven."

"At low water you can walk about the Minquiers?"

"No doubt; there would be sand above water."

"And what of the Dirouilles?"

"The Dirouilles bear no resemblance to the Minquiers."

"They are very dangerous."

"They are near Granville."

"I see that you St. Malo people, like us, enjoy sailing in these seas."

"Yes," replied the St. Malo man, "with the difference that we say, 'We have the habit,' you, 'We are fond.'"

"You make good sailors."

"I am myself a cattle merchant."

"Who was that famous sailor born of St. Malo?"

"Surcouf?"

"Another?"

"Duguay-Trouin."

Here the Parisian commercial man chimed in:

"Duguay-Trouin? He was captured by the English. He was as agreeable as he was brave. A young English lady fell in love with him. It was she who procured him his liberty."

At this moment a voice like thunder was heard crying out:

"You are drunk, man!"

IV

CAPTAIN CLUBIN DISPLAYS ALL HIS GREAT QUALITIES

EVERYBODY TURNED.

It was the captain calling to the helmsman.

Sieur Clubin's tone and manner evidenced that he was extremely angry, or that he wished to appear so.

A well-timed burst of anger sometimes removes responsibility, and sometimes shifts it on to other shoulders.

The captain, standing on the bridge between the two paddle-boxes, fixed his eyes on the helmsman. He repeated, between his teeth, "Drunkard." The unlucky Tangrouille hung his head.

The fog had made progress. It filled by this time nearly one-half of the horizon. It seemed to advance from every quarter at the same time. There is something in a fog of the nature of a drop of oil upon the water. It enlarged insensibly. The light wind moved it onward slowly and silently. By little and little it took possession of the ocean. It was coming chiefly from the northwest, dead ahead: the ship had it before her prow, like a line of cliff moving vast and vague. It rose from the sea like a wall. There was an exact point where the wide waters entered the fog, and were lost to sight.

This line of the commencement of the fog was still above half-a-league distant. The interval was visibly growing less and less. The Durande made way; the fog made way also. It was drawing nearer to the vessel, while the vessel was drawing nearer to it.

Clubin gave the order to put on more steam, and to hold off the coast.

Thus for some time they skirted the edge of the fog; but still it advanced. The vessel, meanwhile, sailed in broad sunlight.

Time was lost in these manœuvres, which had little chance of success. Nightfall comes quickly in February. The native of Guernsey was meditating upon the subject of this fog. He said to the St. Malo men:

"It will be thick!"

"An ugly sort of weather at sea," observed one of the St. Malo men.

The other added:

"A kind of thing which spoils a good passage."

The Guernsey passenger approached Clubin, and said:

"I'm afraid, Captain, that the fog will catch us."

Clubin replied:

"I wished to stay at St. Malo, but I was advised to go."

"By whom?"

"By some old sailors."

"You were certainly right to go," said the Guernsey man. "Who knows whether there will not be a tempest to-morrow? At this season you may wait and find it worse."

A few moments later, the Durande entered the fog bank.

The effect was singular. Suddenly those who were on the after-deck could not see those forward. A soft grey medium divided the ship in two.

Then the entire vessel passed into the fog. The sun became like a dull red moon. Everybody suddenly shivered. The passengers put on their overcoats, and the sailors their tarpaulins. The sea, almost without a ripple, was the more menacing from its cold tranquillity. All was pale and wan. The black funnel and the heavy smoke struggled with the dewy mist which enshrouded the vessel.

Dropping to westward was now useless. The captain kept the vessel's head again towards Guernsey, and gave orders to put on the steam.

The Guernsey passenger, hanging about the engine-room hatchway, heard the negro Imbrancam talking to his engineer comrade. The passenger listened. The negro said:

"This morning, in the sun, we were going half steam on; now, in the fog, we put on steam."

The Guernsey man returned to Clubin.

"Captain Clubin, a look-out is useless; but have we not too much steam on?"

"What can I do, sir? We must make up for time lost through the fault of that drunkard of a helmsman."

"True, Captain Clubin."

And Clubin added:

"I am anxious to arrive. It is foggy enough by day: it would be rather too much at night."

The Guernsey man rejoined his St. Malo fellow-passengers, and remarked: "We have an excellent captain."

At intervals, great waves of mist bore down heavily upon them, and blotted out the sun; which again issued out of them pale and sickly. The little that could be seen of the heavens resembled the long strips of painted sky, dirty and smeared with oil, among the old scenery of a theatre.

The Durande passed close to a cutter which had cast anchor for safety. It was the *Shealtiel* of Guernsey. The master of the cutter remarked the high speed of the steam-vessel. It struck him also, that she was not in her exact course. She seemed to him to bear to westward too much. The apparition of this vessel under full steam in the fog surprised him.

Towards two o'clock the weather had become so thick that the captain was obliged to leave the bridge, and plant himself near the steersman. The sun had vanished, and all was fog. A sort of ashy darkness surrounded the ship. They were navigating in a pale shroud. They could see neither sky nor water.

There was not a breath of wind.

The can of turpentine suspended under the bridge, between the paddle-boxes, did not even oscillate.

The passengers had become silent.

The Parisian, however, hummed between his teeth the song of Béranger— "*Un jour le bon Dieu s'éveillant.*"

One of the St. Malo passengers addressed him:

"You are from Paris, sir?"

"Yes, sir. *Il mit la tête à la fenêtre.*"

"What do they do in Paris?"

"*Leur planète a péri, peut-être.*—In Paris, sir, things are going on very badly."

"Then it's the same ashore as at sea."

"It is true; we have an abominable fog here."

"One which might involve us in misfortunes."

The Parisian exclaimed:

"Yes; and why all these misfortunes in the world? Misfortunes! What are they sent for, these misfortunes? What use do they serve? There was the fire at the Odéon theatre, and immediately a number of families thrown out of employment. Is that just? I don't know what is your religion, sir, but I am puzzled by all this."

VICTOR HUGO

"So am I," said the St. Malo man.

"Everything that happens here below," continued the Parisian, "seems to go wrong. It looks as if Providence, for some reason, no longer watched over the world."

The St. Malo man scratched the top of his head, like one making an effort to understand. The Parisian continued:

"Our guardian angel seems to be absent. There ought to be a decree against celestial absenteeism. He is at his country-house, and takes no notice of us; so all gets in disorder. It is evident that this guardian is not in the government; he is taking holiday, leaving some vicar—some seminarist angel, some wretched creature with sparrows'-wings—to look after affairs."

Captain Clubin, who had approached the speakers during this conversation, laid his hand upon the shoulder of the Parisian.

"Silence, sir," he said. "Keep a watch upon your words. We are upon the sea."

No one spoke again aloud.

After a pause of five minutes, the Guernsey man, who had heard all this, whispered in the ear of the St. Malo passenger:

"A religious man, our captain."

It did not rain, but all felt their clothing wet. The crew took no heed of the way they were making; but there was increased sense of uneasiness. They seemed to have entered into a doleful region. The fog makes a deep silence on the sea; it calms the waves, and stifles the wind. In the midst of this silence, the creaking of the Durande communicated a strange, indefinable feeling of melancholy and disquietude.

They passed no more vessels. If afar off, in the direction of Guernsey or in that of St. Malo, any vessels were at sea outside the fog, the Durande, submerged in the dense cloud, must have been invisible to them; while her long trail of smoke attached to nothing, looked like a black comet in the pale sky.

Suddenly Clubin roared out:

"Hang-dog! you have played us an ugly trick. You will have done us some damage before we are out of this. You deserve to be put in irons. Get you gone, drunkard!"

And he seized the helm himself.

The steersman, humbled, shrunk away to take part in the duties forward.

The Guernsey man said:

"That will save us."

The vessel was still making way rapidly.

Towards three o'clock, the lower part of the fog began to clear, and they could see the sea again.

A mist can only be dispersed by the sun or the wind. By the sun is well; by the wind is not so well. At three o'clock in the afternoon, in the month of February, the sun is always weak. A return of the wind at this critical point in a voyage is not desirable. It is often the forerunner of a hurricane.

If there was any breeze, however, it was scarcely perceptible.

Clubin with his eye on the binnacle, holding the tiller and steering, muttered to himself some words like the following, which reached the ears of the passengers:

"No time to be lost; that drunken rascal has retarded us."

His visage, meanwhile, was absolutely without expression.

The sea was less calm under the mist. A few waves were distinguishable. Little patches of light appeared on the surface of the water. These luminous patches attract the attention of the sailors. They indicate openings made by the wind in the overhanging roof of fog. The cloud rose a little, and then sunk heavier. Sometimes the density was perfect. The ship was involved in a sort of foggy iceberg. At intervals this terrible circle opened a little, like a pair of pincers; showed a glimpse of the horizon, and then closed again.

Meanwhile the Guernsey man, armed with his spyglass, was standing like a sentinel in the fore part of the vessel.

An opening appeared for a moment, and was blotted out again.

The Guernsey man returned alarmed.

"Captain Clubin!"

"What is the matter?"

"We are steering right upon the Hanways."

"You are mistaken," said Clubin, coldly.

The Guernsey man insisted.

"I am sure of it."

"Impossible."

"I have just seen the rock in the horizon."

"Where?"

"Out yonder."

"It is the open sea there. Impossible."

And Clubin kept the vessel's head to the point indicated by the passenger.

The Guernsey man seized his spyglass again.

A moment later he came running aft again.

"Captain!"

"Well."

"Tack about!"

"Why?"

"I am certain of having seen a very high rock just ahead. It is the Great Hanway."

"You have seen nothing but a thicker bank of fog."

"It is the Great Hanway. Tack, in the name of Heaven!"

Clubin gave the helm a turn.

V

CLUBIN REACHES THE CROWNING-POINT OF GLORY

A CRASH WAS HEARD. The ripping of a vessel's side upon a sunken reef in open sea is the most dismal sound of which man can dream. The Durande's course was stopped short.

Several passengers were knocked down with the shock and rolled upon the deck.

The Guernsey man raised his hands to heaven:

"We are on the Hanways. I predicted it."

A long cry went up from the ship.

"We are lost."

The voice of Clubin, dry and short, was heard above all.

"No one is lost! Silence!"

The black form of Imbrancam, naked down to the waist, issued from the hatchway of the engine-room.

The negro said with self-possession:

"The water is gaining, Captain. The fires will soon be out."

The moment was terrible.

The shock was like that of a suicide. If the disaster had been wilfully sought, it could not have been more terrible. The Durande had rushed upon her fate as if she had attacked the rock itself. A point had pierced her sides like a wedge. More than six feet square of planking had gone; the stem was broken, the prow smashed, and the gaping hull drank in the sea with a horrible gulping noise. It was an entrance for wreck and ruin. The rebound was so violent that it had shattered the rudder pendants; the rudder itself hung unhinged and flapping. The rock had driven in her keel. Round about the vessel nothing was visible except a thick, compact fog, now become sombre. Night was gathering fast.

The Durande plunged forward. It was like the effort of a horse pierced through the entrails by the horns of a bull. All was over with her.

Tangrouille was sobered. Nobody is drunk in the moment of a ship-wreck. He came down to the quarter-deck, went up again, and said:

"Captain, the water is gaining rapidly in the hold. In ten minutes it will be up to the scupper-holes."

The passengers ran about bewildered, wringing their hands, leaning over the bulwarks, looking down in the engine-room, and making every other sort of useless movement in their terror. The tourist had fainted.

Clubin made a sign with his hand, and they were silent. He questioned Imbrancam:

"How long will the engines work yet?"

"Five or six minutes, sir."

Then he interrogated the Guernsey passenger:

"I was at the helm. You saw the rock. On which bank of the Hanways are we?"

"On the Mauve. Just now, in the opening in the fog, I saw it clearly."

"If we're on the Mauve," remarked Clubin, "we have the Great Hanway on the port side, and the Little Hanway on the starboard bow; we are a mile from the shore."

The crew and passengers listened, fixing their eyes anxiously and attentively on the captain.

Lightening the ship would have been of no avail, and indeed would have been hardly possible. In order to throw the cargo overboard, they would have had to open the ports and increase the chance of the water entering. To cast anchor would have been equally useless: they were stuck fast. Besides, with such a bottom for the anchor to drag, the chain would probably have fouled. The engines not being injured, and being workable while the fires were not extinguished, that is to say, for a few minutes longer, they could have made an effort, by help of steam and her paddles, to turn her astern off the rocks; but if they had succeeded, they must have settled down immediately. The rock, indeed, in some degree stopped the breach and prevented the entrance of the water. It was at least an obstacle; while the hole once freed, it would have been impossible to stop the leak or to work the pumps. To snatch a poniard from a wound in the heart is instant death to the victim. To free the vessel from the rock would have been simply to founder.

The cattle, on whom the water was gaining in the hold, were lowing piteously.

Clubin issued orders:

"Launch the long boat."

Imbrancam and Tangrouille rushed to execute the order. The boat was eased from her fastenings. The rest of the crew looked on stupefied.

"All hands to assist," cried Clubin.

This time all obeyed.

Clubin, self-possessed, continued to issue his orders in that old sea dialect, which French sailors of the present day would scarcely understand.

"Haul in a rope—Get a cable if the capstan does not work—Stop heaving—Keep the blocks clear—Lower away there—- Bring her down stern and bows—Now then, all together, lads—Take care she don't lower stern first—There's too much strain on there—Hold the laniard of the stock tackle—Stand by there!"

The long boat was launched.

At that instant the Durande's paddles stopped, and the smoke ceased—the fires were drowned.

The passengers slipped down the ladder, and dropped hurriedly into the long boat. Imbrancam lifted the fainting tourist, carried him into the boat, and then boarded the vessel again.

The crew made a rush after the passengers—the cabin boy was knocked down, and the others were trampling upon him.

Imbrancam barred their passage.

"Not a man before the lad," he said.

He kept off the sailors with his two black arms, picked up the boy, and handed him down to the Guernsey man, who was standing upright in the boat.

The boy saved, Imbrancam made way for the others, and said:

"Pass on!"

Meanwhile Clubin had entered his cabin, and had made up a parcel containing the ship's papers and instruments. He took the compass from the binnacle, handed the papers and instruments to Imbrancam, and the compass to Tangrouille, and said to them:

"Get aboard the boat."

They obeyed. The crew had taken their places before them.

"Now," cried Clubin, "push off."

A cry arose from the long boat.

"What about yourself, Captain?"

"I will remain here."

Shipwrecked people have little time to deliberate, and not much for indulging in tender feeling. Those who were in the long boat and in comparative safety, however, felt an emotion which was not altogether selfish. All the voices shouted together:

"Come with us, Captain."

"No: I remain here."

The Guernsey man, who had some experience of the sea, replied:

"Listen to me, Captain. You are wrecked on the Hanways. Swimming, you would have only a mile to cross to Pleinmont. In a boat you can only land at Rocquaine, which is two miles. There are breakers, and there is the fog. Our boat will not get to Rocquaine in less than two hours. It will be a dark night. The sea is rising—the wind getting fresh. A squall is at hand. We are now ready to return and bring you off; but if bad weather comes on, that will be out of our power. You are lost if you stay there. Come with us."

The Parisian chimed in:

"The long boat is full—too full, it is true, and one more will certainly be one too many; but we are thirteen—a bad number for the boat, and it is better to overload her with a man than to take an ominous number. Come, Captain."

Tangrouille added:

"It was all my fault—not yours, Captain. It isn't fair for you to be left behind."

"I have decided to remain here," said Clubin. "The vessel must inevitably go to pieces in the tempest to-night. I won't leave her. When the ship is lost, the captain is already dead. People shall not say I didn't do my duty to the end. Tangrouille, I forgive you."

Then, folding his arms, he cried:

"Obey orders! Let go the rope, and push off."

The long-boat swayed to and fro. Imbrancam had seized the tiller. All the hands which were not rowing were raised towards the captain—every mouth cried, "Cheers for Captain Clubin."

"An admirable fellow!" said the American.

"Sir," replied the Guernsey man, "he is one of the worthiest seamen afloat."

Tangrouille shed tears.

"If I had had the courage," he said, "I would have stayed with him."

The long-boat pushed away, and was lost in the fog.

Nothing more was visible.

The beat of the oars grew fainter, and died away.

Clubin remained alone.

VI

THE INTERIOR OF AN ABYSS SUDDENLY REVEALED

WHEN CLUBIN found himself upon this rock, in the midst of the fog and the wide waters, far from all sound of human life, left for dead, alone with the tide rising around him, and night settling down rapidly, he experienced a feeling of profound satisfaction.

He had succeeded.

His dream was realised. The acceptance which he had drawn upon destiny at so long a date had fallen due at last.

With him, to be abandoned there was, in fact, to be saved.

He was on the Hanways, one mile from the shore; he had about him seventy-five thousand francs. Never was shipwreck more scientifically accomplished. Nothing had failed. It is true, everything had been foreseen. From his early years Clubin had had an idea to stake his reputation for honesty at life's gaming-table; to pass as a man of high honour, and to make that reputation his fulcrum for other things; to bide his time, to watch his opportunity; not to grope about blindly, but to seize boldly; to venture on one great stroke, only one; and to end by sweeping off the stakes, leaving fools behind him to gape and wonder. What stupid rogues fail in twenty times, he meant to accomplish at the first blow; and while they terminated a career on the gallows, he intended to finish with a fortune. The meeting with Rantaine had been a new light to him. He had immediately laid his plan—to compel Rantaine to disgorge; to frustrate his threatened revelations by disappearing; to make the world believe him dead, the best of all modes of concealment; and for this purpose to wreck the Durande. The shipwreck was necessary to his designs. Lastly, he had the satisfaction of vanishing, leaving behind him a great renown, the crowning point of his existence. As he stood meditating on these things amid the wreck, Clubin might have been taken for some demon in a pleasant mood.

He had lived a lifetime for the sake of this one minute.

His whole exterior was expressive of the two words, "At last." A devilish tranquillity reigned in that sallow countenance.

His dull eye, the depth of which generally seemed to be impenetrable, became clear and terrible. The inward fire of his dark spirit was reflected there.

Man's inner nature, like that external world about him, has its electric phenomena. An idea is like a meteor; at the moment of its coming, the confused meditations which preceded it open a way, and a spark flashes forth. Bearing within oneself a power of evil, feeling an inward prey, brings to some minds a pleasure which is like a sparkle of light. The triumph of an evil purpose brightens up their visages. The success of certain cunning combinations, the attainment of certain cherished objects, the gratification of certain ferocious instincts, will manifest themselves in sinister but luminous appearances in their eyes. It is like a threatening dawn, a gleam of joy drawn out of the heart of a storm. These flashes are generated in the conscience in its states of cloud and darkness.

Some such signs were then exhibiting themselves in the pupils of those eyes. They were like nothing else that can be seen shining either above or here below.

All Clubin's pent-up wickedness found full vent now.

He gazed into the vast surrounding darkness, and indulged in a low, irrepressible laugh, full of sinister significance.

He was rich at last! rich at last!

The unknown future of his life was at length unfolding; the problem was solved.

Clubin had plenty of time before him. The sea was rising, and consequently sustained the Durande, and even raised her at last a little. The vessel kept firmly in its place among the rocks; there was no danger of her foundering. Besides, he determined to give the long-boat time to get clear off—to go to the bottom, perhaps. Clubin hoped it might.

Erect upon the deck of the shipwrecked vessel, he folded his arms, apparently enjoying that forlorn situation in the dark night.

Hypocrisy had weighed upon this man for thirty years. He had been evil itself, yoked with probity for a mate. He detested virtue with the feeling of one who has been trapped into a hateful match. He had always had a wicked premeditation; from the time when he attained manhood he had worn the cold and rigid armour of appearances. Underneath this was the demon of self. He had lived like a bandit in the disguise of an honest citizen. He had been the soft-spoken pirate; the bond-slave of honesty. He had been confined in garments of innocence, as in oppressive mummy cloths; had worn those angel wings which the devils find so wearisome in their fallen state. He had been overloaded with public esteem. It is arduous passing for a shining light. To preserve a perpetual equilibrium amid these difficulties, to think evil, to speak goodness—here had been indeed a labour. Such a life of contradictions had been Clubin's fate. It had been his lot—not the less onerous because he had chosen it himself—to preserve a good exterior, to be always presentable, to foam in secret, to smile while grinding his teeth. Virtue presented itself to his mind as something stifling. He had felt, sometimes, as if he could have gnawed those finger-ends which he was compelled to keep before his mouth.

To live a life which is a perpetual falsehood is to suffer unknown tortures. To be premeditating indefinitely a diabolical act, to have to assume austerity;

to brood over secret infamy seasoned with outward good fame; to have continually to put the world off the scent; to present a perpetual illusion, and never to be one's self—is a burdensome task. To be constrained to dip the brush in that dark stuff within, to produce with it a portrait of candour; to fawn, to restrain and suppress one's self, to be ever on the *qui vive*; watching without ceasing to mask latent crimes with a face of healthy innocence: to transform deformity into beauty; to fashion wickedness into the shape of perfection; to tickle, as it were, with the point of a dagger, to put sugar with poison, to keep a bridle on every gesture and keep a watch over every tone, not even to have a countenance of one's own—what can be harder, what can be more torturing. The odiousness of hypocrisy is obscurely felt by the hypocrite himself. Drinking perpetually of his own imposture is nauseating. The sweetness of tone which cunning gives to scoundrelism is repugnant to the scoundrel compelled to have it ever in the mouth; and there are moments of disgust when villainy seems on the point of vomiting its secret. To have to swallow that bitter saliva is horrible. Add to this picture his profound pride. There are strange moments in the history of such a life, when hypocrisy worships itself. There is always an inordinate egotism in roguery. The worm has the same mode of gliding along as the serpent, and the same manner of raising its head. The treacherous villain is the despot curbed and restrained, and only able to attain his ends by resigning himself to play a secondary part. He is summed-up littleness capable of enormities. The perfect hypocrite is a Titan dwarfed.

Clubin had a genuine faith that he had been ill-used. Why had not he the right to have been born rich? It was from no fault of his that it was otherwise. Deprived as he had been of the higher enjoyments of life, why had he been forced to labour—in other words, to cheat, to betray, to destroy? Why had he been condemned to this torture of flattering, cringing, fawning; to be always labouring for men's respect and friendship, and to wear night and day a face which was not his own? To be compelled to dissimulate was in itself to submit to a hardship. Men hate those to whom they have to lie. But now the disguise was at an end. Clubin had taken his revenge.

On whom? On all! On everything!

Lethierry had never done him any but good services; so much the greater his spleen. He was revenged upon Lethierry.

VICTOR HUGO

He was revenged upon all those in whose presence he had felt constraint. It was his turn to be free now. Whoever had thought well of him was his enemy. He had felt himself their captive long enough.

Now he had broken through his prison walls. His escape was accomplished. That which would be regarded as his death, would be, in fact, the beginning of his life. He was about to begin the world again. The true Clubin had stripped off the false. In one hour the spell was broken. He had kicked Rantaine into space; overwhelmed Lethierry in ruin; human justice in night, and opinion in error. He had cast off all humanity; blotted out the whole world.

The name of God, that word of three letters, occupied his mind but little.

He had passed for a religious man. What was he now?

There are secret recesses in hypocrisy; or rather the hypocrite is himself a secret recess.

When Clubin found himself quite alone, that cavern in which his soul had so long lain hidden, was opened. He enjoyed a moment of delicious liberty. He revelled for that moment in the open air. He gave vent to himself in one long breath.

The depth of evil within him revealed itself in his visage. He expanded, as it were, with diabolical joy. The features of Rantaine by the side of his at that moment would have shown like the innocent expression of a newborn child.

What a deliverance was this plucking off of the old mask. His conscience rejoiced in the sight of its own monstrous nakedness, as it stepped forth to take its hideous bath of wickedness. The long restraint of men's respect seemed to have given him a peculiar relish for infamy. He experienced a certain lascivious enjoyment of wickedness. In those frightful moral abysses so rarely sounded, such natures find atrocious delights—they are the obscenities of rascality. The long-endured insipidity of the false reputation for virtue gave him a sort of appetite for shame. In this state of mind men disdain their fellows so much that they even long for the contempt which marks the ending of their unmerited homage. They feel a satisfaction in the freedom of degradation, and cast an eye of envy at baseness, sitting at its ease, clothed in ignominy and shame. Eyes that are forced to droop modestly are familiar with these stealthy glances at sin. From Messalina to Marie-Alacoque the distance is not great. Remember the histories of La Cadière and the nun of Louviers. Clubin, too, had worn the veil. Effrontery had always been the object of his secret admiration. He envied the painted courtesan, and the face of bronze of the professional ruffian. He felt a pride in surpassing her in artifices, and a disgust for the trick of passing for a saint. He had been the Tantalus of cynicism. And now, upon this rock, in the midst of this solitude, he could be frank and open. A bold plunge into wickedness—what a voluptuous sense of relief it brought with it. All the delights known to the fallen angels are summed up in this; and Clubin felt them in that moment. The long arrears of dissimulations were paid at last. Hypocrisy is an investment; the devil reimburses it. Clubin gave himself up to the intoxication of the idea, having no longer any eye upon him but that of Heaven. He whispered within himself, "I am a scoundrel," and felt profoundly satisfied.

Never had human conscience experienced such a full tide of emotions.

He was glad to be entirely alone, and yet would not have been sorry to have had some one there. He would have been pleased to have had a witness of his fiendish joy; gratified to have had opportunity of saying to society, "Thou fool."

The solitude, indeed, assured his triumph; but it made it less.

He was not himself to be spectator of his glory. Even to be in the pillory has its satisfaction, for everybody can see your infamy.

To compel the crowd to stand and gape is, in fact, an exercise of power. A malefactor standing upon a platform in the market-place, with the collar of iron around his neck, is master of all the glances which he constrains the multitude to turn towards him. There is a pedestal on yonder scaffolding. To be there—the centre of universal observation—is not this, too, a triumph? To direct the pupil of the public eye, is this not another form of supremacy? For those who worship an ideal wickedness, opprobrium is glory. It is a height from whence they can look down; a superiority at least of some kind; a pre-eminence in which they can display themselves royally. A gallows standing high in the gaze of all the world is not without some analogy with a throne. To be exposed is, at least, to be seen and studied.

Herein we have evidently the key to the wicked reigns of history. Nero burning Rome, Louis Quatorze treacherously seizing the Palatinate, the

Prince Regent killing Napoleon slowly, Nicholas strangling Poland before the eyes of the civilised world, may have felt something akin to Clubin's joy. Universal execration derives a grandeur even from its vastness.

To be unmasked is a humiliation; but to unmask one's self is a triumph. There is an intoxication in the position, an insolent satisfaction in its contempt for appearances, a flaunting insolence in the nakedness with which it affronts the decencies of life.

These ideas in a hypocrite appear to be inconsistent, but in reality are not. All infamy is logical. Honey is gall. A character like that of Escobar has some affinity with that of the Marquis de Sade. In proof, we have Léotade. A hypocrite, being a personification of vice complete, includes in himself the two poles of perversity. Priest-like on one side, he resembles the courtesan on the other. The sex of his diabolical nature is double. It engenders and transforms itself. Would you see it in its pleasing shape? Look at it. Would you see it horrible? Turn it round.

All this multitude of ideas was floating confusedly in Clubin's mind. He analysed them little, but he felt them much.

A whirlwind of flakes of fire borne up from the pit of hell into the dark night, might fitly represent the wild succession of ideas in his soul.

Clubin remained thus some time pensive and motionless. He looked down upon his cast-off virtues as a serpent on its old skin.

Everybody had had faith in that virtue; even he himself a little.

He laughed again.

Society would imagine him dead, while he was rich. They would believe him drowned, while he was saved. What a capital trick to have played off on the stupidity of the world.

Rantaine, too, was included in that universal stupidity. Clubin thought of Rantaine with an unmeasured disdain: the disdain of the marten for the tiger. The trick had failed with Rantaine; it had succeeded with him.— Rantaine had slunk away abashed; Clubin disappeared in triumph. He had substituted himself for Rantaine—stepped between him and his mistress, and carried off her favours.

As to the future, he had no well-settled plan. In the iron tobacco-box in his girdle he had the three bank-notes. The knowledge of that fact was enough. He would change his name. There are plenty of countries where sixty thousand francs are equal to six hundred thousand. It would be no bad solution to go to one of those corners of the world, and live there honestly on the money disgorged by that scoundrel Rantaine. To speculate, to embark in commerce, to increase his capital, to become really a millionaire, that, too, would be no bad termination to his career.

For example. The great trade in coffee from Costa Rica was just beginning to be developed. There were heaps of gold to be made. He would see.

It was of little consequence. He had plenty of time to think of it. The hardest part of the enterprise was accomplished. Stripping Rantaine, and disappearing with the wreck of the Durande, were the grand achievements. All the rest was for him simple. No obstacle henceforth was likely to stop him. He had nothing more to fear. He could reach the shore with certainty by swimming. He would land at Pleinmont in the darkness; ascend the cliffs; go straight to the old haunted house; enter it easily by the help of the knotted cord, concealed beforehand in a crevice of the rocks; would find in the house his travelling-bag containing provisions and dry clothing. There he could await his opportunity. He had information. A week would not pass without the Spanish smugglers, Blasquito probably, touching at Pleinmont. For a few guineas he would obtain a passage, not to Torbay—as he had said to Blasco, to confound conjecture, and put him off the scent—but to Bilbao or Passages. Thence he could get to Vera Cruz or New Orleans. But the moment had come for taking to the water. The long boat was far enough by this time. An hour's swimming was nothing for Clubin. The distance of a mile only separated him from the land, as he was on the Hanways.

At this point in Clubin's meditations, a clear opening appeared in the fog bank, the formidable Douvres rocks stood before him.

VII
AN UNEXPECTED DENOUEMENT

CLUBIN, haggard, stared straight ahead.

It was indeed those terrible and solitary rocks.

It was impossible to mistake their misshapen outlines. The two twin Douvres reared their forms aloft, hideously revealing the passage between them, like a snare, a cut-throat in ambush in the ocean.

They were quite close to him. The fog, like an artful accomplice, had hidden them until now.

Clubin had mistaken his course in the dense mist. Notwithstanding all his pains, he had experienced the fate of two other great navigators, Gonzalez who discovered Cape Blanco, and Fernandez, who discovered Cape Verd. The fog had bewildered him. It had seemed to him, in the confidence of his seamanship, to favour admirably the execution of his project; but it had its perils. In veering to westward he had lost his reckoning. The Guernsey man, who fancied that he recognised the Hanways, had decided his fate, and determined him to give the final turn to the tiller. Clubin had never doubted that he had steered the vessel on the Hanways.

The Durande, stove in by one of the sunken rocks of the group, was only separated from the two Douvres by a few cables' lengths.

At two hundred fathoms further was a massive block of granite. Upon the steep sides of this rock were some hollows and small projections, which might help a man to climb. The square corners of those rude walls at right angles indicated the existence of a plateau on the summit.

It was the height known by the name of "The Man."

"The Man Rock" rose even higher still than the Douvres. Its platform commanded a view over their two inaccessible peaks. This platform, crumbling at its edges, had every kind of irregularity of shape. No place more desolate or more dangerous could be imagined. The hardly perceptible waves of the open sea lapped gently against the square sides of that dark enormous mass; a sort of rest-place for the vast spectres of the sea and darkness.

All around was calm. Scarcely a breath of air or a ripple. The mind guessed darkly the hidden life and vastness of the depths beneath that quiet surface.

Clubin had often seen the Douvres from afar.

He satisfied himself that he was indeed there.

He could not doubt it.

A sudden and hideous change of affairs. The Douvres instead of the Hanways. Instead of one mile, five leagues of sea! The Douvres to the solitary shipwrecked sailor is the visible and palpable presence of death, the extinction of all hope of reaching land.

Clubin shuddered. He had placed himself voluntarily in the jaws of destruction. No other refuge was left to him than "The Man Rock." It was probable that a tempest would arise in the night, and that the longboat, overloaded as she was, would sink. No news of the shipwreck then would come to land. It would not even be known that Clubin had been left upon the Douvres. No prospect was now before him but death from cold and hunger. His seventy-five thousand francs would not purchase him a mouthful of bread. All the scaffolding he had built up had brought him only to this snare. He alone was the laborious architect of this crowning catastrophe. No resource—no possible escape; his triumph transformed into a fatal precipice. Instead of deliverance, a prison; instead of the long prosperous future, agony. In the glance of an eye, in the moment which the lightning occupies in passing, all his construction had fallen into ruins. The paradise dreamed of by this demon had changed to its true form of a sepulchre.

Meanwhile there had sprung up a movement in the air. The wind was rising. The fog, shaken, driven in, and rent asunder, moved towards the horizon in vast shapeless masses. As quickly as it had disappeared before, the sea became once more visible.

The cattle, more and more invaded by the waters, continued to bellow in the hold.

Night was approaching, probably bringing with it a storm.

The Durande, filling slowly with the rising tide, swung from right to left, then from left to right, and began to turn upon the rock as upon a pivot.

The moment could be foreseen when a wave must move her from her fixed position, and probably roll her over on her beam-ends.

It was not even so dark as at the instant of her striking the rocks. Though the day was more advanced, it was possible to see more clearly. The fog had carried away with it some part of the darkness. The west was without a cloud. Twilight brings a pale sky. Its vast reflection glimmered on the sea.

The Durande's bows were lower than her stern. Her stern was, in fact, almost out of the water. Clubin mounted on the taffrail, and fixed his eyes on the horizon.

It is the nature of hypocrisy to be sanguine. The hypocrite is one who waits his opportunity. Hypocrisy is nothing, in fact, but a horrible hopefulness; the very foundation of its revolting falsehood is composed of that virtue transformed into a vice.

Strange contradiction. There is a certain trustfulness in hypocrisy. The hypocrite confides in some power, unrevealed even to himself, which permits the course of evil.

Clubin looked far and wide over the ocean.

The position was desperate, but that evil spirit did not yet despair.

He knew that after the fog, vessels that had been lying-to or riding at anchor would resume their course; and he thought that perhaps one would pass within the horizon.

And, as he had anticipated, a sail appeared.

She was coming from the east and steering towards the west.

As it approached the cut of the vessel became visible. It had but one mast, and was schooner-rigged. Her bowsprit was almost horizontal. It was a cutter.

Before a half-hour she must pass not very far from the Douvres.

Clubin said within himself, "I am saved!"

In a moment like this, a man thinks at first of nothing but his life.

The cutter was probably a strange craft. Might it not be one of the smuggling vessels on its way to Pleinmont? It might even be Blasquito himself. In that case, not only life, but fortune, would be saved; and the accident of the Douvres, by hastening the conclusion, by dispensing with the necessity for concealment in the haunted house, and by bringing the adventure to a dénouement at sea, would be turned into a happy incident.

All his original confidence of success returned fanatically to his sombre mind.

It is remarkable how easily knaves are persuaded that they deserve to succeed.

There was but one course to take.

The Durande, entangled among the rocks, necessarily mingled her outline with them, and confounded herself with their irregular shapes, among which she formed only one more mass of lines. Thus become indistinct and lost, she would not suffice, in the little light which remained, to attract the attention of the crew of the vessel which was approaching.

But a human form standing up, black against the pale twilight of the sky, upon "the Man Rock," and making signs of distress, would doubtless be perceived, and the cutter would then send a boat to take the shipwrecked man aboard.

"The Man" was only two hundred fathoms off. To reach it by swimming was simple, to climb it easy.

There was not a minute to lose.

The bows of the Durande being low between the rocks, it was from the height of the poop where Clubin stood that he had to jump into the sea. He began by taking a sounding, and discovered that there was great depth just under the stern of the wrecked vessel. The microscopic shells of foraminifera which the adhesive matter on the lead-line brought up were intact, indicating the presence of very hollow caves under the rocks, in which the water was tranquil, however great the agitation of the surface.

He undressed, leaving his clothing on the deck. He knew that he would be able to get clothing when aboard the cutter.

He retained nothing but his leather belt.

As soon as he was stripped he placed his hand upon this belt, buckled it more securely, felt for the iron tobacco-box, took a rapid survey in the direction which he would have to follow among the breakers and the waves to gain "the Man Rock;" then precipitating himself head first, he plunged into the sea.

As he dived from a height, he plunged heavily.

He sank deep in the water, touched the bottom, skirted for a moment the submarine rocks, then struck out to regain the surface.

At that moment he felt himself seized by one foot.

Book VII
The Danger of Opening a Book at Random

✳

I
THE PEARL AT THE FOOT OF THE PRECIPICE

A FEW MOMENTS after his short colloquy with Sieur Landoys, Gilliatt was at St. Sampson.

He was troubled, even anxious. What could it be that had happened.

There was a murmur in St. Sampson like that of a startled hive. Everybody was at his door. The women were talking loud. There were people who seemed relating some occurrence and who were gesticulating. A group had gathered around them. The words could be heard, "What a misfortune!" Some faces wore a smile.

Gilliatt interrogated no one. It was not in his nature to ask questions. He was, moreover, too much moved to speak to strangers. He had no confidence in rumours. He preferred to go direct to the Bravées.

His anxiety was so great that he was not even deterred from entering the house.

The door of the great lower room opening upon the Quay, moreover, stood quite open. There was a swarm of men and women on the threshold. Everybody was going in, and Gilliatt went with the rest.

Entering he found Sieur Landoys standing near the doorposts.

"You have heard, no doubt, of this event?"

"No."

"I did not like to call it out to you on the road. It makes me like a bird of evil omen."

"What has happened?"

"The Durande is lost."

There was a crowd in the great room.

The various groups spoke low, like people in a sick chamber.

The assemblage, which consisted of neighbours, the first comers, curious to learn the news, huddled together near the door with a sort of timidity, leaving clear the bottom of the room, where appeared Déruchette sitting and in tears. Mess Lethierry stood beside her.

His back was against the wall at the end of the room. His sailor's cap came down over his eyebrows. A lock of grey hair hung upon his cheek. He said nothing. His arms were motionless; he seemed scarcely to breathe. He had the look of something lifeless placed against the wall.

It was easy to see in his aspect a man whose life had been crushed within him. The Durande being gone, Lethierry had no longer any object in his existence. He had had a being on the sea; that being had suddenly foundered. What could he do now? Rise every morning: go to sleep every night. Never more to await the coming of the Durande; to see her get under way, or steer again into the port. What was a remainder of existence without object? To drink, to eat, and then?—He had crowned the labours of his life by a masterpiece: won by his devotion a new step in civilisation. The step was lost; the masterpiece destroyed. To live a few vacant years longer! where would be the good? Henceforth nothing was left for him to do. At his age men do not begin life anew. Besides, he was ruined. Poor old man!

Déruchette, sitting near him on a chair and weeping, held one of Mess Lethierry's hands in hers. Her hands were joined: his hand was clenched fast. It was the sign of the shade of difference in their two sorrows. In joined hands there is still some token of hope, in the clenched fist none.

Mess Lethierry gave up his arm to her, and let her do with it what she pleased. He was passive. Struck down by a thunderbolt, he had scarcely a spark of life left within him.

There is a degree of overwhelmment which abstracts the mind entirely from its fellowship with man. The forms which come and go within your room become confused and indistinct. They pass by, even touch you, but never really come near you. You are far away; inaccessible to them, as they to you. The intensities of joy and despair differ in this. In despair, we take cognisance of the world only as something dim and afar off: we are insensible to the things before our eyes; we lose the feeling of our own existence. It is in vain, at such times, that we are flesh and blood; our consciousness of life is none the more real: we are become, even to ourselves, nothing but a dream.

Mess Lethierry's gaze indicated that he had reached this state of absorption.

The various groups were whispering together. They exchanged information as far as they had gathered it. This was the substance of their news.

The Durande had been wrecked the day before in the fog on the Douvres, about an hour before sunset. With the exception of the captain, who refused to leave his vessel, the crew and passengers had all escaped in the long-boat. A squall from the south-west springing up as the fog had cleared, had almost wrecked them a second time, and had carried them out to sea beyond Guernsey. In the night they had had the good fortune to meet with the *Cashmere*, which had taken them aboard and landed them at St. Peter's Port. The disaster was entirely the fault of the steersman Tangrouille, who was in prison. Clubin had behaved nobly.

The pilots, who had mustered in great force, pronounced the words "The Douvres" with a peculiar emphasis. "A dreary half-way house that," said one.

A compass and a bundle of registers and memorandum-books lay on the table; they were doubtless the compass of the Durande and the ship's papers, handed by Clubin to Imbrancam and Tangrouille at the moment of the departure of the long-boat. They were the evidences of the magnificent self-abnegation of that man who had busied himself with saving these documents even in the presence of death itself—a little incident full of moral grandeur; an instance of sublime self-forgetfulness never to be forgotten.

They were unanimous in their admiration of Clubin; unanimous also in believing him to be saved after all. The *Shealtiel* cutter had arrived some hours after the *Cashmere*. It was this vessel which had brought the last items of intelligence. She had passed four-and-twenty hours in the same waters as the Durande. She had lain-to in the fog, and tacked about during the squall. The captain of the *Shealtiel* was present among the company.

This captain had just finished his narrative to Lethierry as Gilliatt entered. The narrative was a true one. Towards the morning, the storm having abated, and the wind becoming manageable, the captain of the *Shealtiel* had heard the lowing of oxen in the open sea. This rural sound in the midst of the waves had naturally startled him. He steered in that direction, and perceived the Durande among the Douvres. The sea had sufficiently subsided for him to approach. He hailed the wreck; the bellowing of the cattle was the sole reply. The captain of the *Shealtiel* was confident that there was no one aboard the Durande. The wreck still held together well, and notwithstanding the violence of the squall, Clubin could have passed the night there. He was not the man to leave go his hold very easily. He was not there, however; and therefore he must have been rescued. It was certain that several sloops and luggers, from Granville and St. Malo, must, after laying-to in the fog on the previous evening, have passed pretty near the rocks. It was evident that one of these had taken Clubin aboard. It was to be remembered that the long-boat of the Durande was full when it left the unlucky vessel; that it was certain to encounter great risks; that another man aboard would have overloaded her, and perhaps caused her to founder; and that these circumstances had no doubt weighed with Clubin in coming to his determination to remain on the wreck. His duty, however, once fulfilled, and a vessel at hand, Clubin assuredly would not have scrupled to avail himself of its aid. A hero is not necessarily an idiot. The idea of a suicide was absurd in connection with a man of Clubin's irreproachable character. The culprit, too, was Tangrouille, not Clubin. All this was conclusive. The captain of the *Shealtiel* was evidently right, and everybody expected to see Clubin reappear very shortly. There was a project abroad to carry him through the town in triumph.

Two things appeared certain from the narrative of the captain: Clubin was saved, the Durande lost.

As regarded the Durande, there was nothing for it but to accept the fact; the catastrophe was irremediable. The captain of the *Shealtiel* had witnessed the last moments of the wreck. The sharp rock on which the vessel had been, as it were, nailed, had held her fast during the night, and resisted the shock of the tempest as if reluctant to part with its prey; but in the morning, at the moment when the captain of the *Shealtiel* had convinced himself that there was no one aboard to be saved, and was about to wear off again, one of those seas which are like the last angry blows of a tempest had struck her. The wave lifted her violently from her place, and with the swiftness and directness of an arrow from a bow had thrown her against the two Douvres rocks. "An infernal crash was heard," said the captain. The vessel, lifted by the wave to a certain height, had plunged between the two rocks up to her midship frame. She had stuck fast again; but more firmly than on the submarine rocks. She must have remained there suspended, and exposed to every wind and sea.

The Durande, according to the statements of the crew of the *Shealtiel*, was already three parts broken up. She would evidently have foundered during the night, if the rocks had not kept her up. The captain of the *Shealtiel* had watched her a long time with his spyglass. He gave, with naval precision, the details of her disaster. The starboard quarter beaten in, the masts maimed, the sails blown from the bolt-ropes, the shrouds torn away, the cabin sky-lights smashed by the falling of one of the booms, the dome of the cuddy-house beaten in, the chocks of the long-boat struck away, the round-house overturned, the hinges of the rudder broken, the trusses wrenched away, the quarter-cloths demolished, the bits gone, the cross-beam destroyed, the shear-rails knocked off, the stern-post broken. As to the parts of the cargo made fast before the foremast, all destroyed, made a clean sweep of, gone to ten thousand shivers, with top ropes, iron pulleys, and chains. The Durande had broken her back; the sea now must break her up piecemeal. In a few days there would be nothing of her remaining.

It appeared that the engine was scarcely injured by all these ravages—a remarkable fact, and one which proved its excellence. The captain of the *Shealtiel* thought he could affirm that the crank had received no serious injury. The vessel's masts had given way, but the funnel had resisted everything. Only the iron guards of the captain's gangway were twisted; the paddle boxes had suffered, the frames were bruised, but the paddles had not a float missing. The machinery was intact. Such was the conviction of the captain of the *Shealtiel*. Imbrancam, the engineer, who was among the crowd, had the same conviction. The negro, more intelligent than many of his white companions, was proud of his engines. He lifted up his arms, opening the ten fingers of his black hands, and said to Lethierry, as he sat there silent, "Master, the machinery is alive still!"

The safety of Clubin seeming certain, and the hull of the Durande being already sacrificed, the engines became the topic of conversation among the crowd. They took an interest in it as in a living thing. They felt a delight in praising its good qualities. "That's what I call a well-built machine," said a French sailor. "Something like a good one," cried a Guernsey fisherman.

"She must have some good stuff in her," said the captain of the *Shealtiel*, "to come out of that affair with only a few scratches."

By degrees the machinery of the Durande became the absorbing object of their thoughts. Opinions were warm for and against. It had its enemies and its friends. More than one who possessed a good old sailing cutter, and who hoped to get a share of the business of the Durande, was not sorry to find that the Douvres rock had disposed of the new invention. The whispering became louder. The discussion grew noisy, though the hubbub was evidently a little restrained; and now and then there was a simultaneous lowering of voices out of respect to Lethierry's death-like silence.

The result of the colloquy, so obstinately maintained on all sides, was as follows:—

The engines were the vital part of the vessel. To rescue the Durande was impossible; but the machinery might still be saved. These engines were unique. To construct others similar, the money was wanting; but to find the artificer would have been still more difficult. It was remembered that the constructor of the machinery was dead. It had cost forty thousand francs. No one would risk again such a sum upon such a chance: particularly as it was now discovered that steamboats could be lost like other vessels. The accident of the Durande destroyed the prestige of all her previous success. Still, it was deplorable to think that at that very moment this valuable mechanism was still entire and in good condition, and that in five or six days it would probably go to pieces, like the vessel herself. As long as this existed, it might almost be said that there was no shipwreck. The loss of the engines was alone irreparable. To save the machinery would be almost to repair the disaster.

Save the machinery! It was easy to talk of it; but who would undertake to do it? Was it possible, even? To scheme and to execute are two different things; as different as to dream and to do. Now if ever a dream had appeared wild and impracticable, it was that of saving the engines then embedded between the Douvres. The idea of sending a ship and a crew to work upon those rocks was absurd. It could not be thought of. It was the season of heavy seas. In the first gale the chains of the anchors would be worn away and snapped upon the submarine peaks, and the vessel must be shattered on the rocks. That would be to send a second shipwreck to the relief of the first. On the miserable narrow height where the legend of the place described the shipwrecked sailor as having perished of hunger, there was scarcely room for one person. To save the engines, therefore, it would be necessary for a man to go to the Douvres, to be alone in that sea, alone in that desert, alone at five leagues from the coast, alone in that region of terrors, alone for entire weeks, alone in the presence of dangers foreseen and unforeseen—without supplies in the face of hunger and nakedness, without succour in the time of distress, without token of human life around him save the bleached bones of the miserable being who had perished there in his misery, without companionship save that of death. And besides, how was it possible to extricate the machinery? It would require not only a sailor, but an engineer; and for what trials must he not prepare. The man who would attempt such a task must be more than a hero. He must be a madman: for in certain enterprises, in which superhuman power appears necessary, there is a sort of madness which is more potent than courage. And after all, would it not be a folly to immolate oneself for a mass of rusted iron. No: it was certain that nobody would undertake to go to the Douvres on such an errand. The engine must be abandoned like the rest. The engineer for such a task would assuredly not be forthcoming. Where, indeed, should they look for such a man?

All this, or similar observations, formed the substance of the confused conversations of the crowd.

The captain of the *Shealtiel*, who had been a pilot, summed up the views of all by exclaiming aloud:—

"No; it is all over. The man does not exist who could go there and rescue the machinery of the Durande."

"If I don't go," said Imbrancam, "it is because nobody could do it."

The captain of the *Shealtiel* shook his left hand in the air with that sudden movement which expresses a conviction that a thing is impossible.

"If he existed—" continued the captain.

Déruchette turned her head impulsively, and interrupted.

"I would marry him," she said, innocently.

There was a pause.

A man made his way out of the crowd, and standing before her, pale and anxious, said:

"You would marry him, Miss Déruchette?"

It was Gilliatt.

All eyes were turned towards him. Mess Lethierry had just before stood upright, and gazed about him. His eyes glittered with a strange light.

He took off his sailor's cap, and threw it on the ground: then looked solemnly before him, and without seeing any of the persons present, said:

"Déruchette should be his. I pledge myself to it in God's name."

II

MUCH ASTONISHMENT ON THE WESTERN COAST

THE FULL MOON ROSE at ten o'clock on the following night; but however fine the night, however favourable the wind and sea, no fisherman thought of going out that evening either from Hogue la Perre, or Bourdeaux harbour, or Houmet Benet, or Platon, or Port Grat, or Vazon Bay, or Perrelle Bay, or Pezeries, or the Tielles or Saints' Bay, or Little Bo, or any other port or little harbour in Guernsey; and the reason was very simple. A cock had been heard to crow at noonday.

When the cock is heard to crow at an extraordinary hour, fishing is suspended.

At dusk on that evening, however, a fisherman returning to Omptolle, met with a remarkable adventure. On the height above Houmet Paradis, beyond the Two Brayes and the Two Grunes, stands to the left the beacon of the Plattes Tougères, representing a tub reversed; and to the right, the beacon of St. Sampson, representing the face of a man. Between these two, the fisherman thought that he perceived for the first time a third beacon. What could be the meaning of this beacon? When had it been erected on that point? What shoal did it indicate? The beacon responded immediately to these interrogations. It moved, it was a mast. The astonishment of the fisherman did not diminish. A beacon would have been remarkable; a mast was still more so: it could not be a fishing-boat. When everybody else was returning, some boat was going out. Who could it be? and what was he about?

Ten minutes later the vessel, moving slowly, came within a short distance of the Omptolle fisherman. He did not recognise it. He heard the sound of rowing: there were evidently only two oars. There was probably, then, only one man aboard. The wind was northerly. The man, therefore, was evidently paddling along in order to take the wind off Point Fontenelle. There he would probably take to his sails. He intended then to double the Ancresse and Mount Crevel. What could that mean?

The vessel passed, the fisherman returned home. On that same night, at different hours, and at different points, various persons scattered and isolated on the western coast of Guernsey, observed certain facts.

As the Omptolle fisherman was mooring his bark, a carter of seaweed about half-a-mile off, whipping his horses along the lonely road from the Clôtures near the Druid stones, and in the neighbourhood of the Martello Towers 6 and 7, saw far off at sea, in a part little frequented, because it requires much knowledge of the waters, and in the direction of North Rock and the Jablonneuse, a sail being hoisted. He paid little attention to the circumstance, not being a seaman, but a carter of seaweed.

Half-an-hour had perhaps elapsed since the carter had perceived this vessel, when a plasterer returning from his work in the town, and passing round Pelée Pool, found himself suddenly opposite a vessel sailing boldly among the rocks of the Quenon, the Rousse de Mer, and the Gripe de Rousse. The night was dark, but the sky was light over the sea, an effect common enough; and he could distinguish a great distance in every direction. There was no sail visible except this vessel.

A little lower, a gatherer of crayfish, preparing his fish wells on the beach which separates Port Soif from the Port Enfer, was puzzled to make out the movements of a vessel between the Boue Corneille and the Moubrette. The man must have been a good pilot, and in great haste to reach some destination to risk his boat there.

Just as eight o'clock was striking at the Catel, the tavern-keeper at Cobo Bay observed with astonishment a sail out beyond the Boue du Jardin and the Grunettes, and very near the Susanne and the Western Grunes.

Not far from Cobo Bay, upon the solitary point of the Houmet of Vason Bay, two lovers were lingering, hesitating before they parted for the night. The young woman addressed the young man with the words, "I am not going because I don't care to stay with you: I've a great deal to do." Their farewell kiss was interrupted by a good sized sailing boat which passed very near them, making for the direction of the Messellettes.

Monsieur le Peyre des Norgiots, an inhabitant of Cotillon Pipet, was engaged about nine o'clock in the evening in examining a hole made by some trespassers in the hedge of his property called La Jennerotte, and his "*friquet* planted with trees." Even while ascertaining the amount of the damage, he could not help observing a fishing-boat audaciously making its way round the Crocq Point at that hour of night.

On the morrow of a tempest, when there is always some agitation upon the sea, that route was extremely unsafe. It was rash to choose it, at least, unless the steersman knew all the channels by heart.

At half-past nine o'clock, at L'Equerrier, a trawler carrying home his net stopped for a time to observe between Colombelle and the Soufleresse something which looked like a boat. The boat was in a dangerous position. Sudden gusts of wind of a very dangerous kind are very common in that spot. The *Soufleresse*, or Blower, derives its name from the sudden gusts of wind which it seems to direct upon the vessels, which by rare chance find their way thither.

At the moment when the moon was rising, the tide being high and the sea being quiet, in the little strait of Li-Hou, the solitary keeper of the island of Li-Hou was considerably startled. A long black object slowly passed between the moon and him. This dark form, high and narrow, resembled a winding-sheet spread out and moving. It glided along the line of the top of the wall formed by the ridges of rock. The keeper of Li-Hou fancied that he had beheld the Black Lady.

The White Lady inhabits the Tau de Pez d'Amont; the Grey Lady, the Tau de Pez d'Aval; the Red Lady, the Silleuse, to the north of the Marquis Bank; and the Black Lady, the Grand Etacré, to the west of Li-Houmet. At night, when the moon shines, these ladies stalk abroad, and sometimes meet.

That dark form might undoubtedly be a sail. The long groups of rocks on which she appeared to be walking, might in fact be concealing the hull of a bark navigating behind them, and allowing only her sail to be seen. But the keeper asked himself, what bark would dare, at that hour, to venture

herself between Li-Hou and the Pécheresses, and the Anguillières and Lérée
Point? And what object could she have? It seemed to him much more
probable that it was the Black Lady.

As the moon was passing the clock-tower of St. Peter in the Wood, the
serjeant at Castle Rocquaine, while in the act of raising the drawbridge
of the castle, distinguished at the end of the bay beyond the Haute Canée,
but nearer than the Sambule, a sailing-vessel which seemed to be steadily
dropping down from north to south.

On the southern coast of Guernsey behind Pleinmont, in the curve of
a bay composed entirely of precipices and rocky walls rising peak-shaped
from the sea, there is a singular landing-place, to which a French gentleman,
a resident of the island since 1855, has given the name of "The Port on the
Fourth Floor," a name now generally adopted. This port, or landing-place,
which was then called the Moie, is a rocky plateau half-formed by nature,
half by art, raised about forty feet above the level of the waves, and communicating with the water by two large beams laid parallel in the form of an
inclined plane. The fishing-vessels are hoisted up there by chains and pulleys
from the sea, and are let down again in the same way along these beams,
which are like two rails. For the fishermen there is a ladder. The port was,
at the time of our story, much frequented by the smugglers. Being difficult
of access, it was well suited to their purposes.

Towards eleven o'clock, some smugglers—perhaps the same upon
whose aid Clubin had counted—stood with their bales of goods on the
summit of this platform of the Moie. A smuggler is necessarily a man on
the look out, it is part of his business to watch. They were astonished to
perceive a sail suddenly make its appearance beyond the dusky outline of
Cape Pleinmont. It was moonlight. The smugglers observed the sail narrowly,
suspecting that it might be some coast-guard cutter about to lie in ambush
behind the Great Hanway. But the sail left the Hanways behind, passed to
the north-west of the Boue Blondel, and was lost in the pale mists of the
horizon out at sea.

"Where the devil can that boat be sailing?" asked the smuggler.

That same evening, a little after sunset, some one had been heard knocking at the door of the old house of the Bû de la Rue. It was a boy wearing
brown clothes and yellow stockings, a fact that indicated that he was a little

parish clerk. An old fisherwoman prowling about the shore with a lantern in her hand, had called to the boy, and this dialogue ensued between the fisherwoman and the little clerk, before the entrance to the Bû de la Rue:—

"What d'ye want, lad?"

"The man of this place."

"He's not there."

"Where is he?"

"I don't know."

"Will he be there to-morrow?"

"I don't know."

"Is he gone away?"

"I don't know."

"I've come, good woman, from the new rector of the parish, the Reverend Ebenezer Caudray, who desires to pay him a visit."

"I don't know where he is."

"The rector sent me to ask if the man who lives at the Bû de la Rue would be at home to-morrow morning."

"I don't know."

III
A QUOTATION FROM THE BIBLE

DURING THE twenty-four hours which followed, Mess Lethierry slept not, ate nothing, drank nothing. He kissed Déruchette on the forehead, asked after Clubin, of whom there was as yet no news, signed a declaration certifying that he had no intention of preferring a charge against anyone, and set Tangrouille at liberty.

All the morning of the next day he remained half supporting himself on the table of the office of the Durande, neither standing nor sitting: answering kindly when anyone spoke to him. Curiosity being satisfied, the Bravées had become a solitude. There is a good deal of curiosity generally mingled with the haste of condolences. The door had closed again, and left the old man again alone with Déruchette. The strange light that had shone in Lethierry's eyes was extinguished. The mournful look which filled them after the first news of the disaster had returned.

Déruchette, anxious for his sake, had, on the advice of Grace and Douce, laid silently beside him a pair of stockings, which he had been knitting, sailor fashion, when the bad news had arrived.

He smiled bitterly, and said:

"They must think me foolish."

After a quarter of an hour's silence, he added:

"These things are well when you are happy."

Déruchette carried away the stockings, and took advantage of the opportunity to remove also the compass and the ship's papers which Lethierry had been brooding over too long.

In the afternoon, a little before tea-time, the door opened and two strangers entered, attired in black. One was old, the other young.

The young one has, perhaps, already been observed in the course of this story.

The two men had each a grave air; but their gravity appeared different. The old man possessed what might be called state gravity; the gravity of the young man was in his nature. Habit engenders the one; thought the other.

They were, as their costume indicated, two clergymen, each belonging to the Established Church.

The first fact in the appearance of the younger man which might have first struck the observer was, that his gravity, though conspicuous in the expression of his features, and evidently springing from the mind, was not indicated by his person. Gravity is not inconsistent with passion, which it exalts by purifying it; but the idea of gravity could with difficulty be associated with an exterior remarkable above all for personal beauty. Being in holy orders, he must have been at least four-and-twenty, but he seemed scarcely more than eighteen. He possessed those gifts at once in harmony with, and in opposition to, each other. A soul which seemed created for exalted passion, and a body created for love. He was fair, rosy-fresh, slim, and elegant in his severe attire, and he had the cheeks of a young girl, and delicate hands. His movements were natural and lively, though subdued. Everything about him was pleasing, elegant, almost voluptuous. The beauty of his expression served to correct this excess of personal attraction. His open smile, which showed his teeth, regular and white as those of a child, had something in it pensive, even devotional. He had the gracefulness of a page, mingled with the dignity of a bishop.

His fair hair, so fair and golden as to be almost effeminate, clustered over his white forehead, which was high and well-formed. A slight double line between the eyebrows awakened associations with studious thought.

Those who saw him felt themselves in the presence of one of those natures, benevolent, innocent, and pure, whose progress is in inverse sense with that of vulgar minds; natures whom illusion renders wise, and whom experience makes enthusiasts.

His older companion was no other than Doctor Jaquemin Hérode. Doctor Jaquemin Hérode belonged to the High Church; a party whose system is a sort of popery without a pope. The Church of England was at that epoch labouring with the tendencies which have since become strengthened and condensed in the form of Puseyism. Doctor Jaquemin Hérode belonged to that shade of Anglicanism which is almost a variety of the Church of Rome. He was haughty, precise, stiff, and commanding. His inner sight scarcely penetrated outwardly. He possessed the letter in the place of the spirit. His manner was arrogant; his presence imposing. He had less the appearance of a "Reverend" than of a *Monsignore*. His frock-coat was cut somewhat in the fashion of a cassock. His true centre would have been Rome. He was a born Prelate of the Antechamber. He seemed to have been created expressly to fill a part in the Papal Court, to walk behind the Pontifical litter, with all the Court of Rome in *abitto paonazzo*. The accident of his English birth and his theological education, directed more towards the Old than the New Testament, had deprived him of that destiny. All his splendours were comprised in his preferments as Rector of St. Peter's Port, Dean of the Island of Guernsey, and Surrogate of the Bishop of Winchester. These were, undoubtedly, not without their glories. These glories did not prevent M. Jaquemin Hérode being, on the whole, a worthy man.

As a theologian he was esteemed by those who were able to judge of such matters; he was almost an authority in the Court of Arches—that Sorbonne of England.

He had the true air of erudition; a learned contraction of the eyes; bristling nostrils; teeth which showed themselves at all times; a thin upper lip and a thick lower one. He was the possessor of several learned degrees, a valuable prebend, titled friends, the confidence of the bishop, and a Bible, which he carried always in his pocket.

Mess Lethierry was so completely absorbed that the entrance of the two priests produced no effect upon him, save a slight movement of the eyebrows.

M. Jaquemin Hérode advanced, bowed, alluded in a few sober and dignified words to his recent promotion, and mentioned that he came according to custom to introduce among the inhabitants, and to Mess Lethierry in particular, his successor in the parish, the new Rector of St. Sampson, the Rev. Ebenezer Caudray, henceforth the pastor of Mess Lethierry.

Déruchette rose.

The young clergyman, who was the Rev. Ebenezer, saluted her.

Mess Lethierry regarded Monsieur Ebenezer Caudray, and muttered, "A bad sailor."

Grace placed chairs. The two visitors seated themselves near the table.

Doctor Hérode commenced a discourse. It had reached his ears that a serious misfortune had befallen his host. The Durande had been lost. He came as Lethierry's pastor to offer condolence and advice. This shipwreck was unfortunate, and yet not without compensations. Let us examine our own hearts. Are we not puffed up with prosperity? The waters of felicity are dangerous. Troubles must be submitted to cheerfully. The ways of Providence are mysterious. Mess Lethierry was ruined, perhaps. But riches were a danger. You may have false friends; poverty will disperse them, and leave you alone. The Durande was reported to have brought a revenue of one thousand pounds sterling per annum. It was more than enough for the wise. Let us fly from temptations; put not our faith in gold; bow the head to losses and neglect. Isolation is full of good fruits. It was in solitude that Ajah discovered the warm springs while leading the asses of his father Zibeon. Let us not rebel against the inscrutable decrees of Providence. The holy man Job, after his misery, had put faith in riches. Who can say that the loss of the Durande may not have its advantages even of a temporal kind. He, for instance, Doctor Jaquemin Hérode had invested some money in an excellent enterprise, now in progress at Sheffield. If Mess Lethierry, with the wealth which might still remain to him, should choose to embark in the same affair, he might transfer his capital to that town. It was an extensive manufactory of arms for the supply of the Czar, now engaged in repressing insurrection in Poland. There was a good prospect of obtaining three hundred per cent. profit.

The word Czar appeared to awaken Lethierry. He interrupted Dr. Hérode.

"I want nothing to do with the Czar."

The Reverend Jaquemin Hérode replied:

"Mess Lethierry, princes are recognised by God. It is written, 'Render unto Cæsar the things which are Cæsar's.' The Czar is Cæsar."

Lethierry partly relapsed into his dream and muttered:

"Cæsar? who is Cæsar? I don't know."

The Rev. Jaquemin Hérode continued his exhortations. He did not press the question of Sheffield.

To contemn a Cæsar was republicanism. He could understand a man being a republican. In that case he could turn his thoughts towards a re-public. Mess Lethierry might repair his fortune in the United States, even better than in England. If he desired to invest what remained to him at great profit, he had only to take shares in the great company for developing the resources of Texas, which employed more than twenty thousand negroes.

"I want nothing to do with slavery," said Lethierry.

"Slavery," replied the Reverend Hérode, "is an institution recognised by Scripture. It is written, 'If a man smite his slave, he shall not be punished, for he is his money.'"

Grace and Douce at the door of the room listened in a sort of ecstacy to the words of the Reverend Doctor.

The doctor continued. He was, all things considered, as we have said, a worthy man; and whatever his differences, personal or connected with caste, with Mess Lethierry, he had come very sincerely to offer him that spiritual and even temporal aid which he, Doctor Jaquemin Hérode, dispensed.

If Mess Lethierry's fortune had been diminished to that point that he was unable to take a beneficial part in any speculation, Russian or Amer-ican, why should he not obtain some government appointment suited to him? There were many very respectable places open to him, and the reverend gentleman was ready to recommend him. The office of Depu-ty-Vicomte was just vacant. Mess Lethierry was popular and respected, and the Reverend Jaquemin Hérode, Dean of Guernsey and Surrogate of the Bishop, would make an effort to obtain for Mess Lethierry this post. The Deputy-Vicomte is an important officer. He is present as the representative of His Majesty at the holding of the Sessions, at the debates of the *Cohue*, and at executions of justice.

Lethierry fixed his eye upon Doctor Hérode.

"I don't like hanging," he said.

Doctor Hérode, who, up to this point, had pronounced his words with the same intonation, had now a fit of severity; his tone became slightly changed.

"Mess Lethierry, the pain of death is of divine ordination. God has placed the sword in the hands of governors. It is written, 'An eye for an eye, a tooth for a tooth.'"

The Reverend Ebenezer imperceptibly drew his chair nearer to the Reverend Doctor and said, so as to be heard only by him:

"What this man says, is dictated to him."

"By whom? By what?" demanded the Reverend Jaquemin Hérode, in the same tone.

The young man replied in a whisper, "By his conscience."

The Reverend Jaquemin Hérode felt in his pocket, drew out a thick little bound volume with clasps, and said aloud:

"Conscience is here."

The book was a Bible.

Then Doctor Hérode's tone became softer. "His wish was to render a service to Mess Lethierry, whom he respected much. As his pastor, it was his right and duty to offer counsel. Mess Lethierry, however, was free."

Mess Lethierry, plunged once more in his overwhelming absorption, no longer listened. Déruchette, seated near him, and thoughtful, also did not raise her eyes, and by her silent presence somewhat increased the embarrassment of a conversation not very animated. A witness who says nothing is a species of indefinable weight. Doctor Hérode, however, did not appear to feel it.

Lethierry no longer replying, Doctor Hérode expatiated freely. Counsel is from man; inspiration is from God. In the counsels of the priests there is inspiration. It is good to accept, dangerous to refuse them. Sochoh was seized by eleven devils for disdaining the exhortations of Nathaniel. Tiburianus was struck with a leprosy for having driven from his house the Apostle Andrew. Barjesus, a magician though he was, was punished with blindness for having mocked at the words of St. Paul. Elxai and his sisters, Martha and Martena, are in eternal torments for despising the warnings of Valentianus, who proved to them clearly that their Jesus Christ, thirty-eight leagues in height, was a demon. Aholibamah, who is also called Judith, obeyed the Councils, Reuben and Peniel listened to the counsels from on high, as their names indeed indicate. Reuben signifies son of the vision; and Peniel, "the face of God."

Mess Lethierry struck the table with his fist.

"Parbleu!" he cried; "it was my fault."

"What do you mean?" asked M. Jaquemin Hérode.

"I say that it is my fault."

"Your fault? Why?"

"Because I allowed the Durande to return on Fridays."

M. Jaquemin Hérode whispered in Caudray's ear:

"This man is superstitious."

He resumed, raising his voice, and in a didactic tone:

"Mess Lethierry, it is puerile to believe in Fridays. You ought not to put faith in fables. Friday is a day just like any other. It is very often a propitious day. Melendez founded the city of Saint Augustin on a Friday; it was on a Friday that Henry the Seventh gave his commission to John Cabot; the Pilgrims of the *Mayflower* landed at Province Town on a Friday. Washington was born on Friday, the 22nd of February 1732; Christopher Columbus discovered America on Friday, the 12th of October 1492."

Having delivered himself of these remarks, he rose.

Caudray, whom he had brought with him, rose also.

Grace and Douce, perceiving that the two clergymen were about to take their leave, opened the folding-doors.

Mess Lethierry saw nothing; heard nothing.

M. Jaquemin Hérode said, apart to M. Caudray:

"He does not even salute us. This is not sorrow; it is vacancy. He must have lost his reason."

He took his little Bible, however, from the table, and held it between his hands outstretched, as one holds a bird in fear that it may fly away. This attitude awakened among the persons present a certain amount of attention. Grace and Douce leaned forward eagerly.

His voice assumed all the solemnity of which it was capable.

"Mess Lethierry," he began, "let us not part without reading a page of the Holy Book. It is from books that wise men derive consolation in the troubles of life. The profane have their oracles; but believers have their ready resource in the Bible. The first book which comes to hand, opened by chance may afford counsel; but the Bible, opened at any page, yields a revelation. It is, above all, a boon to the afflicted. Yes, Holy Scripture is an unfailing balm for their wounds. In the presence of affliction, it is good to consult its sacred pages—to open even without choosing the place, and to read with faith the passage which we find. What man does not choose is chosen by God. He knoweth best what suiteth us. His finger pointeth invisibly to that which we read. Whatever be the page, it will infallibly enlighten. Let us seek, then, no other light; but hold fast to His. It is the word from on high. In the text which is evoked with confidence and reverence, often do we find a mysterious significance in our present troubles. Let us hearken, then, and obey. Mess Lethierry, you are in affliction, but I hold here the book of consolation. You are sick at heart, but I have here the book of spiritual health."

The Reverend Jaquemin Hérode touched the spring of the clasp, and let his finger slip between the leaves. Then he placed his hand a moment upon the open volume, collected his thoughts, and, raising his eyes impressively, began to read in a loud voice.

The passage which he had lighted on was as follows:

"And Isaac went out to meditate in the field at the eventide, and he lifted up his eyes and saw and beheld the camels were coming.

"And Rebekah lifted up her eyes, and when she saw Isaac she lighted off the camel.

"For she had said unto the servant, What man is this that walketh in the field to meet us?

"And Isaac brought her into his mother Sarah's tent, and took Rebekah, and she became his wife, and he loved her; and Isaac was comforted after his mother's death."

Caudray and Déruchette glanced at each other.

Part II

Malicious Gilliatt

Book I
The Rock

✳

I
THE PLACE WHICH IS DIFFICULT TO REACH, AND DIFFICULT TO LEAVE

THE BARK which had been observed at so many points on the coast of Guernsey on the previous evening was, as the reader has guessed, the old Dutch barge or sloop. Gilliatt had chosen the channel along the coast among the rocks. It was the most dangerous way, but it was the most direct. To take the shortest route was his only thought. Shipwrecks will not wait; the sea is a pressing creditor; an hour's delay may be irreparable. His anxiety was to go quickly to the rescue of the machinery in danger.

One of his objects in leaving Guernsey was to avoid arousing attention. He set out like one escaping from justice, and seemed anxious to hide from human eyes. He shunned the eastern coast, as if he did not care to pass in sight of St. Sampson and St. Peter's Port, and glided silently along the opposite coast, which is comparatively uninhabited. Among the breakers, it was necessary to ply the oars; but Gilliatt managed them on scientific principles; taking the water quietly, and dropping it with exact regularity, he was able to move in the darkness with as little noise and as rapidly as possible. So stealthy were his movements, that he might have seemed to be bent upon some evil errand.

In truth, though embarking desperately in an enterprise which might well be called impossible, and risking his life with nearly every chance against him, he feared nothing but the possibility of some rival in the work which he had set before him.

As the day began to break, those unknown eyes which look down upon the world from boundless space might have beheld, at one of the most dangerous and solitary spots at sea, two objects, the distance between which was gradually decreasing, as the one was approaching the other. One, which was almost imperceptible in the wide movement of the waters, was a sailing boat. In this was a man. It was the sloop. The other, black, motionless, colossal, rose above the waves, a singular form. Two tall pillars issuing from the sea bore aloft a sort of cross-beam which was like a bridge between them. This bridge, so singular in shape that it was impossible to imagine what it was from a distance, touched each of the two pillars. It resembled a vast portal. Of what use could such an erection be in that open plain, the sea, which stretched around it far and wide? It might have been imagined to be a Titanic Cromlech, planted there in mid-ocean by an imperious whim, and built up by hands accustomed to proportion their labours to the great deep. Its wild outline stood well-defined against the clear sky.

The morning light was growing stronger in the east; the whiteness in the horizon deepened the shadow on the sea. In the opposite sky the moon was sinking.

The two perpendicular forms were the Douvres. The huge mass held fast between them, like an architrave between two pillars, was the wreck of the Durande.

The rock, thus holding fast and exhibiting its prey, was terrible to behold. Inanimate things look sometimes as if endowed with a dark and hostile spirit towards man. There was a menace in the attitude of the rocks. They seemed to be biding their time.

Nothing could be more suggestive of haughtiness and arrogance than their whole appearance: the conquered vessel; the triumphant abyss. The two rocks, still streaming with the tempest of the day before, were like two wrestlers sweating from a recent struggle. The wind had sunk; the sea rippled gently; here and there the presence of breakers might be detected in the graceful streaks of foam upon the surface of the waters. A sound came from the sea like the murmuring of bees. All around was level except the Douvres, rising straight, like two black columns. Up to a certain height they were completely bearded with seaweed; above this their steep haunches glittered at points like polished armour. They seemed ready to commence the strife again. The beholder felt that they were rooted deep in mountains whose summits were beneath the sea. Their aspect was full of a sort of tragic power.

Ordinarily the sea conceals her crimes. She delights in privacy. Her unfathomable deeps keep silence. She wraps herself in a mystery which rarely consents to give up its secrets. We know her savage nature, but who can tell the extent of her dark deeds? She is at once open and secret; she hides away carefully, and cares not to divulge her actions; wrecks a vessel, and, covering it with the waves, engulfs it deep, as if conscious of her guilt. Among her crimes is hypocrisy. She slays and steals, conceals her booty, puts on an air of unconsciousness, and smiles.

Here, however, was nothing of the kind. The Douvres, lifting above the level of the waters the shattered hull of the Durande, had an air of triumph. The imagination might have pictured them as two monstrous arms, reaching upwards from the gulf, and exhibiting to the tempest the lifeless body of the ship. Their aspect was like that of an assassin boasting of his evil deeds.

The solemnity of the hour contributed something to the impression of the scene. There is a mysterious grandeur in the dawn, as of the border-land between the region of consciousness and the world of our dreams. There is something spectral in that confused transition time. The immense form of the two Douvres, like a capital letter H, the Durande forming its cross stroke, appeared against the horizon in all their twilight majesty.

Gilliatt was attired in his seaman's clothing: a Guernsey shirt, woollen stockings, thick shoes, a homespun jacket, trousers of thick stuff, with pockets, and a cap upon his head of red worsted, of a kind then much in use among sailors, and known in the last century as a *galérienne*.

He recognised the rocks, and steered towards them.

The situation of the Durande was exactly the contrary of that of a vessel gone to the bottom: it was a vessel suspended in the air.

No problem more strange was ever presented to a salvor.

It was broad daylight when Gilliatt arrived in the waters about the rock.

As we have said, there was but little sea. The slight agitation of the water was due almost entirely to its confinement among the rocks. Every passage, small or large, is subject to this chopping movement. The inside of a channel is always more or less white with foam. Gilliatt did not approach the Douvres without caution.

He cast the sounding lead several times.

He had a cargo to disembark.

Accustomed to long absences, he had at home a number of necessaries always ready. He had brought a sack of biscuit, another of rye-meal, a basket of salt fish and smoked beef, a large can of fresh water; a Norwegian chest painted with flowers, containing several coarse woollen shirts, his tarpaulin and his waterproof overalls, and a sheepskin which he was accustomed to throw at night over his clothes. On leaving the Bû de la Rue he had put all these things hastily into the barge, with the addition of a large loaf. In his hurry he had brought no other tools but his huge forge-hammer, his chopper and hatchet, and a knotted rope. Furnished with a grappling-iron and with a ladder of that sort, the steepest rocks become accessible, and a good sailor will find it possible to scale the rudest escarpment. In the island of Sark the visitor may see what the fishermen of the Havre Gosselin can accomplish with a knotted cord.

His nets and lines and all his fishing apparatus were in the barge. He had placed them there mechanically and by habit; for he intended, if his enterprise continued, to sojourn for some time in an archipelago of rocks and breakers, where fishing nets and tackle are of little use.

At the moment when Gilliatt was skirting the great rock the sea was retiring; a circumstance favourable to his purpose. The departing tide laid bare, at the foot of the smaller Douvre, one or two table-rocks, horizontal, or only slightly inclined, and bearing a fanciful resemblance to boards supported by crows. These table-rocks, sometimes narrow, sometimes broad, standing at unequal distances along the side of the great perpendicular column, were continued in the form of a thin cornice up to a spot just beneath the Durande, the hull of which stood swelling out between the two rocks. The wreck was held fast there as in a vice.

This series of platforms was convenient for approaching and surveying the position. It was convenient also for disembarking the contents of the barge provisionally; but it was necessary to hasten, for it was only above water for a few hours. With the rising tide the table-rocks would be again beneath the foam.

It was before these table-rocks, some level, some slanting, that Gilliatt pushed in and brought the barge to a stand. A thick mass of wet and slippery sea-wrack covered them, rendered more slippery here and there by their inclined surfaces.

Gilliatt pulled off his shoes and sprang bare-footed on to the slimy weeds, and made fast the barge to a point of rock.

Then he advanced as far as he could along the granite cornice, reached the rock immediately beneath the wreck, looked up, and examined it.

The Durande had been caught suspended, and, as it were, fitted in between the two rocks, at about twenty feet above the water. It must have been a heavy sea which had cast her there.

Such effects from furious seas have nothing surprising for those who are familiar with the ocean. To cite one example only:—On the 25th January 1840, in the Gulf of Stora, a tempest struck with its expiring force a brig, and casting it almost intact completely over the broken wreck of the corvette *La Marne*, fixed it immovable, bowsprit first, in a gap between the cliffs.

The Douvres, however, held only a part of the Durande.

The vessel snatched from the waves had been, as it were, uprooted from the waters by the hurricane. A whirlwind had wrenched it against the counteracting force of the rolling waves, and the vessel thus caught in contrary directions by the two claws of the tempest had snapped like a lath. The afterpart with the engine and the paddles, lifted out of the foam and driven by all the fury of the cyclone into the defile of the Douvres, had plunged in up to her midship beam, and remained there. The blow had been well directed. To drive it in this fashion between the two rocks, the storm had struck it as with an enormous hammer. The forecastle carried away and rolled down by the sea, had gone to fragments among the breakers.

The hold, broken in, had scattered out the bodies of the drowned cattle upon the sea.

A large portion of the forward side and bulwarks still hung to the riders by the larboard paddle-box, and by some shattered braces easy to strike off with the blow of a hatchet.

Here and there, among beams, planks, rags of canvas, pieces of chains, and other remains of wreck were seen lying about among the rugged fragments of shattered rock.

Gilliatt surveyed the Durande attentively. The keel formed a roofing over his head.

A serene sky stretched far and wide over the waters, scarcely wrinkled with a passing breath. The sun rose gloriously in the midst of the vast azure circle.

From time to time a drop of water was detached from the wreck and fell into the sea.

II
A CATALOGUE OF DISASTERS

THE DOUVRES differed in shape as well as in height.

Upon the Little Douvre, which was curved and pointed, long veins of reddish-coloured rock, of a comparatively soft kind, could be seen branching out and dividing the interior of the granite. At the edges of these red dykes were fractures, favourable to climbing. One of these fractures, situated a little above the wreck, had been so laboriously worn and scooped out by the splashing of the waves, that it had become a sort of niche, in which it would have been quite possible to place a statue. The granite of the Little Douvre was rounded at the surface, and, to the feel at least, soft like touchstone; but this feeling detracted nothing from its durability. The Little Douvre terminated in a point like a horn. The Great Douvre, polished, smooth, glossy, perpendicular, and looking as if cut out by the builder's square, was in one piece, and seemed made of black ivory. Not a hole, not a break in its smooth surface. The escarpment looked inhospitable. A convict could not have used it for escape, nor a bird for a place for its nest. On the summit there was a horizontal surface as upon "The Man Rock;" but the summit of the Great Douvre was inaccessible.

It was possible to scale the Little Douvre, but not to remain on the summit; it would have been possible to rest on the summit of the Great Douvre, but impossible to scale it.

Gilliatt, having rapidly surveyed the situation of affairs, returned to the barge, landed its contents upon the largest of the horizontal cornice rocks, made of the whole compact mass a sort of bale, which he rolled up in tarpaulin, fitted a sling rope to it with a hoisting block, pushed the package into a corner of the rocks where the waves could not reach it, and then clutching the Little Douvre with his hands, and holding on with his naked feet, he clambered from projection to projection, and from niche to niche, until he found himself level with the wrecked vessel high up in the air.

Having reached the height of the paddles, he sprang upon the poop.

The interior of the wreck presented a mournful aspect.

Traces of a great struggle were everywhere visible. There were plainly to be seen the frightful ravages of the sea and wind. The action of the tempest resembles the violence of a band of pirates. Nothing is more like the victim of a criminal outrage than a wrecked ship violated and stripped by those terrible accomplices, the storm-cloud, the thunder, the rain, the squall, the waves, and the breakers.

Standing upon the dismantled deck, it was natural to dream of the presence of something like a furious stamping of the spirits of the storm. Everywhere around were the marks of their rage. The strange contortions of certain portions of the ironwork bore testimony to the terrific force of the winds. The between-decks were like the cell of a lunatic, in which everything has been broken.

No wild beast can compare with the sea for mangling its prey. The waves are full of talons. The north wind bites, the billows devour, the waves are like hungry jaws. The ocean strikes like a lion with its heavy paw, seizing and dismembering at the same moment.

The ruin conspicuous in the Durande presented the peculiarity of being detailed and minute. It was a sort of horrible stripping and plucking. Much of it seemed done with design. The beholder was tempted to exclaim, "What wanton mischief!" The ripping of the planking was edged here and there artistically. This peculiarity is common with the ravages of the cyclone. To chip and tear away is the caprice of the great devastator. Its ways are like those of the professional torturer. The disasters which it causes wear a look of ingenious punishments. One might fancy it actuated by the worst passions of man. It refines in cruelty like a savage. While it is exterminating it dissects bone by bone. It torments its victim, avenges itself, and takes delight in its work. It even appears to descend to petty acts of malice.

Cyclones are rare in our latitudes, and are, for that reason, the more dangerous, being generally unexpected. A rock in the path of a heavy wind may become the pivot of a storm. It is probable that the squall had thus rotated upon the point of the Douvres, and had turned suddenly into a waterspout on meeting the shock of the rocks, a fact which explained the casting of the vessel so high among them. When the cyclone blows, a vessel is of no more weight in the wind than a stone in a sling.

The damage received by the Durande was like the wound of a man cut in twain. It was a divided trunk from which issued a mass of *débris* like the entrails of a body. Various kinds of cordage hung floating and trembling, chains swung chattering; the fibres and nerves of the vessel were there naked and exposed. What was not smashed was disjointed.

Fragments of the sheeting resembled currycombs bristling with nails; everything bore the appearance of ruin; a handspike had become nothing but a piece of iron; a sounding-lead, nothing but a lump of metal; a dead-eye had become a mere piece of wood; a halliard, an end of rope; a strand of cord, a tangled skein; a bolt-rope, a thread in the hem of a sail. All around was the lamentable work of demolition. Nothing remained that was not unhooked, unnailed, cracked, wasted, warped, pierced with holes, destroyed: nothing hung together in the dreadful mass, but all was torn, dislocated, broken. There was that air of drift which characterises the scene of all struggles—from the melées of men, which are called battles, to the melées of the elements, to which we give the name of chaos. Everything was sinking and dropping away; a rolling mass of planks, panelling, ironwork, cables, and beams had been arrested just at the great fracture of the hull, whence the least additional shock must have precipitated them into the sea. What remained of her powerful frame, once so triumphant, was cracked here and there, showing through large apertures the dismal gloom within.

The foam from below spat its flakes contemptuously upon this broken and forlorn outcast of the sea.

III
SOUND; BUT NOT SAFE

GILLIATT DID NOT expect to find only a portion of the ship existing. Nothing in the description, in other respects so precise, of the captain of the *Shealtiel* had led him to anticipate this division of the vessel in the centre. It was probable that the "diabolical crash" heard by the captain of the *Shealtiel* marked the moment when this destruction had taken place under the blows of a tremendous sea. The captain had, doubtless, worn ship just before this last heavy squall; and what he had taken for a great sea was probably a waterspout. Later, when he drew nearer to observe the wreck, he had only been able to see the stern of the vessel—the remainder, that is to say, the large opening where the fore-part had given way, having been concealed from him among the masses of rock.

With that exception, the information given by the captain of the *Shealtiel* was strictly correct. The hull was useless, but the engine remained intact.

Such chances are common in the history of shipwreck. The logic of disaster at sea is beyond the grasp of human science.

The masts having snapped short, had fallen over the side; the chimney was not even bent. The great iron plating which supported the machinery had kept it together, and in one piece. The planks of the paddle-boxes were disjointed, like the leaves of wooden sunblinds; but through their apertures the paddles themselves could be seen in good condition. A few of their floats only were missing.

Besides the machinery, the great stern capstan had resisted the destruction. Its chain was there, and, thanks to its firm fixture in a frame of joists, might still be of service, unless the strain of the voyal should break away the planking. The flooring of the deck bent at almost every point, and was tottering throughout.

On the other hand, the trunk of the hull, fixed between the Douvres, held together, as we have already said, and it appeared strong.

There was something like derision in this preservation of the machinery; something which added to the irony of the misfortune. The sombre malice of the unseen powers of mischief displays itself sometimes in such bitter mockeries. The machinery was saved, but its preservation did not make it any the less lost. The ocean seemed to have kept it only to demolish it at leisure. It was like the playing of the cat with her prey.

Its fate was to suffer there and to be dismembered day by day. It was to be the plaything of the savage amusements of the sea. It was slowly to dwindle, and, as it were, to melt away. For what could be done? That this vast block of mechanism and gear, at once massive and delicate, condemned to fixity by its weight, delivered up in that solitude to the destructive elements, exposed in the gripe of the rock to the action of the wind and wave, could, under the frown of that implacable spot, escape from slow destruction, seemed a madness even to imagine.

The Durande was the captive of the Douvres.

How could she be extricated from that position?

How could she be delivered from her bondage?

The escape of a man is difficult; but what a problem was this—the escape of a vast and cumbrous machine.

IV
A PRELIMINARY SURVEY

GILLIATT WAS pressed on all sides by demands upon his labours. The most pressing, however, was to find a safe mooring for the barge; then a shelter for himself.

The Durande having settled down more on the larboard than on the starboard side, the right paddle-box was higher than the left.

Gilliatt ascended the paddle-box on the right. From that position, although the gut of rocks stretching in abrupt angles behind the Douvres had several elbows, he was able to study the ground-plan of the group.

This survey was the preliminary step of his operations.

The Douvres, as we have already described them, were like two high gable-ends, forming the narrow entrance to a straggling alley of small cliffs with perpendicular faces. It is not rare to find in primitive submarine formations these singular kinds of passages, which seem cut out with a hatchet.

This defile was extremely tortuous, and was never without water even in the low tides. A current, much agitated, traversed it at all times from end to end. The sharpness of its turnings was favourable or unfavourable, according to the nature of the prevailing wind; sometimes it broke the swell and caused it to fall; sometimes it exasperated it. This latter effect was the most frequent. An obstacle arouses the anger of the sea, and pushes it to excesses. The foam is the exaggeration of the waves.

The stormy winds in these narrow and tortuous passages between the rocks are subjected to a similar compression, and acquire the same malignant character. The tempest frets in its sudden imprisonment. Its bulk is still immense, but sharpened and contracted; and it strikes with the massiveness of a huge club and the keenness of an arrow. It pierces even while it strikes down. It is a hurricane contracted, like the draught through the crevice of a door.

The two chains of rocks, leaving between them this kind of street in the sea, formed stages at a lower level than the Douvres, gradually decreasing, until they sunk together at a certain distance beneath the waves.

There was another such gullet of less height than the gullet of the Douvres, but narrower still, and which formed the eastern entrance of the defile. It was evident that the double prolongation of the ridge of rocks continued the kind of street under the water as far as "The Man Rock," which stood like a square citadel at the extremity of the group.

At low water, indeed, which was the time at which Gilliatt was observing them, the two rows of sunken rock showed their tips, some high and dry, and all visible and preserving their parallel without interruption.

"The Man" formed the boundary, and buttressed on the eastern side the entire mass of the group, which was protected on the opposite side by the two Douvres.

The whole, from a bird's-eye view, appeared like a winding chaplet of rocks, having the Douvres at one extremity and "The Man" at the other.

The Douvres, taken together, were merely two gigantic shafts of granite protruding vertically and almost touching each other, and forming the crest of one of the mountainous ranges lying beneath the ocean. Those immense ridges are not only found rising out of the unfathomable deep. The surf and the squall had broken them up and divided them like the teeth of a saw. Only the tip of the ridge was visible; this was the group of rocks. The remainder, which the waves concealed, must have been enormous. The passage in which the storm had planted the Durande was the way between these two colossal shafts.

This passage, zigzag in form as the forked lightning, was of about the same width in all parts. The ocean had so fashioned it. Its eternal commotion produces sometimes those singular regularities. There is a sort of geometry in the action of the sea.

From one extremity to the other of the defile, the two parallel granite walls confronted each other at a distance which the midship frame of the Durande measured exactly. Between the two Douvres, the widening of the Little Douvre, curved and turned back as it was, had formed a space for the paddles. In any other part they must have been shattered to fragments.

The high double façade of rock within the passage was hideous to the sight. When, in the exploration of the desert of water which we call the ocean, we come upon the unknown world of the sea, all is uncouth and shapeless. So much as Gilliatt could see of the defile from the height of the wreck, was appalling. In the rocky gorges of the ocean we may often trace a strange permanent impersonation of shipwreck. The defile of the Douvres was one of these gorges, and its effect was exciting to the imagination. The oxydes of the rock showed on the escarpment here and there in red places, like marks of clotted blood; it resembled the splashes on the walls of an abattoir. Associations of the charnel-house haunted the place. The rough marine stones, diversely tinted—here by the decomposition of metallic amalgams mingling with the rock, there by the mould of dampness, manifested in places by purple scales, hideous green blotches, and ruddy splashes, awakened ideas of murder and extermination. It was like the unwashed walls of a chamber which had been the scene of an assassination; or it might have been imagined that men had been crushed to death there, leaving traces of their fate. The peaked rocks produced an indescribable impression of accumulated agonies. Certain spots appeared to be still dripping with the carnage; here the wall was wet, and it looked impossible to touch it without leaving the fingers bloody. The blight of massacre seemed everywhere. At the base of the double parallel escarpment, scattered along the water's edge, or just below the waves, or in the worn hollows of the rocks, were monstrous rounded masses of shingle, some scarlet, others black or purple, which bore a strange resemblance to internal organs of the body; they might have been taken for human lungs, or heart, or liver, scattered and putrefying in that dismal place. Giants might have been disembowelled there. From top to bottom of the granite ran long red lines, which might have been compared to oozings from a funeral bier.

Such aspects are frequent in sea caverns.

V
A WORD UPON THE SECRET CO-OPERATIONS OF THE ELEMENTS

THOSE WHO, by the disastrous chances of sea-voyages, happen to be condemned to a temporary habitation upon a rock in mid-ocean, find that the form of their inhospitable refuge is by no means a matter of indifference. There is the pyramidal-shaped rock, a single peak rising from the water; there is the circle rock somewhat resembling a round of great stones; and there is the corridor-rock. The latter is the most alarming of all. It is not only the ceaseless agony of the waves between its walls, or the tumult of the imprisoned sea; there are also certain obscure meteorological characteristics which appear to appertain to this parallelism of two marine rocks. The two straight sides seem a veritable electric battery.

The first result of the peculiar position of these corridor-rocks is an action upon the air and the water. The corridor-rock acts upon the waves and the wind mechanically by its form; galvanically, by the different magnetic action rendered possible by its vertical height, its masses in juxtaposition and contrary to each other.

This form of rock attracts to itself all the forces scattered in the winds, and exercises over the tempest a singular power of concentration.

Hence there is in the neighbourhood of these breakers a certain accentuation of storms.

It must be borne in mind that the wind is composite. The wind is believed to be simple; but it is by no means simple. Its power is not merely dynamic, it is chemical also; but this is not all, it is magnetic. Its effects are often inexplicable. The wind is as much electrical as aerial. Certain winds coincide with the *aurores boreales*. The wind blowing from the bank of the Aiguilles rolls the waves one hundred feet high; a fact observed with astonishment by Dumont-d'Urville. The corvette, he says, "knew not what to obey."

In the south seas the waters will sometimes become inflated like an outbreak of immense tumours; and at such times the ocean becomes so terrible that the savages fly to escape the sight of it. The blasts in the north seas are different. They are mingled with sharp points of ice; and their gusts, unfit to breathe, will blow the sledges of the Esquimaux backwards in the snow. Other winds burn. The simoon of Africa is the typhoon of China and the samiel of India. Simoon, typhoon, and samiel, are believed to be the names of demons. They descend from the heights of the mountains. A storm vitrified the volcano of Toluca. This hot wind, a whirlwind of inky colour, rushing upon red clouds, is alluded to in the Vedas: "Behold the black god, who comes to steal the red cows." In all these facts we trace the presence of the electric mystery.

The wind indeed is full of it; so are the waves. The sea, too, is composite in its nature. Under its waves of water which we see, it has its waves of force which are invisible. Its constituents are innumerable. Of all the elements the ocean is the most indivisible and the most profound.

Endeavour to conceive this chaos so enormous that it dwarfs all other things to one level. It is the universal recipient, reservoir of germs of life, and mould of transformations. It amasses and then disperses, it accumulates and then sows, it devours and then creates. It receives all the waste and refuse waters of the earth, and converts them into treasure. It is solid in the iceberg, liquid in the wave, fluid in the estuary. Regarded as matter, it is a mass; regarded as a force, it is an abstraction. It equalises and unites all phenomena. It may be called the infinite in combination. By force and disturbance, it arrives at transparency. It dissolves all differences, and absorbs them into its own unity. Its elements are so numerous that it becomes identity. One of its drops is complete, and represents the whole. From the abundance of its tempests, it attains equilibrium. Plato beheld the mazy dances of the spheres. Strange fact, though not the less real, the ocean, in the vast terrestrial journey round the sun, becomes, with its flux and reflux, the balance of the globe.

In a phenomenon of the sea, all other phenomena are resumed. The sea is blown out of a waterspout as from a syphon; the storm observes the principle of the pump; the lightning issues from the sea as from the air. Aboard ships dull shocks are sometimes felt, and an odour of sulphur issues from the receptacles of chain cables. The ocean boils. "The devil has put the sea in his cauldron," said De Ruyter. In certain tempests, which characterise the equinoxes and the return to equilibrium of the prolific power of nature, vessels breasting the foam seem to give out a kind of fire, phosphoric lights chase each other along the rigging, so close sometimes to the sailors at their work that the latter stretch forth their hands and try to catch, as they fly, these birds of flame. After the great earthquake of Lisbon, a blast of hot air, as from a furnace, drove before it towards the city a wave sixty feet high. The oscillation of the ocean is closely related to the convulsions of the earth.

These immeasurable forces produce sometimes extraordinary inundations. At the end of the year 1864, one of the Maldive Islands, at a hundred leagues from the Malabar coast, actually foundered in the sea. It sunk to the bottom like a shipwrecked vessel. The fishermen who sailed from it in the morning, found nothing when they returned at night; scarcely could they distinguish their villages under the sea. On this occasion boats were the spectators of the wrecks of houses.

In Europe, where nature seems restrained by the presence of civilisation, such events are rare and are thought impossible. Nevertheless, Jersey and Guernsey originally formed part of Gaul, and at the moment while we are writing these lines, an equinoctial gale has demolished a great portion of the cliff of the Firth of Forth in Scotland.

Nowhere do these terrific forces appear more formidably conjoined than in the surprising strait known as the Lyse-Fiord. The Lyse-Fiord is the most terrible of all the gut rocks of the ocean. Their terrors are there complete. It is in the northern sea, near the inhospitable Gulf of Stavanger, and in the 59th degree of latitude. The water is black and heavy, and subject to intermitting storms. In this sea, and in the midst of this solitude, rises a great sombre street—a street for no human footsteps. None ever pass through there; no ship ever ventures in. It is a corridor ten leagues in length, between two rocky walls of three thousand feet in height. Such is the passage which presents an entrance to the sea. The defile has its elbows and angles like all these streets of the sea—never straight, having been formed by the irregular action of the water. In the Lyse-Fiord, the sea is almost always tranquil; the sky above is serene; the place terrible. Where is the wind? Not on high. Where is the thunder? Not in the heavens. The wind is under the sea; the lightnings within the rock. Now and then there is a convulsion of the water. At certain moments, when there is perhaps not a cloud in the sky, nearly half way up the perpendicular rock, at a thousand or fifteen hundred feet above the water, and rather on the southern than on the northern side, the rock suddenly thunders, lightnings dart forth, and then retire like those toys which lengthen out and spring back again in the hands of children. They contract and enlarge;

strike the opposite cliff, re-enter the rock, issue forth again, recommence their play, multiply their heads and tips of flame, grow bristling with points, strike wherever they can, recommence again, and then are extinguished with a sinister abruptness. Flocks of birds fly wide in terror. Nothing is more mysterious than that artillery issuing out of the invisible. One cliff attacks the other, raining lightning blows from side to side. Their war concerns not man. It signals the ancient enmity of two rocks in the impassable gulf.

In the Lyse-Fiord, the wind whirls like the water in an estuary; the rock performs the function of the clouds; and the thunder breaks forth like volcanic fire. This strange defile is a voltaic pile; the plates of which are the double line of cliffs.

VI
A STABLE FOR THE HORSE

GILLIATT WAS sufficiently familiar with marine rocks to grapple in earnest with the Douvres. Before all, as we have just said, it was necessary to find a safe shelter for the barge.

The double row of reefs, which stretched in a sinuous form behind the Douvres, connected itself here and there with other rocks, and suggested the existence of blind passages and hollows opening out into the straggling way, and joining again to the principal defile like branches to a trunk.

The lower part of these rocks was covered with kelp, the upper part with lichens. The uniform level of the seaweed marked the line of the water at the height of the tide, and the limit of the sea in calm weather. The points which the water had not touched presented those silver and golden hues communicated to marine granite by the white and yellow lichen.

A crust of conoidical shells covered the rock at certain points, the dry rot of the granite.

At other points in the retreating angles, where fine sand had accumulated, ribbed on its surface rather by the wind than by the waves, appeared tufts of blue thistles.

In the indentations, sheltered from the winds, could be traced the little perforations made by the sea-urchin. This shelly mass of prickles, which moves about a living ball, by rolling on its spines, and the armour of which is composed of ten thousand pieces, artistically adjusted and welded together—the sea-urchin, which is popularly called, for some unknown reason, "Aristotle's lantern," wears away the granite with his five teeth, and lodges himself in the hole. It is in such holes that the samphire gatherers find them. They cut them in halves and eat them raw, like an oyster. Some steep their bread in the soft flesh. Hence its other name, "Sea-egg."

The tips of the further reefs, left out of the water by the receding tide, extended close under the escarpment of "The Man" to a sort of creek, enclosed nearly on all sides by rocky walls. Here was evidently a possible harbourage. It had the form of a horse-shoe, and opened only on one side to the east wind, which is the least violent of all winds in that sea labyrinth. The water was shut in there, and almost motionless. The shelter seemed comparatively safe. Gilliatt, moreover, had not much choice.

If he wished to take advantage of the low water, it was important to make haste.

The weather continued to be fine and calm. The insolent sea was for a while in a gentle mood.

Gilliatt descended, put on his shoes again, unmoored the cable, re-embarked, and pushed out into the water. He used the oars, coasting the side of the rock.

Having reached "The Man Rock," he examined the entrance to the little creek.

A fixed, wavy line in the motionless sea, a sort of wrinkle, imperceptible to any eye but that of a sailor, marked the channel.

Gilliatt studied for a moment its lineament, almost indistinct under the water; then he held off a little in order to veer at ease, and steer well into channel; and suddenly with a stroke of the oars he entered the little bay.

He sounded.

The anchorage appeared to be excellent.

The sloop would be protected there against almost any of the contingencies of the season.

The most formidable reefs have quiet nooks of this sort. The ports which are thus found among the breakers are like the hospitality of the fierce Bedouin—friendly and sure.

Gilliatt placed the sloop as near as he could to "The Man," but still far enough to escape grazing the rock; and he cast his two anchors.

That done, he crossed his arms, and reflected on his position.

The sloop was sheltered. Here was one problem solved. But another remained. Where could he now shelter himself?

He had the choice of two places: the sloop itself, with its corner of cabin, which was scarcely habitable, and the summit of "The Man Rock," which was not difficult to scale.

From one or other of these refuges it was possible at low water, by jumping from rock to rock, to gain the passage between the Douvres where the Durande was fixed, almost without wetting the feet.

But low water lasts but a short while, and all the rest of the time he would be cut off either from his shelter or from the wreck by more than two hundred fathoms. Swimming among breakers is difficult at all times; if there is the least commotion in the sea it is impossible.

He was driven to give up the idea of shelter in the sloop or on "The Man."

No resting-place was possible among the neighbouring rocks.

The summits of the lower ones disappeared twice a day beneath the rising tide.

The summits of the higher ones were constantly swept by the flakes of foam, and promised nothing but an inhospitable drenching.

No choice remained but the wreck itself.

Was it possible to seek refuge there?

Gilliatt hoped it might be.

VII
A CHAMBER FOR THE VOYAGER

HALF-AN-HOUR AFTERWARDS, Gilliatt having returned to the wreck, climbed to the deck, went below, and descended into the hold, completing the summary survey of his first visit.

By the help of the capstan he had raised to the deck of the Durande the package which he had made of the lading of the sloop. The capstan had worked well. Bars for turning it were not wanting. Gilliatt had only to take his choice among the heap of wreck.

He found among the fragments a chisel, dropped, no doubt, from the carpenter's box, and which he added to his little stock of tools.

Besides this—for in poverty of appliances so complete everything counts for a little—he had his jack-knife in his pocket.

Gilliatt worked the whole day long on the wreck, clearing away, propping, arranging.

At nightfall he observed the following facts:

The entire wreck shook in the wind. The carcass trembled at every step he took. There was nothing stable or strong except the portion of the hull jammed between the rocks which contained the engine. There the beams were powerfully supported by the granite walls.

Fixing his home in the Durande would be imprudent. It would increase the weight; but far from adding to her burden, it was important to lighten it. To burden the wreck in any way was indeed the very contrary of what he wanted.

The mass of ruin required, in fact, the most careful management. It was like a sick man at the approach of dissolution. The wind would do sufficient to help it to its end.

It was, moreover, unfortunate enough to be compelled to work there. The amount of disturbance which the wreck would have to withstand would necessarily distress it, perhaps beyond its strength.

Besides, if any accident should happen in the night while Gilliatt was sleeping, he must necessarily perish with the vessel. No assistance was possible; all would be over. In order to help the shattered vessel, it was absolutely necessary to remain outside it.

How to be outside and yet near it, this was the problem.

The difficulty became more complicated as he considered it.

Where could he find a shelter under such conditions?

Gilliatt reflected.

There remained nothing but the two Douvres. They seemed hopeless enough.

From below, it was possible to distinguish upon the upper plateau of the Great Douvre a sort of protuberance.

High rocks with flattened summits, like the Great Douvre and "The Man," are a sort of decapitated peaks. They abound among the mountains and in the ocean. Certain rocks, particularly those which are met with in the open sea, bear marks like half-felled trees. They have the appearance of having received blows from a hatchet. They have been subjected, in fact, to the blows of the gale, that indefatigable pioneer of the sea.

There are other still more profound causes of marine convulsions. Hence the innumerable bruises upon these primeval masses of granite. Some of these sea giants have their heads struck off.

Sometimes these heads, from some inexplicable cause, do not fall, but remain shattered on the summit of the mutilated trunk. This singularity is by no means rare. The Devil's Rock, at Guernsey, and the Table, in the Valley of Anweiler, illustrate some of the most surprising features of this strange geological enigma.

Some such phenomena had probably fashioned the summit of the Great Douvre.

If the protuberance which could be observed on the plateau were not a natural irregularity in the stone, it must necessarily be some remaining fragment of the shattered summit.

Perhaps the fragment might contain some excavation—some hole into which a man could creep for cover. Gilliatt asked for no more.

But how could he reach the plateau? How could he scale that perpendicular wall, hard and polished as a pebble, half covered with the growth of glutinous confervæ, and having the slippery look of a soapy surface?

The ridge of the plateau was at least thirty feet above the deck of the Durande.

Gilliatt took out of his box of tools the knotted cord, hooked it to his belt by the grapnel, and set to work to scale the Little Douvre. The ascent became more difficult as he climbed. He had forgotten to take off his shoes, a fact which increased the difficulty. With great labour and straining, however, he reached the point. Safely arrived there, he raised himself and stood erect. There was scarcely room for his two feet. To make it his lodging would be difficult. A Stylite might have contented himself there; Gilliatt, more luxurious in his requirements, wanted something more commodious.

The Little Douvre, leaning towards the great one, looked from a distance as if it was saluting it, and the space between the Douvres, which was some score of feet below, was only eight or ten at the highest points.

From the spot to which he had climbed, Gilliatt saw more distinctly the rocky excrescence which partly covered the plateau of the Great Douvre.

This plateau rose three fathoms at least above his head.

A precipice separated him from it. The curved escarpment of the Little Douvre sloped away out of sight beneath him.

He detached the knotted rope from his belt, took a rapid glance at the dimensions of the rock, and slung the grapnel up to the plateau.

The grapnel scratched the rock, and slipped. The knotted rope with the hooks at its end fell down beneath his feet, swinging against the side of the little Douvre.

He renewed the attempt; slung the rope further, aiming at the granite protuberance, in which he could perceive crevices and scratches.

The cast was, this time, so neat and skilful, that the hooks caught.

He pulled from below. A portion of the rock broke away, and the knotted rope with its heavy iron came down once more, striking the escarpment beneath his feet.

He slung the grapnel a third time.

It did not fall.

He put a strain upon the rope; it resisted. The grapnel was firmly anchored.

The hooks had caught in some fracture of the plateau which he could not see.

It was necessary to trust his life to that unknown support.

He did not hesitate.

The matter was urgent. He was compelled to take the shortest route.

Moreover, to descend again to the deck of the Durande, in order to devise some other step, was impossible. A slip was probable, and a fall almost certain. It was easier to climb than to descend.

Gilliatt's movements were decisive, as are those of all good sailors. He never wasted force. He always proportioned his efforts to the work in hand. Hence the prodigies of strength which he executed with ordinary muscles. His biceps were no more powerful than that of ordinary men; but his heart was firmer. He added, in fact, to strength which is physical, energy which belongs to the moral faculties.

The feat to be accomplished was appalling.

It was to cross the space between the two Douvres, hanging only by this slender line.

Oftentimes in the path of duty and devotedness, the figure of death rises before men to present these terrible questions:

Wilt thou do this? asks the shadow.

Gilliatt tested the cord again; the grappling-iron held firm.

Wrapping his left hand in his handkerchief, he grasped the knotted cord with his right hand, which he covered with his left; then stretching out one foot, and striking out sharply with the other against the rock, in order that the impetus might prevent the rope twisting, he precipitated himself from the height of the Little Douvre on to the escarpment of the great one.

The shock was severe.

There was a rebound.

His clenched fists struck the rocks in their turn; the handkerchief had loosened, and they were scratched; they had indeed narrowly escaped being crushed.

Gilliatt remained hanging there a moment dizzy.

He was sufficiently master of himself not to let go his hold of the cord.

A few moments passed in jerks and oscillations before he could catch the cord with his feet; but he succeeded at last.

Recovering himself, and holding the cord at last between his naked feet as with two hands, he gazed into the depth below.

He had no anxiety about the length of the cord, which had many a time served him for great heights. The cord, in fact, trailed upon the deck of the Durande.

Assured of being able to descend again, he began to climb hand over hand, and still clinging with his feet.

In a few moments he had gained the summit.

Never before had any creature without wings found a footing there. The plateau was covered in parts with the dung of birds. It was an irregular trapezium, a mass struck off from the colossal granitic prism of the Great Douvre. This block was hollowed in the centre like a basin—a work of the rain.

Gilliatt, in fact, had guessed correctly.

At the southern angle of the block, he found a mass of superimposed rocks, probably fragments of the fallen summit. These rocks, looking like a heap of giant paving-stones, would have left room for a wild beast, if one could have found its way there, to secrete himself between them. They supported themselves confusedly one against the other, leaving interstices like a heap of ruins. They formed neither grottoes nor caves, but the pile was full of holes like a sponge. One of these holes was large enough to admit a man.

This recess had a flooring of moss and a few tufts of grass. Gilliatt could fit himself in it as in a kind of sheath. The recess at its entrance was about two feet high. It contracted towards the bottom. Stone coffins sometimes have this form. The mass of rocks behind lying towards the south-west, the recess was sheltered from the showers, but was open to the cold north wind.

Gilliatt was satisfied with the place.

The two chief problems were solved; the sloop had a harbour, and he had found a shelter.

The chief merit of his cave was its accessibility from the wreck.

The grappling-iron of the knotted cord having fallen between two blocks, had become firmly hooked, but Gilliatt rendered it more difficult to give way by rolling a huge stone upon it.

He was now free to operate at leisure upon the Durande.

Henceforth he was at home.

The Great Douvre was his dwelling; the Durande was his workshop.

Nothing was more simple for him than going to and fro, ascending and descending.

He dropped down easily by the knotted cord on to the deck.

The day's work was a good one, the enterprise had begun well; he was satisfied, and began to feel hungry.

He untied his basket of provisions, opened his knife, cut a slice of smoked beef, took a bite out of his brown loaf, drank a draught from his can of fresh water, and supped admirably.

To do well and eat well are two satisfactions. A full stomach resembles an easy conscience.

This supper was ended, and there was still before him a little more daylight. He took advantage of it to begin the lightening of the wreck—an urgent necessity.

He had passed part of the day in gathering up the fragments. He put on one side, in the strong compartment which contained the machine, all that might become of use to him, such as wood, iron, cordage, and canvas. What was useless he cast into the sea.

The cargo of the sloop hoisted on to the deck by the capstan, compact as he had made it, was an encumbrance. Gilliatt surveyed the species of niche, at a height within his reach, in the side of the Little Douvre. These natural closets, not shut in, it is true, are often seen in the rocks. It struck him that it was possible to trust some stores to this depôt, and he accordingly placed in the back of the recess his two boxes containing his tools and his clothing, and his two bags holding the rye-meal and the biscuit. In the front—a little too near the edge perhaps, but he had no other place—he rested his basket of provisions.

He had taken care to remove from the box of clothing his sheepskin, his loose coat with a hood, and his waterproof overalls.

To lessen the hold of the wind upon the knotted cord, he made the lower extremity fast to one of the riders of the Durande.

The Durande being much driven in, this rider was bent a good deal, and it held the end of the cord as firmly as a tight hand.

There was still the difficulty of the upper end of the cord. To control the lower part was well, but at the summit of the escarpment at the spot where the knotted cord met the ridge of the plateau, there was reason to fear that it would be fretted and worn away by the sharp angle of the rock.

Gilliatt searched in the heap of rubbish in reserve, and took from it some rags of sail-cloth, and from a bunch of old cables he pulled out some strands of rope-yarn with which he filled his pockets.

A sailor would have guessed that he intended to bind with these pieces of sail-cloth and ends of yarn the part of the knotted rope upon the edge of the rock, so as to preserve it from all friction—an operation which is called "keckling."

Having provided himself with these things, he drew on his overalls over his legs, put on his waterproof coat over his jacket, drew its hood over his red cap, hung the sheepskin round his neck by the two legs, and clothed in this complete panoply, he grasped the cord, now firmly fixed to the side of the Great Douvre, and mounted to the assault of that sombre citadel in the sea.

In spite of his scratched hands, Gilliatt easily regained the summit.

The last pale tints of sunset were fading in the sky. It was night upon the sea below. A little light still lingered upon the height of the Douvre.

Gilliatt took advantage of this remains of daylight to bind the knotted rope. He wound it round again and again at the part which passed over the edge of the rock, with a bandage of several thicknesses of canvas strongly tied at every turn. The whole resembled in some degree the padding which actresses place upon their knees, to prepare them for the agonies and supplications of the fifth act.

This binding completely accomplished, Gilliatt rose from his stooping position.

For some moments, while he had been busied in his task, he had had a confused sense of a singular fluttering in the air.

It resembled, in the silence of the evening, the noise which an immense bat might make with the beating of its wings.

Gilliatt raised his eyes.

A great black circle was revolving over his head in the pale twilight sky.

Such circles are seen in pictures round the heads of saints. These, however, are golden on a dark ground, while the circle around Gilliatt was dark upon a pale ground. The effect was strange. It spread round the Great Douvre like the aureole of night.

The circle drew nearer, then retired; grew narrower, and then spread wide again.

It was an immense flight of gulls, seamews, and cormorants; a vast multitude of affrighted sea birds.

The Great Douvre was probably their lodging, and they were coming to rest for the night. Gilliatt had taken a chamber in their home. It was evident that their unexpected fellow-lodger disturbed them.

A man there was an object they had never beheld before.

Their wild flutter continued for some time.

They seemed to be waiting for the stranger to leave the place.

Gilliatt followed them dreamily with his eyes.

The flying multitude seemed at last to give up their design. The circle suddenly took a spiral form, and the cloud of sea birds came down upon "The Man Rock" at the extremity of the group, where they seemed to be conferring and deliberating.

Gilliatt, after settling down in his alcove of granite, and covering a stone for a pillow for his head, could hear the birds for a long time chattering one after the other, or croaking, as if in turns.

Then they were silent, and all were sleeping—the birds upon their rock, Gilliatt upon his.

VIII
IMPORTUNÆQUE VOLUCRES

GILLIATT slept well; but he was cold, and this awoke him from time to time. He had naturally placed his feet at the bottom, and his head at the entrance to his cave. He had not taken the precaution to remove from his couch a number of angular stones, which did not by any means conduce to sleep.

Now and then he half-opened his eyes.

At intervals he heard loud noises. It was the rising tide entering the caverns of the rocks with a sound like the report of a cannon.

All the circumstances of his position conspired to produce the effect of a vision. Hallucinations seemed to surround him. The vagueness of night increased this effect; and Gilliatt felt himself plunged into some region of unrealities. He asked himself if all were not a dream?

Then he dropped to sleep again; and this time, in a veritable dream, found himself at the Bû de la Rue, at the Bravées, at St. Sampson. He heard Déruchette singing; he was among realities. While he slept he seemed to wake and live; when he awoke again he appeared to be sleeping.

In truth, from this time forward he lived in a dream.

Towards the middle of the night a confused murmur filled the air. Gilliatt had a vague consciousness of it even in his sleep. It was perhaps a breeze arising.

Once, when awakened by a cold shiver, he opened his eyes a little wider than before. Clouds were moving in the zenith; the moon was flying through the sky, with one large star following closely in her footsteps.

Gilliatt's mind was full of the incidents of his dreams. The wild outlines of things in the darkness were exaggerated by this confusion with the impressions of his sleeping hours.

At daybreak he was half-frozen; but he slept soundly.

The sudden daylight aroused him from a slumber which might have been dangerous. The alcove faced the rising sun.

Gilliatt yawned, stretched himself, and sprang out of his sleeping place.

His sleep had been so deep that he could not at first recall the circumstances of the night before.

By degrees the feeling of reality returned, and he began to think of breakfast.

The weather was calm; the sky cool and serene. The clouds were gone; the night wind had cleared the horizon, and the sun rose brightly. Another fine day was commencing. Gilliatt felt joyful.

He threw off his overcoat and his leggings; rolled them up in the sheepskin with the wool inside, fastened the roll with a length of rope-yarn, and pushed it into the cavern for a shelter in case of rain.

This done, he made his bed—an operation which consisted in removing the stones which had annoyed him in the night.

His bed made, he slid down the cord on to the deck of the Durande, and approached the niche where he had placed his basket of provisions. As it was very near the edge, the wind in the night had swept it down, and rolled it into the sea.

It was evident that it would not be easy to recover it. There was a spirit of mischief and malice in a wind which had sought out his basket in that position.

It was the commencement of hostilities. Gilliatt understood the token.

To those who live in a state of rude familiarity with the sea, it becomes natural to regard the wind as an individuality, and the rocks as sentient beings.

Nothing remained but the biscuit and the rye-meal, except the shellfish, on which the shipwrecked sailor had supported a lingering existence upon "The Man Rock."

It was useless to think of subsisting by net or line fishing. Fish are naturally averse to the neighbourhood of rocks. The drag and bow net fishers would waste their labour among the breakers, the points of which would be destructive only to their nets.

Gilliatt breakfasted on a few limpets which he plucked with difficulty from the rocks. He narrowly escaped breaking his knife in the attempt.

While he was making his spare meal, he was sensible of a strange disturbance on the sea. He looked around.

It was a swarm of gulls and seamews which had just alighted upon some low rocks, and were beating their wings, tumbling over each other, screaming, and shrieking. All were swarming noisily upon the same point. This horde with beaks and talons were evidently pillaging something.

It was Gilliatt's basket.

Rolled down upon a sharp point by the wind, the basket had burst open. The birds had gathered round immediately. They were carrying off in their beaks all sorts of fragments of provisions. Gilliatt recognised from the distance his smoked beef and his salted fish.

It was their turn now to be aggressive. The birds had taken to reprisals. Gilliatt had robbed them of their lodging, they deprived him of his supper.

IX
THE ROCK, AND HOW GILLIATT USED IT

A WEEK PASSED.

Although it was in the rainy season no rain fell, a fact for which Gilliatt felt thankful. But the work he had entered upon surpassed, in appearance at least, the power of human hand or skill. Success appeared so improbable that the attempt seemed like madness.

It is not until a task is fairly grappled with that its difficulties and perils become fully manifest. There is nothing like making a commencement for making evident how difficult it will be to come to the end. Every beginning is a struggle against resistance. The first step is an exorable undeceiver. A difficulty which we come to touch pricks like a thorn.

Gilliatt found himself immediately in the presence of obstacles.

In order to raise the engine of the Durande from the wreck in which it was three-fourths buried, with any chance of success—in order to accomplish a salvage in such a place and in such a season, it seemed almost necessary to be a legion of men. Gilliatt was alone; a complete apparatus of carpenters' and engineers' tools and implements were wanted. Gilliatt had a saw, a hatchet, a chisel, and a hammer. He wanted both a good workshop and a good shed; Gilliatt had not a roof to cover him. Provisions, too, were necessary, but he had not even bread.

Any one who could have seen Gilliatt working on the rock during all that first work might have been puzzled to determine the nature of his operations. He seemed to be no longer thinking either of the Durande or the two Douvres. He was busy only among the breakers: he seemed absorbed in saving the smaller parts of the shipwreck. He took advantage of every high tide to strip the reefs of everything which the shipwreck had distributed among them. He went from rock to rock, picking up whatever the sea had scattered—tatters of sail-cloth, pieces of iron, splinters of panels, shattered planking, broken yards—here a beam, there a chain, there a pulley.

At the same time he carefully surveyed all the recesses of the rocks. To his great disappointment none were habitable. He had suffered from the cold in the night, where he lodged between the stones on the summit of the rock, and he would gladly have found some better refuge.

Two of those recesses were somewhat extensive. Although the natural pavement of rock was almost everywhere oblique and uneven it was possible to stand upright, and even to walk within them. The wind and the rain wandered there at will, but the highest tides did not reach them. They were near the Little Douvre, and were approachable at any time. Gilliatt decided that one should serve him as a storehouse, the other as a forge.

With all the sail, rope-bands, and all the reef-earrings he could collect, he made packages of the fragments of wreck, tying up the wood and iron in bundles, and the canvas in parcels. He lashed all these together carefully. As the rising tide approached these packages, he began to drag them across the reefs to his storehouse. In the hollow of the rocks he had found a top rope, by means of which he had been able to haul even the large pieces of timber. In the same manner he dragged from the sea the numerous portions of chains which he found scattered among the breakers.

Gilliatt worked at these tasks with astonishing activity and tenacity. He accomplished whatever he attempted—nothing could withstand his ant-like perseverance.

At the end of the week he had gathered into this granite warehouse of marine stores, and ranged into order, all this miscellaneous and shapeless mass of salvage. There was a corner for the tacks of sails and a corner for sheets. Bow-lines were not mixed with halliards; parrels were arranged according to their number of holes. The coverings of rope-yarn, unwound from the broken anchorings, were tied in bunches; the dead-eyes without pulleys were separated from the tackle-blocks. Belaying-pins, bullseyes, preventer-shrouds, down-hauls, snatch-blocks, pendents, kevels, trusses, stoppers, sailbooms, if they were not completely damaged by the storm, occupied different compartments. All the cross-beams, timber-work, up-rights, stanchions, mast-heads, binding-strakes, portlids, and clamps, were heaped up apart. Wherever it was possible, he had fixed the fragments of planks, from the vessel's bottom, one in the other. There was no confusion between reef-points and nippers of the cable, nor of crow's-feet with towlines; nor of pulleys of the small with pulleys of the large ropes; nor of fragments from the waist with fragments from the stern. A place had been reserved for a portion of the cat-harpings of the Durande, which had supported the shrouds of the topmast and the futtock-shrouds. Every portion had its place. The entire wreck was there classed and ticketed. It was a sort of chaos in a storehouse.

A stay-sail, fixed by huge stones, served, though torn and damaged, to protect what the rain might have injured.

Shattered as were the bows of the wreck, he had succeeded in saving the two cat-heads with their three pulley-blocks.

He had found the bowsprit too, and had had much trouble in unrolling its gammoning; it was very hard and tight, having been, according to custom, made by the help of the windlass, and in dry weather. Gilliatt, however, persevered until he had detached it, this thick rope promising to be very useful to him.

He had been equally successful in discovering the little anchor which had become fast in the hollow of a reef, where the receding tide had left it uncovered.

In what had been Tangrouille's cabin he had found a piece of chalk, which he preserved carefully. He reflected that he might have some marks to make.

A fire-bucket and several pails in pretty good condition completed this stock of working materials.

All that remained of the store of coal of the Durande he carried into the warehouse.

In a week this salvage of débris was finished; the rock was swept clean, and the Durande was lightened. Nothing remained now to burden the hull except the machinery.

The portion of the fore-side bulwarks which hung to it did not distress the hull. The mass hung without dragging, being partly sustained by a ledge of rock. It was, however, large and broad, and heavy to drag, and would have encumbered his warehouse too much. This bulwarking looked something like a boat-builder's stocks. Gilliatt left it where it was.

He had been profoundly thoughtful during all this labour. He had sought in vain for the figure-head—the "doll," as the Guernsey folks called it, of the Durande. It was one of the things which the waves had carried away for ever. Gilliatt would have given his hands to find it—if he had not had such peculiar need of them at that time.

At the entrance to the storehouse and outside were two heaps of refuse—a heap of iron good for forging, and a heap of wood good for burning.

Gilliatt was always at work at early dawn. Except his time of sleep, he did not take a moment of repose.

The wild sea birds, flying hither and thither, watched him at his work.

X
THE FORGE

THE WAREHOUSE COMPLETED, Gilliatt constructed his forge.

The other recess which he had chosen had within it a species of passage like a gallery in a mine of pretty good depth. He had had at first an idea of making this his lodging, but the draught was so continuous and so persevering in this passage that he had been compelled to give it up. This current of air, incessantly renewed, first gave him the notion of the forge. Since it could not be his chamber, he was determined that this cabin should be his smithy. To bend obstacles to our purposes is a great step towards triumph. The wind was Gilliatt's enemy. He had set about making it his servant.

The proverb applied to certain kinds of men—"Fit for everything, good for nothing"—may also be applied to the hollows of rocks. They give no advantages gratuitously. On one side we find a hollow fashioned conveniently in the shape of a bath; but it allows the water to run away through a fissure. Here is a rocky chamber, but without a roof; here a bed of moss, but oozy with wet; here an arm-chair, but one of hard stone.

The forge which Gilliatt intended was roughly sketched out by nature; but nothing could be more troublesome than to reduce this rough sketch to manageable shape, to transform this cavern into a laboratory and smith's shop. With three or four large rocks, shaped like a funnel, and ending in a narrow fissure, chance had constructed there a species of vast ill-shapen blower, of very different power to those huge old forge bellows of fourteen feet long, which poured out at every breath ninety-eight thousand inches of air. This was quite a different sort of construction. The proportions of the hurricane cannot be definitely measured.

This excess of force was an embarrassment. The incessant draught was difficult to regulate.

The cavern had two inconveniences; the wind traversed it from end to end; so did the water.

This was not the water of the sea, but a continual little trickling stream, more like a spring than a torrent.

The foam, cast incessantly by the surf upon the rocks and sometimes more than a hundred feet in the air, had filled with sea water a natural cave situated among the high rocks overlooking the excavation. The overflowings of this reservoir caused, a little behind the escarpment, a fall of water of about an inch in breadth, and descending four or five fathoms. An occasional contribution from the rains also helped to fill the reservoir. From time to time a passing cloud dropped a shower into the rocky basin, always over-flowing. The water was brackish, and unfit to drink, but clear. This rill of water fell in graceful drops from the extremities of the long marine grasses, as from the ends of a length of hair.

He was struck with the idea of making this water serve to regulate the draught in the cave. By the means of a funnel made of planks roughly and hastily put together to form two or three pipes, one of which was fitted with a valve, and of a large tub arranged as a lower reservoir, without checks or counterweight, and completed solely by air-tight stuffing above and air-holes below, Gilliatt, who, as we have already said, was handy at the forge and at the mechanic's bench, succeeded in constructing, instead of the forge-bellows, which he did not possess, an apparatus less perfect than what is known now-a-days by the name of a "cagniardelle," but less rude than what the people of the Pyrenees anciently called a "trompe."

He had some rye-meal, and he manufactured with it some paste. He had also some white rope, which picked out into tow. With this paste and tow, and some bits of wood, he stopped all the crevices of the rock, leaving only a little air passage made of a powder-flask which he had found aboard the Durande, and which had served for loading the signal gun. This powder-flask was directed horizontally to a large stone, which Gilliatt made the hearth of the forge. A stopper made of a piece of tow served to close it in case of need.

After this, he heaped up the wood and coal upon the hearth, struck his steel against the bare rock, caught a spark upon a handful of loose tow, and having ignited it, soon lighted his forge fire.

He tried the blower: it worked well.

Gilliatt felt the pride of a Cyclops: he was the master of air, water, and fire. Master of the air; for he had given a kind of lungs to the wind, and changed the rude draught into a useful blower. Master of water, for he had converted the little cascade into a "trompe." Master of fire, for out of this moist rock he had struck a flame.

The cave being almost everywhere open to the sky, the smoke issued freely, blackening the curved escarpment. The rocks which seemed destined for ever to receive only the white foam, became now familiar with the blackening smoke.

Gilliatt selected for an anvil a large smooth round stone, of about the required shape and dimensions. It formed a base for the blows of his hammer; but one that might fly and was very dangerous. One of the extremities of this block, rounded and ending in a point, might, for want of anything better, serve instead of a conoid bicorn; but the other kind of bicorn of the

pyramidal form was wanting. It was the ancient stone anvil of the Troglo-
dytes. The surface, polished by the waves, had almost the firmness of steel.

He regretted not having brought his anvil. As he did not know that the
Durande had been broken in two by the tempest, he had hoped to find the
carpenter's chest and all his tools generally kept in the forehold. But it was
precisely the fore-part of the vessel which had been carried away.

These two excavations which he had found in the rock were contiguous.
The warehouse and the forge communicated with each other.

Every evening, when his work was ended, he supped on a little biscuit,
moistened in water, a sea-urchin or a crab, or a few *châtaignes de mer*, the
only food to be found among those rocks; and shivering like his knotted
cord, mounted again to sleep in his cell upon the Great Douvre.

The very materialism of his daily occupation increased the kind of
abstraction in which he lived. To be steeped too deeply in realities is in itself
a cause of visionary moods. His bodily labour, with its infinite variety of
details, detracted nothing from the sensation of stupor which arose from the
strangeness of his position and his work. Ordinary bodily fatigue is a thread
which binds man to the earth; but the very peculiarity of the enterprise he
was engaged in kept him in a sort of ideal twilight region. There were times
when he seemed to be striking blows with his hammer in the clouds. At
other moments his tools appeared to him like arms. He had a singular feeling,
as if he was repressing or providing against some latent danger of attack.
Untwisting ropes, unravelling threads of yarn in a sail, or propping up a
couple of beams, appeared to him at such times like fashioning engines of
war. The thousand minute pains which he took about his salvage operations
produced at last in his mind the effect of precautions against aggressions
little concealed, and easy to anticipate. He did not know the words which
express the ideas, but he perceived them. His instincts became less and less
those of the worker; his habits more and more those of the savage man.

His business there was to subdue and direct the powers of nature. He
had an indistinct perception of it. A strange enlargement of his ideas!

Around him, far as eye could reach, was the vast prospect of endless
labour wasted and lost. Nothing is more disturbing to the mind than the
contemplation of the diffusion of forces at work in the unfathomable and
illimitable space of the ocean. The mind tends naturally to seek the object

of these forces. The unceasing movement in space, the unwearying sea, the clouds that seem ever hurrying somewhere, the vast mysterious prodigality of effort, all this is a problem. Whither does this perpetual movement tend? What do these winds construct? What do these giant blows build up? These howlings, shocks, and sobbings of the storm, what do they end in? and what is the business of this tumult? The ebb and flow of these questionings is eternal, as the flux and reflux of the sea itself. Gilliatt could answer for himself; his work he knew, but the agitation which surrounded him far and wide at all times perplexed him confusedly with its eternal questionings. Unknown to himself, mechanically, by the mere pressure of external things, and without any other effect than a strange, unconscious bewilderment, Gilliatt, in this dreamy mood, blended his own toil somehow with the prodigious wasted labour of the sea-waves. How, indeed, in that position, could he escape the influence of that mystery of the dread, laborious ocean? how do other than meditate, so far as meditation was possible, upon the vacillation of the waves, the perseverance of the foam, the imperceptible wearing down of rocks, the furious beatings of the four winds? How terrible that perpetual recommencement, that ocean bed, those Danaïdes-like clouds, all that travail and weariness for no end!

For no end? Not so! But for what? O Thou Infinite Unknown, Thou only knowest!

XI
DISCOVERY

A ROCK NEAR the coast is sometimes visited by men; a rock in mid-ocean never. What object could any one have there? No supplies can be drawn thence; no fruit-trees are there, no pasturage, no beasts, no springs of water fitted for man's use. It stands aloft, a rock with its steep sides and summits above water, and its sharp points below. Nothing is to be found there but inevitable shipwreck.

This kind of rocks, which in the old sea dialect were called *Isolés*, are, as we have said, strange places. The sea is alone there; she works her own will. No token of terrestrial life disturbs her. Man is a terror to the sea; she is shy of his approach, and hides from him her deeds. But she is bolder among the lone sea rocks. The everlasting soliloquy of the waves is not troubled there. She labours at the rock, repairs its damage, sharpens its peaks, makes them rugged or renews them. She pierces the granite, wears down the soft stone, and denudes the hard; she rummages, dismembers, bores, perforates, and grooves; she fills the rock with cells, and makes it sponge-like, hollows out the inside, or sculptures it without. In that secret mountain which is hers, she makes to herself caves, sanctuaries, palaces. She has her splendid and monstrous vegetation, composed of floating plants which bite, and of monsters which take root; and she hides away all this terrible magnificence in the twilight of her deeps. Among the isolated rocks no eye watches over her; no spy embarrasses her movements. It is there that she develops at liberty her mysterious side, which is inaccessible to man. Here she keeps all strange secretions of life. Here that the unknown wonders of the sea are assembled.

Promontories, forelands, capes, headlands, breakers, and shoals are veritable constructions. The geological changes of the earth are trifling compared with the vast operations of the ocean. These breakers, these habitations in the sea, these pyramids, and spouts of the foam are the practicers of a mysterious art which the author of this book has somewhere called "the Art of Nature." Their style is known by its vastness. The effects of chance seem here design. Its works are multiform. They abound in the mazy entanglement of the rock-coral groves, the sublimity of the cathedral, the extravagance of the pagoda, the amplitude of the mountain, the delicacy of the jeweller's work, the horror of the sepulchre. They are filled with cells like the wasps' nest, with dens like menageries, with subterranean passages like the haunts of moles, with dungeons like Bastiles, with ambuscades like a camp. They have their doors, but they are barricaded; their columns, but they are shattered; their towers, but they are tottering; their bridges, but they are broken. Their compartments are unaccommodating; these are fitted for the birds only, those only for fish. They are impassable. Their architectural style is variable and inconsistent; it regards or disregards at will the laws of equilibrium, breaks off, stops short, begins in the form of an archivolt, and ends in an architrave, block on block. Enceladus is the mason. A wondrous science of dynamics exhibits here its problems ready solved. Fearful overhanging blocks threaten, but fall not: the human mind cannot guess what power supports their bewildering masses. Blind entrances, gaps, and ponderous suspensions multiply and vary infinitely. The laws which regulate this Babel baffle human induction. The great unknown architect plans nothing, but succeeds in all. Rocks massed together in confusion form a monstrous monument, defy reason, yet maintain equilibrium. Here is something more than strength; it is eternity. But order is wanting. The wild tumult of the waves seems to have passed into the wilderness of stone. It is like a tempest petrified and fixed for ever. Nothing is more impressive than that wild architecture; always standing, yet always seeming to fall; in which everything appears to give support, and yet to withdraw it. A struggle between opposing lines has resulted in the construction of an edifice, filled with traces of the efforts of those old antagonists, the ocean and the storm.

This architecture has its terrible masterpieces, of which the Douvres rock was one.

The sea had fashioned and perfected it with a sinister solicitude. The snarling waters licked it into shape. It was hideous, treacherous, dark, full of hollows.

It had a complete system of submarine caverns ramifying and losing themselves in unfathomed depths. Some of the orifices of this labyrinth of passages were left exposed by the low tides. A man might enter there, but at his risk and peril.

Gilliatt determined to explore all these grottoes, for the purpose of his salvage labour. There was not one which was not repulsive. Everywhere about the caverns that strange aspect of an abattoir, those singular traces of slaughter, appeared again in all the exaggeration of the ocean. No one who has not seen in excavations of this kind, upon the walls of everlasting granite, these hideous natural frescoes, can form a notion of their singularity.

These pitiless caverns, too, were false and sly. Woe betide him who would loiter there. The rising tide filled them to their roofs.

Rock limpets and edible mosses abounded among them.

They were obstructed by quantities of shingle, heaped together in their recesses. Some of their huge smooth stones weighed more than a ton. They were of every proportion, and of every hue; but the greater part were blood coloured. Some, covered with a hairy and glutinous seaweed, seemed like large green moles boring a way into the rock.

Several of the caverns terminated abruptly in the form of a demi-cupola. Others, main arteries of a mysterious circulation, lengthened out in the rock in dark and tortuous fissures. They were the alleys of the submarine city; but they gradually contracted from their entrances, and at length left no way for a man to pass. Peering in by the help of a lighted torch, he could see nothing but dark hollows dripping with moisture.

One day, Gilliatt, exploring, ventured into one of these fissures. The state of the tide favoured the attempt. It was a beautiful day of calm and sunshine. There was no fear of any accident from the sea to increase the danger.

Two necessities, as we have said, compelled him to undertake these explorations. He had to gather fragments of wreck and other things to aid him in his labour, and to search for crabs and crayfish for his food. Shell-fish had begun to fail him on the rocks.

The fissure was narrow, and the passage difficult. Gilliatt could see daylight beyond. He made an effort, contorted himself as much as he could, and penetrated into the cave as far as he was able.

He had reached, without suspecting it, the interior of the rock, upon the point of which Clubin had steered the Durande. Though abrupt and almost inaccessible without, it was hollowed within. It was full of galleries, pits, and chambers, like the tomb of an Egyptian king. This network of caverns was one of the most complicated of all that labyrinth, a labour of the water, the undermining of the restless sea. The branches of the subterranean maze probably communicated with the sea without by more than one issue, some gaping at the level of the waves, the others profound and invisible. It was near here, but Gilliatt knew it not, that Clubin had dived into the sea.

In this crocodile cave—where crocodiles, it is true, were not among the dangers—Gilliatt wound about, clambered, struck his head occasionally, bent low and rose again, lost his footing and regained it many times, advancing laboriously. By degrees the gallery widened; a glimmer of daylight appeared, and he found himself suddenly at the entrance to a cavern of a singular kind.

XII

THE INTERIOR OF AN EDIFICE UNDER THE SEA

THE GLEAM of daylight was fortunate.

One step further, and Gilliatt must have fallen into a pool, perhaps without bottom. The waters of these cavern pools are so cold and paralysing as to prove fatal to the strongest swimmers.

There is, moreover, no means of remounting or of hanging on to any part of their steep walls.

He stopped short. The crevice from which he had just issued ended in a narrow and slippery projection, a species of corbel in the peaked wall. He leaned against the side and surveyed it.

He was in a large cave. Over his head was a roofing not unlike the inside of a vast skull, which might have been imagined to have been recently dissected. The dripping ribs of the striated indentations of the roof seemed to imitate the branching fibres and jagged sutures of the bony cranium. A stony ceiling and a watery floor. The rippled waters between the four walls of the cave were like wavy paving tiles. The grotto was shut in on all sides. Not a window, not even an air-hole visible. No breach in the wall, no crack in the roof. The light came from below and through the water, a strange, sombre light.

Gilliatt, the pupils of whose eyes had contracted during his explorations of the dusky corridor, could distinguish everything about him in the pale glimmer.

He was familiar, from having often visited them, with the caves of Plémont in Jersey, the Creux-Maillé at Guernsey, the Boutiques at Sark; but none of these marvellous caverns could compare with the subterranean and submarine chamber into which he had made his way.

Under the water at his feet he could see a sort of drowned arch. This arch, a natural ogive, fashioned by the waves, was glittering between its two dark and profound supports. It was by this submerged porch that the daylight entered into the cavern from the open sea. A strange light shooting upward from a gulf.

The glimmer spread out beneath the waters like a large fan, and was reflected on the rocks. Its direct rays, divided into long, broad shafts, appeared in strong relief against the darkness below, and becoming brighter or more dull from one rock to another, looked as if seen here and there through plates of glass. There was light in that cave it is true; but it was the light that was unearthly. The beholder might have dreamed that he had descended in some other planet. The glimmer was an enigma, like the glaucous light from the eye-pupil of a Sphinx. The whole cave represented the interior of a death's-head of enormous proportions, and of a strange splendour. The vault was the hollow of the brain, the arch the mouth; the sockets of the eyes were wanting. The cavern, alternately swallowing and rendering up the flux and reflux through its mouth wide opened to the full noonday without, seemed to drink in the light and vomit forth bitterness; a type of some beings intelligent and evil. The light, in traversing this inlet through the vitreous medium of the sea-water, became green, like a ray of starlight from Aldebaran. The water, filled with the moist light, appeared like a liquid emerald. A tint of aqua-marina of marvellous delicacy spread a soft hue throughout the cavern. The roof, with its cerebral lobes, and its rampant ramifications, like the fibres of nerves, gave out a tender reflection of chrys-oprase. The ripples reflected on the roof were falling in order and dissolving again incessantly, and enlarging and contracting their glittering scales in a mysterious and mazy dance. They gave the beholder an impression of something weird and spectral: he wondered what prey secured, or what ex-pectation about to be realised, moved with a joyous thrill this magnificent network of living fire. From the projections of the vault, and the angles of the rock, hung lengths of delicate fibrous plants, bathing their roots probably through the granite in some upper pool of water, and distilling from their silky ends one after the other, a drop of water like a pearl. These drops fell in the water now and then with a gentle splash. The effect of the scene was singular. Nothing more beautiful could be imagined; nothing more mournful could anywhere be found.

It was a wondrous palace, in which death sat smiling and content.

XIII
WHAT WAS SEEN THERE; AND WHAT PERCEIVED DIMLY

A PLACE OF SHADE, which yet was dazzling to the eyes—such was this surprising cavern.

The beating of the sea made itself felt throughout the cavern. The oscillation without raised and depressed the level of the waters within, with the regularity of respiration. A mysterious spirit seemed to fill this great organism, as it swelled and subsided in silence.

The water had a magical transparency, and Gilliatt distinguished at various depths submerged recesses, and surfaces of jutting rocks ever of a deeper and a deeper green. Certain dark hollows, too, were there, probably too deep for soundings.

On each side of the submarine porch, rude elliptical arches, filled with shallows, indicated the position of small lateral caves, low alcoves of the central cavern, accessible, perhaps, at certain tides. These openings had roofs in the form of inclined planes, and at angles more or less acute. Little sandy beaches of a few feet wide, laid bare by the action of the water, stretched inward, and were lost in these recesses.

Here and there seaweeds of more than a fathom in length undulated beneath the water, like the waving of long tresses in the wind; and there were glimpses of a forest of sea plants.

Above and below the surface of the water, the wall of the cavern from top to bottom—from the vault down to the depth at which it became invisible—was tapestried with that prodigious efflorescence of the sea, rarely perceived by human eyes, which the old Spanish navigators called *praderias del mar*. A luxuriant moss, having all the tints of the olive, enlarged and concealed the protuberances of granite. From all the jutting points swung the thin fluted strips of varech, which sailors use as their barometers. The light breath which stirred in the cavern waved to and fro their glossy bands.

Under these vegetations there showed themselves from time to time some of the rarest *bijoux* of the casket of the ocean; ivory shells, strombi, purple-fish, univalves, struthiolaires, turriculated cerites. The bell-shaped limpet shells, like tiny huts, were everywhere adhering to the rocks, distributed in settlements, in the alleys between which prowled oscabrions, those beetles of the sea. A few large pebbles found their way into the cavern; shell-fish took refuge there. The crustacea are the grandees of the sea, who, in their lacework and embroidery, avoid the rude contact of the pebbly crowd. The glittering heap of their shells, in certain spots under the wave, gave out singular irradiations, amidst which the eye caught glimpses of confused azure and gold, and mother-of-pearl, of every tint of the water.

Upon the side of the cavern, a little above the water-line, a magnificent and singular plant, attaching itself, like a fringe, to the border of seaweed, continued and completed it. This plant, thick, fibrous, inextricably intertwined, and almost black, exhibited to the eye large confused and dusky festoons, everywhere dotted with innumerable little flowers of the colour of lapis-lazuli. In the water they seemed to glow like small blue flames. Out of the water they were flowers; beneath it they were sapphires. The water rising and inundating the basement of the grotto clothed with these plants, seemed to cover the rock with gems.

At every swelling of the wave these flowers increased in splendour, and at every subsidence grew dull again. So it is with the destiny of man; aspiration is life, the outbreathing of the spirit is death.

One of the marvels of the cavern was the rock itself. Forming here a wall, there an arch, and here again a pillar or pilaster, it was in places rough and bare, and sometimes close beside, was wrought with the most delicate natural carving. Strange evidences of mind mingled with the massive stolidity of the granite. It was the wondrous art-work of the ocean. Here a sort of panel, cut square, and covered with round embossments in various positions, simulated a vague bas-relief. Before this sculpture, with its obscure designs, a man might have dreamed of Prometheus roughly sketching for Michael Angelo. It seemed as if that great genius with a few blows of his mallet could have finished the indistinct labours of the giant. In other places the rock was damasked like a Saracen buckler, or engraved like a Florentine vase. There were portions which appeared like Corinthian brass, then like arabesques, as on the door of a mosque; then like Runic stones with obscure and mystic prints of claws. Plants with twisted creepers and tendrils, crossing and recrossing upon the groundwork of golden lichens, covered it with filigree. The grotto resembled in some wise a Moorish palace. It was a union of barbarism and of goldsmith's work, with the imposing and rugged architecture of the elements.

The magnificent stains and moulderings of the sea covered, as with velvet, the angles of granite. The escarpments were festooned with large-flowered bindweed, sustaining itself with graceful ease, and ornamenting the walls as by intelligent design. Wall-pellitories showed their strange clusters in tasteful arrangement. The wondrous light which came from beneath the water, at once a submarine twilight and an Elysian radiance, softened down and blended all harsh lineaments. Every wave was a prism. The outlines of things under these rainbow-tinted undulations produced the chromatic effects of optical glasses made too convex. Solar spectra shot through the waters. Fragments of rainbows seemed floating in that transparent dawn. Elsewhere—in other corners—there was discernible a kind of moonlight in the water. Every kind of splendour seemed to mingle there, forming a strange sort of twilight. Nothing could be more perplexing or enigmatical than the sumptuous beauties of this cavern. Enchantment reigned over all. The fantastic vegetation, the rude masonry of the place seemed to harmonise. It was a happy marriage this, between these strange wild things. The branches seeming but to touch one another clung closely each to each. The stern rock and the pale flower met in a passionate embrace. Massive pillars had capitals and entwining wreaths of delicate garlands, that quivered through every fibre, suggestive of fairy fingers tickling the feet of a Behemoth, and the rock upheld the plant, and the plant clasped the rock with unnatural joy of attraction.

The effect produced by the mysterious reconciliation of these strange forms was of a supreme and inexpressible beauty.

The works of nature, not less than the works of genius, contain the absolute, and produce an impression of awe. Something unexpected about them imperiously insists on our mental submission; we are conscious of a premeditation beyond our human scope, and at no time are they more startling than when we suddenly become aware of the beauty that is mingled with their terror.

This hidden grotto was, if we may use the expression, siderealised. There was everything in it to surprise and overwhelm. An apocalyptic light illuminated this crypt. One could not tell if that which the eyes looked upon was a reality, for reality bore the impress of the impossible. One could see, and touch, and know that one was standing there, and yet it was difficult to believe in it all.

Was it daylight which entered by this casement beneath the sea? Was it indeed water which trembled in this dusky pool? Were not these arched roofs and porches fashioned out of sunset clouds to imitate a cavern to men's eyes? What stone was that beneath the feet? Was not this solid shaft about to melt and pass into thin air? What was that cunning jewellery of glittering shells, half seen beneath the wave? How far away were life, and the green earth, and human faces? What strange enchantment haunted that mystic twilight? What blind emotion, mingling its sympathies with the uneasy restlessness of plants beneath the wave?

At the extremity of the cavern, which was oblong, rose a Cyclopean archivolte, singularly exact in form. It was a species of cave within a cave, of tabernacle within a sanctuary. Here, behind a sheet of bright verdure, interposed like the veil of a temple, arose a stone out of the waves, having square sides, and bearing some resemblance to an altar. The water surrounded it in all parts. It seemed as if a goddess had just descended from it. One might have dreamed there that some celestial form beneath that crypt or upon that altar dwelt for ever pensive in naked beauty, but grew invisible at the approach of mortals. It was hard to conceive that majestic chamber without a vision within. The day-dream of the intruder might evoke again the marvellous apparition. A flood of chaste light falling upon white shoulders scarcely seen; a forehead bathed with the light of dawn; an Olympian visage oval-shaped; a bust full of mysterious grace; arms modestly drooping; tresses unloosened in the aurora; a body delicately modelled of pure whiteness, half-wrapped in a sacred cloud, with the glance of a virgin; a Venus rising from the sea, or Eve issuing from chaos; such was the dream which filled the mind.

It seemed improbable that no phantom figure haunted this abode. Some woman's form, the embodiment of a star, had no doubt but shortly left the altar. Enveloped in this atmosphere of mute adoration the mind pictured an Amphitryon, a Tethys, some Diana capable of passion, some idealistic figure formed of light, looking softly down in the surrounding dusk. It was she who had left behind in the cave this perfumed luminosity, an emanation from her star-body. The dazzling phantom was no longer visible, she was only revealed by the invisible, and the sense of her presence lingered, setting the whole being voluptuously a-quiver. The goddess had departed, but divinity remained.

The beauty of the recess seemed made for this celestial presence. It was for the sake of this deity, this fairy of the pearl caverns, this queen of the Zephyrs, this Grace born of the waves, it was for her—as the mind, at least, imagined—that this subterranean dwelling had been thus religiously walled in, so that nothing might ever trouble the reverent shadows and the majestic silence round about that divine spirit.

Gilliatt, who was a kind of seer amid the secrets of nature, stood there musing, and sensible of confused emotions.

Suddenly, at a few feet below him, in the delightful transparence of that water like liquid jewels, he became sensible of the approach of something of mystic shape. A species of long ragged band was moving amidst the oscillation of the waves. It did not float, but darted about of its own will. It had an object; was advancing somewhere rapidly. The object had something of the form of a jester's bauble with points, which hung flabby and undulating. It seemed covered with a dust incapable of being washed away by the water. It was more than horrible; it was foul. The beholder felt that it was something monstrous. It was a living thing; unless, indeed, it were but an illusion. It seemed to be seeking the darker portion of the cavern, where at last it vanished. The heavy shadows grew darker as its sinister form glided into them, and disappeared.

Book II
The Labour

❄

I
THE RESOURCES OF ONE WHO HAS NOTHING

THE CAVERN DID NOT easily part with its explorers. The entry had been difficult; going back was more difficult still. Gilliatt, however, succeeded in extricating himself; but he did not return there. He had found nothing of what he was in quest of, and he had not the time to indulge curiosity.

He put the forge in operation at once. Tools were wanting; he set to work and made them.

For fuel he had the wreck; for motive force the water; for his bellows the wind; for his anvil a stone; for art his instinct; for power his will.

He entered with ardour upon his sombre labours.

The weather seemed to smile upon his work. It continued to be dry and free from equinoctial gales. The month of March had come, but it was tranquil. The days grew longer. The blue of the sky, the gentleness of all the movements of the scene, the serenity of the noontide, seemed to exclude the idea of mischief. The waves danced merrily in the sunlight. A Judas kiss is the first step to treachery; of such caresses the ocean is prodigal. Her smile, like that of woman's sometimes, cannot be trusted.

There was little wind. The hydraulic bellows worked all the better for that reason. Much wind would have embarrassed rather than aided it. Gilliatt had a saw; he manufactured for himself a file. With the saw he attacked the wood; with the file the metal. Then he availed himself of the two iron hands of the smith—the pincers and the pliers. The pincers gripe, the pliers handle; the one is like the closed hand, the other like the fingers. By degrees he made for himself a number of auxiliaries, and constructed his armour. With a piece of hoop-wood he made a screen for his forge-fire.

One of his principal labours was the sorting and repair of pulleys. He mended both the blocks and the sheaves of tackle. He cut down the irregularities of all broken joists, and reshaped the extremities. He had, as we have said, for the necessities of his carpentry, a quantity of pieces of wood, stored away, and arranged according to the forms, the dimensions, and the nature of their grain; the oak on one side, the pine on the other; the short pieces like riders, separated from the straight pieces like binding strakes. This formed his reserve of supports and levers, of which he might stand in great need at any moment.

Any one who intends to construct hoisting tackle ought to provide himself with beams and small cables. But that is not sufficient. He must have cordage. Gilliatt restored the cables, large and small. He frayed out the tattered sails, and succeeded in converting them into an excellent yarn, of which he made twine. With this he joined the ropes. The joins, however, were liable to rot. It was necessary, therefore, to hasten to make use of these cables. He had only been able to make white tow, for he was without tar.

The ropes mended, he proceeded to repair the chains.

Thanks to the lateral point of the stone anvil, which served the part of the conoid bicorn, he was able to forge rings rude in shape but strong. With these he fastened together the severed lengths of chains, and made long pieces.

To work at a forge without assistance is something more than troublesome. He succeeded nevertheless. It is true that he had only to forge and shape articles of comparatively small size, which he was able to handle with the pliers in one hand, while he hammered with the other.

He cut into lengths the iron bars of the captain's bridge on which Clubin used to pass to and fro from paddle-box to paddle-box giving his orders; forged at one extremity of each piece a point, and at the other a flat head. By this means he manufactured large nails of about a foot in length. These nails, much used in pontoon making, are useful in fixing anything in rocks.

What was his object in all these labours? We shall see.

He was several times compelled to renew the blade of his hatchet and the teeth of his saw. For renotching the saw he had manufactured a three-sided file.

Occasionally he made use of the capstan of the Durande. The hook of the chain broke: he made another.

By the aid of his pliers and pincers, and by using his chisel as a screwdriver, he set to work to remove the two paddle-wheels of the vessel; an object which he accomplished. This was rendered practicable by reason of a peculiarity in their construction. The paddle-boxes which covered them served him to stow them away. With the planks of these paddle-boxes, he made two cases in which he deposited the two paddles, piece by piece, each part being carefully numbered.

His lump of chalk became precious for this purpose.

He kept the two cases upon the strongest part of the wreck.

When these preliminaries were completed, he found himself face to face with the great difficulty. The problem of the engine of the Durande was now clearly before him.

Taking the paddle-wheels to pieces had proved practicable. It was very different with the machinery.

In the first place, he was almost entirely ignorant of the details of the mechanism. Working thus blindly he might do some irreparable damage. Then, even in attempting to dismember it, if he had ventured on that course, far other tools would be necessary than such as he could fabricate with a cavern for a forge, a wind-draught for bellows, and a stone for an anvil. In attempting, therefore, to take to pieces the machinery, there was the risk of destroying it.

The attempt seemed at first sight wholly impracticable.

The apparent impossibility of the project rose before him like a stone wall, blocking further progress.

What was to be done?

II
WHEREIN SHAKESPEARE AND ÆSCHYLUS MEET

GILLIATT HAD A NOTION.

Since the time of the carpenter-mason of Salbris, who, in the sixteenth century, in the dark ages of science—long before Amontons had discovered the first law of electricity, or Lahire the second, or Coulomb the third—

without other helper than a child, his son, with ill-fashioned tools, in the chamber of the great clock of La Charité-sur-Loire, resolved at one stroke five or six problems in statics and dynamics inextricably intervolved like the wheels in a block of carts and waggons—since the time of that grand and marvellous achievement of the poor workman, who found means, without breaking a single piece of wire, without throwing one of the teeth of the wheels out of gear, to lower in one piece, by a marvellous simplification, from the second story of the clock-tower to the first, that massive monitor of the hours, made all of iron and brass, "large as the room in which the man watches at night from the tower," with its motion, its cylinders, its barrels, its drum, its hooks, and its weights, the barrel of its spring steel-yard, its horizontal pendulum, the holdfasts of its escapement, its reels of large and small chains, its stone weights, one of which weighed five hundred pounds, its bells, its peals, its jacks that strike the hours—since the days, I say, of the man who accomplished this miracle, and of whom posterity knows not even the name—nothing that could be compared with the project which Gilliatt was meditating had ever been attempted.

The ponderousness, the delicacy, the involvement of the difficulties were not less in the machinery of the Durande than in the clock of La Charité-sur-Loire.

The untaught mechanic had his helpmate—his son; Gilliatt was alone.

A crowd gathered together from Meung-sur-Loire, from Nevers, and even from Orleans, able at time of need to assist the mason of Salbris, and to encourage him with their friendly voices. Gilliatt had around him no voices but those of the wind; no crowd but the assemblage of waves.

There is nothing more remarkable than the timidity of ignorance, unless it be its temerity. When ignorance becomes daring, she has sometimes a sort of compass within herself—the intuition of the truth, clearer oftentimes in a simple mind than in a learned brain.

Ignorance invites to an attempt. It is a state of wonderment, which, with its concomitant curiosity, forms a power. Knowledge often enough disconcerts and makes over-cautious. Gama, had he known what lay before him, would have recoiled before the Cape of Storms. If Columbus had been a great geographer, he might have failed to discover America.

The second successful climber of Mont Blanc was the savant, Saussure; the first the goatherd, Balmat.

These instances I admit are exceptions, which detract nothing from science, which remains the rule. The ignorant man may discover; it is the learned who invent.

The sloop was still at anchor in the creek of "The Man Rock," where the sea left it in peace. Gilliatt, as will be remembered, had arranged everything for maintaining constant communication with it. He visited the sloop and measured her beam carefully in several parts, but particularly her midship frame. Then he returned to the Durande and measured the diameter of the floor of the engine-room. This diameter, of course, without the paddles, was two feet less than the broadest part of the deck of his bark. The machinery, therefore, might be put aboard the sloop.

But how could it be got there?

III

GILLIATT'S MASTERPIECE COMES TO THE RESCUE OF THAT OF LETHIERRY

ANY FISHERMAN who had been mad enough to loiter in that season in the neighbourhood of Gilliatt's labours about this time would have been repaid for his hardihood, by a singular sight between the two Douvres.

Before his eyes would have appeared four stout beams, at equal distances, stretching from one Douvre to the other, and apparently forced into the rock, which is the firmest of all holds. On the Little Douvre, their extremities were laid and buttressed upon the projections of rock. On the Great Douvre, they had been driven in by blows of a hammer, by the powerful hand of a workman standing upright upon the beam itself. These supports were a little longer than the distance between the rocks. Hence the firmness of their hold; and hence, also, their slanting position. They touched the Great Douvre at an acute, and the Little Douvre at an obtuse angle. Their inclination was only slight; but it was unequal, which was a defect. But for this defect, they might have been supposed to be prepared to receive the planking of a deck. To these four beams were attached four sets of hoisting apparatus, each having its pendent and its tackle-fall, with the bold peculiarity of having the tackle-blocks with two sheaves at one extremity of the beam, and the simple pulleys at the opposite end. This distance, which was too great not to be perilous, was necessitated by the operations to be effected. The blocks were firm, and the pulleys strong. To this tackle-gear cables were attached, which from a distance looked like threads; while beneath this apparatus of tackle and carpentry, in the air, the massive hull of the Durande seemed suspended by threads.

She was not yet suspended, however. Under the cross beams, eight perpendicular holes had been made in the deck, four on the port, and four on the starboard side of the engine; eight other holes had been made beneath them through the keel. The cables, descending vertically from the four tackle-blocks, through the deck, passed out at the keel, and under the machinery, re-entered the ship by the holes on the other side, and passing again upward through the deck, returned, and were wound round the beams. Here a sort of jigger-tackle held them in a bunch bound fast to a single cable, capable of being directed by one arm. The single cable passed over a hook, and through a dead-eye, which completed the apparatus, and kept it in check. This combination compelled the four tacklings to work together, and acting as a complete restraint upon the suspending powers, became a sort of dynamical rudder in the hand of the pilot of the operation, maintaining the movements in equilibrium. The ingenious adjustment of this system of tackling had some of the simplifying qualities of the Weston pulley of these times, with a mixture of the antique polyspaston of Vitruvius. Gilliatt had discovered this, although he knew nothing of the dead Vitruvius or of the still unborn Weston. The length of the cables varied, according to the unequal declivity of the cross-beams. The ropes were dangerous, for the untarred hemp was liable to give way. Chains would have been better in this respect, but chains would not have passed well through the tackle-blocks.

The apparatus was full of defects; but as the work of one man, it was surprising. For the rest, it will be understood that many details are omitted which would render the construction perhaps intelligible to practical mechanics, but obscure to others.

The top of the funnel passed between the two beams in the middle.

Gilliatt, without suspecting it, had reconstructed, three centuries later, the mechanism of the Salbris carpenter—a mechanism rude and incorrect, and hazardous for him who would dare to use it.

Here let us remark, that the rudest defects do not prevent a mechanism from working well or ill. It may limp, but it moves. The obelisk in the square of St. Peter's at Rome is erected in a way which offends against all the principles of statics. The carriage of the Czar Peter was so constructed that it appeared about to overturn at every step; but it travelled onward for all that. What deformities are there in the machinery of Marly! Everything that is heterodox in hydraulics. Yet it did not supply Louis XIV. any the less with water.

Come what might, Gilliatt had faith. He had even anticipated success so confidently as to fix in the bulwarks of the sloop, on the day when he measured its proportions, two pairs of corresponding iron rings on each side, exactly at the same distances as the four rings on board the Durande, to which were attached the four chains of the funnel.

He had in his mind a very complete and settled plan. All the chances being against him, he had evidently determined that all the precautions at least should be on his side.

He did some things which seemed useless; a sign of attentive premeditation.

His manner of proceeding would, as we have said, have puzzled an observer, even though familiar with mechanical operations.

A witness of his labour who had seen him, for example, with enormous efforts, and at the risk of breaking his neck, driving with blows of his hammer eight or ten great nails which he had forged into the base of the two Douvres at the entrance of the defile between them, would have had some difficulty in understanding the object of these nails, and would probably have wondered what could be the use of all that trouble.

If he had then seen him measuring the portion of the fore bulwark which had remained, as we have described it, hanging on by the wreck, then attaching a strong cable to the upper edge of that portion, cutting away with strokes of his hatchet the dislocated fastenings which held it, then dragging it out of the defile, pushing the lower part by the aid of the receding tide, while he dragged the upper part; finally, by great labour, fastening with the cable this heavy mass of planks and piles wider than the entrance of the defile itself, with the nails driven into the base of the Little Douvre, the observer would perhaps have found it still more difficult to comprehend, and might have wondered why Gilliatt, if he wanted for the purpose of his operations to disencumber the space between the two rocks of this mass, had not allowed it to fall into the sea, where the tide would have carried it away.

Gilliatt had probably his reasons.

In fixing the nails in the basement of the rocks, he had taken advantage of all the cracks in the granite, enlarged them where needful, and driven in first of all wedges of wood, in which he fixed the nails. He made a rough commencement of similar preparations in the two rocks which rose at the other extremity of the narrow passage on the eastern side. He furnished with plugs of wood all the crevices, as if he desired to keep these also ready to hold nails or clamps; but this appeared to be a simple precaution, for he did not use them further. He was compelled to economise, and only to use his materials as he had need, and at the moment when the necessity for them came. This was another addition to his numerous difficulties.

As fast as one labour was accomplished another became necessary. Gilliatt passed without hesitation from task to task, and resolutely accomplished his giant strides.

IV
SUB RE

THE ASPECT OF the man who accomplished all these labours became terrible.

Gilliatt in his multifarious tasks expended all his strength at once, and regained it with difficulty.

Privations on the one hand, lassitude on the other, had much reduced him. His hair and beard had grown long. He had but one shirt which was not in rags. He went about bare-footed, the wind having carried away one of his shoes and the sea the other. Fractures of the rude and dangerous stone anvil which he used had left small wounds upon his hands and arms, the marks of labour. These wounds, or rather scratches, were superficial; but the keen air and the salt sea irritated them continually.

He was generally hungry, thirsty, and cold.

His store of fresh water was gone; his rye-meal was used or eaten. He had nothing left but a little biscuit.

This he broke with his teeth, having no water in which to steep it.

By little and little, and day by day, his powers decreased.

The terrible rocks were consuming his existence.

How to obtain food was a problem; how to get drink was a problem; how to find rest was a problem.

He ate when he was fortunate enough to find a crayfish or a crab; he drank when he chanced to see a sea-bird descend upon a point of rock; for on climbing up to the spot he generally found there a hollow with a little fresh water. He drank from it after the bird; sometimes with the bird; for the gulls and seamews had become accustomed to him, and no longer flew away at his approach. Even in his greatest need of food he did not attempt to molest them. He had, as will be remembered, a superstition about birds. The birds on their part—now that his hair was rough and wild and his beard long—had no fear of him. The change in his face gave them confidence; he had lost resemblance to men, and taken the form of the wild beast.

The birds and Gilliatt, in fact, had become good friends. Companions in poverty, they helped each other. As long as he had had any meal, he had crumbled for them some little bits of the cakes he made. In his deeper distress they showed him in their turn the places where he might find the little pools of water.

He ate the shell-fish raw. Shell-fish help in a certain degree to quench the thirst. The crabs he cooked. Having no kettle, he roasted them between two stones made red-hot in his fire, after the manner of the savages of the Feroe islands.

Meanwhile signs of the equinoctial season had begun to appear. There came rain—an angry rain. No showers or steady torrents, but fine, sharp, icy, penetrating points which pierced to his skin through his clothing, and to his bones through his skin. It was a rain which yielded little water for drinking, but which drenched him none the less.

Chary of assistance, prodigal of misery—such was the character of these rains. During one week Gilliatt suffered from them all day and all night.

At night, in his rocky recess, nothing but the overpowering fatigue of his daily work enabled him to get sleep. The great sea-gnats stung him, and he awakened covered with blisters.

He had a kind of low fever, which sustained him; this fever is a succour which destroys. By instinct he chewed the mosses, or sucked the leaves of wild cochlearia, scanty tufts of which grew in the dry crevices of the rocks. Of his suffering, however, he took little heed. He had no time to spare from his work to the consideration of his own privations. The rescue of the machinery of the Durande was progressing well. That sufficed for him.

Every now and then, for the necessities of his work, he jumped into the water, swam to some point, and gained a footing again. He simply plunged into the sea and left it, as a man passes from one room in his dwelling to another.

His clothing was never dry. It was saturated with rain water, which had no time to evaporate, and with sea water, which never dries. He lived perpetually wet.

Living in wet clothing is a habit which may be acquired. The poor groups of Irish people—old men, mothers, girls almost naked, and infants— who pass the winter in the open air, under the snow and rain, huddled together, sometimes at the corners of houses in the streets of London, live and die in this condition.

To be soaked with wet, and yet to be thirsty: Gilliatt grew familiar with this strange torture. There were times when he was glad to suck the sleeve of his loose coat.

The fire which he made scarcely warmed him. A fire in open air yields little comfort. It burns on one side, and freezes on the other.

Gilliatt often shivered even while sweating over his forge.

Everywhere about him rose resistance amidst a terrible silence. He felt himself the enemy of an unseen combination. There is a dismal *non possumus* in nature. The inertia of matter is like a sullen threat. A mysterious persecution environed him. He suffered from heats and shiverings. The fire ate into his flesh; the water froze him; feverish thirst tormented him; the wind tore his clothing; hunger undermined the organs of the body. The oppression of all these things was constantly exhausting him. Obstacles silent, immense, seemed to converge from all points, with the blind irresponsibility of fate, yet full of a savage unanimity. He felt them pressing inexorably upon him. No means were there of escaping from them. His sufferings produced the impression of some living persecutor. He had a constant sense of something working against him, of a hostile form ever present, ever labouring to circumvent and to subdue him. He could have fled from the struggle; but since he remained, he had no choice but to war with this impenetrable hostility. He asked himself what it was. It took hold of him, grasped him tightly, overpowered him, deprived him of breath. The invisible persecutor was destroying him by slow degrees. Every day the oppression became greater, as if a mysterious screw had received another turn.

His situation in this dreadful spot resembled a duel, in which a suspicion of some treachery haunts the mind of one of the combatants.

Now it seemed a coalition of obscure forces which surrounded him. He felt that there was somewhere a determination to be rid of his presence. It is thus that the glacier chases the loitering ice-block.

Almost without seeming to touch him this latent coalition had reduced him to rags; had left him bleeding, distressed, and, as it were, *hors de combat*, even before the battle. He laboured, indeed, not the less—without pause or rest; but as the work advanced, the workman himself lost ground. It might have been fancied that Nature, dreading his bold spirit, adopted the plan of slowly undermining his bodily power. Gilliatt kept his ground, and left the rest to the future. The sea had begun by consuming him; what would come next?

The double Douvres—that dragon made of granite, and lying in ambush in mid-ocean—had sheltered him. It had allowed him to enter, and to do his will; but its hospitality resembled the welcome of devouring jaws.

The desert, the boundless surface, the unfathomable space around him and above, so full of negatives to man's will; the mute, inexorable determination of phenomena following their appointed course; the grand general law of things, implacable and passive; the ebbs and flows; the rocks themselves, dark Pleiades whose points were each a star amid vortices, a centre of an irradiation of currents; the strange, indefinable conspiracy to stifle with indifference the temerity of a living being; the wintry winds, the clouds, and the beleaguering waves enveloped him, closed round him slowly, and in a measure shut him in, and separated him from companionship, like a dungeon built up by degrees round a living man. All against him; nothing for him; he felt himself isolated, abandoned, enfeebled, sapped, forgotten.

His storehouse empty, his tools broken or defective; he was tormented with hunger and thirst by day, with cold by night. His sufferings had left him with wounds and tatters, rags covering sores, torn hands, bleeding feet, wasted limbs, pallid cheeks, and eyes bright with a strange light; but this was the steady flame of his determination.

The virtue of a man is betrayed by his eyes. How much of the man there is in us may be read in their depths. We make ourselves known by the light that gleams beneath our brows. The petty natures wink at us, the larger send forth flashes. If there is no brilliancy under the lids, there is no thought in the brain, no love in the heart. Those who love desire, and those who desire sparkle and flash. Determination gives a fire to the glance, a magnificent fire that consumes all timid thoughts.

It is the self-willed ones who are sublime. He who is only brave, has but a passing fit, he who is only valiant has temperament and nothing more, he who is courageous has but one virtue. He who persists in the truth is the grand character. The secret of great hearts may be summed up in the word: Perseverando. Perseverance is to courage what the wheel is to the lever; it is the continual renewing of the centre of support. Let the desired goal be on earth or in heaven, only make for the goal. Everything is in that; in the first case one is a Columbus, in the second a god. Not to allow conscience to argue or the will to fail—this is the way to suffering and glory. In the world of ethics to fall does not exclude the possibility of soaring, rather does it give impetus to flight. The mediocrities allow themselves to be dissuaded by the specious obstacles—the great ones never. To perish is their perhaps, to conquer their conviction. You may propose many good reasons to the martyr why he should not allow himself to be stoned to death. Disdain of every reasonable objection begets that sublime victory of the vanquished which we call martyrdom.

All his efforts seemed to tend to the impossible. His success was trifling and slow. He was compelled to expend much labour for very little results. This it was that gave to his struggle its noble and pathetic character.

That it should have required so many preparations, so much toil, so many cautious experiments, such nights of hardship, and such days of danger, merely to set up four beams over a shipwrecked vessel, to divide and isolate the portion that could be saved, and to adjust to that wreck within a wreck four tackle-blocks with their cables was only the result of his solitary labour. Fate had decreed him the work, and necessity obliged him to carry it out.

That solitary position Gilliatt had more than accepted; he had deliberately chosen it. Dreading a competitor, because a competitor might have proved a rival, he had sought for no assistance. The overwhelming enterprise, the risk, the danger, the toil multiplied by itself, the possible destruction of the salvor in his work, famine, fever, nakedness, distress—he had chosen all these for himself! Such was his selfishness. He was like a man placed in some terrible chamber which is being slowly exhausted of air. His vitality was leaving him by little and little. He scarcely perceived it.

Exhaustion of the bodily strength does not necessarily exhaust the will. Faith is only a secondary power; the will is the first. The mountains, which faith is proverbially said to move, are nothing beside that which the will can accomplish. All that Gilliatt lost in vigour, he gained in tenacity. The destruction of the physical man under the oppressive influence of that wild surrounding sea, and rock, and sky, seemed only to reinvigorate his moral nature.

Gilliatt felt no fatigue; or, rather, would not yield to any. The refusal of the mind to recognise the failings of the body is in itself an immense power.

He saw nothing, except the steps in the progress of his labours.

His object—now seeming so near attainment—wrapped him in perpetual illusions.

He endured all this suffering without any other thought than is comprised in the word "Forward." His work flew to his head; the strength of the will is intoxicating. Its intoxication is called heroism.

He had become a kind of Job, having the ocean for the scene of his sufferings. But he was a Job wrestling with difficulty, a Job combating and making head against afflictions; a Job conquering! a combination of Job and Prometheus, if such names are not too great to be applied to a poor sailor and fisher of crabs and crayfish.

V

SUB UMBRA

SOMETIMES IN THE NIGHT-TIME Gilliatt woke and peered into the darkness.

He felt a strange emotion.

His eyes were opened upon the black night; the situation was dismal; full of disquietude.

There is such a thing as the pressure of darkness.

A strange roof of shadow; a deep obscurity, which no diver can explore; a light mingled with that obscurity, of a strange, subdued, and sombre kind; floating atoms of rays, like a dust of seeds or of ashes; millions of lamps, but no illumining; a vast sprinkling of fire, of which no man knows the secret; a diffusion of shining points, like a drift of sparks arrested in their course; the disorder of the whirlwind, with the fixedness of death; a mysterious and abyssmal depth; an enigma, at once showing and concealing its face; the Infinite in its mask of darkness—these are the synonyms of night. Its weight lies heavily on the soul of man.

This union of all mysteries—the mystery of the Cosmos and the mystery of Fate—oppresses human reason.

The pressure of darkness acts in inverse proportion upon different kinds of natures. In the presence of night man feels his own incompleteness. He perceives the dark void and is sensible of infirmity. It is like the vacancy of blindness. Face to face with night, man bends, kneels, prostrates himself, crouches on the earth, crawls towards a cave, or seeks for wings. Almost always he shrinks from that vague presence of the Infinite Unknown. He asks himself what it is; he trembles and bows the head. Sometimes he desires to go to it.

To go whither?

He can only answer, "Yonder."

But what is that? and what is there?

This curiosity is evidently forbidden to the spirit of man; for all around him the roads which bridge that gulf are broken up or gone. No arch exists for him to span the Infinite. But there is attraction in forbidden knowledge, as in the edge of the abyss. Where the footstep cannot tread, the eye may reach; where the eye can penetrate no further, the mind may soar. There is no man, however feeble or insufficient his resources, who does not essay. According to his nature he questions or recoils before that mystery. With some it has the effect of repressing; with others it enlarges the soul. The spectacle is sombre, indefinite.

Is the night calm and cloudless? It is then a depth of shadow. Is it stormy? It is then a sea of cloud. Its limitless deeps reveal themselves to us, and yet baffle our gaze: close themselves against research, but open to conjecture. Its innumerable dots of light only make deeper the obscurity beyond. Jewels, scintillations, stars; existences revealed in the unknown universes; dread defiances to man's approach; landmarks of the infinite creation; boundaries there, where there are no bounds; sea-marks impossible, and yet real, numbering the fathoms of those infinite deeps. One microscopic glittering point; then another; then another; imperceptible, yet enormous. Yonder light is a focus; that focus is a star; that star is a sun; that sun is a universe; that universe is nothing. For all numbers are as zero in the presence of the Infinite.

These worlds, which yet are nothing, exist. Through this fact we feel the difference which separates the *being nothing* from the *not to be*.

The inaccessible joined to the inexplicable, such is the universe. From the contemplation of the universe is evolved a sublime phenomenon: the soul growing vast through its sense of wonder. A reverent fear is peculiar to man; the beasts know no such fear.

His intelligence becomes conscious in this august terror of its own power and its own weakness.

Darkness has unity, hence arises horror; at the same time it is complex, and hence terror. Its unity weighs on the spirit and destroys all desire of resistance. Its complexity causes us to look around on all sides; apparently we have reason to fear sudden happenings. We yield and yet are on guard. We are in presence of the whole, hence submission; and of the many, hence defiance.

The unity of darkness contains a multiple, a mysterious plurality—visible in matter, realised in thought. Silence rules all; another reason for watchfulness.

Night—and he who writes this has said it elsewhere—is the right and normal condition of that special part of creation to which we belong. Light, brief of duration here as throughout space, is but the nearness of a star. This universal, prodigious night does not fulfil itself, without friction, and all such friction in such a mechanism means what we call evil. We feel this darkness to be evil, a latent denial of divine order, the implicit blasphemy of the real rebelling against the ideal. Evil complicates, by one knows not what hydra-headed monstrosity, the vast, cosmic whole.

Everywhere it arises and resists.

It is the tempest, and hinders the hastening ship; it is chaos, and trammels the birth of a world. Good is one; evil is ubiquitous. Evil dislocates the logic of Life. It causes the bird to devour the fly and the comet to destroy the planet. Evil is a blot on the page of creation.

The darkness of night is full of vertiginous uncertainty.

Whoso would sound its depths is submerged, and struggles therein.

What fatigue to be compared to this contemplation of shadows. It is the study of annihilation.

There is no sure hold on which the soul may rest. There are ports of departure, and no havens for arrival. The interlacing of contradictory solutions; all the branches of doubt seen at a glance; the ramifications of phenomena budding limitlessly from some undefined impulse; laws intersecting each other; an incomprehensible promiscuity causing the mineral to become vegetable; the vegetable to rise to higher life; thought to gather weight; love to shine and gravitation to attract; the immense range presented to view by all questions, extending itself into the limitless obscurity; the half seen, suggesting the unknown; the cosmic correlation appearing clearly, not to sight but to intelligence, in the vast, dim space; the invisible become visible—these are the great overshadowing! Man lives beneath it. He is ignorant of detail, but he carries, in such proportion as he is able to bear, the weight of the monstrous whole. This obsession prompted the astronomy of the Chaldean shepherds. Involuntary revelations flow from creation; hints of science fall from it unconsciously and are absorbed by the ignorant. Every solitary, impregnated in this mysterious way, becomes, without being aware of it, a natural philosopher.

The darkness is indivisible. It is inhabited. Inhabited by the changeless absolute; inhabited also by change. Action exists there, disquieting thought! An awful creative will works out its phases. Premeditations, Powers, fore-ordained Destinies, elaborate there together an incommensurable work. A life of horror and terror is hidden therein. There are vast evolutions of suns; the stellar family, the planetary family; zodiacal pollen; the *Quid Divinum* of currents; effluvia, polarisations, and attractions; there are embraces and antagonisms; a magnificent flux and reflux of universal antithesis; the imponderable, free-floating around fixed centres; there is the sap of globes and light beyond globes; the wandering atom, the scattered germ, the processes of fecundity, meetings for union and for combat; unimagined profusion, distances which are as a dream, vertiginous orbits, the rush of worlds into the incalculable; marvels following each other in the obscurity. One mechanism works throughout in the breath of fleeing spheres, and the wheels that we know are turning. The sage conjectures; the ignorant man believes and trembles. These things exist and yet are hidden; they are inexpugnable, beyond reach, beyond approach.

We are convinced and oppressed—we feel, we know not what dark evidence within us; we realise nothing, but are crushed by the impalpable.

All is incomprehensible, but nothing is unintelligible.

And add to all that, the tremendous question: Is this immanent universe a Being?

We exist beneath the shadow. We look; we listen. And meanwhile the dark earth rolls onward. The flowers are conscious of this tremendous motion; the one opens at eleven in the evening and the other at five in the morning. Astounding sense of law! And in other depths of wonder, the drop of water is a world; the infusoria breed; animalculæ display gigantic fecundity, the imperceptible reveals its grandeur, immensity manifests itself, in an inverse sense; there are algæ that produce in an hour thirteen hundred millions of their kind. Every enigma is propounded in one. The irreducible is before us. Hence we are constrained to some kind of faith. An involuntary belief is the result. But belief does not ensure peace of mind. Faith has an extraordinary desire to take shape. Hence religions. Nothing is so overwhelming as a formless faith.

And despite of thought or desire or inward resistance, to look at the darkness is to fall into profound and wondering meditation. What can we make of these phenomena! How should we act beneath their united forces? To divide such weight of oppression is impossible. What reverie can follow all these mystic vistas? What abstruse revelations arise, stammering, and are obscure from their very mass, as a hesitating speech. Darkness is silence, but such a silence suggests everything. One majestic thought is the result: God—God is the irrepressible idea that springs within man's soul. Syllogisms, feuds, negations, systems, religions cannot destroy it. This idea is affirmed by the whole dark universe. Yet unrest is everywhere in fearful immanence. The wondrous correlation of forces is manifested in the upholding of the balanced darkness. The universe is suspended and nothing falls. Incessant and immeasurable changes operate without accident or destruction. Man participates in the constant changes, and in experiencing such he names them Destiny. But where does destiny begin? And where does nature end? What difference is there between an event and a season? between a sorrow and a rainfall? between a virtue and a star? An hour, is it not a rolling wave? The wheels of creation revolve mechanically regardless of man. The starry sky is a vision of wheels, pendulums, and counterpoise.

He who contemplates it cannot but ponder upon it.

It is the whole reality and yet the whole abstraction. And nothing more. We are in prison and at the mercy of the darkness, and no evasion is possible.

We are an integral part of the working of this unknown whole; and we feel the mystery within us fraternising with the mystery beyond us. Hence the sublimity of Death. What anguish! And yet what bliss to belong to the Infinite, and through the sense of the Infinite to recognise our inevitable immortality, the possibility of an eternity; to grasp amid this prodigious deluge of universal life, the persistent, imperishable *Me*; to look at the stars and say, The living soul within me is akin to you; to gaze into darkness and cry, I am as unfathomable as thou! Such immensity is of night, and, added to solitude, weighed heavily on Gilliatt's mind.

Did he understand it? No.

Did he feel it? Yes.

All these vague imaginings, increased and intensified by solitude, weighed upon Gilliatt.

He understood them little, but he felt them. His was a powerful intellect clouded; a great spirit wild and untaught.

VI

GILLIATT PLACES THE SLOOP IN READINESS

THIS RESCUE of the machinery of the wreck as meditated by Gilliatt was, as we have already said, like the escape of a criminal from a prison—necessitating all the patience and industry recorded of such achievements; industry carried to the point of a miracle, patience only to be compared with a long agony. A certain prisoner named Thomas, at the Mont Saint Michel, found means of secreting the greater part of a wall in his paillasse. Another at Tulle, in 1820, cut away a quantity of lead from the terrace where the prisoners walked for exercise. With what kind of knife? No one would guess. And melted this lead with what fire? None have ever discovered; but it is known that he cast it in a mould made of the crumbs of bread. With this lead and this mould he made a key, and with this key succeeded in opening a lock of which he had never seen anything but the keyhole. Some of this marvellous ingenuity Gilliatt possessed. He had once climbed and descended from the cliff at Boisrosé. He was the Baron Trenck of the wreck, and the Latude of her machinery.

The sea, like a jailor, kept watch over him.

For the rest, mischievous and inclement as the rain had been, he had contrived to derive some benefit from it. He had in part replenished his stock of fresh water; but his thirst was inextinguishable, and he emptied his can as fast as he filled it.

One day—it was on the last day of April or the first of May—all was at length ready for his purpose.

The engine-room was, as it were, enclosed between the eight cables hanging from the tackle-blocks, four on one side, four on the other. The sixteen holes upon the deck and under the keel, through which the cables passed, had been hooped round by sawing. The planking had been sawed, the timber cut with the hatchet, the ironwork with a file, the sheathing with the chisel. The part of the keel immediately under the machinery was cut squarewise, and ready to descend with it while still supporting it. All this frightful swinging mass was held only by one chain, which was itself only kept in position by a filed notch. At this stage, in such a labour and so near its completion, haste is prudence.

The water was low; the moment favourable.

Gilliatt had succeeded in removing the axle of the paddles, the extremities of which might have proved an obstacle and checked the descent. He had contrived to make this heavy portion fast in a vertical position within the engine-room itself.

It was time to bring his work to an end. The workman, as we have said, was not weary, for his will was strong; but his tools were. The forge was by degrees becoming impracticable. The blower had begun to work badly. The little hydraulic fall being of sea-water, saline deposits had encrusted the joints of the apparatus, and prevented its free action.

Gilliatt visited the creek of "The Man Rock," examined the sloop, and assured himself that all was in good condition, particularly the four rings fixed to starboard and to larboard; then he weighed anchor, and worked the heavy barge-shaped craft with the oars till he brought it alongside the two Douvres. The defile between the rocks was wide enough to admit it. There was also depth enough. On the day of his arrival he had satisfied himself that it was possible to push the sloop under the Durande.

The feat, however, was difficult; it required the minute precision of a watchmaker. The operation was all the more delicate from the fact that, for his objects, he was compelled to force it in by the stern, rudder first. It was necessary that the mast and the ringing of the sloop should project beyond the wreck in the direction of the sea.

These embarrassments rendered all Gilliatt's operations awkward. It was not like entering the creek of "The Man," where it was a mere affair of the tiller. It was necessary here to push, drag, row, and take soundings all together. Gilliatt consumed but a quarter of an hour in these manœuvres; but he was successful.

In fifteen or twenty minutes the sloop was adjusted under the wreck. It was almost wedged in there. By means of his two anchors he moored the boat by head and stern. The strongest of the two was placed so as to be efficient against the strongest wind that blows, which was that from the south-west. Then by the aid of a lever and the capstan, he lowered into the sloop the two cases containing the pieces of the paddle-wheel, the slings of which were all ready. The two cases served as ballast.

Relieved of these encumbrances, he fastened to the hook of the chain of the capstan the sling of the regulating tackle-gear, intending to check the pulleys.

Owing to the peculiar objects of this labour, the defects of the old sloop became useful qualities. It had no deck; her burden therefore would have greater depth, and could rest upon the hold. Her mast was very forward—too far forward indeed for general purposes; her contents therefore would have more room, and the mast standing thus beyond the mass of the wreck, there would be nothing to hinder its disembarkation. It was a mere shell, or case for receiving it; but nothing is more stable than this on the sea.

While engaged in these operations, Gilliatt suddenly perceived that the sea was rising. He looked around to see from what quarter the wind was coming.

VII
SUDDEN DANGER

THE BREEZE was scarcely perceptible; but what there was came from the west. A disagreeable habit of the winds during the equinoxes.

The rising sea varies much in its effects upon the Douvres rocks, depending upon the quarter of the wind.

According to the gale which drives them before it, the waves enter the rocky corridor either from the east or from the west. Entering from the east, the sea is comparatively gentle; coming from the west, it is always furious. The reason of this is, that the wind from the east blowing from the land has not had time to gather force; while the westerly winds, coming from the Atlantic, blow unchecked from a vast ocean. Even a very slight breeze, if it comes from the west, is serious. It rolls the huge billows from the illimitable space and dashes the waves against the narrow defile in greater bulk than can find entrance there.

A sea which rolls into a gulf is always terrible. It is the same with a crowd of people: a multitude is a sort of fluid body. When the quantity which can enter is less than the quantity endeavouring to force a way, there is a fatal crush among the crowd, a fierce convulsion on the water. As long as the west wind blows, however slight the breeze, the Douvres are twice a day subjected to that rude assault. The sea rises, the tide breasts up, the narrow gullet gives little entrance, the waves, driven against it violently, rebound and roar, and a tremendous surf beats the two sides of the gorge. Thus the Douvres, during the slightest wind from the west, present the singular spectacle of a sea comparatively calm without, while within the rocks a storm is raging. This tumult of waters, altogether confined and circumscribed, has nothing of the character of a tempest. It is a mere local outbreak among the waves, but a terrible one. As regards the winds from the north and south, they strike the rocks crosswise, and cause little surf in the passage. The entrance by the east, a fact which must be borne in mind, was close to "The Man Rock." The dangerous opening to the west was at the opposite extremity, exactly between the two Douvres.

It was at this western entrance that Gilliatt found himself with the wrecked Durande, and the sloop made fast beneath it.

A catastrophe seemed inevitable. There was not much wind, but it was sufficient for the impending mischief.

Before many hours, the swell which was rising would be rushing with full force into the gorge of the Douvres. The first waves were already breaking. This swell, and eddy of the entire Atlantic, would have behind it the immense sea. There would be no squall; no violence, but a simple overwhelming wave, which commencing on the coasts of America, rolls towards the shores of Europe with an impetus gathered over two thousand leagues. This wave, a gigantic ocean barrier, meeting the gap of the rocks, must be caught between the two Douvres, standing like watch-towers at the entrance, or like pillars of the defile. Thus swelled by the tide, augmented by resistance, driven back by the shoals, and urged on by the wind, it would strike the rock with violence, and with all the contortions from the obstacles it had encountered, and all the frenzy of a sea confined in limits, would rush between the rocky walls, where it would reach the sloop and the Durande, and, in all probability, destroy them.

A shield against this danger was wanting. Gilliatt had one.

The problem was to prevent the sea reaching it at one bound; to obstruct it from striking, while allowing it to rise; to bar the passage without refusing it admission; to prevent the compression of the water in the gorge, which was the whole danger; to turn an eruption into a simple flood; to extract as it were from the waves all their violence, and constrain the furies to be gentle; it was, in fact, to substitute an obstacle which will appease, for an obstacle which irritates.

Gilliatt, with all that dexterity which he possessed, and which is so much more efficient than mere force, sprang upon the rocks like a chamois among the mountains or a monkey in the forest; using for his tottering and dizzy strides the smallest projecting stone; leaping into the water, and issuing from it again; swimming among the shoals and clambering the rocks, with a rope between his teeth and a mallet in his hand. Thus he detached the cable which kept suspended and also fast to the basement of the Little Douvre the end of the forward side of the Durande; fashioned out of some ends of hawsers a sort of hinges, holding this bulwark to the huge nails fixed in the granite; swung this apparatus of planks upon them, like the gates of a great dock, and turned their sides, as he would turn a rudder, outward to the waves, which pushed the extremities upon the Great Douvre, while the rope hinges detained the other extremities upon the Little Douvre; next he contrived, by means of the huge nails placed beforehand for the purpose, to fix the same kind of fastenings upon the Great Douvre as on the little one; made completely fast the vast mass of woodwork against the two pillars of the gorge, slung a chain across this barrier like a baldric upon a cuirass; and in less than an hour, this barricade against the sea was complete and the gullet of the rocks closed as by a folding-door.

This powerful apparatus, a heavy mass of beams and planks, which laid flat would have made a raft, and upright formed a wall, had by the aid of the water been handled by Gilliatt with the adroitness of a juggler. It might almost have been said that the obstruction was complete before the rising sea had the time to perceive it.

It was one of those occasions on which Jean Bart would have employed the famous expression which he applied to the sea every time he narrowly escaped shipwreck. "We have cheated the Englishman;" for it is well known that when that famous admiral meant to speak contemptuously of the ocean he called it "the Englishman."

The entrance to the defile being thus protected, Gilliatt thought of the sloop. He loosened sufficient cable for the two anchors to allow her to rise with the tide; an operation similar to what the mariners of old called "*mouiller avec des embossures.*" In all this, Gilliatt was not taken the least by surprise; the necessity had been foreseen. A seaman would have perceived it by the two pulleys of the top ropes cut in the form of snatch-blocks, and fixed behind the sloop, through which passed two ropes, the ends of which were slung through the rings of the anchors.

Meanwhile the tide was rising fast; the half flood had arrived, a moment when the shock of the waves, even in comparatively moderate weather, may become considerable. Exactly what Gilliatt expected came to pass. The waves rolled violently against the barrier, struck it, broke heavily and passed beneath. Outside was the heavy swell; within, the waters ran quietly. He had devised a sort of marine *Furculæ caudinæ*. The sea was conquered.

VIII
MOVEMENT RATHER THAN PROGRESS

THE MOMENT so long dreaded had come.

The problem now was to place the machinery in the bark.

Gilliatt remained thoughtful for some moments, holding the elbow of his left arm in his right hand, and applying his left hand to his forehead.

Then he climbed upon the wreck, one part of which, containing the engine, was to be parted from it, while the other remained.

He severed the four slings which fixed the four chains from the funnel on the larboard and the starboard sides. The slings being only of cord, his knife served him well enough for this purpose.

The four chains set free, hung down along the sides of the funnel.

From the wreck he climbed up to the apparatus which he had constructed, stamped with his feet upon the beams, inspected the tackle-blocks, looked to the pulleys, handled the cables, examined the eking-pieces, assured himself that the untarred hemp was not saturated through, found that nothing was wanting and nothing giving way; then springing from the height of the suspending props on to the deck, he took up his position near the capstan, in the part of the Durande which he intended to leave jammed in between the two Douvres. This was to be his post during his labours.

Earnest, but troubled with no impulses but what were useful to his work, he took a final glance at the hoisting-tackle, then seized a file and began to saw with it through the chain which held the whole suspended.

The rasping of the file was audible amidst the roaring of the sea.

The chain from the capstan, attached to the regulating gear, was within his reach, quite near his hand.

Suddenly there was a crash. The link which he was filing snapped when only half cut through: the whole apparatus swung violently. He had only just time sufficient to seize the regulating gear.

The severed chain beat against the rock; the eight cables strained; the huge mass, sawed and cut through, detached itself from the wreck; the belly of the hull opened, and the iron flooring of the engine-room was visible below the keel.

If he had not seized the regulating tackle at that instant it would have fallen. But his powerful hand was there, and it descended steadily.

When the brother of Jean Bart, Peter Bart, that powerful and sagacious toper, that poor Dunkirk fisherman, who used to talk familiarly with the Grand Admiral of France, went to the rescue of the galley *Langeron*, in distress in the Bay of Ambleteuse, endeavouring to save the heavy floating mass in the midst of the breakers of that furious bay, he rolled up the mainsail, tied it with sea-reeds, and trusted to the ties to break away of themselves, and give the sail to the wind at the right moment. Just so Gilliatt trusted to the breaking of the chain; and the same eccentric feat of daring was crowned with the same success.

The tackle, taken in hand by Gilliatt, held out and worked well. Its function, as will be remembered, was to moderate the powers of the apparatus, thus reduced from many to one, by bringing them into united action. The gear had some similarity to a bridle of a bowline, except that instead of trimming a sail it served to balance a complicated mechanism.

Erect, and with his hand upon the capstan, Gilliatt, so to speak, was enabled to feel the pulse of the apparatus.

It was here that his inventive genius manifested itself.

A remarkable coincidence of forces was the result.

While the machinery of the Durande, detached in a mass, was lowering to the sloop, the sloop rose slowly to receive it. The wreck and the salvage vessel assisting each other in opposite ways, saved half the labour of the operation.

The tide swelling quietly between the two Douvres raised the sloop and brought it nearer to the Durande. The sea was more than conquered; it was tamed and broken in. It became, in fact, part and parcel of the organisation of power.

The rising waters lifted the vessel without any sort of shock, gently, and almost with precaution, as one would handle porcelain.

Gilliatt combined and proportioned the two labours, that of the water and that of the apparatus; and standing steadfast at the capstan, like some terrible statue obeyed by all the movement around it at the same moment, regulated the slowness of the descent by the slow rise of the sea.

There was no jerk given by the waters, no slip among the tackle. It was a strange collaboration of all the natural forces subdued. On one side, gravitation lowering the huge bulk, on the other the sea raising the bark. The attraction of heavenly bodies which causes the tide, and the attractive force of the earth, which men call weight, seemed to conspire together to aid his plans. There was no hesitation, no stoppage in their service; under the dominance of mind these passive forces became active auxiliaries. From minute to minute the work advanced; the interval between the wreck and the sloop diminished insensibly. The approach continued in silence, and as in a sort of terror of the man who stood there. The elements received his orders and fulfilled them.

Nearly at the moment when the tide ceased to raise it, the cable ceased to slide. Suddenly, but without commotion, the pulleys stopped. The vast machine had taken its place in the bark, as if placed there by a powerful hand. It stood straight, upright, motionless, firm. The iron floor of the engine-room rested with its four corners evenly upon the hold.

The work was accomplished.

Gilliatt contemplated it, lost in thought.

He was not the spoiled child of success. He bent under the weight of his great joy. He felt his limbs, as it were, sinking; and contemplating his triumph, he, who had never been shaken by danger, began to tremble.

He gazed upon the sloop under the wreck and at the machinery in the sloop. He seemed to feel it hard to believe it true. It might have been supposed that he had never looked forward to that which he had accomplished. A miracle had been wrought by his hands, and he contemplated it in bewilderment.

His reverie lasted but a short time.

Starting like one awakening from a deep sleep, he seized his saw, cut the eight cables, separated now from the sloop, thanks to the rising of the tide, by only about ten feet; sprang aboard, took a bunch of cord, made four slings, passed them through the rings prepared beforehand, and fixed on both sides aboard the sloop the four chains of the funnel which only an hour before had been still fastened to their places aboard the Durande.

The funnel being secured, he disengaged the upper part of the machinery. A square portion of the planking of the Durande was adhering to it; he struck off the nails and relieved the sloop of this encumbrance of planks and beams; which fell over on to the rocks—a great assistance in lightening it.

For the rest, the sloop, as has been foreseen, behaved well under the burden of the machinery. It had sunk in the water, but only to a good waterline. Although massive, the engine of the Durande was less heavy than the pile of stones and the cannon which he had once brought back from Herm in the sloop.

All then was ended; he had only to depart.

IX

A SLIP BETWEEN CUP AND LIP

ALL WAS NOT ENDED.

To re-open the gorge thus closed by the portion of the Durande's bulwarks, and at once to push out with the sloop beyond the rocks, nothing could appear more clear and simple. On the ocean every minute is urgent. There was little wind; scarcely a wrinkle on the open sea. The afternoon was beautiful, and promised a fine night. The sea, indeed, was calm, but the ebb had begun. The moment was favourable for starting. There would be the ebb-tide for leaving the Douvres; and the flood would carry him into Guernsey. It would be possible to be at St. Sampson's at daybreak.

But an unexpected obstacle presented itself. There was a flaw in his arrangements which had baffled all his foresight.

The machinery was freed; but the chimney was not.

The tide, by raising the sloop to the wreck suspended in the air, had diminished the dangers of the descent, and abridged the labour. But this diminution of the interval had left the top of the funnel entangled in the kind of gaping frame formed by the open hull of the Durande. The funnel was held fast there as between four walls.

The services rendered by the sea had been accompanied by that unfortunate drawback. It seemed as if the waves, constrained to obey, had avenged themselves by a malicious trick.

It is true that what the flood-tide had done, the ebb would undo.

The funnel, which was rather more than three fathoms in height, was buried more than eight feet in the wreck. The water-level would fall about twelve feet. Thus the funnel descending with the falling tide would have four feet of room to spare, and would clear itself easily.

But how much time would elapse before that release would be completed? Six hours.

In six hours it would be near midnight. What means would there be of attempting to start at such an hour? What channel could he find among all those breakers, so full of dangers even by day? How was he to risk his vessel in the depth of black night in that inextricable labyrinth, that ambuscade of shoals?

There was not help for it. He must wait for the morrow. These six hours lost, entailed a loss of twelve hours at least.

He could not even advance the labour by opening the mouth of the gorge. His breakwater was necessary against the next tide.

He was compelled to rest. Folding his arms was almost the only thing which he had not yet done since his arrival on the rocks.

This forced inaction irritated, almost vexed him with himself, as if it had been his fault. He thought "what would Déruchette say of me if she saw me thus doing nothing?"

And yet this interval for regaining his strength was not unnecessary.

The sloop was now at his command; he determined to pass the night in it.

He mounted once more to fetch his sheepskin upon the Great Douvre; descended again, supped off a few limpets and *châtaignes de mer*, drank, being very thirsty, a few draughts of water from his can, which was nearly empty, enveloped himself in the skin, the wool of which felt comforting, lay down like a watch-dog beside the engine, drew his red cap over his eyes and slept.

His sleep was profound. It was such sleep as men enjoy who have completed a great labour.

X
SEA-WARNINGS

IN THE MIDDLE of the night he awoke suddenly and with a jerk like the recoil of a spring.

He opened his eyes.

The Douvres, rising high over his head, were lighted up as by the white glow of burning embers. Over all the dark escarpment of the rock there was a light like the reflection of a fire.

Where could this fire come from?

It was from the water.

The aspect of the sea was extraordinary.

The water seemed a-fire. As far as the eye could reach, among the reefs and beyond them, the sea ran with flame. The flame was not red; it had nothing in common with the grand living fires of volcanic craters or of great furnaces. There was no sparkling, no glare, no purple edges, no noise. Long trails of a pale tint simulated upon the water the folds of a winding-sheet. A trembling glow was spread over the waves. It was the spectre of a great fire, rather than the fire itself. It was in some degree like the glow of unearthly flames lighting the inside of a sepulchre. A burning darkness.

The night itself, dim, vast, and wide-diffused, was the fuel of that cold flame. It was a strange illumination issuing out of blindness. The shadows even formed part of that phantom-fire.

The sailors of the Channel are familiar with those indescribable phosphorescences, full of warning for the navigator. They are nowhere more surprising than in the "Great V," near Isigny.

By this light, surrounding objects lose their reality. A spectral glimmer renders them, as it were, transparent. Rocks become no more than outlines. Cables of anchors look like iron bars heated to a white heat. The nets of the fishermen beneath the water seem webs of fire. The half of the oar above the waves is dark as ebony, the rest in the sea like silver. The drops from the blades uplifted from the water fall in starry showers upon the sea. Every boat leaves a furrow behind it like a comet's tail. The sailors, wet and luminous, seem like men in flames. If you plunge a hand into the water, you withdraw it clothed in flame. The flame is dead, and is not felt. Your arm becomes a firebrand. You see the forms of things in the sea roll beneath the waves as in liquid fire. The foam twinkles. The fish are tongues of fire, or fragments of the forked lightning, moving in the depths.

The reflection of this brightness had passed over the closed eyelids of Gilliatt in the sloop. It was this that had awakened him.

His awakening was opportune.

The ebb tide had run out, and the waters were beginning to rise again. The funnel, which had become disengaged during his sleep, was about to enter again into the yawning hollow above it.

It was rising slowly.

A rise of another foot would have entangled it in the wreck again. A rise of one foot is equivalent to half-an-hour's tide. If he intended, therefore, to take advantage of that temporary deliverance once more within his reach, he had just half-an-hour before him.

He leaped to his feet.

Urgent as the situation was, he stood for a few moments meditative, contemplating the phosphorescence of the waves.

Gilliatt knew the sea in all its phases. Notwithstanding all her tricks, and often as he had suffered from her terrors, he had long been her companion. That mysterious entity which we call the ocean had nothing in its secret thoughts which he could not divine. Observation, meditation, and solitude, had given him a quick perception of coming changes, of wind, or cloud, or wave.

Gilliatt hastened to the top ropes and payed out some cable; then being no longer held fast by the anchors, he seized the boat-hook of the sloop, and pushed her towards the entrance to the gorge some fathoms from the

Durande, and quite near to the breakwater. Here, as the Guernsey sailors say, it had *du rang*. In less than ten minutes the sloop was withdrawn from beneath the carcase of the wreck. There was no further danger of the funnel being caught in a trap. The tide might rise now.

And yet Gilliatt's manner was not that of one about to take his departure.

He stood considering the light upon the sea once more; but his thoughts were not of starting. He was thinking of how to fix the sloop again, and how to fix it more firmly than ever, though near to the exit from the defile.

Up to this time he had only used the two anchors of the sloop and had not yet employed the little anchor of the Durande, which he had found, as will be remembered, among the breakers. This anchor had been deposited by him in readiness for any emergency, in a corner of the sloop, with a quantity of hawsers, and blocks of top-ropes, and his cable, all furnished beforehand with large knots, which prevented its dragging. He now let go this third anchor, taking care to fasten the cable to a rope, one end of which was slung through the anchor ring, while the other was attached to the windlass of the sloop. In this manner he made a kind of triangular, triple anchorage, much stronger than the moorings with two anchors. All this indicated keen anxiety, and a redoubling of precautions. A sailor would have seen in this operation something similar to an anchorage in bad weather, when there is fear of a current which might carry the vessel under the wind.

The phosphorescence which he had been observing, and upon which his eye was now fixed once more, was threatening, but serviceable at the same time. But for it he would have been held fast locked in sleep, and deceived by the night. The strange appearance upon the sea had awakened him, and made things about him visible.

The light which it shed among the rocks was, indeed, ominous; but disquieting as it appeared to be to Gilliatt, it had served to show him the dangers of his position, and had rendered possible his operations in extricating the sloop. Henceforth, whenever he should be able to set sail, the vessel, with its freight of machinery, would be free.

And yet the idea of departing was further than ever from his mind. The sloop being fixed in its new position, he went in quest of the strongest chain which he had in his store-cavern, and attaching it to the nails driven into the two Douvres, he fortified from within with this chain the rampart of planks and beams, already protected from without by the cross chain. Far from opening the entrance to the defile, he made the barrier more complete.

The phosphorescence lighted him still, but it was diminishing. The day, however, was beginning to break.

Suddenly he paused to listen.

XI
A WORD TO THE WISE IS ENOUGH

A FEEBLE, indistinct sound seemed to reach his ear from somewhere in the far distance.

At certain hours the great deeps give forth a murmuring noise.

He listened a second time. The distant noise recommenced. Gilliatt shook his head like one who recognises at last something familiar to him.

A few minutes later he was at the other extremity of the alley between the rocks, at the entrance facing the east, which had remained open until then, and by heavy blows of his hammer was driving large nails into the sides of the gullet near "The Man Rock," as he had done at the gullet of the Douvres.

The crevices of these rocks were prepared and well furnished with timber, almost all of which was heart of oak. The rock on this side being much broken up, there were abundant cracks, and he was able to fix even more nails there than in the base of the two Douvres.

Suddenly, and as if some great breath had passed over it, the luminous appearance on the waters vanished. The twilight becoming paler every moment, assumed its functions.

The nails being driven, Gilliatt dragged beams and cords, and then chains to the spot; and without taking his eyes off his work, or permitting his mind to be diverted for a moment, he began to construct across the gorge of "The Man" with beams fixed horizontally, and made fast by cables, one of those open barriers which science has now adopted under the name of breakwaters.

Those who have witnessed, for example, at La Rocquaine in Guernsey, or at Bourg-d'Eau in France, the effect produced by a few posts fixed in the rock, will understand the power of these simple preparations. This sort of breakwater is a combination of what is called in France *épi* with what is known in England as "a dam." The breakwater is the chevaux-de-frise of fortifications against tempests. Man can only struggle against the sea by taking advantage of this principle of dividing its forces.

Meanwhile, the sun had risen, and was shining brightly. The sky was clear, the sea calm.

Gilliatt pressed on his work. He, too, was calm; but there was anxiety in his haste. He passed with long strides from rock to rock, and returned dragging wildly sometimes a rider, sometimes a binding strake. The utility of all this preparation of timbers now became manifest. It was evident that he was about to confront a danger which he had foreseen.

A strong iron bar served him as a lever for moving the beams.

The work was executed so fast that it was rather a rapid growth than a construction. He who has never seen a military pontooner at his work can scarcely form an idea of this rapidity.

The eastern gullet was still narrower than the western. There were but five or six feet of interval between the rocks. The smallness of this opening was an assistance. The space to be fortified and closed up being very little, the apparatus would be stronger, and might be more simple. Horizontal beams, therefore, sufficed, the upright ones being useless.

The first cross pieces of the breakwater being fixed, Gilliatt mounted upon them and listened once more.

The murmurs had become significant.

He continued his construction. He supported it with the two cat-heads of the Durande, bound to the frame of beams by cords passed through the three pulley-sheaves. He made the whole fast by chains.

The construction was little more than a colossal hurdle, having beams for rods and chains in the place of wattles.

It seemed woven together, quite as much as built.

He multiplied the fastenings, and added nails where they were necessary.

Having obtained a great quantity of bar iron from the wreck, he had been able to make a large number of these heavy nails.

While still at work, he broke some biscuit with his teeth. He was thirsty, but he could not drink, having no more fresh water. He had emptied the can at his meal of the evening before.

He added afterwards four or five more pieces of timber; then climbed again upon the barrier and listened.

The noises from the horizon had ceased; all was still.

The sea was smooth and quiet; deserving all those complimentary phrases which worthy citizens bestow upon it when satisfied with a trip. "A mirror," "a pond," "like oil," and so forth. The deep blue of the sky responded to the deep green tint of the ocean. The sapphire and the emerald hues vied with each other. Each were perfect. Not a cloud on high, not a line of foam below. In the midst of all this splendour, the April sun rose magnificently. It was impossible to imagine a lovelier day.

On the verge of the horizon a flight of birds of passage formed a long dark line against the sky. They were flying fast as if alarmed.

Gilliatt set to work again to raise the breakwater.

He raised it as high as he could; as high, indeed, as the curving of the rocks would permit.

Towards noon the sun appeared to him to give more than its usual warmth. Noon is the critical time of the day. Standing upon the powerful frame which he had built up, he paused again to survey the wide expanse.

The sea was more than tranquil. It was a dull dead calm. No sail was visible. The sky was everywhere clear; but from blue it had become white. The whiteness was singular. To the west, and upon the horizon, was a little spot of a sickly hue. The spot remained in the same place, but by degrees grew larger. Near the breakers the waves shuddered; but very gently.

Gilliatt had done well to build his breakwater.

A tempest was approaching.

The elements had determined to give battle.

Book III
The Struggle

❋

I
EXTREMES MEET

NOTHING is more threatening than a late equinox.

The appearance of the sea presents a strange phenomenon, resulting from what may be called the arrival of the ocean winds.

In all seasons, but particularly at the epoch of the Syzygies, at the moment when least expected, the sea sometimes becomes singularly tranquil. That vast perpetual movement ceases; a sort of drowsiness and languor overspreads it; and it seems weary and about to rest. Every rag of bunting, from the tiny streamer of the fishing-boat to the great flag of ships of war, droops against the mast. The admiral's flag, the Royal and Imperial ensigns sleep alike.

Suddenly all these streamers begin to flutter gently.

If there happen to be clouds, the moment has then come for marking the formation of the *cirri*; if the sun is setting, for observing the red tints of the horizon; or if it be night and there is a moon, for looking attentively for the halo.

It is then that the captain or commander of a squadron, if he happen to possess one of those storm indicators, the inventor of which is unknown, notes his instrument carefully and takes his precautions against the south wind, if the clouds have an appearance like dissolved sugar; or against the north, if they exfoliate in crystallisations like brakes of brambles, or like fir woods. Then, too, the poor Irish or Breton fisherman, after having consulted some mysterious gnomon engraved by the Romans or by demons upon one of those straight enigmatical stones, which are called in Brittany *Menhir*, and in Ireland *Cruach*, hauls his boat up on the shore.

Meanwhile the serenity of sky and ocean continues. The day dawns radiant, and Aurora smiles. It was this which filled the old poets and seers with religious horror; for men dared to suspect the falsity of the sun. *Solem quis dicere falsum audeat?*

The sombre vision of nature's secret laws is interdicted to man by the fatal opacity of surrounding things. The most terrible and perfidious of her aspects is that which masks the convulsions of the deep.

Some hours, and even days sometimes, pass thus. Pilots raise their telescopes here and there. The faces of old seamen have always an expression of severity left upon them by the vexation of perpetually looking out for changes.

Suddenly a great confused murmur is heard. A sort of mysterious dialogue takes place in the air.

Nothing unusual is seen.

The wide expanse is tranquil.

Yet the noises increase. The dialogue becomes more audible.

There is something beyond the horizon.

Something terrible. It is the wind.

The wind; or rather that populace of Titans which we call the gale. The unseen multitude.

India knew them as the Maroubs, Judea as the Keroubim, Greece as the Aquilones. They are the invisible winged creatures of the Infinite. Their blasts sweep over the earth.

II
THE OCEAN WINDS

THEY COME FROM the immeasurable deep. Their wide wings need the breadth of the ocean gulf; the spaciousness of desert solitudes. The Atlantic, the Pacific—those vast blue plains—are their delight. They hasten thither in flocks. Commander Page witnessed, far out at sea, seven waterspouts at once. They wander there, wild and terrible! The ever-ending yet eternal flux and reflux is their work. The extent of their power, the limits of their will, none know. They are the Sphinxes of the abyss: Gama was their Œdipus. In that dark, ever-moving expanse, they appear with faces of cloud. He who perceives their pale lineaments in that wide dispersion, the horizon of the sea, feels himself in presence of an unsubduable power. It might be imagined that the proximity of human intelligence disquieted them, and that they revolted against it. The mind of man is invincible, but the elements baffle him. He can do nothing against the power which is everywhere, and which none can bind. The gentle breath becomes a gale, smites with the force of a war-club, and then becomes gentle again. The winds attack with a terrible crash, and defend themselves by fading into nothingness. He who would encounter them must use artifice. Their varying tactics, their swift redoubled blows, confuse. They fly as often as they attack. They are tenacious and impalpable. Who can circumvent them? The prow of the *Argo*, cut from an oak of Dodona's grove, that mysterious pilot of the bark, spoke to them, and they insulted that pilot-goddess. Columbus, beholding their approach at *La Pinta*, mounted upon the poop, and addressed them with the first verses of St. John's Gospel. Surcouf defied them: "Here come the gang," he used to say. Napier greeted them with cannon-balls. They assume the dictatorship of chaos.

Chaos is theirs, in which to wreak their mysterious vengeance: the den of the winds is more monstrous than that of lions. How many corpses lie in its deep recesses, where the howling gusts sweep without pity over that obscure and ghastly mass! The winds are heard wheresoever they go, but they give ear to none. Their acts resemble crimes. None know on whom they cast their hoary surf; with what ferocity they hover over shipwrecks, looking at times as if they flung their impious foam-flakes in the face of heaven. They are the tyrants of unknown regions. "*Luoghi spaventosi*," murmured the Venetian mariners.

The trembling fields of space are subjected to their fierce assaults. Things unspeakable come to pass in those deserted regions. Some horseman rides in the gloom; the air is full of a forest sound; nothing is visible; but the tramp of cavalcades is heard. The noonday is overcast with sudden night; a tornado passes. Or it is midnight, which suddenly becomes bright as day; the polar lights are in the heavens. Whirlwinds pass in opposite ways, and in a sort of hideous dance, a stamping of the storms upon the waters. A cloud overburdened opens and falls to earth. Other clouds, filled with red light, flash and roar; then frown again ominously. Emptied of their lightnings, they are but as spent brands. Pent-up rains dissolve in mists. Yonder sea appears a fiery furnace in which the rains are falling: flames seem to issue from the waves. The white gleam of the ocean under the shower is reflected to marvellous distances. The different masses transform themselves into uncouth shapes. Monstrous whirlpools make strange hollows in the sky. The vapours revolve, the waves spin, the giddy Naiads roll; sea and sky are livid; noises as of cries of despair are in the air.

Great sheaves of shadow and darkness are gathered up, trembling in the far depths of the sky. Now and then there is a convulsion. The rumour becomes tumult as the wave becomes surge. The horizon, a confused mass of strata, oscillating ceaselessly, murmurs in a continual undertone. Strange and sudden outbursts break through the monotony. Cold airs rush forth, succeeded by warm blasts. The trepidation of the sea betokens anxious expectation, agony, terror profound. Suddenly the hurricane comes down, like a wild beast, to drink of the ocean: a monstrous draught! The sea rises to the invisible mouth; a mound of water is formed; the swell increases, and the waterspout appears; the Prester of the ancients, stalactite above, stalagmite below, a whirling double-inverted cone, a point in equilibrium upon another, the embrace of two mountains—a mountain of foam ascending, a mountain of vapour descending—terrible coition of the cloud and the wave. Like the column in Holy Writ, the waterspout is dark by day and luminous by night. In its presence the thunder itself is silent and seems cowed.

The vast commotion of those solitudes has its gamut, a terrible crescendo. There are the gust, the squall, the storm, the gale, the tempest, the whirlwind, the waterspout—the seven chords of the lyre of the winds, the seven notes of the firmament. The heavens are a clear space, the sea a vast round; but a breath passes, they have vanished, and all is fury and wild confusion.

Such are these inhospitable realms.

The winds rush, fly, swoop down, dwindle away, commence again; hover above, whistle, roar, and smile; they are frenzied, wanton, unbridled, or sinking at ease upon the raging waves. Their howlings have a harmony of their own. They make all the heavens sonorous. They blow in the cloud as in a trumpet; they sing through the infinite space with the mingled tones of clarions, horns, bugles, and trumpets—a sort of Promethean fanfare.

Such was the music of ancient Pan. Their harmonies are terrible. They have a colossal joy in the darkness. They drive and disperse great ships.

Night and day, in all seasons, from the tropics to the pole, there is no truce; sounding their fatal trumpet through the tangled thickets of the clouds and waves, they pursue the grim chase of vessels in distress. They have their packs of bloodhounds, and take their pleasure, setting them to bark among the rocks and billows. They huddle the clouds together, and drive them diverse. They mould and knead the supple waters as with a million hands.

The water is supple because it is incompressible. It slips away without effort. Borne down on one side, it escapes on the other. It is thus that waters become waves, and that the billows are a token of their liberty.

III
THE NOISES EXPLAINED

THE GRAND DESCENT of winds upon the world takes place at the equinoxes. At this period the balance of tropic and pole librates, and the vast atmospheric tides pour their flood upon one hemisphere and their ebb upon another. The signs of Libra and Aquarius have reference to these phenomena.

It is the time of tempests.

The sea awaits their coming, keeping silence.

Sometimes the sky looks sickly. Its face is wan. A thick dark veil obscures it. The mariners observe with uneasiness the angry aspect of the clouds.

But it is its air of calm contentment which they dread the most. A smiling sky in the equinoxes is the tempest in gay disguise. It was under skies like these that "The Tower of Weeping Women," in Amsterdam, was filled with wives and mothers scanning the far horizon.

When the vernal or autumnal storms delay to break, they are gathering strength; hoarding up their fury for more sure destruction. Beware of the gale that has been long delayed. It was Angot who said that "the sea pays well old debts."

When the delay is unusually long, the sea betokens her impatience only by a deeper calm, but the magnetic intensity manifests itself by what might be called a fiery humour in the sea. Fire issues from the waves; electric air, phosphoric water. The sailors feel a strange lassitude. This time is particularly perilous for iron vessels; their hulls are then liable to produce variations of the compass, leading them to destruction. The transatlantic steam-vessel *Iowa* perished from this cause.

To those who are familiar with the sea, its aspect at these moments is singular. It may be imagined to be both desiring and fearing the approach of the cyclone. Certain unions, though strongly urged by nature, are attended by this strange conjunction of terror and desire. The lioness in her tenderest moods flies from the lion. Thus the sea, in the fire of her passion, trembles at the near approach of her union with the tempest. The nuptials are prepared. Like the marriages of the ancient emperors, they are celebrated with immolations. The fête is heralded with disasters.

Meanwhile, from yonder deeps, from the great open sea, from the unapproachable latitudes, from the lurid horizon of the watery waste, from the utmost bounds of the free ocean, the winds pour down.

Listen; for this is the famous equinox.

The storm prepares mischief. In the old mythology these entities were recognised, indistinctly moving, in the grand scene of nature. Eolus plotted with Boreas. The alliance of element with element is necessary; they divide their task. One has to give impetus to the wave, the cloud, the stream: night is an auxiliary, and must be employed. There are compasses to be falsified, beacons to be extinguished, lanterns of lighthouses to be masked, stars to be hidden. The sea must lend her aid. Every storm is preceded by a murmur. Behind the horizon line there is a premonitory whispering among the hurricanes.

This is the noise which is heard afar off in the darkness amidst the terrible silence of the sea.

It was this significant whispering which Gilliatt had noted. The phosphorescence on the water had been the first warning: this murmur the second.

If the demon Legion exists, he is assuredly no other than the wind.

The wind is complex, but the air is one.

Hence it follows that all storms are mixed—a principle which results from the unity of the air.

The entire abyss of heaven takes part in a tempest: the entire ocean also. The totality of its forces is marshalled for the strife. A wave is the ocean gulf;

a gust is a gulf of the atmosphere. A contest with a storm is a contest with all the powers of sea and sky.

It was Messier, that great authority among naval men, the pensive astronomer of the little lodge at Cluny, who said, "The wind comes from everywhere and is everywhere." He had no faith in the idea of winds imprisoned even in inland seas. With him there were no Mediterranean winds; he declared that he recognised them as they wandered about the earth. He affirmed that on a certain day, at a certain hour, the Föhn of the Lake of Constance, the ancient Favonius of Lucretius, had traversed the horizon of Paris; on another day, the Bora of the Adriatic; on another day, the whirling Notus, which is supposed to be confined in the round of the Cyclades. He indicated their currents. He did not believe it impossible that the "Autan," which circulates between Corsica and the Balearic Isles, could escape from its bounds. He did not admit the theory of winds imprisoned like bears in their dens. It was he, too, who said that "every rain comes from the tropics, and every flash of lightning from the pole." The wind, in fact, becomes saturated with electricity at the intersection of the colures which marks the extremity of the axis, and with water at the equator; bringing moisture from the equatorial line and the electric fluid from the poles.

The wind is ubiquitous.

It is certainly not meant by this that the winds never move in zones. Nothing is better established than the existence of those continuous air currents; and aerial navigation by means of the wind boats, to which the passion for Greek terminology has given the name of "aeroscaphes," may one day succeed in utilising the chief of these streams of wind. The regular course of air streams is an incontestable fact. There are both rivers of wind and rivulets of wind, although their branches are exactly the reverse of water currents: for in the air it is the rivulets which flow out of the rivers, and the smaller rivers which flow out of the great streams instead of falling into them. Hence instead of concentration we have dispersion.

The united action of the winds and the unity of the atmosphere result from this dispersion. The displacement of one molecule produces the displacement of another. The vast body of air becomes subject to one agitation. To these profound causes of coalition we must add the irregular surface of the earth, whose mountains furrow the atmosphere, contorting and diverting the winds from their course, and determining the directions of counter currents in infinite radiations.

The phenomenon of the wind is the oscillation of two oceans one against the other; the ocean of air, superimposed upon the ocean of water, rests upon these currents, and is convulsed with this vast agitation.

The indivisible cannot produce separate action. No partition divides wave from wave. The islands of the Channel feel the influence of the Cape of Good Hope. Navigation everywhere contends with the same monster; the sea is one hydra. The waves cover it as with a coat of scales. The ocean is Ceto.

Upon that unity reposes an infinite variety.

IV
TURBA TURMA

ACCORDING TO THE compass there are thirty-two winds, that is to say, thirty-two points. But these directions may be subdivided indefinitely. Classed by its directions, the wind is incalculable; classed by its kinds, it is infinite. Homer himself would have shrunk from the task of enumerating them.

The polar current encounters the tropical current. Heat and cold are thus combined; the equilibrium is distributed by a shock, the wave of wind issues forth and is distended, scattered and broken up in every direction in fierce streams. The dispersion of the gusts shakes the streaming locks of the wind upon the four corners of the horizon.

All the winds which blow are there. The wind of the Gulf Stream, which disgorges the great fogs of Newfoundland; the wind of Peru, in the region of silent heavens, where no man ever heard the thunder roar; the wind of Nova Scotia, where flies the great auk (*Alca impennis*) with his furrowed beak; the iron whirlwinds of the Chinese seas; the wind of Mozambique, which destroys the canoes and junks; the electric wind, which the people of Japan denounce by the beating of a gong; the African wind, which blows between Table Mountain and the Devil's Peak, where it gains its liberty; the currents of the equator, which pass over the trade winds, describing a parabola, the summit of which is always to the west; the Plutonian wind, which issues from craters, the terrible breath of flames; the singular wind peculiar to the volcano Awa, which occasions a perpetual olive tint in the north; the Java monsoon, against which the people construct those casemates known as hurricane houses; the branching north winds called by the English "Bush winds;" the curved squalls of the Straits of Malacca, observed by Horsburgh; the powerful south-west wind, called Pampero in Chili, and Rebojo at Buenos Ayres, which carries the great condor out to sea, and saves him from the pit where the Indian, concealed under a bullock-hide newly stripped, watches for him, lying on his back and bending his great bow with his feet; the chemical wind, which, according to Lemery, produces thunder-bolts from the clouds; the Harmattan of the Caffres; the Polar snow-driver, which harnesses itself to the everlasting icebergs; the wind of the Gulf of Bengal, which sweeps over a continent to pillage the triangular town of wooden booths at Nijni-Novogorod, in which is held the great fair of Asia; the wind of the Cordilleras, agitator of great waves and forests; the wind of the Australian Archipelago, where the bee-hunters take the wild hives hidden under the forks of the branches of the giant eucalyptus; the Sirocco, the Mistral, the Hurricane, the dry winds, the inundating and diluvian winds, the torrid winds, which scatter dust from the plains of Brazil upon the streets of Genoa, which both obey and revolt against diurnal rotation, and of which Herrara said, "*Malo viento torna contra el sol;*" those winds which hunt in couples, conspiring mischief, the one undoing the work of the other; and those old winds which assailed Columbus on the coast of Veragua, and which during forty days, from the 21st of October to the 28th of November 1520, delayed and nearly frustrated Magellan's approach to the Pacific; and those which dismasted the Armada and confounded Philip II. Others, too, there are, of the names of which there is no end. The winds, for instance, which carry showers of frogs and locusts, and drive before them clouds of living things across the ocean; those which blow in what are called "Wind-leaps," and whose function is to destroy ships at sea; those which at a single blast throw the cargo out of trim, and compel the vessel to continue her course half broadside over; the winds which construct the circum-cumuli; the winds which mass together the circum-strati; the dark heavy winds swelled with rains; the winds of the hailstorms; the fever winds, whose approach sets the salt springs and sulphur springs of Calabria boiling; those which give a glittering appearance to the fur of African panthers, prowling among the bushes of Cape Ferro; those which come shaking from the cloud, like the tongue of a trigonocephal, the terrible forked lightning; and those which bring whirlwinds of black snow. Such is the legion of winds.

The Douvres rock heard their distant tramp at the moment when Gilliatt was constructing his breakwater.

As we have said, the wind means the combination of all the winds of the earth.

V
GILLIATT'S ALTERNATIVES

THE MYSTERIOUS FORCES had chosen their time well.

Chance, if chance exists, is sometimes far-seeing.

While the sloop had been anchored in the little creek of "The Man Rock," and as long as the machinery had been prisoned in the wreck, Gilliatt's position had been impregnable. The sloop was in safety; the machinery sheltered. The Douvres, which held the hull of the Durande fast, condemned it to slow destruction, but protected it against unexpected accidents. In any event, one resource had remained to him. If the engine had been destroyed, Gilliatt would have been uninjured. He had still the sloop by which to escape.

But to wait till the sloop was removed from the anchorage where she was inaccessible; to allow it to be fixed in the defile of the Douvres; to watch until the sloop, too, was, as it were, entangled in the rocks; to permit him to complete the salvage, the moving, and the final embarkation of the machinery; to do no damage to that wonderful construction by which one man was enabled to put the whole aboard his bark; to acquiesce, in fact, in the success of his exploits so far; this was but the trap which the elements had laid for him. Now for the first time he began to perceive in all its sinister characteristics the trick which the sea had been meditating so long.

The machinery, the sloop, and their master were all now within the gorge of the rocks. They formed but a single point. One blow, and the sloop might be dashed to pieces on the rock, the machinery destroyed, and Gilliatt drowned.

The situation could not have been more critical.

The sphinx, which men have imagined concealing herself in the cloud, seemed to mock him with a dilemma.

"Go or stay."

To go would have been madness; to remain was terrible.

VI
THE COMBAT

GILLIATT ascended to the summit of the Great Douvre.

From hence he could see around the horizon.

The western side was appalling. A wall of cloud spread across it, barring the wide expanse from side to side, and ascending slowly from the horizon towards the zenith. This wall, straight lined, vertical, without a crevice in its height, without a rent in its structure, seemed built by the square and measured by the plumb-line. It was cloud in the likeness of granite. Its escarpment, completely perpendicular at the southern extremity, curved a little towards the north, like a bent sheet of iron, presenting the steep slippery face of an inclined plane. The dark wall enlarged and grew; but its entablature never ceased for a moment to be parallel with the horizon line, which was almost indistinguishable in the gathering darkness. Silently, and altogether, the airy battlements ascended. No undulation, no wrinkle, no projection changed its shape or moved its place. The aspect of this immobility in movement was impressive. The sun, pale in the midst of a strange sickly transparence, lighted up this outline of the Apocalypse. Already the cloudy bank had blotted out one half the space of the sky: shelving like the fearful talus of the abyss. It was the uprising of a dark mountain between earth and heaven.

It was night falling suddenly upon midday.

There was a heat in the air as from an oven door, coming from that mysterious mass on mass. The sky, which from blue had become white, was now turning from white to a slatey grey. The sea beneath was leaden-hued and dull. There was no breath, no wave, no noise. Far as eye could reach, the desert ocean. No sail was visible on any side. The birds had disappeared. Some monstrous treason seemed abroad.

The wall of cloud grew visibly larger.

This moving mountain of vapours, which was approaching the Douvres, was one of those clouds which might be called the clouds of battle. Sinister appearances; some strange, furtive glance seemed cast upon the beholder through that obscure mass up-piled.

The approach was terrible.

Gilliatt observed it closely, and muttered to himself, "I am thirsty enough, but you will give me plenty to drink."

He stood there motionless a few moments, his eye fixed upon the cloud bank, as if mentally taking a sounding of the tempest.

His *galérienne* was in the pocket of his jacket; he took it out and placed it on his head. Then he fetched from the cave, which had so long served him for a sleeping-place, a few things which he had kept there in reserve; he put on his overalls, and attired himself in his waterproof overcoat, like a knight who puts on his armour at the moment of battle. He had no shoes; but his naked feet had become hardened to the rocks.

This preparation for the storm being completed, he looked down upon his breakwater, grasped the knotted cord hurriedly, descended from the plateau of the Douvre, stepped on to the rocks below, and hastened to his store cavern. A few moments later he was at work. The vast silent cloud might have heard the strokes of his hammer. With the nails, ropes, and beams which still remained, he constructed for the eastern gullet a second frame, which he succeeded in fixing at ten or twelve feet from the other.

The silence was still profound. The blades of grass between the cracks of the rocks were not stirred.

The sun disappeared suddenly. Gilliatt looked up.

The rising cloud had just reached it. It was like the blotting out of day, succeeded by a mingled pale reflection.

The immense wall of cloud had changed its appearance. It no longer
retained its unity. It had curved on reaching the zenith, whence it spread
horizontally over the rest of the heavens. It had now its various stages. The
tempest formation was visible, like the strata in the side of a trench. It was
possible to distinguish the layers of the rain from the beds of hail. There
was no lightning, but a horrible, diffused glare; for the idea of horror may
be attached to light. The vague breathing of the storm was audible; the
silence was broken by an obscure palpitation. Gilliatt, silent also, watched the
giant blocks of vapour grouping themselves overhead forming the shapeless
mass of clouds. Upon the horizon brooded and lengthened out a band of
mist of ashen hue; in the zenith, another band of lead colour. Pale, ragged
fragments of cloud hung from the great mass above upon the mist below.
The pile of cloud which formed the background was wan, dull, gloomy. A
thin, whitish transverse cloud, coming no one could tell whither, cut the
high dark wall obliquely from north to south. One of the extremities of this
cloud trailed along the surface of the sea. At the point where it touched the
waters, a dense red vapour was visible in the midst of the darkness. Below
it, smaller clouds, quite black and very low, were flying as if bewildered or
moved by opposite currents of air. The immense cloud beyond increased
from all points at once, darkened the eclipse, and continued to spread its
sombre pall. In the east, behind Gilliatt, there was only one clear porch in
the heavens, which was rapidly being closed. Without any feeling of wind
abroad, a strange flight of grey downy particles seemed to pass; they were
fine and scattered as if some gigantic bird had been plucked of its plum-
age behind the bank of cloud. A dark compact roof had gradually formed
itself, which on the verge of the horizon touched the sea, and mingled in
darkness with it. The beholder had a vague sense of something advancing
steadily towards him. It was vast, heavy, ominous. Suddenly an immense peal
of thunder burst upon the air.

Gilliatt himself felt the shock. The rude reality in the midst of that visionary region has something in it terrific. The listener might fancy that he
hears something falling in the chamber of giants. No electric flash accompanied the report. It was a blind peal. The silence was profound again. There
was an interval, as when combatants take up their position. Then appeared
slowly, one after the other, great shapeless flashes; these flashes were silent.

The wall of cloud was now a vast cavern, with roofs and arches. Outlines of forms were traceable among them; monstrous heads were vaguely shadowed forth; rocks seemed to stretch out; elephants bearing turrets, seen for a moment, vanished. A column of vapour, straight, round, and dark, and surmounted by a white mist, simulated the form of a colossal steam-vessel engulfed, hissing, and smoking beneath the waves. Sheets of cloud undulated like folds of giant flags. In the centre, under a thick purple pall, a nucleus of dense fog sunk motionless, inert, impenetrable by the electric fires; a sort of hideous fœtus in the bosom of the tempest.

Suddenly Gilliatt felt a breath moving his hair. Two or three large spots of rain fell heavily around him on the rock. Then there was a second thunderclap. The wind was rising.

The terror of darkness was at its highest point. The first peal of thunder had shaken the sea; the second rent the wall of cloud from top to base; breach was visible; the pent-up deluge rushed towards it; the rent became like a gulf filled with rain. The outpouring of the tempest had begun.

The moment was terrible.

Rain, wind, lightnings, thunder, waves swirling upwards to the clouds, foam, hoarse noises, whistlings, mingled together like monsters suddenly unloosened.

For a solitary man, imprisoned with an overloaded vessel, between two dangerous rocks in mid-ocean, no crisis could have been more menacing. The danger of the tide, over which he had triumphed, was nothing compared with the danger of the tempest.

Surrounded on all sides by dangers, Gilliatt, at the last moment, and before the crowning peril, had developed an ingenious strategy. He had secured his basis of operations in the enemies' territory; had pressed the rock into his service. The Douvres, originally his enemy, had become his second in that immense duel. Out of that sepulchre he had constructed a fortress. He was built up among those formidable sea ruins. He was blockaded, but well defended. He had, so to speak, set his back against the wall, and stood face to face with the hurricane. He had barricaded the narrow strait, that highway of the waves. This, indeed, was the only possible course. It seemed as if the ocean, like other despots, might be brought to reason by the aid of barricades. The sloop might be considered secure on three sides.

Closely wedged between the two interior walls of the rock, made fast by three anchorings, she was sheltered from the north by the Little Douvre, on the south by the Great one; terrible escarpments, more accustomed to wreck vessels than to save them. On the western side she was protected by the frame of timbers made fast and nailed to the rocks—a tried barrier which had withstood the rude flood-tide of the sea; a veritable citadel-gate, having for its sides the columns of the rock—the two Douvres themselves. Nothing was to be feared from that side. It was on the eastern side only that there was danger.

On that side there was no protection but the breakwater. A breakwater is an apparatus for dividing and distributing. It requires at least two frames. Gilliatt had only had time to construct one. He was compelled to build the second in the very presence of the tempest.

Fortunately the wind came from the north-west. The wind is not always adroit in its attacks. The north-west wind, which is the ancient "galerno," had little effect upon the Douvres. It assailed the rocks in flank, and drove the waves neither against the one nor the other of the two gullets; so that instead of rushing into a defile, they dashed themselves against a wall.

But the currents of the wind are curved, and it was probable that there would be some sudden change. If it should veer to the east before the second frame could be constructed the peril would be great. The irruption of the sea into the gorge would be complete, and all would probably be lost.

The wildness of the storm went on increasing. The essence of a tempest is the rapid succession of its blows. That is its strength; but it is also its weakness. Its fury gives the opportunity to human intelligence, and man spies its weak points for his defence; but under what overwhelming assaults! No respite, no interruption, no truce, no pause for taking breath. There seems an unspeakable cowardice in that prodigality of inexhaustible resources.

All the tumult of the wide expanse rushed towards the Douvres. Voices were heard in the darkness. What could they be? The ancient terror of the sea was there. At times they seemed to speak as if some one was uttering words of command. There were clamours, strange trepidations, and then that majestic roar which the mariners call the "Ocean cry." The indefinite and flying eddies of the wind whistled, while curling the waves and flinging them like giant quoits, cast by invisible athletes, against the breakers.

The enormous surf streamed over all the rocks; torrents above; foam below. Then the roaring was redoubled. No uproar of men or beasts could yield an idea of that din which mingled with the incessant breaking of the sea. The clouds cannonaded, the hailstones poured their volleys, the surf mounted to the assault. As far as eye could reach, the sea was white; ten leagues of yeasty water filled the horizon. Doors of fire were opened, clouds seemed burnt by clouds, and showed like smoke above a nebulous red mass, resembling burning embers. Floating conflagrations rushed together and amalgamated, each changing the shape of the other. From the midst of the dark roof a terrible arsenal appeared to be emptied out, hurling downward from the gulf, pell-mell, waterspouts, hail torrents, purple fire, phosphoric gleams, darkness, and lightnings.

Meanwhile Gilliatt seemed to pay no attention to the storm. His head was bent over his work. The second framework began to approach completion. To every clap of thunder he replied with a blow of his hammer, making a cadence which was audible even amidst that tumult. He was bareheaded, for a gust had carried away his *galérienne*.

He suffered from a burning thirst. Little pools of rain had formed in the rocks around him. From time to time he took some water in the hollow of his hand and drank. Then, without even looking upward to observe the storm, he applied himself anew to his task.

All might depend upon a moment. He knew the fate that awaited him if his breakwater should not be completed in time. Of what avail could it be to lose a moment in looking for the approach of death?

The turmoil around him was like that of a vast bubbling cauldron. Crash and uproar were everywhere. Sometimes the lightning seemed to descend a sort of ladder. The electric flame returned incessantly to the same points of the rock, where there were probably metallic veins. Hailstones fell of enormous size. Gilliatt was compelled to shake the folds of his overcoat, even the pockets of which became filled with hail.

The storm had now rotated to the west, and was expending its fury upon the barricades of the two Douvres. But Gilliatt had faith in his breakwaters, and with good reason. These barricades, made of a great portion of the fore-part of the Durande, took the shock of the waves easily. Elasticity is a resistance. The experiments of Stephenson establish the fact that against the waves, which are themselves elastic, a raft of timber, joined and chained together in a certain fashion, will form a more powerful obstacle than a breakwater of masonry. The barriers of the Douvres fulfilled these conditions. They were, moreover, so ingeniously made fast, that the waves striking them beneath were like hammers beating in nails, pressing and consolidating the work upon the rocks. To demolish them it would have been necessary to overthrow the Douvres themselves. The surf, in fact, was only able to cast over upon the sloop some flakes of foam. On that side, thanks to the barrier, the tempest ended only in harmless insult. Gilliatt turned his back upon the scene. He heard composedly its useless rage upon the rocks behind him.

The foam-flakes coming from all sides were like flights of down. The vast irritated ocean deluged the rocks, dashed over them and raged within, penetrated into the network of their interior fissures, and issued again from the granitic masses by the narrow chinks, forming a kind of inexhaustible fountains playing peacefully in the midst of that deluge. Here and there a silvery network fell gracefully from these spouts in the sea.

The second frame of the eastern barrier was nearly completed. A few more knots of rope and ends of chains and this new rampart would be ready to play its part in barring out the storm.

Suddenly there was a great brightness; the rain ceased; the clouds rolled asunder; the wind had just shifted; a sort of high, dark window opened in the zenith, and the lightnings were extinguished. The end seemed to have come. It was but the commencement.

The change of wind was from the north-west to the north-east.

The storm was preparing to burst forth again with a new legion of hurricanes. The north was about to mount to the assault. Sailors call this dreaded moment of transition the "Return storm." The southern wind brings most rain, the north wind most lightning.

The attack, coming now from the east, was directed against the weak point of the position.

This time Gilliatt interrupted his work and looked around him.

He stood erect, upon a curved projection of the rock behind the second barrier, which was nearly finished. If the first frame had been carried away, it would have broken down the second, which was not yet consolidated, and must have crushed him. Gilliatt, in the place that he had chosen, must in that case have been destroyed before seeing the sloop, the machinery, and all his work shattered and swallowed up in the gulf. Such was the possibility which awaited him. He accepted it, and contemplated it sternly.

In that wreck of all his hope, to die at once would have been his desire; to die first, as he would have regarded it—for the machinery produced in his mind the effect of a living being. He moved aside his hair, which was beaten over his eyes by the wind, grasped his trusty mallet, drew himself up in a menacing attitude, and awaited the event.

He was not kept long in suspense.

A flash of lightning gave the signal; the livid opening in the zenith closed; a driving torrent of rain fell; then all became dark, save where the lightnings broke forth once more. The attack had recommenced in earnest.

A heavy swell, visible from time to time in the blaze of the lightning, was rolling in the east beyond "The Man Rock." It resembled a huge wall of glass. It was green and without foam, and it stretched across the wide expanse. It was advancing towards the breakwater, increasing as it approached. It was a singular kind of gigantic cylinder, rolling upon the ocean. The thunder kept up a hollow rumbling.

The great wave struck "The Man Rock," broke in twain, and passed beyond. The broken wave, rejoined, formed a mountain of water, and instead of advancing in parallel line as before, came down perpendicularly upon the breakwater.

The shock was terrific: the whole wave became a roaring surf.

It is impossible for those who have not witnessed them to imagine those snowy avalanches which the sea thus precipitates, and under which it engulfs for the moment rocks of more than a hundred feet in height, such, for example, as the Great Anderlo at Guernsey, and the Pinnacle at Jersey. At Saint Mary of Madagascar it passes completely over the promontory of Tintingue.

For some moments the sea drowned everything. Nothing was visible except the furious waters, an enormous breadth of foam, the whiteness of a winding-sheet blowing in the draught of a sepulchre; nothing was heard but the roaring storm working devastation around.

When the foam subsided, Gilliatt was still standing at his post.

The barrier had stood firm. Not a chain was broken, not a nail displaced. It had exhibited under the trial the two chief qualities of a breakwater; it had proved flexible as a hurdle and firm as a wall. The surf falling upon it had dissolved into a shower of drops.

A river of foam rushing along the zigzags of the defile subsided as it approached the sloop.

The man who had put this curb upon the fury of the ocean took no rest.

The storm fortunately turned aside its fury for a moment. The fierce attack of the waves was renewed upon the wall of the rock. There was a respite, and Gilliatt took advantage of it to complete the interior barrier.

The daylight faded upon his labours. The hurricane continued its violence upon the flank of the rocks with a mournful solemnity. The stores of fire and water in the sky poured out incessantly without exhausting themselves. The undulations of the wind above and below were like the movements of a dragon.

Nightfall brought scarcely any deeper night. The change was hardly felt, for the darkness was never complete. Tempests alternately darkening and illumining by their lightnings, are merely intervals of the visible and invisible. All is pale glare, and then all is darkness. Spectral shapes issue forth suddenly, and return as suddenly into the deep shade.

A phosphoric zone, tinged with the hue of the aurora borealis, appeared like ghastly flames behind the dense clouds, giving to all things a wan aspect, and making the rain-drifts luminous.

This uncertain light aided Gilliatt, and directed him in his operations. By its help he was enabled to raise the forward barrier. The breakwater was now almost complete. As he was engaged in making fast a powerful cable to the last beam, the gale blew directly in his face. This compelled him to raise his head. The wind had shifted abruptly to the north-east. The assault upon the eastern gullet recommenced. Gilliatt cast his eyes around the horizon. Another great wall of water was approaching.

The wave broke with a great shock; a second followed; then another and another still; then five or six almost together; then a last shock of tremendous force.

This last wave, which was an accumulation of forces, had a singular resemblance to a living thing. It would not have been difficult to imagine in the midst of that swelling mass the shapes of fins and gill-coverings. It fell heavily and broke upon the barriers. Its almost animal form was torn to pieces in the shape of spouts and gushes, resembling the crushing to death of some sea hydra upon that block of rocks and timbers. The swell rushed through, subsiding but devastating as it went. The huge wave seemed to bite and cling to its victim as it died. The rock shook to its base. A savage howling mingled with the roar; the foam flew far like the spouting of a leviathan.

The subsidence exhibited the extent of the ravages of the surf. This last escalade had not been ineffectual. The breakwater had suffered this time. A long and heavy beam, torn from the first barrier, had been carried over the second, and hurled violently upon the projecting rock on which Gilliatt had stood but a moment before. By good fortune he had not returned there. Had he done so, his death had been inevitable.

There was a remarkable circumstance in the fall of this beam, which by preventing the framework rebounding, saved Gilliatt from greater dangers. It even proved useful to him, as will be seen, in another way.

Between the projecting rock and the interior wall of the defile there was a large interval, something like the notch of an axe, or the split of a wedge. One of the extremities of the timber hurled into the air by the waves had stuck fast into this notch in falling. The gap had become enlarged.

Gilliatt was struck with an idea. It was that of bearing heavily on the other extremity.

The beam caught by one end in the nook, which it had widened, projected from it straight as an outstretched arm. This species of arm projected parallel with the anterior wall of the defile, and the disengaged end stretched from its resting place about eighteen or twenty inches. A good distance for the object to be attained.

Gilliatt raised himself by means of his hands, feet, and knees to the escarpment, and then turned his back, pressing both his shoulders against the enormous lever. The beam was long, which increased its raising power. The rock was already loosened; but he was compelled to renew his efforts again and again. The sweat-drops rolled from his forehead as rapidly as the spray. The fourth attempt exhausted all his powers. There was a cracking noise; the gap spreading in the shape of a fissure, opened its vast jaws, and the heavy mass fell into the narrow space of the defile with a noise like the echo of the thunder.

The mass fell straight, and without breaking; resting in its bed like a Druid cromlech precipitated in one piece.

The beam which had served as a lever descended with the rock, and Gilliatt, stumbling forward as it gave way, narrowly escaped falling.

The bed of the pass at this part was full of huge round stones, and there was little water. The monolith lying in the boiling foam, the flakes of which fell on Gilliatt where he stood, stretched from side to side of the great parallel rocks of the defile, and formed a transversal wall, a sort of cross-stroke between the two escarpments. Its two ends touched the rocks. It had been a little too long to lie flat, but its summit of soft rock was struck off with the fall. The result of this fall was a singular sort of *cul-de-sac*, which may still be seen. The water behind this stony barrier is almost always tranquil.

This was a rampart more invincible still than the forward timbers of the Durande fixed between the two Douvres.

The barrier came opportunely.

The assaults of the sea had continued. The obstinacy of the waves is always increased by an obstacle. The first frame began to show signs of breaking up. One breach, however small, in a breakwater, is always serious. It inevitably enlarges, and there is no means of supplying its place, for the sea would sweep away the workmen.

A flash which lighted up the rocks revealed to Gilliatt the nature of the mischief; the beams broken down, the ends of rope and fragments of chain swinging in the winds, and a rent in the centre of the apparatus. The second frame was intact.

Though the block of stone so powerfully overturned by Gilliatt in the defile behind the breakwater was the strongest possible barrier, it had a defect. It was too low. The surge could not destroy, but could sweep over it.

It was useless to think of building it higher. Nothing but masses of rock could avail upon a barrier of stone; but how could such masses be detached? or, if detached, how could they be moved, or raised, or piled, or fixed? Timbers may be added, but rocks cannot.

Gilliatt was not Enceladus.

The very little height of this rocky isthmus rendered him anxious.

The effects of this fault were not long in showing themselves. The assaults upon the breakwater were incessant; the heavy seas seemed not merely to rage, but to attack with determination to destroy it. A sort of trampling noise was heard upon the jolted framework.

Suddenly the end of a binding strake, detached from the dislocated frame, was swept away over the second barrier and across the transversal rock, falling in the defile, where the water seized and carried it into the sinuosities of the pass. Gilliatt lost sight of it. It seemed probable that it would do some injury to the sloop. Fortunately, the water in the interior of the rocks, shut in on all sides, felt little of the commotion without. The waves there were comparatively trifling, and the shock was not likely to be very severe. For the rest, he had little time to spare for reflection upon this mishap. Every variety of danger was arising at once; the tempest was concentrated upon the vulnerable point; destruction was imminent.

The darkness was profound for a moment: the lightnings paused—a sort of sinister connivance. The cloud and the sea became one: there was a dull peal.

This was followed by a terrible outburst. The frame which formed the front of the barriers was swept away. The fragments of beams were visible in the rolling waters. The sea was using the first breakwater as an engine for making a breach in the second.

Gilliatt experienced the feeling of a general who sees his advanced guard driven in.

The second construction of beams resisted the shock. The apparatus behind it was powerfully secured and buttressed. But the broken frame was heavy, and was at the mercy of the waves, which were incessantly hurling it forward and withdrawing it. The ropes and chains which remained unsevered prevented its entirely breaking up, and the qualities which Gilliatt had given it as a means of defence made it, in the end, a more effective weapon of destruction. Instead of a buckler, it had become a battering-ram. Besides this, it was now full of irregularities from breaking; ends of timbers projected from all parts; and it was, as it were, covered with teeth and spikes. No sort of arm could have been more effective, or more fitted for the handling of the tempest. It was the projectile, while the sea played the part of the catapult.

The blows succeeded each other with a dismal regularity. Gilliatt, thoughtful and anxious, behind that barricaded portal, listened to the sound of death knocking loudly for admittance.

He reflected with bitterness that, but for the fatal entanglement of the funnel of the Durande in the wreck, he would have been at that very moment, and even since the morning, once more at Guernsey, in the port, with the sloop out of danger and with the machinery saved.

The dreaded moment arrived. The destruction was complete. There was a sound like a death-rattle. The entire frame of the breakwater, the double apparatus crushed and mingled confusedly, came in a whirl of foam, rushing upon the stone barricade like chaos upon a mountain, where it stopped. Here the fragments lay together, a mass of beams penetrable by the waves, but still breaking their force. The conquered barrier struggled nobly against destruction. The waves had shattered it, and in their turn were shattered against it. Though overthrown, it still remained in some degree effective. The rock which barred its passage, an immovable obstacle held it fast. The defile, as we have said, was very narrow at that point; the victorious whirlwind had driven forward, mingled and piled up the wreck of the breakwater in this narrow pass. The very violence of the assault, by heaping up the mass and driving the broken ends one into the other, had contributed to make the pile firm. It was destroyed, but immovable. A few pieces of timber only were swept away and dispersed by the waves. One passed through the air very near to Gilliatt. He felt the counter current upon his forehead.

Some waves, however, of that kind which in great tempests return with an imperturbable regularity, swept over the ruins of the breakwater. They fell into the defile, and in spite of the many angles of the passage, set the waters within in commotion. The waters began to roll through the gorge ominously. The mysterious embraces of the waves among the rocks were audible.

What means were there of preventing this agitation extending as far as the sloop? It would not require a long time for the blast of wind to create a tempest through all the windings of the pass. A few heavy seas would be sufficient to stave in the sloop and scatter her burden.

Gilliatt shuddered as he reflected.

But he was not disconcerted. No defeat could daunt his soul.

The hurricane had now discovered the true plan of attack, and was rushing fiercely between the two walls of the strait.

Suddenly a crash was heard, resounding and prolonging itself through the defile at some distance behind him: a crash more terrible than any he had yet heard.

It came from the direction of the sloop.

Something disastrous was happening there.

Gilliatt hastened towards it.

From the eastern gullet where he was, he could not see the sloop on account of the sharp turns of the pass. At the last turn he stopped and waited for the lightning.

The first flash revealed to him the position of affairs.

The rush of the sea through the eastern entrance had been met by a blast of wind from the other end. A disaster was near at hand.

The sloop had received no visible damage; anchored as she was, the storm had little power over her, but the carcase of the Durande was distressed.

In such a tempest, the wreck presented a considerable surface. It was entirely out of the sea in the air, exposed. The breach which Gilliatt had made, and which he had passed the engine through, had rendered the hull still weaker. The keelson was snapped, the vertebral column of the skeleton was broken.

The hurricane had passed over it. Scarcely more than this was needed to complete its destruction. The planking of the deck had bent like an opened book. The dismemberment had begun. It was the noise of this dislocation which had reached Gilliatt's ears in the midst of the tempest.

The disaster which presented itself as he approached appeared almost irremediable.

The square opening which he had cut in the keel had become a gaping wound. The wind had converted the smooth-cut hole into a ragged fracture. This transverse breach separated the wreck in two. The after-part, nearest to the sloop, had remained firm in its bed of rocks. The forward portion which faced him was hanging. A fracture, while it holds, is a sort of hinge. The whole mass oscillated, as the wind moved it, with a doleful noise. Fortunately the sloop was no longer beneath it.

But this swinging movement shook the other portion of the hull, still wedged and immovable as it was between the two Douvres. From shaking to casting down the distance is not far. Under the obstinate assaults of the gale, the dislocated part might suddenly carry away the other portion, which almost touched the sloop. In this case, the whole wreck, together with the sloop and the engine, must be swept into the sea and swallowed up.

All this presented itself to his eyes. It was the end of all. How could it be prevented?

Gilliatt was one of those who are accustomed to snatch the means of safety out of danger itself. He collected his ideas for a moment. Then he hastened to his arsenal and brought his hatchet.

The mallet had served him well, it was now the turn of the axe.

He mounted upon the wreck, got a footing on that part of the planking which had not given way, and leaning over the precipice of the pass between the Douvres, he began to cut away the broken joists and the planking which supported the hanging portion of the hull.

His object was to effect the separation of the two parts of the wreck, to disencumber the half which remained firm, to throw overboard what the waves had seized, and thus share the prey with the storm. The hanging portion of the wreck, borne down by the wind and by its own weight, adhered only at one or two points. The entire wreck resembled a folding-screen, one leaf of which, half-hanging, beat against the other. Five or six pieces of the planking only, bent and started, but not broken, still held. Their fractures creaked and enlarged at every gust, and the axe, so to speak, had but to help the labour of the wind. This more than half-severed condition, while it increased the facility of the work, also rendered it dangerous. The whole might give way beneath him at any moment.

The tempest had reached its highest point. The convulsion of the sea reached the heavens. Hitherto the storm had been supreme, it had seemed to work its own imperious will, to give the impulse, to drive the waves to frenzy, while still preserving a sort of sinister lucidity. Below was fury— above, anger. The heavens are the breath, the ocean only foam, hence the authority of the wind. But the intoxication of its own horrors had confused it. It had become a mere whirlwind; it was a blindness leading to night. There are times when tempests become frenzied, when the heavens are attacked with a sort of delirium; when the firmament raves and hurls its lightnings blindly. No terror is greater than this. It is a hideous moment. The trembling of the rock was at its height. Every storm has a mysterious course, but now it loses its appointed path. It is the most dangerous point of the tempest. "At that moment," says Thomas Fuller, "the wind is a furious maniac." It is at that instant that that continuous discharge of electricity takes place which Piddington calls "the cascade of lightnings." It is at that instant that in the blackest spot of the clouds, none know why, unless it be to spy the universal terror, a circle of blue light appears, which the Spanish sailors of ancient times called the eye of the tempest, *el ojo de la tempestad*. That terrible eye looked down upon Gilliatt.

Gilliatt on his part was surveying the heavens. He raised his head now. After every stroke of his hatchet he stood erect and gazed upwards, almost haughtily. He was, or seemed to be, too near destruction not to feel self-sustained. Would he despair? No! In the presence of the wildest fury of the ocean he was watchful as well as bold. He planted his feet only where the wreck was firm. He ventured his life, and yet was careful; for his determined spirit, too, had reached its highest point. His strength had grown tenfold greater. He had become heated with his own intrepidity. The strokes of his hatchet were like blows of defiance. He seemed to have gained in directness what the tempest had lost. A pathetic struggle! On the one hand, an indefatigable will; on the other, inexhaustible power. It was a contest with the elements for the prize at his feet. The clouds took the shape of Gorgon masks in the immensity of the heavens; every possible form of terror appeared; the rain came from the sea, the surf from the cloud; phantoms of the wind bent down; meteoric faces revealed themselves and were again eclipsed, leaving the darkness more monstrous: then there was nothing seen but the torrents coming from all sides—a boiling sea; cumuli heavy with hail, ashen-hued, ragged-edged, appeared seized with a sort of whirling frenzy; strange rattlings filled the air; the inverse currents of electricity observed by Volta darted their sudden flashes from cloud to cloud. The prolongation of the lightnings was terrible; the flashes passed near to Gilliatt. The very ocean seemed astonished. He passed to and fro upon the tottering wreck, making the deck tremble under his steps, striking, cutting, hacking with the hatchet in his hand, pallid in the gleam of the lightning, his long hair streaming, his feet naked, in rags, his face covered with the foam of the sea, but grand still amid that maelstrom of the thunderstorm.

Against these furious powers man has no weapon but his invention. Invention was Gilliatt's triumph. His object was to allow all the dislocated portions of the wreck to fall together. For this reason he cut away the broken portions without entirely separating them, leaving some parts on which they still swung. Suddenly he stopped, holding his axe in the air. The operation was complete. The entire portion went with a crash.

The mass rolled down between the two Douvres, just below Gilliatt, who stood upon the wreck, leaning over and observing the fall. It fell perpendicularly into the water, struck the rocks, and stopped in the de-file before touching the bottom. Enough remained out of the water to rise more than twelve feet above the waves. The vertical mass of planking formed a wall between the two Douvres; like the rock overturned crosswise higher up the defile, it allowed only a slight stream of foam to pass through at its two extremities, and thus was a fifth barricade improvised by Gilliatt against the tempest in that passage of the seas.

The hurricane itself, in its blind fury, had assisted in the construction of this last barrier.

It was fortunate that the proximity of the two walls had prevented the mass of wreck from falling to the bottom. This circumstance gave the barri-cade greater height; the water, besides, could flow under the obstacle, which diminished the power of the waves. That which passes below cannot pass over. This is partly the secret of the floating breakwater.

Henceforth, let the storm do what it might, there was nothing to fear for the sloop or the machinery. The water around them could not become agitated again. Between the barrier of the Douvres, which covered them on the west, and the barricade which protected them from the east, no heavy sea or wind could reach them.

Gilliatt had plucked safety out of the catastrophe itself. The storm had been his fellow-labourer in the work.

This done, he took a little water in the palm of his hand from one of the rain-pools, and drank: and then, looking upward at the storm, said with a smile, "Bungler!"

Human intelligence combating with brute force experiences an ironical joy in demonstrating the stupidity of its antagonist, and compelling it to serve the very objects of its fury, and Gilliatt felt something of that immemorial desire to insult his invisible enemy, which is as old as the heroes of the *Iliad*.

He descended to the sloop and examined it by the gleam of the lightning. The relief which he had been able to give to his distressed bark was well-timed. She had been much shaken during the last hour, and had begun to give way. A hasty glance revealed no serious injury. Nevertheless, he was certain that the vessel had been subjected to violent shocks. As soon as the waves had subsided, the hull had righted itself; the anchors had held fast; as to the machine, the four chains had supported it admirably.

While Gilliatt was completing this survey, something white passed before his eyes and vanished in the gloom. It was a sea-mew.

No sight could be more welcome in tempestuous weather. When the birds reappear the storm is departing. The thunder redoubled; another good sign.

The violent efforts of the storm had broken its force. All mariners know that the last ordeal is severe, but short. The excessive violence of the thunderstorm is the herald of the end.

The rain stopped suddenly. Then there was only a surly rumbling in the heavens. The storm ceased with the suddenness of a plank falling to the ground. The immense mass of clouds became disorganised. A strip of clear sky appeared between them. Gilliatt was astonished: it was broad daylight.

The tempest had lasted nearly twenty hours.

The wind which had brought the storm carried it away. A dark pile was diffused over the horizon, the broken clouds were flying in confusion across the sky. From one end to the other of the line there was a movement of retreat: a long muttering was heard, gradually decreasing, a few last drops of rain fell, and all those dark masses charged with thunder, departed like a terrible multitude of chariots.

Suddenly the wide expanse of sky became blue.

Gilliatt perceived that he was wearied. Sleep swoops down upon the exhausted frame like a bird upon its prey. He drooped and sank upon the deck of the bark without choosing his position, and there slept. Stretched at length and inert, he remained thus for some hours, scarcely distinguishable from the beams and joists among which he lay.

Book IV
Pitfalls in the Way

*

I
HE WHO IS HUNGRY IS NOT ALONE

WHEN HE AWAKENED he was hungry.

The sea was growing calmer. But there was still a heavy swell, which made his departure, for the present at least, impossible. The day, too, was far advanced. For the sloop with its burden to get to Guernsey before midnight, it was necessary to start in the morning.

Although pressed by hunger, Gilliatt began by stripping himself, the only means of getting warmth. His clothing was saturated by the storm, but the rain had washed out the sea-water, which rendered it possible to dry them.

He kept nothing on but his trousers, which he turned up nearly to the knees.

His overcoat, jacket, overalls, and sheepskin he spread out and fixed with large round stones here and there.

Then he thought of eating.

He had recourse to his knife, which he was careful to sharpen, and to keep always in good condition; and he detached from the rocks a few limpets, similar in kind to the *clonisses* of the Mediterranean. It is well known that these are eaten raw: but after so many labours, so various and so rude, the pittance was meagre. His biscuit was gone; but of water he had now abundance.

He took advantage of the receding tide to wander among the rocks in search of crayfish. There was extent enough of rock to hope for a successful search.

But he had not reflected that he could do nothing with these without fire to cook them. If he had taken the trouble to go to his store-cavern, he would have found it inundated with the rain. His wood and coal were drowned, and of his store of tow, which served him for tinder, there was not a fibre which was not saturated. No means remained of lighting a fire.

For the rest, his blower was completely disorganised. The screen of the hearth of his forge was broken down; the storm had sacked and devastated his workshop. With what tools and apparatus had escaped the general wreck, he could still have done carpentry work; but he could not have accomplished any of the labours of the smith. Gilliatt, however, never thought of his workshop for a moment.

Drawn in another direction by the pangs of hunger, he had pursued without much reflection his search for food. He wandered, not in the gorge of the rocks, but outside among the smaller breakers. It was there that the Durande, ten weeks previously, had first struck upon the sunken reef.

For the search that Gilliatt was prosecuting, this part was more favourable than the interior. At low water the crabs are accustomed to crawl out into the air. They seem to like to warm themselves in the sun, where they swarm sometimes to the disgust of loiterers, who recognise in these creatures, with their awkward sidelong gait, climbing clumsily from crack to crack the lower stages of the rocks like the steps of a staircase, a sort of sea vermin.

For two months Gilliatt had lived upon these vermin of the sea.

On this day, however, the crayfish and crabs were both wanting. The tempest had driven them into their solitary retreats; and they had not yet mustered courage to venture abroad. Gilliatt held his open knife in his hand, and from time to time scraped a cockle from under the bunches of seaweed, which he ate while still walking.

He could not have been far from the very spot where Sieur Clubin had perished.

As Gilliatt was determining to content himself with the sea-urchins and the *châtaignes de mer*, a little clattering noise at his feet aroused his attention. A large crab, startled by his approach, had just dropped into a pool. The water was shallow, and he did not lose sight of it.

He chased the crab along the base of the rock; the crab moved fast.

Suddenly it was gone.

It had buried itself in some crevice under the rock.

Gilliatt clutched the projections of the rock, and stretched out to observe where it shelved away under the water.

As he suspected, there was an opening there in which the creature had evidently taken refuge. It was more than a crevice; it was a kind of porch.

The sea entered beneath it, but was not deep. The bottom was visible, covered with large pebbles. The pebbles were green and clothed with *confervæ*, indicating that they were never dry. They were like the tops of a number of heads of infants, covered with a kind of green hair.

Holding his knife between his teeth, Gilliatt descended, by the help of feet and hands, from the upper part of the escarpment, and leaped into the water. It reached almost to his shoulders.

He made his way through the porch, and found himself in a blind passage, with a roof in the form of a rude arch over his head. The walls were polished and slippery. The crab was nowhere visible. He gained his feet and advanced in daylight growing fainter, so that he began to lose the power to distinguish objects.

At about fifteen paces the vaulted roof ended overhead. He had penetrated beyond the blind passage. There was here more space, and consequently more daylight. The pupils of his eyes, moreover, had dilated; he could see pretty clearly. He was taken by surprise.

He had made his way again into the singular cavern which he had visited in the previous month. The only difference was that he had entered by the way of the sea.

It was through the submarine arch, that he had remarked before, that he had just entered. At certain low tides it was accessible.

His eyes became more accustomed to the place. His vision became clearer and clearer. He was astonished. He found himself again in that extraordinary palace of shadows; saw again before his eyes that vaulted roof, those columns, those purple and blood-like stains, that vegetation rich with gems, and at the farther end, that crypt or sanctuary, and that altar-like stone. He took little notice of these details, but their impression was in his mind, and he saw that the place was unchanged.

He observed before him, at a certain height in the wall, the crevice through which he had penetrated the first time, and which, from the point where he now stood, appeared inaccessible.

Near the moulded arch, he remarked those low dark grottoes, a sort of caves within a cavern, which he had already observed from a distance. He now stood nearer to them. The entrance to the nearest to him was out of the water, and easily approachable. Nearer still than this recess he noticed, above the level of the water, and within reach of his hand, a horizontal fissure. It seemed to him probable that the crab had taken refuge there, and he plunged his hand in as far as he was able, and groped about in that dusky aperture.

Suddenly he felt himself seized by the arm. A strange indescribable horror thrilled through him.

Some living thing, thin, rough, flat, cold, slimy, had twisted itself round his naked arm, in the dark depth below. It crept upward towards his chest. Its pressure was like a tightening cord, its steady persistence like that of a screw. In less than a moment some mysterious spiral form had passed round his wrist and elbow, and had reached his shoulder. A sharp point penetrated beneath the armpit.

Gilliatt recoiled; but he had scarcely power to move! He was, as it were, nailed to the place. With his left hand, which was disengaged, he seized his knife, which he still held between his teeth, and with that hand, holding the knife, he supported himself against the rocks, while he made a desperate effort to withdraw his arm. He succeeded only in disturbing his persecutor, which wound itself still tighter. It was supple as leather, strong as steel, cold as night.

A second form, sharp, elongated, and narrow, issued out of the crevice, like a tongue out of monstrous jaws. It seemed to lick his naked body. Then suddenly stretching out, it became longer and thinner, as it crept over his skin, and wound itself round him. At the same time a terrible sense of pain, comparable to nothing he had ever known, compelled all his muscles to contract. He felt upon his skin a number of flat rounded points. It seemed as if innumerable suckers had fastened to his flesh and were about to drink his blood.

A third long undulating shape issued from the hole in the rock; seemed to feel its way about his body; lashed round his ribs like a cord, and fixed itself there.

Agony when at its height is mute. Gilliatt uttered no cry. There was sufficient light for him to see the repulsive forms which had entangled themselves about him. A fourth ligature, but this one swift as an arrow, darted towards his stomach, and wound around him there.

It was impossible to sever or tear away the slimy bands which were twisted tightly round his body, and were adhering by a number of points. Each of the points was the focus of frightful and singular pangs. It was as if numberless small mouths were devouring him at the same time.

A fifth long, slimy, riband-shaped strip issued from the hole. It passed over the others, and wound itself tightly around his chest. The compression increased his sufferings. He could scarcely breathe.

These living thongs were pointed at their extremities, but broadened like a blade of a sword towards its hilt. All belonged evidently to the same centre. They crept and glided about him; he felt the strange points of pressure, which seemed to him like mouths, change their places from time to time.

Suddenly a large, round, flattened, glutinous mass issued from beneath the crevice. It was the centre; the five thongs were attached to it like spokes to the nave of a wheel. On the opposite side of this disgusting monster appeared the commencement of three other tentacles, the ends of which remained under the rock. In the middle of this slimy mass appeared two eyes.

The eyes were fixed on Gilliatt.

He recognised the Devil-Fish.

II
THE MONSTER

IT IS DIFFICULT for those who have not seen it to believe in the existence of the devil-fish.

Compared to this creature, the ancient hydras are insignificant.

At times we are tempted to imagine that the vague forms which float in our dreams may encounter in the realm of the Possible attractive forces, having power to fix their lineaments, and shape living beings, out of these creatures of our slumbers. The Unknown has power over these strange visions, and out of them composes monsters. Orpheus, Homer, and Hesiod imagined only the Chimera: Providence has created this terrible creature of the sea.

Creation abounds in monstrous forms of life. The wherefore of this perplexes and affrights the religious thinker.

If terror were the object of its creation, nothing could be imagined more perfect than the devil-fish.

The whale has enormous bulk, the devil-fish is comparatively small; the jararaca makes a hissing noise, the devil-fish is mute; the rhinoceros has a horn, the devil-fish has none; the scorpion has a dart, the devil-fish has no dart; the shark has sharp fins, the devil-fish has no fins; the vespertilio-bat has wings with claws, the devil-fish has no wings; the porcupine has his spines, the devil-fish has no spines; the sword-fish has his sword, the devil-fish has none; the torpedo has its electric spark, the devil-fish has none; the toad has its poison, the devil-fish has none; the viper has its venom, the devil-fish has no venom; the lion has its talons, the devil-fish has no talons; the griffon has its beak, the devil-fish has no beak; the crocodile has its jaws, the devil-fish has no teeth.

The devil-fish has no muscular organisation, no menacing cry, no breastplate, no horn, no dart, no claw, no tail with which to hold or bruise; no cutting fins, or wings with nails, no prickles, no sword, no electric discharge, no poison, no talons, no beak, no teeth. Yet he is of all creatures the most formidably armed.

What, then, is the devil-fish? It is the sea vampire.

The swimmer who, attracted by the beauty of the spot, ventures among breakers in the open sea, where the still waters hide the splendours of the deep, or in the hollows of unfrequented rocks, in unknown caverns abounding in sea plants, testacea, and crustacea, under the deep portals of the ocean, runs the risk of meeting it. If that fate should be yours, be not curious, but fly. The intruder enters there dazzled; but quits the spot in terror.

This frightful apparition, which is always possible among the rocks in the open sea, is a greyish form which undulates in the water. It is of the thickness of a man's arm, and in length nearly five feet. Its outline is ragged. Its form resembles an umbrella closed, and without handle. This irregular mass advances slowly towards you. Suddenly it opens, and eight radii issue abruptly from around a face with two eyes. These radii are alive: their undulation is like lambent flames; they resemble, when opened, the spokes of a wheel, of four or five feet in diameter. A terrible expansion! It springs upon its prey.

The devil-fish harpoons its victim.

It winds around the sufferer, covering and entangling him in its long folds. Underneath it is yellow; above, a dull, earthy hue: nothing could render that inexplicable shade dust coloured. Its form is spider-like, but its tints are like those of the chamelion. When irritated it becomes violet. Its most horrible characteristic is its softness.

Its folds strangle, its contact paralyses.

It has an aspect like gangrened or scabrous flesh. It is a monstrous embodiment of disease.

It adheres closely to its prey, and cannot be torn away; a fact which is due to its power of exhausting air. The eight antennæ, large at their roots, diminish gradually, and end in needle-like points. Underneath each of these feelers range two rows of pustules, decreasing in size, the largest ones near the head, the smaller at the extremities. Each row contains twenty-five of these. There are, therefore, fifty pustules to each feeler, and the creature possesses in the whole four hundred. These pustules are capable of acting like cupping-glasses. They are cartilaginous substances, cylindrical, horny, and livid. Upon the large species they diminish gradually from the diameter of a five-franc piece to the size of a split pea. These small tubes can be thrust out and withdrawn by the animal at will. They are capable of piercing to a depth of more than an inch.

This sucking apparatus has all the regularity and delicacy of a key-board. It stands forth at one moment and disappears the next. The most perfect sensitiveness cannot equal the contractibility of these suckers; always proportioned to the internal movement of the animal, and its exterior circumstances. The monster is endowed with the qualities of the sensitive plant.

This animal is the same as those which mariners call Poulps; which science designates Cephalopteræ, and which ancient legends call Krakens. It is the English sailors who call them "Devil-fish," and sometimes Bloodsuckers. In the Channel Islands they are called *pieuvres*.

They are rare at Guernsey, very small at Jersey; but near the island of Sark are numerous as well as very large.

An engraving in Sonnini's edition of Buffon represents a Cephaloptera crushing a frigate. Denis Montfort, in fact, considers the Poulp, or Octopod, of high latitudes, strong enough to destroy a ship. Bory Saint Vincent doubts this; but he shows that in our regions they will attack men. Near Brecq-Hou, in Sark, they show a cave where a devil-fish a few years since seized and drowned a lobster-fisher. Peron and Lamarck are in error in their belief that the "poulp" having no fins cannot swim. He who writes these lines has seen with his own eyes, at Sark, in the cavern called the Boutiques, a pieuvre swimming and pursuing a bather. When captured and killed, this specimen was found to be four English feet broad, and it was possible to count its four hundred suckers. The monster thrust them out convulsively in the agony of death.

According to Denis Montfort, one of those observers whose marvellous intuition sinks or raises them to the level of magicians, the poulp is almost endowed with the passions of man: it has its hatreds. In fact, in the Absolute to be hideous is to hate.

Hideousness struggles under the natural law of elimination, which necessarily renders it hostile.

When swimming, the devil-fish rests, so to speak, in its sheath. It swims with all its parts drawn close. It may be likened to a sleeve sewn up with a closed fist within. The protuberance, which is the head, pushes the water aside and advances with a vague undulatory movement. Its two eyes, though large, are indistinct, being of the colour of the water.

When in ambush, or seeking its prey, it retires into itself, grows smaller and condenses itself. It is then scarcely distinguishable in the submarine twilight.

At such times, it looks like a mere ripple in the water. It resembles anything except a living creature.

The devil-fish is crafty. When its victim is unsuspicious, it opens suddenly.

A glutinous mass, endowed with a malignant will, what can be more horrible?

It is in the most beautiful azure depths of the limpid water that this hideous, voracious polyp delights. It always conceals itself, a fact which increases its terrible associations. When they are seen, it is almost invariably after they have been captured.

At night, however, and particularly in the hot season, it becomes phosphorescent. These horrible creatures have their passions; their submarine nuptials. Then it adorns itself, burns and illumines; and from the height of some rock, it may be seen in the deep obscurity of the waves below, expanding with a pale irradiation—a spectral sun.

The devil-fish not only swims, it walks. It is partly fish, partly reptile. It crawls upon the bed of the sea. At these times, it makes use of its eight feelers, and creeps along in the fashion of a species of swift-moving caterpillar.

It has no blood, no bones, no flesh. It is soft and flabby; a skin with nothing inside. Its eight tentacles may be turned inside out like the fingers of a glove.

It has a single orifice in the centre of its radii, which appears at first to be neither the vent nor the mouth. It is, in fact, both one and the other. The orifice performs a double function. The entire creature is cold.

The jelly-fish of the Mediterranean is repulsive. Contact with that animated gelatinous substance which envelopes the bather, in which the hands sink, and the nails scratch ineffectively; which can be torn without killing it, and which can be plucked off without entirely removing it—that fluid and yet tenacious creature which slips through the fingers, is disgusting; but no horror can equal the sudden apparition of the devil-fish, that Medusa with its eight serpents.

No grasp is like the sudden strain of the cephaloptera.

It is with the sucking apparatus that it attacks. The victim is oppressed by a vacuum drawing at numberless points: it is not a clawing or a biting, but an indescribable scarification. A tearing of the flesh is terrible, but less terrible than a sucking of the blood. Claws are harmless compared with the horrible action of these natural air-cups. The talons of the wild beast enter into your flesh; but with the cephaloptera it is you who enter into the creature. The muscles swell, the fibres of the body are contorted, the skin cracks under the loathsome oppression, the blood spurts out and mingles horribly with the lymph of the monster, which clings to its victim by innumerable hideous mouths. The hydra incorporates itself with the man; the man becomes one with the hydra. The spectre lies upon you: the tiger can only devour you; the devil-fish, horrible, sucks your life-blood away. He draws you to him, and into himself; while bound down, glued to the ground, powerless, you feel yourself gradually emptied into this horrible pouch, which is the monster itself.

These strange animals, Science, in accordance with its habit of excessive caution even in the face of facts, at first rejects as fabulous; then she decides to observe them; then she dissects, classifies, catalogues, and labels; then procures specimens, and exhibits them in glass cases in museums. They enter then into her nomenclature; are designated mollusks, invertebrata, radiata: she determines their position in the animal world a little above the calamaries, a little below the cuttle-fish; she finds for these hydras of the sea an analogous creature in fresh water called the argyronecte: she divides them into great, medium, and small kinds; she admits more readily the existence of the small than of the large species, which is, however, the tendency of science in all countries, for she is by nature more microscopic than telescopic. She regards them from the point of view of their construction, and calls them Cephaloptera; counts their antennæ, and calls them Octopedes. This done, she leaves them. Where science drops them, philosophy takes them up.

Philosophy in her turn studies these creatures. She goes both less far and further. She does not dissect, but meditate. Where the scalpel has laboured, she plunges the hypothesis. She seeks the final cause. Eternal perplexity of the thinker. These creatures disturb his ideas of the Creator. They are hideous surprises. They are the death's-head at the feast of contemplation. The philosopher determines their characteristics in dread. They are the concrete forms of evil. What attitude can he take towards this treason of creation against herself? To whom can he look for the solution of these riddles? The Possible is a terrible matrix. Monsters are mysteries in their concrete form. Portions of shade issue from the mass, and something within detaches itself, rolls, floats, condenses, borrows elements from the ambient darkness, becomes subject to unknown polarisations, assumes a kind of life, furnishes itself with some unimagined form from the obscurity, and with some terrible spirit from the miasma, and wanders ghostlike among living things. It is as if night itself assumed the forms of animals. But for what good? with what object? Thus we come again to the eternal questioning.

These animals are indeed phantoms as much as monsters. They are proved and yet improbable. Their fate is to exist in spite of *à priori* reasonings. They are the amphibia of the shore which separates life from death. Their unreality makes their existence puzzling. They touch the frontier of man's domain and people the region of chimeras. We deny the possibility of the vampire, and the cephaloptera appears. Their swarming is a certainty which disconcerts our confidence. Optimism, which is nevertheless in the right, becomes silenced in their presence. They form the visible extremity of the dark circles. They mark the transition of our reality into another. They seem to belong to that commencement of terrible life which the dreamer sees confusedly through the loophole of the night.

That multiplication of monsters, first in the Invisible, then in the Possible, has been suspected, perhaps perceived by magi and philosophers in their austere ecstasies and profound contemplations. Hence the conjecture of a material hell. The demon is simply the invisible tiger. The wild beast which devours souls has been presented to the eyes of human beings by St. John, and by Dante in his vision of Hell.

If, in truth, the invisible circles of creation continue indefinitely, if after one there is yet another, and so forth in illimitable progression; if that chain, which for our part we are resolved to doubt, really exist, the cephaloptera at one extremity proves Satan at the other. It is certain that the wrongdoer at one end proves the existence of wrong at the other.

Every malignant creature, like every perverted intelligence, is a sphinx. A terrible sphinx propounding a terrible riddle; the riddle of the existence of Evil.

It is this perfection of evil which has sometimes sufficed to incline powerful intellects to a faith in the duality of the Deity, towards that terrible bifrons of the Manichæans.

A piece of silk stolen during the last war from the palace of the Emperor of China represents a shark eating a crocodile, who is eating a serpent, who is devouring an eagle, who is preying on a swallow, who in his turn is eating a caterpillar.

All nature which is under our observation is thus alternately devouring and devoured. The prey prey on each other.

Learned men, however, who are also philosophers, and therefore optimists in their view of creation, find, or believe they find, an explanation. Among others, Bonnet of Geneva, that mysterious exact thinker, who was opposed to Buffon, as in later times Geoffrey St. Hilaire has been to Cuvier, was struck with the idea of the final object. His notions may be summed up thus: universal death necessitates universal sepulture; the devourers are the sextons of the system of nature. All created things enter into and form the elements of other. To decay is to nourish. Such is the terrible law from which not even man himself escapes.

In our world of twilight this fatal order of things produces monsters. You ask for what purpose. We find the solution here.

But *is* this the solution? Is this the answer to our questionings? And if so, why not some different order of things? Thus the question returns.

Let us live: be it so.

But let us endeavour that death shall be progress. Let us aspire to an existence in which these mysteries shall be made clear. Let us follow that conscience which leads us thither.

For let us never forget that the highest is only attained through the high.

III
ANOTHER KIND OF SEA-COMBAT

SUCH WAS THE creature in whose power Gilliatt had fallen for some minutes.

The monster was the inhabitant of the grotto; the terrible genii of the place. A kind of sombre demon of the water.

All the splendours of the cavern existed for it alone.

On the day of the previous month when Gilliatt had first penetrated into the grotto, the dark outline, vaguely perceived by him in the ripples of the secret waters, was this monster. It was here in its home.

When entering for the second time into the cavern in pursuit of the crab, he had observed the crevice in which he supposed that the crab had taken refuge, the pieuvre was there lying in wait for prey.

Is it possible to imagine that secret ambush?

No bird would brood, no egg would burst to life, no flower would dare to open, no breast to give milk, no heart to love, no spirit to soar, under the influence of that apparition of evil watching with sinister patience in the dusk.

Gilliatt had thrust his arm deep into the opening; the monster had snapped at it. It held him fast, as the spider holds the fly.

He was in the water up to his belt; his naked feet clutching the slippery roundness of the huge stones at the bottom; his right arm bound and rendered powerless by the flat coils of the long tentacles of the creature, and his body almost hidden under the folds and cross folds of this horrible bandage.

Of the eight arms of the devil-fish three adhered to the rock, while five encircled Gilliatt. In this way, clinging to the granite on the one hand, and with the other to its human prey, it enchained him to the rock. Two hundred and fifty suckers were upon him, tormenting him with agony and loathing. He was grasped by gigantic hands, the fingers of which were each nearly a yard long, and furnished inside with living blisters eating into the flesh.

As we have said, it is impossible to tear oneself from the folds of the devil-fish. The attempt ends only in a firmer grasp. The monster clings with more determined force. Its effort increases with that of its victim; every struggle produces a tightening of its ligatures.

Gilliatt had but one resource, his knife.

His left hand only was free; but the reader knows with what power he could use it. It might have been said that he had two right hands.

His open knife was in his hand.

The antenna of the devil-fish cannot be cut; it is a leathery substance impossible to divide with the knife, it slips under the edge; its position in attack also is such that to cut it would be to wound the victim's own flesh.

The creature is formidable, but there is a way of resisting it. The fishermen of Sark know this, as does any one who has seen them execute certain movements in the sea. The porpoises know it also; they have a way of biting the cuttle-fish which decapitates it. Hence the frequent sight on the sea of pen-fish, poulps, and cuttle-fish without heads.

The cephaloptera, in fact, is only vulnerable through the head.

Gilliatt was not ignorant of this fact.

He had never seen a devil-fish of this size. His first encounter was with one of the larger species. Another would have been powerless with terror.

With the devil-fish, as with a furious bull, there is a certain moment in the conflict which must be seized. It is the instant when the bull lowers the neck; it is the instant when the devil-fish advances its head. The movement is rapid. He who loses that moment is destroyed.

The things we have described occupied only a few moments. Gilliatt, however, felt the increasing power of its innumerable suckers.

The monster is cunning; it tries first to stupefy its prey. It seizes and then pauses awhile.

Gilliatt grasped his knife; the sucking increased.

He looked at the monster, which seemed to look at him.

Suddenly it loosened from the rock its sixth antenna, and darting it at him, seized him by the left arm.

At the same moment it advanced its head with a violent movement. In one second more its mouth would have fastened on his breast. Bleeding in the sides, and with his two arms entangled, he would have been a dead man.

But Gillian was watchful. He avoided the antenna, and at the moment when the monster darted forward to fasten on his breast, he struck it with the knife clenched in his left hand. There were two convulsions in opposite directions; that of the devil-fish and that of its prey. The movement was rapid as a double flash of lightnings.

He had plunged the blade of his knife into the flat slimy substance, and by a rapid movement, like the flourish of a whip in the air, describing a circle round the two eyes, he wrenched the head off as a man would draw a tooth.

The struggle was ended. The folds relaxed. The monster dropped away, like the slow detaching of bands. The four hundred suckers, deprived of their sustaining power, dropped at once from the man and the rock. The mass sank to the bottom of the water.

Breathless with the struggle, Gilliatt could perceive upon the stones at his feet two shapeless, slimy heaps, the head on one side, the remainder of the monster on the other.

Fearing, nevertheless, some convulsive return of his agony, he recoiled to avoid the reach of the dreaded tentacles.

But the monster was quite dead.

Gilliatt closed his knife.

IV

NOTHING IS HIDDEN, NOTHING LOST

IT WAS TIME that he killed the devil-fish. He was almost suffocated. His right arm and his chest were purple. Numberless little swellings were distinguishable upon them; the blood flowed from them here and there. The remedy for these wounds is sea-water. Gilliatt plunged into it, rubbing himself at the same time with the palms of his hands. The swellings disappeared under the friction.

By stepping further into the waters he had, without perceiving, approached to the species of recess already observed by him near the crevice where he had been attacked by the devil-fish.

This recess stretched obliquely under the great walls of the cavern, and was dry. The large pebbles which had become heaped up there had raised the bottom above the level of ordinary tides. The entrance was a rather large elliptical arch; a man could enter by stooping. The green light of the submarine grotto penetrated into it and lighted it feebly.

It happened that, while hastily rubbing his skin, Gilliatt raised his eyes mechanically.

He was able to see far into the cavern.

He shuddered.

He fancied that he perceived, in the furthest depth of the dusky recess, something smiling.

Gilliatt had never heard the word "hallucination," but he was familiar with the idea. Those mysterious encounters with the invisible, which, for the sake of avoiding the difficulty of explaining them, we call hallucinations, are in nature. Illusions or realities, visions are a fact. He who has the gift will see them. Gilliatt, as we have said, was a dreamer. He had, at times, the faculty of a seer. It was not in vain that he had spent his days in musing among solitary places.

He imagined himself the dupe of one of those mirages which he had more than once beheld when in his dreamy moods.

The opening was somewhat in the shape of a chalk-burner's oven. It was a low niche with projections like basket-handles. Its abrupt groins contracted gradually as far as the extremity of the crypt, where the heaps of round stones and the rocky roof joined.

Gilliatt entered, and lowering his head, advanced towards the object in the distance.

There was indeed something smiling.

It was a death's head; but it was not only the head. There was the entire skeleton. A complete human skeleton was lying in the cavern.

In such a position a bold man will continue his researches.

Gilliatt cast his eyes around. He was surrounded by a multitude of crabs. The multitude did not stir. They were but empty shells.

These groups were scattered here and there among the masses of pebbles in irregular constellations.

Gilliatt, having his eyes fixed elsewhere, had walked among them without perceiving them.

At this extremity of the crypt, where he had now penetrated, there was a still greater heap of remains. It was a confused mass of legs, antennæ, and mandibles. Claws stood wide open; bony shells lay still under their bristling prickles; some reversed showed their livid hollows. The heap was like a *mêlée* of besiegers who had fallen, and lay massed together.

The skeleton was partly buried in this heap.

Under this confused mass of scales and tentacles, the eye perceived the cranium with its furrows, the vertebræ, the thigh bones, the tibias, and the long-jointed finger bones with their nails. The frame of the ribs was filled with crabs. Some heart had once beat there. The green mould of the sea had settled round the sockets of the eyes. Limpets had left their slime upon the bony nostrils. For the rest, there were not in this cave within the rocks either sea-gulls, or weeds, or a breath of air. All was still. The teeth grinned.

The sombre side of laughter is that strange mockery of expression which is peculiar to a human skull.

This marvellous palace of the deep, inlaid and incrusted with all the gems of the sea, had at length revealed and told its secret. It was a savage haunt; the devil-fish inhabited it; it was also a tomb, in which the body of a man reposed.

The skeleton and the creatures around it oscillated vaguely in the reflections of the subterranean water which trembled upon the roof and wall.

The horrible multitude of crabs looked as if finishing their repast. These crustacea seemed to be devouring the carcase. Nothing could be more strange than the aspect of the dead vermin upon their dead prey.

Gilliatt had beneath his eyes the storehouse of the devil-fish.

It was a dismal sight. The crabs had devoured the man: the devil-fish had devoured the crabs.

There were no remains of clothing anywhere visible. The man must have been seized naked.

Gilliatt, attentively examining, began to remove the shells from the skeleton. What had this man been? The body was admirably dissected; it looked as if prepared for the study of anatomy; all the flesh was stripped; not a muscle remained; not a bone was missing. If Gilliatt had been learned in science, he might have demonstrated the fact. The periostea, denuded of their covering, were white and smooth, as if they had been polished. But for some green mould of sea-mosses here and there, they would have been like ivory. The cartilaginous divisions were delicately inlaid and arranged. The tomb sometimes produces this dismal mosaic work.

The body was, as it were, interred under the heap of dead crabs. Gilliatt disinterred it.

Suddenly he stooped, and examined more closely.

He had perceived around the vertebral column a sort of belt.

It was a leathern girdle, which had evidently been worn buckled upon the waist of the man when alive.

The leather was moist; the buckle rusty.

Gilliatt pulled the girdle; the vertebra of the skeleton resisted, and he was compelled to break through them in order to remove it. A crust of small shells had begun to form upon it.

He felt it, and found a hard substance within, apparently of square form. It was useless to endeavour to unfasten the buckle, so he cut the leather with his knife.

The girdle contained a little iron box and some pieces of gold. Gilliatt counted twenty guineas.

The iron box was an old sailor's tobacco-box, opening and shutting with a spring. It was very tight and rusty. The spring being completely oxidised would not work.

Once more the knife served Gilliatt in a difficulty. A pressure with the point of the blade caused the lid to fly up.

The box was open.

There was nothing inside but pieces of paper.

A little roll of very thin sheets, folded in four, was fitted in the bottom of the box. They were damp, but not injured. The box, hermetically sealed, had preserved them. Gilliatt unfolded them.

They were three bank-notes of one thousand pounds sterling each; making together seventy-five thousand francs.

Gilliatt folded them again, replaced them in the box, taking advantage of the space which remained to add the twenty guineas; and then reclosed the box as well as he could.

Next he examined the girdle.

The leather, which had originally been polished outside, was rough within. Upon this tawny ground some letters had been traced in black thick ink. Gilliatt deciphered them, and read the words, "Sieur Clubin."

V
THE FATAL DIFFERENCE BETWEEN SIX INCHES AND TWO FEET

GILLIATT REPLACED THE BOX in the girdle, and placed the girdle in the pocket of his trousers.

He left the skeleton among the crabs, with the remains of the devil-fish beside it.

While he had been occupied with the devil-fish and the skeleton, the rising tide had submerged the entrance to the cave. He was only enabled to leave it by plunging under the arched entrance. He got through without difficulty; for he knew the entrance well, and was master of these gymnastics in the sea.

It is easy to understand the drama which had taken place there during the ten weeks preceding. One monster had preyed upon another; the devil-fish had seized Clubin.

These two embodiments of treachery had met in the inexorable darkness. There had been an encounter at the bottom of the sea between these two compounds of mystery and watchfulness; the monster had destroyed the man: a horrible fulfilment of justice.

The crab feeds on carrion, the devil-fish on crabs. The devil-fish seizes as it passes any swimming animal—an otter, a dog, a man if it can—sucks the blood, and leaves the body at the bottom of the water. The crabs are the spider-formed scavengers of the sea. Putrefying flesh attracts them; they crowd round it, devour the body, and are in their turn consumed by the devil-fish. Dead creatures disappear in the crab, the crab disappears in the pieuvre. This is the law which we have already pointed out.

The devil-fish had laid hold of him, and drowned him. Some wave had carried his body into the cave, and deposited it at the extremity of the inner cavern, where Gilliatt had discovered it.

He returned searching among the rocks for sea-urchins and limpets. He had no desire for crabs; to have eaten them now would have seemed to him like feeding upon human flesh.

For the rest, he thought of nothing but of eating what he could before starting. Nothing now interposed to prevent his departure. Great tempests are always followed by a calm, which lasts sometimes several days. There was, therefore, no danger from the sea. Gilliatt had resolved to leave the rocks on the following day. It was important, on account of the tide, to keep the barrier between the two Douvres during the night, but he intended to remove it at daybreak, to push the sloop out to sea, and set sail for St. Sampson. The light breeze which was blowing came from the south-west, which was precisely the wind which he would want.

It was in the first quarter of the moon, in the month of May; the days were long.

When Gilliatt, having finished his wanderings among the rocks, and appeased his appetite to some extent, returned to the passage between the two Douvres, where he had left the sloop, the sun had set, the twilight was increased by that pale light which comes from a crescent moon; the tide had attained its height, and was beginning to ebb. The funnel standing upright above the sloop had been covered by the foam during the tempest with a coating of salt which glittered white in the light of the moon.

This circumstance reminded Gilliatt that the storm had inundated the sloop, both with surf and rain-water, and that if he meant to start in the morning, it would be necessary to bail it out.

Before leaving to go in quest of crabs, he had ascertained that it had about six inches of water in the hold. The scoop which he used for the purpose would, he thought, be sufficient for throwing the water overboard.

On arriving at the barrier, Gilliatt was struck with terror. There were nearly two feet of water in the sloop. A terrible discovery; the bark had sprung a leak.

She had been making water gradually during his absence. Burdened as she was, two feet of water was a perilous addition. A little more, and she must inevitably founder. If he had returned but an hour later, he would probably have found nothing above water but the funnel and the mast.

There was not a minute to be lost in deliberation. It was absolutely necessary to find the leakage, stop it, and then empty the vessel, or at all events, lighten it. The pumps of the Durande had been lost in the break-up of the wreck. He was reduced to use the scoop of the bark.

To find the leak was the most urgent necessity.

Gilliatt set to work immediately, and without even giving himself time to dress. He shivered; but he no longer felt either hunger or cold.

The water continued to gain upon his vessel. Fortunately there was no wind. The slightest swell would have been fatal.

The moon went down.

Bent low, and plunged in the water deeper than his waist he groped about for a long time. He discovered the mischief at last.

During the gale, at the critical moment when the sloop had swerved, the strong bark had bumped and grazed rather violently on the rocks. One of the projections of the Little Douvre had made a fracture in the starboard side of the hull.

The leak unluckily—it might almost have been said, maliciously—had been made near the joint of the two riders, a fact which, joined with the fury of the hurricane, had prevented him perceiving it during his dark and rapid survey in the height of the storm.

The fracture was alarming on account of its size; but fortunately, although the vessel was sunk lower than usual by the weight of water, it was still above the ordinary water-line.

At the moment when the accident had occurred, the waves had rolled heavily into the defile, and had flooded through the breach; and the vessel had sunk a few inches under the additional weight, so that, even after the subsidence of the water, the weight having raised the water-line, had kept the hole still under the surface. Hence the imminence of the danger. But if he could succeed in stopping the leak, he could empty the sloop; the hole once staunched, the vessel would rise to its usual water-line, the fracture would be above water, and in this position the repair would be easy, or at least possible. He had still, as we have already said, his carpenters' tools in good condition.

But meanwhile what uncertainty must he not endure! What perils, what chances of accidents! He heard the water rising inexorably. One shock, and all would have perished. What misery seemed in store for him. Perhaps his endeavours were even now too late.

He reproached himself bitterly. He thought that he ought to have seen the damage immediately. The six inches of water in the hold ought to have suggested it to him. He had been stupid enough to attribute these six inches of water to the rain and the foam. He was angry with himself for having slept and eaten; he taxed himself even with his weariness, and almost with the storm and the dark night. All seemed to him to have been his own fault.

These bitter self-reproaches filled his mind while engaged in his labour, but they did not prevent his considering well the work he was engaged in.

The leak had been found; that was the first step: to staunch it was the second. That was all that was possible for the moment. Joinery work cannot be carried on under water.

It was a favourable circumstance that the breach in the hull was in the space between the two chains which held the funnel fast on the starboard side. The stuffing with which it was necessary to stop it could be fixed to these chains.

The water meanwhile was gaining. Its depth was now between two and three feet; and it reached above his knees.

VI

DE PROFUNDIS AD ALTUM

GILLIATT HAD to his hand among his reserve of rigging for the sloop a pretty large tarpaulin, furnished with long laniards at the four corners.

He took this tarpaulin, made fast the two corners by the laniards to the two rings of the chains of the funnel on the same side as the leak, and threw it over the gunwale. The tarpaulin hung like a sheet between the Little Douvre and the bark, and sunk in the water. The pressure of the water endeavouring to enter into the hold, kept it close to the hull upon the gap. The heavier the pressure the closer the sail adhered. It was stuck by the water itself right upon the fracture. The wound of the bark was staunched.

The tarred canvas formed an effectual barrier between the interior of the hold and the waves without. Not a drop of water entered. The leak was masked, but was not stopped. It was a respite only.

Gilliatt took the scoop and began to bale the sloop. It was time that she were lightened. The labour warmed him a little, but his weariness was extreme. He was forced to acknowledge to himself that he could not complete the work of staunching the hold. He had scarcely eaten anything, and he had the humiliation of feeling himself exhausted.

He measured the progress of his work by the sinking of the level of water below his knees. The fall was slow.

Moreover, the leakage was only interrupted; the evil was moderated, not repaired. The tarpaulin pushed into the gap began to bulge inside; looking as if a fist were under the canvas, endeavouring to force it through. The canvas, strong and pitchy, resisted; but the swelling and the tension increased; it was not certain that it would not give way, and at any moment the swelling might become a rent. The irruption of water must then recommence.

In such a case, as the crews of vessels in distress know well, there is no other remedy than stuffing. The sailors take rags of every kind which they can find at hand, everything, in fact, which in their language is called "service;" and with this they push the bulging sail-cloth as far as they can into the leak.

Of this "service," Gilliatt had none. All the rags and tow which he had stored up had been used in his operations, or carried away by the storm.

If necessary, he might possibly have been able to find some remains by searching among the rocks. The sloop was sufficiently lightened for him to leave it with safety for a quarter of an hour; but how could he make this search without a light? The darkness was complete. There was no longer any moon; nothing but the starry sky. He had no dry tow with which to make a match, no tallow to make a candle, no fire to light one, no lantern to shelter it from the wind. In the sloop and among the rocks all was confused and indistinct. He could hear the water lapping against the wounded hull, but he could not even see the crack. It was with his hands that he had ascertained the bulging of the tarpaulin. In that darkness it was impossible to make any useful search for rags of canvas or pieces of tow scattered among the breakers. Who could glean these waifs and strays without being able to see his path? Gilliatt looked sorrowfully at the sky; all those stars, he thought, and yet no light!

The water in the bark having diminished, the pressure from without increased. The bulging of the canvas became larger, and was still increasing, like a frightful abscess ready to burst. The situation, which had been improved for a short time, began to be threatening.

Some means of stopping it effectually was absolutely necessary. He had nothing left but his clothes, which he had stretched to dry upon the projecting rocks of the Little Douvre.

He hastened to fetch them, and placed them upon the gunwale of the sloop.

Then he took his tarpaulin overcoat, and kneeling in the water, thrust it into the crevice, and pushing the swelling of the sail outward, emptied it of water. To the tarpaulin coat he added the sheepskin, then his Guernsey shirt, and then his jacket. The hole received them all. He had nothing left but his sailor's trousers, which he took off, and pushed in with the other articles. This enlarged and strengthened the stuffing.

The stopper was made, and it appeared to be sufficient.

These clothes passed partly through the gap, the sail-cloth outside enveloping them. The sea making an effort to enter, pressed against the obstacle, spread it over the gap, and blocked it. It was a sort of exterior compression.

THE TOILERS OF THE SEA321

Inside, the centre only of the bulging having been driven out, there remained all around the gap and the stuffing just thrust through a sort of circular pad formed by the tarpaulin, which was rendered still firmer by the irregularities of the fracture with which it had become entangled.

The leak was staunched, but nothing could be more precarious. Those sharp splinters of the gap which fixed the tarpaulin might pierce it and make holes, by which the water would enter; while he would not even perceive it in the darkness. There was little probability of the stoppage lasting until daylight. Gilliatt's anxiety changed its form; but he felt it increasing at the same time that he found his strength leaving him.

He had again set to work to bale out the hold, but his arms, in spite of all his efforts, could scarcely lift a scoopfull of water. He was naked and shivering. He felt as if the end were now at hand.

One possible chance flashed across his mind. There might be a sail in sight. A fishing-boat which should by any accident be in the neighbourhood of the Douvres, might come to his assistance. The moment had arrived when a helpmate was absolutely necessary. With a man and a lantern all might yet be saved. If there were two persons, one might easily bale the vessel. Since the leak was temporarily staunched, as soon as she could be relieved of this burden, she would rise, and regain her ordinary water-line. The leak would then be above the surface of the water, the repairs would be practicable, and he would be able immediately to replace the stuff by a piece of planking, and thus substitute for the temporary stoppage a complete repair. If not, it would be necessary to wait till daylight—to wait the whole night long; a delay which might prove ruinous. If by chance some ship's lantern should be in sight, Gilliatt would be able to signal it from the height of the Great Douvre. The weather was calm, there was no wind or rolling sea; there was a possibility of the figure of a man being observed moving against the background of the starry sky. A captain of a ship, or even the master of a fishing-boat, would not be at night in the waters of the Douvres without directing his glass upon the rock, by way of precaution.

Gilliatt hoped that some one might perceive him.

He climbed upon the wreck, grasped the knotted rope, and mounted upon the Great Douvre.

Not a sail was visible around the horizon; not a boat's lantern. The wide expanse, as far as eye could reach, was a desert. No assistance was possible, and no resistance possible.

Gilliatt felt himself without resources; a feeling which he had not felt until then.

A dark fatality was now his master. With all his labour, all his success, all his courage, he and his bark, and its precious burden, were about to become the sport of the waves. He had no other means of continuing the struggle; he became listless. How could he prevent the tide from returning, the water from rising, the night from continuing? The temporary stoppage which he had made was his sole reliance. He had exhausted and stripped himself in constructing and completing it; he could neither fortify nor add to it. The stopgap was such that it must remain as it was; and every further effort was useless. The apparatus, hastily constructed, was at the mercy of the waves. How would this inert obstacle work? It was this obstacle now, not Gilliatt, which had to sustain the combat, that handfull of rags, not that intelligence. The swell of a wave would suffice to re-open the fracture. More or less of pressure; the whole question was comprised in that formula.

All depended upon a brute struggle between two mechanical quantities. Henceforth he could neither aid his auxiliary, nor stop his enemy. He was no longer any other than a mere spectator of this struggle, which was one for him of life or death. He who had ruled over it, a supreme intelligence, was at the last moment compelled to resign all to a mere blind resistance.

No trial, no terror that he had yet undergone, could bear comparison with this.

From the time when he had taken up his abode upon the Douvres, he had found himself environed, and, as it were, possessed by solitude. This solitude more than surrounded, it enveloped him. A thousand menaces at once had met him face to face. The wind was always there, ready to become furious; the sea, ready to roar. There was no stopping that terrible mouth the wind, no imprisoning that dread monster the sea. And yet he had striven, he, a solitary man, had combated hand to hand with the ocean, had wrestled even with the tempest.

Many other anxieties, many other necessities had he made head against. There was no form of distress with which he had not become familiar. He had been compelled to execute great works without tools, to move vast burdens without aid, without science to resolve problems, without provisions to find food, without bed or roof to cover it, to find shelter and sleep.

Upon that solitary rock he had been subjected by turns to all the varied and cruel tortures of nature; oftentimes a gentle mother, not less often a pitiless destroyer.

He had conquered his isolation, conquered hunger, conquered thirst, conquered cold, conquered fever, conquered labour, conquered sleep. He had encountered a mighty coalition of obstacles formed to bar his progress. After his privations there were the elements; after the sea the tempest, after the tempest the devil-fish, after the monster the spectre.

A dismal irony was then the end of all. Upon this rock, whence he had thought to arise triumphant, the spectre of Clubin had only arisen to mock him with a hideous smile.

The grin of the spectre was well founded. Gilliatt saw himself ruined; saw himself no less than Clubin in the grasp of death.

Winter, famine, fatigue, the dismemberment of the wreck, the removal of the machinery, the equinoctial gale, the thunder, the monster, were all as nothing compared with this small fracture in a vessel's planks. Against the cold one could procure—and he had procured—fire; against hunger, the shell-fish of the rocks; against thirst, the rain; against the difficulties of his great task, industry and energy; against the sea and the storm, the breakwater; against the devil-fish, the knife; but against the terrible leak he had no weapon.

The hurricane had bequeathed him this sinister farewell. The last struggle, the traitorous thrust, the treacherous side blow of the vanquished foe. In its flight the tempest had turned and shot this arrow in the rear. It was the final and deadly stab of his antagonist.

It was possible to combat with the tempest, but how could he struggle with that insidious enemy who now attacked him.

If the stoppage gave way, if the leak re-opened, nothing could prevent the sloop foundering. It would be the bursting of the ligature of the artery; and once under the water with its heavy burden, no power could raise it. The noble struggle, with two months' Titanic labour, ended then in annihilation. To recommence would be impossible. He had neither forge nor materials. At daylight, in all probability, he was about to see all his work sink slowly and irrecoverably into the gulf. Terrible, to feel that sombre power beneath. The sea snatched his prize from his hands.

With his bark engulfed, no fate awaited him but to perish of hunger and cold, like the poor shipwrecked sailor on "The Man Rock."

During two long months the intelligences which hover invisibly over the world had been the spectators of these things; on one hand the wide expanse, the waves, the winds, the lightnings, the meteors; on the other a man. On one hand the sea, on the other a human mind; on the one hand the infinite, on the other an atom.

The battle had been fierce, and behold the abortive issue of these prodigies of valour.

Thus did this heroism without parallel end in powerlessness; thus ended in despair that formidable struggle; that struggle of a nothing against all; that Iliad against one.

Gilliatt gazed wildly into space.

He had no clothing. He stood naked in the midst of that immensity.

Then overwhelmed by the sense of that unknown infinity, like one bewildered by a strange persecution, confronting the shadows of night, in the presence of that impenetrable darkness, in the midst of the murmur of the waves, the swell, the foam, the breeze, under the clouds, under that vast diffusion of force, under that mysterious firmament of wings, of stars, of gulfs, having around him and beneath him the ocean, above him the constellations, under the great unfathomable deep, he sank, gave up the struggle, lay down upon the rock, his face towards the stars, humbled, and uplifting his joined hands towards the terrible depths, he cried aloud, "Have mercy."

Weighed down to earth by that immensity, he prayed.

He was there alone, in the darkness upon the rock, in the midst of that sea, stricken down with exhaustion like one smitten by lightning, naked like the gladiator in the circus, save that for circus he had the vast horizon, instead of wild beasts the shadows of darkness, instead of the faces of the crowd the eyes of the Unknown, instead of the Vestals the stars, instead of Cæsar the All-powerful.

His whole being seemed to dissolve in cold, fatigue, powerlessness, prayer, and darkness, and his eyes closed.

VII

THE APPEAL IS HEARD

SOME HOURS PASSED.

The sun rose in an unclouded sky.

Its first ray shone upon a motionless form upon the Great Douvre. It was Gilliatt.

He was still outstretched upon the rock.

He was naked, cold, and stiff; but he did not shiver. His closed eyelids were wan. It would have been difficult for a beholder to say whether the form before him was not a corpse.

The sun seemed to look upon him.

If he were not dead, he was already so near death that the slightest cold wind would have sufficed to extinguish life.

The wind began to breathe, warm and animating: it was the opening breath of May.

Meanwhile the sun ascended in the deep blue sky; its rays, less horizontal, flushed the sky. Its light became warmth. It enveloped the slumbering form.

Gilliatt moved not. If he breathed, it was only that feeble respiration which could scarcely tarnish the surface of a mirror.

The sun continued its ascent, its rays striking less and less obliquely upon the naked man. The gentle breeze which had been merely tepid became hot.

The rigid and naked body remained still without movement; but the skin seemed less livid.

The sun, approaching the zenith, shone almost perpendicularly upon the plateau of the Douvres. A flood of light descended from the heavens; the vast reflection from the glassy sea increased its splendour: the rock itself imbibed the rays and warmed the sleeper.

A sigh raised his breast.

He lived.

The sun continued its gentle offices. The wind, which was already the breath of summer and of noon, approached him like loving lips that breathed upon him softly.

Gilliatt moved.

The peaceful calm upon the sea was perfect. Its murmur was like the droning of the nurse beside the sleeping infant. The rock seemed cradled in the waves.

The sea-birds, who knew that form, fluttered above it; not with their old wild astonishment, but with a sort of fraternal tenderness. They uttered plaintive cries: they seemed to be calling to him. A sea-mew, who no doubt knew him, was tame enough to come near him. It began to caw as if speaking to him. The sleeper seemed not to hear. The bird hopped upon his shoulder, and pecked his lips softly.

Gilliatt opened his eyes.

The birds dispersed, chattering wildly.

Gilliatt arose, stretched himself like a roused lion, ran to the edge of the platform, and looked down into the space between the two Douvres.

The sloop was there, intact; the stoppage had held out; the sea had probably disturbed it but little.

All was saved.

He was no longer weary. His powers had returned. His swoon had ended in a deep sleep.

He descended and baled out the sloop, emptied the hold, raised the leakage above the water-line, dressed himself, ate, drank some water, and was joyful.

The gap in the side of his vessel, examined in broad daylight, proved to require more labour than he had thought. It was a serious fracture. The entire day was not too much for its repair.

At daybreak on the morrow, after removing the barrier and re-opening the entrance to the defile, dressed in the tattered clothing which had served to stop the leak, having about him Clubin's girdle and the seventy-five thousand francs, standing erect in the sloop, now repaired, by the side of the machinery which he had rescued, with a favourable breeze and a good sea, Gilliatt pushed off from the Douvres.

He put the sloop's head for Guernsey.

At the moment of his departure from the rocks, any one who had been there might have heard him singing, in an undertone, the air of "Bonnie Dundee."

Part III

Déruchette

Book I
Night and the Moon

❋

I
THE HARBOUR BELL

THE ST. SAMPSON of the present day is almost a city; the St. Sampson of forty years since was almost a village.

When the winter evenings were ended and spring had come, the inhabitants were not long out of bed after sundown. St. Sampson was an ancient parish which had long been accustomed to the sound of the curfew-bell, and which had a traditional habit of blowing out the candle at an early hour. Those old Norman villages are famous for early roosting, and the villagers are generally great rearers of poultry.

The people of St. Sampson, except a few rich families among the townsfolk, are also a population of quarriers and carpenters. The port is a port of ship repairing. The quarrying of stone and the fashioning of timber go on all day long; here the labourer with the pickaxe, there the workman with the mallet. At night they sink with fatigue, and sleep like lead. Rude labours bring heavy slumbers.

One evening, in the commencement of the month of May, after watching the crescent moon for some instants through the trees, and listening to the step of Déruchette, walking alone in the cool air in the garden of the Bravées, Mess Lethierry had returned to his room looking on the harbour, and had retired to rest; Douce and Grace were already a-bed. Except Déruchette, the whole household were sleeping. Doors and shutters were everywhere closed. Footsteps were silent in the streets. Some few lights, like winking eyes about to close in rest, showed here and there in windows in the roofs, indicating the hour of domestics going to bed. Nine had already struck in the old Romanesque belfry, surrounded by ivy, which shares with

the church of St. Brélade at Jersey the peculiarity of having for its date four
ones (IIII), which are used to signify eleven hundred and eleven.

The popularity of Mess Lethierry at St. Sampson had been founded on
his success. The success at an end, there had come a void. It might be imagined that ill-fortune is contagious, and that the unsuccessful have a plague,
so rapidly are they put in quarantine. The young men of well-to-do families
avoided Déruchette. The isolation around the Bravées was so complete that
its inmates had not even yet heard the news of the great local event which
had that day set all St. Sampson in a ferment. The rector of the parish,
the Rev. Ebenezer Caudray, had become rich. His uncle, the magnificent
Dean of St. Asaph, had just died in London. The news had been brought
by the mail sloop, the *Cashmere*, arrived from England that very morning,
and the mast of which could be perceived in the roads of St. Peter's Port.
The *Cashmere* was to depart for Southampton at noon on the morrow,
and, so the rumour ran, to convey the reverend gentleman, who had been
suddenly summoned to England, to be present at the official opening of
the will, not to speak of other urgent matters connected with an important
inheritance. All day long St. Sampson had been conversing on this subject.
The *Cashmere*, the Rev. Ebenezer, his deceased uncle, his riches, his departure, his possible preferment in the future, had formed the foundations of
that perpetual buzzing. A solitary house, still uninformed on these matters,
had remained at peace. This was the Bravées.

Mess Lethierry had jumped into his hammock, and lay down in his
clothing.

Since the catastrophe of the Durande, to get into his hammock had
been his resource. Every captive has recourse to stretching himself upon his
pallet, and Mess Lethierry was the captive of his grief. To go to bed was a
truce, a gain in breathing time, a suspension of ideas. He neither slept nor
watched. Strictly speaking, for two months and a half—for so long was it
since his misfortune—Mess Lethierry had been in a sort of somnambulism.
He had not yet regained possession of his faculties. He was in that cloudy
and confused condition of intellect with which those are familiar who have
undergone overwhelming afflictions. His reflections were not thought, his
sleep was no repose. By day he was not awake, by night not asleep. He was
up, and then gone to rest, that was all. When he was in his hammock forget-

fulness came to him a little. He called that sleeping. Chimeras floated about
him, and within him. The nocturnal cloud, full of confused faces, traversed
his brain. Sometimes it was the Emperor Napoleon dictating to him the
story of his life; sometimes there were several Déruchettes; strange birds
were in the trees; the streets of Lons-le-Saulnier became serpents. Nightmares were the brief respites of despair. He passed his nights in dreaming,
and his days in reverie.

Sometimes he remained all the afternoon at the window of his room,
which looked out upon the port, with his head drooping, his elbows on the
stone, his ears resting on his fists, his back turned to the whole world, his
eye fixed on the old massive iron ring fastened in the wall of the house, at
only a few feet from his window, where in the old days he used to moor the
Durande. He was looking at the rust which gathered on the ring.

He was reduced to the mere mechanical habit of living.

The bravest men, when deprived of their most cherished idea, will
come to this. His life had become a void. Life is a voyage; the idea is the
itinerary. The plan of their course gone, they stop. The object is lost, the
strength of purpose gone. Fate has a secret discretionary power. It is able to
touch with its rod even our moral being. Despair is almost the destitution
of the soul. Only the greatest minds resist, and for what?

Mess Lethierry was always meditating, if absorption can be called meditation, in the depth of a sort of cloudy abyss. Broken words sometimes
escaped him like these, "There is nothing left for me now, but to ask yonder
for leave to go."

There was a certain contradiction in that nature, complex as the sea, of
which Mess Lethierry was, so to speak, the product. Mess Lethierry's grief
did not seek relief in prayer.

To be powerless is a certain strength. In the presence of our two great
expressions of this blindness—destiny and nature—it is in his powerlessness
that man has found his chief support in prayer.

Man seeks succour from his terror; his anxiety bids him kneel. Prayer,
that mighty force of the soul, akin to mystery. Prayer addresses itself to the
magnanimity of the Shades; prayer regards mystery with eyes themselves
overshadowed by it, and beneath the power of its fixed and appealing gaze,
we feel the possibility of the great Unknown unbending to reply.

The mere thought of such a possibility becomes a consolation.

But Mess Lethierry prayed not.

In the time when he was happy, God existed for him almost in visible contact. Lethierry addressed Him, pledged his word to Him, seemed at times to hold familiar intercourse with Him. But in the hour of his misfortune, a phenomenon not infrequent—the idea of God had become eclipsed in his mind. This happens when the mind has created for itself a deity clothed with human qualities.

In the state of mind in which he existed, there was for Lethierry only one clear vision—the smile of Déruchette. Beyond this all was dark.

For some time, apparently on account of the loss of the Durande, and of the blow which it had been to them, this pleasant smile had been rare. She seemed always thoughtful. Her birdlike playfulness, her childlike ways, were gone. She was never seen now in the morning, at the sound of the cannon which announced daybreak, saluting the rising sun with "Boom! Daylight! Come in, please!" At times her expression was very serious, a sad thing for that sweet nature. She made an effort, however, sometimes to laugh before Mess Lethierry and to divert him; but her cheerfulness grew tarnished from day to day—gathered dust like the wing of a butterfly with a pin through its body. Whether through sorrow for her uncle's sorrow—for there are griefs which are the reflections of other griefs—or whether for any other reasons, she appeared at this time to be much inclined towards religion. In the time of the old rector, M. Jaquemin Hérode, she scarcely went to church, as has been already said, four times a year. Now she was, on the contrary, assiduous in her attendance. She missed no service, neither of Sunday nor of Thursday. Pious souls in the parish remarked with satisfaction that amendment. For it is a great blessing when a girl who runs so many dangers in the world turns her thoughts towards God. That enables the poor parents at least to be easy on the subject of love-making and what not.

In the evening, whenever the weather permitted, she walked for an hour or two in the garden of the Bravées. She was almost as pensive there as Mess Lethierry, and almost always alone. Déruchette went to bed last. This, however, did not prevent Douce and Grace watching her a little, by that instinct for spying which is common to servants; spying is such a relaxation after household work.

As to Mess Lethierry, in the abstracted state of his mind, these little changes in Déruchette's habits escaped him. Moreover, his nature had little in common with the Duenna. He had not even remarked her regularity at the church. Tenacious of his prejudices against the clergy and their sermons, he would have seen with little pleasure these frequent attendances at the parish church. It was not because his own moral condition was not undergoing change. Sorrow is a cloud which changes form.

Robust natures, as we have said, are sometimes almost overthrown by sudden great misfortunes; but not quite. Manly characters such as Lethierry's experience a reaction in a given time. Despair has its backward stages. From overwhelmment we rise to dejection; from dejection to affliction; from affliction to melancholy. Melancholy is a twilight state; suffering melts into it and becomes a sombre joy. Melancholy is the pleasure of being sad.

These elegiac moods were not made for Lethierry. Neither the nature of his temperament nor the character of his misfortune suited those delicate shades. But at the moment at which we have returned to him, the reverie of his first despair had for more than a week been tending to disperse; without, however, leaving him less sad. He was more inactive, was always dull; but he was no longer overwhelmed. A certain perception of events and circumstances was returning to him, and he began to experience something of that phenomenon which may be called the return to reality.

Thus by day in the great lower room, he did not listen to the words of those about him, but he heard them. Grace came one morning quite triumphant to tell Déruchette that he had undone the cover of a newspaper.

This half acceptance of realities is in itself a good symptom, a token of convalescence. Great afflictions produce a stupor; it is by such little acts that men return to themselves. This improvement, however, is at first only an aggravation of the evil. The dreamy condition of mind in which the sufferer has lived, has served, while it lasted, to blunt his grief. His sight before was thick. He felt little. Now his view is clear, nothing escapes him; and his wounds re-open. Each detail that he perceives serves to remind him of his sorrow. He sees everything again in memory, every remembrance is a regret. All kinds of bitter aftertastes lurk in that return to life. He is better, and yet worse. Such was the condition of Lethierry. In returning to full consciousness, his sufferings had become more distinct.

A sudden shock first recalled him to a sense of reality.

One afternoon, between the 15th and 20th of April, a double-knock at the door of the great lower room of the Bravées had signalled the arrival of the postman. Douce had opened the door; there was a letter.

The letter came from beyond sea; it was addressed to Mess Lethierry, and bore the postmark "Lisbon."

Douce had taken the letter to Mess Lethierry, who was in his room. He had taken it, placed it mechanically upon the table, and had not looked at it.

The letter remained an entire week upon the table without being unsealed.

It happened, however, one morning that Douce said to Mess Lethierry: "Shall I brush the dust off your letter, sir?"

Lethierry seemed to arouse from his lethargy.

"Ay, ay! You are right," he said; and he opened the letter, and read as follows:—

"At Sea, *10th March*.

"To Mess Lethierry of St. Sampson.

"You will be gratified to receive news of me. I am aboard the *Tamaulipas*, bound for the port of 'No-return.' Among the crew is a sailor named Ahier-Tostevin, from Guernsey, who will return and will have some facts to communicate to you. I take the opportunity of our speaking a vessel, the *Herman Cortes*, bound for Lisbon, to forward you this letter.

"You will be astonished to learn that I am going to be honest.

"As honest as Sieur Clubin.

"I am bound to believe that you know of certain recent occurrences; nevertheless, it is, perhaps, not altogether superfluous to send you a full account of them,

"To proceed then.

"I have returned you your money.

"Some years ago, I borrowed from you, under somewhat irregular circumstances, the sum of fifty thousand francs. Before leaving St. Malo lately, I placed in the hands of your confidential man of business, Sieur Clubin, on your account three bank-notes of one thousand pounds each; making together seventy-five thousand francs. You will no doubt find this reimbursement sufficient.

"Sieur Clubin acted for you, and received your money, including interest, in a remarkably energetic manner. He appeared to me, indeed, singularly zealous. This is, in fact, my reason for apprising you of the facts.

"Your other confidential man of business,

"RANTAINE.

"*Postscript*—Sieur Clubin was in possession of a revolver, which will explain to you the circumstance of my having no receipt."

He who has ever touched a torpedo, or a Leyden-jar fully charged, may have a notion of the effect produced on Mess Lethierry by the reading of this letter.

Under that envelope, in that sheet of paper folded in four, to which he had at first paid so little attention, lay the elements of an extraordinary commotion.

He recognised the writing and the signature. As to the facts which the letter contained, at first he understood nothing.

The excitement of the event, however, soon gave movement to his faculties.

The effective part of the shock he had received lay in the phenomenon of the seventy-five thousand francs entrusted by Rantaine to Clubin; this was a riddle which compelled Lethierry's brain to work. Conjecture is a healthy occupation for the mind. Reason is awakened: logic is called into play.

For some time past public opinion in Guernsey had been undergoing a reaction on the subject of Clubin: that man of such high reputation for honour during many years; that man so unanimously regarded with esteem. People had begun to question and to doubt; there were wagers pro and con. Some light had been thrown on the question in singular ways. The figure of Clubin began to become clearer, that is to say, he began to be blacker in the eyes of the world.

A judicial inquiry had taken place at St. Malo, for the purpose of ascertaining what had become of the coast-guardman, number 619. Legal perspicacity had got upon a false scent, a thing which happens not unfrequently. It had started with the hypothesis that the man had been enticed by Zuela, and shipped aboard the *Tamaulipas* for Chili. This ingenious supposition had led to a considerable amount of wasted conjecture. The shortsightedness of justice had failed to take note of Rantaine; but in the progress of inquiry the authorities had come upon other clues. The affair, so obscure, became complicated. Clubin had become mixed up with the enigma. A coincidence, perhaps a direct connection, had been found between the departure of the *Tamaulipas* and the loss of the Durande. At the wine-shop near the Dinan Gate, where Clubin thought himself entirely unknown, he had been recognised. The wine-shop keeper had talked; Clubin had bought a bottle of brandy that night. For whom? The gunsmith of St. Vincent Street, too, had talked. Clubin had purchased a revolver. For what object? The landlord of the "Jean Auberge" had talked. Clubin had absented himself in an inexplicable manner. Captain Gertrais-Gaboureau had talked; Clubin had determined to start, although warned, and knowing that he might expect a great fog. The crew of the Durande had talked. In fact, the collection of the freight had been neglected, and the stowage badly arranged, a negligence easy to comprehend, if the captain had determined to wreck the ship. The Guernsey passenger, too, had spoken. Clubin had evidently imagined that he had run upon the Hanways. The Torteval people had spoken. Clubin had visited that neighbourhood a few days before the loss of the Durande, and had been seen walking in the direction of Pleinmont, near the Hanways. He had with him a travelling-bag. "He had set out with it, and come back without it." The birds'-nesters had spoken: their story seemed to be possibly connected with Clubin's disappearance, if instead of ghosts they supposed smugglers. Finally, the haunted house of Pleinmont itself had spoken. Persons who had determined to get information had climbed and entered the windows, and had found inside—what? The very travelling-bag which had been seen in Sieur Clubin's possession. The authorities of the *Douzaine* of Torteval had taken possession of the bag and had it opened. It was found to contain provisions, a telescope, a chronometer, a man's clothing, and linen marked with Clubin's initials. All this in the gossip of St. Malo and Guernsey became more and more like a case of fraud. Obscure hints were brought together; there appeared to have been a singular disregard of advice; a willingness to encounter the dangers of the fog; a suspected negligence in the stowage of the cargo. Then there was the mysterious bottle of brandy; a drunken helmsman; a substitution of the captain for the helmsman; a management of the rudder, to say the least, unskilful. The heroism of remaining behind upon the wreck began to look like roguery. Clubin besides had evidently been deceived as to the rock he was on. Granted an intention to wreck the vessel, it was easy to understand the choice of the Hanways, the shore easily reached by swimming, and the intended concealment in the haunted house awaiting the opportunity for flight. The travelling-bag, that suspicious preparative, completed the demonstration. By what link this affair connected itself with the other affair of the disappearance of the coast-guardman nobody knew. People imagined some connection, and that was all. They had a glimpse in their minds of the look-out-man, number 619, alongside of the mysterious Clubin—quite a tragic drama. Clubin possibly was not an actor in it, but his presence was visible in the side scenes.

The supposition of a wilful destruction of the Durande did not explain everything. There was a revolver in the story, with no part yet assigned to it. The revolver, probably, belonged to the other affair.

The scent of the public is keen and true. Its instinct excels in those discoveries of truth by pieces and fragments. Still, amidst these facts, which seemed to point pretty clearly to a case of barratry, there were serious difficulties.

Everything was consistent; everything coherent; but a basis was wanting.

People do not wreck vessels for the pleasure of wrecking them. Men do not run all those risks of fog, rocks, swimming, concealment, and flight without an interest. What could have been Clubin's interest?

The act seemed plain, but the motive was puzzling.

Hence a doubt in many minds. Where there is no motive, it is natural to infer that there was no act.

The missing link was important. The letter from Rantaine seemed to supply it.

This letter furnished a motive for Clubin's supposed crime: seventy-five thousand francs to be appropriated.

Rantaine was the *Deus ex machina*. He had descended from the clouds with a lantern in his hand. His letter was the final light upon the affair. It explained everything, and even promised a witness in the person of Ahier-Tostevin.

The part which it at once suggested for the revolver was decisive. Rantaine was undoubtedly well informed. His letter pointed clearly the explanation of the mystery.

There could be no possible palliation of Clubin's crime. He had premeditated the shipwreck; the proofs were the preparations discovered in the haunted house. Even supposing him innocent, and admitting the wreck to have been accidental, would he not, at the last moment, when he had determined to sacrifice himself with the vessel, have entrusted the seventy-five thousand francs to the men who escaped in the long-boat. The evidence was strikingly complete. Now what had become of Clubin? He had probably been the victim of his blunder. He had doubtless perished upon the Douvres.

All this construction of surmises, which were not far from the reality, had for several days occupied the mind of Mess Lethierry. The letter from Rantaine had done him the service of setting him to think. He was at first shaken by his surprise; then he made an effort to reflect. He made another effort more difficult still, that of inquiry. He was induced to listen, and even seek conversation. At the end of a week, he had become, to a certain degree, in the world again; his thoughts had regained their coherence, and he was almost restored. He had emerged from his confused and troubled state.

Rantaine's letter, even admitting that Mess Lethierry could ever have entertained any hope of the reimbursement of his money, destroyed that last chance.

It added to the catastrophe of the Durande this new wreck of seventy-five thousand francs. It put him in possession of that amount just so far as to make him sensible of its loss. The letter revealed to him the extreme point in his ruin.

Hence he experienced a new and very painful sensation, which we have already spoken of. He began to take an interest in his household— what it was to be in the future—how he was to set things in order; matters of which he had taken no heed for two months past. These trifling cares wounded him with a thousand tiny points, worse in their aggregate than the old despair. A sorrow is doubly burdensome which has to be endured in each item, and while disputing inch by inch with fate for ground already lost. Ruin is endurable in the mass, but not in the dust and fragments of the fallen edifice. The great fact may overwhelm, but the details torture. The catastrophe which lately fell like a thunderbolt, becomes now a cruel persecution. Humiliation comes to aggravate the blow. A second desolation succeeds the first, with features more repulsive. You descend one degree nearer to annihilation. The winding-sheet becomes changed to sordid rags.

No thought is more bitter than that of one's own gradual fall from a social position.

Ruin is simple enough. A violent shock; a cruel turn of fate; a catastrophe once for all. Be it so. We submit, and all is over. You are ruined: it is well; you are dead? No; you are still living. On the morrow you know it well. By what? By the pricking of a pin. Yonder passer-by omits to recognise you; the tradesmen's bills rain down upon you; and yonder is one of your enemies, who is smiling. Perhaps he is thinking of Arnal's last pun; but it is all the same. The pun would not have appeared to him so inimitable but for your ruin. You read your own sudden insignificance even in looks of indifference. Friends who used to dine at your table become of opinion that three courses were an extravagance. Your faults are patent to the eyes of everybody; ingratitude having nothing more to expect, proclaims itself openly; every idiot has foreseen your misfortunes. The malignant pull you to pieces; the more malignant profess to pity. And then come a hundred paltry details. Nausea succeeds to grief. You have been wont to indulge in wine; you must now drink cider. Two servants, too! Why, one will be too many. It will be necessary to discharge this one, and get rid of that. Flowers in your garden are superfluous; you will plant it with potatoes. You used to make presents of your fruits to friends; you will send them henceforth to market. As to the poor, it will be absurd to think of giving anything to them. Are you not poor yourself? And then there is the painful question of dress. To have to refuse a wife a new ribbon, what a torture! To have to refuse one who has made you a gift of her beauty a trifling article; to haggle over such matters, like a miser! Perhaps she will say to you, "What! rob my garden of its flowers, and now refuse one for my bonnet!" Ah me! to have to condemn her to shabby dresses. The family table is silent. You fancy that those around it think harshly of you. Beloved faces have become clouded. This is what is meant by falling fortunes. It is to die day by day. To be struck down is like the blast of the furnace; to decay like this is the torture of the slow fire.

An overwhelming blow is a sort of Waterloo, a slow decay, a St. Helena. Destiny, incarnate in the form of Wellington, has still some dignity; but how sordid in the shape of Hudson Lowe. Fate becomes then a paltry huckster. We find the man of Campo Formio quarrelling about a pair of stockings; we see that dwarfing of Napoleon which makes England less. Waterloo and St. Helena! Reduced to humbler proportions, every ruined man has traversed those two phases.

On the evening we have mentioned, and which was one of the first evenings in May, Lethierry, leaving Déruchette to walk by moonlight in the garden, had gone to bed more depressed than ever.

All these mean and repulsive details, peculiar to worldly misfortune; all these trifling cares, which are at first insipid, and afterwards harassing, were revolving in his mind. A sullen load of miseries! Mess Lethierry felt that his fall was irremediable. What could he do? What would become of them? What sacrifices should he be compelled to impose on Déruchette? Whom should he discharge—Douce or Grace? Would they have to sell the Bravées? Would they not be compelled to leave the island? To be nothing where he had been everything; it was a terrible fall indeed.

And to know that the old times had gone for ever! To recall those journeys to and fro, uniting France with those numberless islands; the Tuesday's departure, the Friday's return, the crowd on the quay, those great cargoes, that industry, that prosperity, that proud direct navigation, that machinery embodying the will of man, that all-powerful boiler, that smoke, all that reality! The steamboat had been the final crown of the compass; the needle indicating the direct track, the steam-vessel following it. One proposing, the other executing. Where was she now, his Durande, that mistress of the seas, that queen who had made him a king? To have been so long the man of ideas in his own country, the man of success, the man who revolutionised navigation; and then to have to give up all, to abdicate! To cease to exist, to become a bye-word, an empty bag which once was full. To belong to the past, after having so long represented the future. To come down to be an object of pity to fools, to witness the triumph of routine, obstinacy, conservatism, selfishness, ignorance. To see the old barbarous sailing cutters crawling to and fro upon the sea: the outworn old-world prejudices young again; to have wasted a whole life; to have been a light, and to suffer this eclipse.

Ah! what a sight it was upon the waves, that noble funnel, that prodigious cylinder, that pillar with its capital of smoke, that column grander than any in the Place Vendôme, for on that there was only a man, while on this stood Progress. The ocean was subdued; it was certainty upon the open sea. And had all this been witnessed in that little island, in that little harbour, in that little town of St. Sampson? Yes; it had been witnessed. And could it be that, having seen it, all had vanished to be seen no more.

All this series of regrets tortured Lethierry. There is such a thing as a mental sobbing. Never, perhaps, had he felt his misfortune more bitterly. A certain numbness follows this acute suffering. Under the weight of his sorrow he gradually dosed.

For about two hours he remained in this state, feverish, sleeping a little, meditating much. Such torpors are accompanied by an obscure labour of the brain, which is inexpressibly wearying. Towards the middle of the night, about midnight, a little before or a little after, he shook off his lethargy. He aroused, and opened his eyes. His window was directly in front of his hammock. He saw something extraordinary.

A form was before the window; a marvellous form. It was the funnel of a steam-vessel.

Mess Lethierry started, and sat upright in his bed. The hammock oscillated like a swing in a tempest. Lethierry stared. A vision filled the window-frame. There was the harbour flooded with the light of the moon, and against that glitter, quite close to his house, stood forth, tall, round, and black, a magnificent object.

The funnel of a steam-vessel was there.

Lethierry sprang out of his hammock, ran to the window, lifted the sash, leaned out, and recognised it.

The funnel of the Durande stood before him.

It was in the old place.

Its four chains supported it, made fast to the bulwarks of a vessel in which, beneath the funnel, he could distinguish a dark mass of irregular outline.

Lethierry recoiled, turned his back to the window, and dropped in a sitting posture into his hammock again.

Then he returned, and once more he saw the vision.

An instant afterwards, or in about the time occupied by a flash of lightning, he was out upon the quay, with a lantern in his hand.

A bark carrying a little backward a massive block from which issued the straight funnel before the window of the Bravées, was made fast to the mooring-ring of the Durande. The bows of the bark stretched beyond the corner of the wall of the house, and were level with the quay.

There was no one aboard.

The vessel was of a peculiar shape. All Guernsey would have recognised it. It was the old Dutch sloop.

Lethierry jumped aboard; and ran forward to the block which he saw beyond the mast.

It was there, entire, complete, intact, standing square and firm upon its cast-iron flooring; the boiler had all its rivets, the axle of the paddle-wheels was raised erect, and made fast near the boiler; the brine-pump was in its place; nothing was wanting.

Lethierry examined the machinery.

The lantern and the moon helped him in his examination. He went over every part of the mechanism.

He noticed the two cases at the sides. He examined the axle of the wheels.

He went into the little cabin; it was empty.

He returned to the engine, and felt it, looked into the boiler, and knelt down to examine it inside.

He placed his lantern within the furnace, where the light, illuminating all the machinery, produced almost the illusion of an engine-room with its fire.

Then he burst into a wild laugh, sprang to his feet, and with his eye fixed on the engine, and his arms outstretched towards the funnel, he cried aloud, "Help."

The harbour bell was upon the quay, at a few paces distance. He ran to it, seized the chain, and began to pull it violently.

II

THE HARBOUR BELL AGAIN

GILLIATT, in fact, after a passage without accident, but somewhat slow on account of the heavy burden of the sloop, had arrived at St. Sampson after dark, and nearer ten than nine o'clock.

He had calculated the time. The half-flood had arrived. There was plenty of water, and the moon was shining; so that he was able to enter the port.

The little harbour was silent. A few vessels were moored there, with their sails brailed up to the yards, their tops over, and without lanterns. At the far end a few others were visible, high and dry in the careenage, where they were undergoing repairs; large hulls dismasted and stripped, with their planking open at various parts, lifting high the ends of their timbers, and looking like huge dead beetles lying on their backs with their legs in the air.

As soon as he had cleared the harbour mouth, Gilliatt examined the port and the quay. There was no light to be seen either at the Bravées or elsewhere. The place was deserted, save, perhaps, by some one going to or returning from the parsonage-house; nor was it possible to be sure even of this; for the night blurred every outline, and the moonlight always gives to objects a vague appearance. The distance added to the indistinctness. The parsonage-house at that period was situated on the other side of the harbour, where there stands at the present day an open mast-house.

Gilliatt had approached the Bravées quietly, and had made the sloop fast to the ring of the Durande, under Mess Lethierry's window.

He leaped over the bulwarks, and was ashore.

Leaving the sloop behind him by the quay, he turned the angle of the house, passed along a little narrow street, then along another, did not even notice the pathway which branched off leading to the Bû de la Rue, and in a few minutes found himself at that corner of the wall where there were wild mallows with pink flowers in June, with holly, ivy, and nettles. Many a time concealed behind the bushes, seated on a stone, in the summer days, he had watched here through long hours, even for whole months, often tempted to climb the wall, over which he contemplated the garden of the Bravées and the two windows of a little room seen through the branches of the trees. The stone was there still; the bushes, the low wall, the angle, as quiet and dark as ever. Like an animal returning to its hole, gliding rather than walking, he made his way in. Once seated there, he made no movement. He looked around; saw again the garden, the pathways, the beds of flowers, the house, the two windows of the chamber. The moonlight fell upon this dream. He felt it horrible to be compelled to breathe, and did what he could to prevent it.

He seemed to be gazing on a vision of paradise, and was afraid that all would vanish. It was almost impossible that all these things could be really before his eyes; and if they were, it could only be with that imminent danger of melting into air which belongs to things divine. A breath, and all must be dissipated. He trembled with the thought.

Before him, not far off, at the side of one of the alleys in the garden, was a wooden seat painted green. The reader will remember this seat.

Gilliatt looked up at the two windows. He thought of the slumber of some one possibly in that room. Behind that wall she was no doubt sleeping. He wished himself elsewhere, yet would sooner have died than go away. He thought of a gentle breathing moving a woman's breast. It was she, that vision, that purity in the clouds, that form haunting him by day and night. She was there! He thought of her so far removed, and yet so near as to be almost within reach of his delight; he thought of that impossible ideal drooping in slumber, and like himself, too, visited by visions; of that being so long desired, so distant, so impalpable—her closed eyelids, her face resting on her hand; of the mystery of sleep in its relations with that pure spirit, of what dreams might come to one who was herself a dream. He dared not think beyond, and yet he did. He ventured on those familiarities which the fancy may indulge in; the notion of how much was feminine in that angelic being disturbed his thoughts. The darkness of night emboldens timid imaginations to take these furtive glances. He was vexed within himself, feeling on reflection as if it were profanity to think of her so boldly; yet still constrained, in spite of himself, he tremblingly gazed into the invisible. He shuddered almost with a sense of pain as he imagined her room, a petticoat on a chair, a mantle fallen on the carpet, a band unbuckled, a handkerchief. He imagined her corset with its lace hanging to the ground, her stockings, her boots. His soul was among the stars.

The stars are made for the human heart of a poor man like Gilliatt not less than for that of the rich and great. There is a certain degree of passion by which every man becomes wrapped in a celestial light. With a rough and primitive nature, this truth is even more applicable. An uncultivated mind is easily touched with dreams.

Delight is a fulness which overflows like any other. To see those windows was almost too much happiness for Gilliatt.

Suddenly, he looked and saw her.

From the branches of a clump of bushes, already thickened by the spring, there issued with a spectral slowness a celestial figure, a dress, a divine face, almost a shining light beneath the moon.

Gilliatt felt his powers failing him: it was Déruchette.

Déruchette approached. She stopped. She walked back a few paces, stopped again, then returned and sat upon the wooden bench. The moon was in the trees, a few clouds floated among the pale stars; the sea murmured to the shadows in an undertone, the town was sleeping, a thin haze was rising from the horizon, the melancholy was profound. Déruchette inclined her head, with those thoughtful eyes which look attentive yet see nothing. She was seated sideways, and had nothing on her head but a little cap untied, which showed upon her delicate neck the commencement of her hair. She twirled mechanically a ribbon of her cap around one of her fingers; the half light showed the outline of her hands like those of a statue; her dress was of one of those shades which by night looked white: the trees stirred as if they felt the enchantment which she shed around her. The tip of one of her feet was visible. Her lowered eyelids had that vague contraction which suggests a tear checked in its course, or a thought suppressed. There was a charming indecision in the movements of her arms, which had no support to lean on; a sort of floating mingled with every posture. It was rather a gleam than a light—rather a grace than a goddess; the folds of her dress were exquisite; her face which might inspire adoration, seemed meditative, like portraits of the Virgin. It was terrible to think how near she was: Gilliatt could hear her breathe.

A nightingale was singing in the distance. The stirring of the wind among the branches set in movement, the inexpressible silence of the night. Déruchette, beautiful, divine, appeared in the twilight like a creation from those rays and from the perfumes in the air. That widespread enchantment seemed to concentre and embody itself mysteriously in her; she became its living manifestation. She seemed the outblossoming of all that shadow and silence.

But the shadow and silence which floated lightly about her weighed heavily on Gilliatt. He was bewildered; what he experienced is not to be told in words. Emotion is always new, and the word is always enough. Hence the impossibility of expressing it. Joy is sometimes overwhelming. To see Déruchette, to see herself, to see her dress, her cap, her ribbon, which she twined around her finger, was it possible to imagine it? Was it possible to be thus near her; to hear her breathe? She breathed! then the stars might breathe also. Gilliatt felt a thrill through him. He was the most miserable and yet the happiest of men. He knew not what to do. His delirious joy at seeing her annihilated him. Was it indeed Déruchette there, and he so near? His thoughts, bewildered and yet fixed, were fascinated by that figure as by a dazzling jewel. He gazed upon her neck—her hair. He did not even say to himself that all that would now belong to him, that before long—to-morrow, perhaps—he would have the right to take off that cap, to unknot that ribbon. He would not have conceived for a moment the audacity of thinking even so far. Touching in idea is almost like touching with the hand. Love was with Gilliatt like honey to the bear. He thought confusedly; he knew not what possessed him. The nightingale still sang. He felt as if about to breathe his life out.

The idea of rising, of jumping over the wall, of speaking to Déruchette, never came into his mind. If it had he would have turned and fled. If anything resembling a thought had begun to dawn in his mind, it was this: that Déruchette was there, that he wanted nothing more, and that eternity had begun.

A noise aroused them both—her from her reverie—him from his ecstasy.

Some one was walking in the garden. It was not possible to see who was approaching on account of the trees. It was the footstep of a man.

Déruchette raised her eyes.

The steps drew nearer, then ceased. The person walking had stopped. He must have been quite near. The path beside which was the bench wound between two clumps of trees. The stranger was there in the alley between the trees, at a few paces from the seat.

Accident had so placed the branches, that Déruchette could see the newcomer while Gilliatt could not.

The moon cast on the ground beyond the trees a shadow which reached to the garden seat.

Gilliatt could see this shadow.

He looked at Déruchette.

She was quite pale; her mouth was partly open, as with a suppressed cry of surprise. She had just half risen from the bench, and sunk again upon it. There was in her attitude a mixture of fascination with a desire to fly. Her surprise was enchantment mingled with timidity. She had upon her lips almost the light of a smile, with the fulness of tears in her eyes. She seemed as if transfigured by that presence; as if the being whom she saw before her belonged not to this earth. The reflection of an angel was in her look.

The stranger, who was to Gilliatt only a shadow, spoke. A voice issued from the trees, softer than the voice of a woman; yet it was the voice of a man. Gilliatt heard these words:

"I see you, mademoiselle, every Sunday and every Thursday. They tell me that once you used not to come so often. It is a remark that has been made. I ask your pardon. I have never spoken to you; it was my duty; but I come to speak to you to-day, for it is still my duty. It is right that I speak to you first. The *Cashmere* sails to-morrow. This is why I have come. You walk every evening in your garden. It would be wrong of me to know your habits so well, if I had not the thought that I have. Mademoiselle, you are poor; since this morning I am rich. Will you have me for your husband?"

Déruchette joined her two hands in a suppliant attitude, and looked at the speaker, silent, with fixed eyes, and trembling from head to foot.

The voice continued:

"I love you. God made not the heart of man to be silent. He has promised him eternity with the intention that he should not be alone. There is for me but one woman upon earth. It is you. I think of you as of a prayer. My faith is in God, and my hope in you. What wings I have you bear. You are my life, and already my supreme happiness."

"Sir," said Déruchette, "there is no one to answer in the house!"

The voice rose again:

"Yes, I have encouraged that dream. Heaven has not forbidden us to dream. You are like a glory in my eyes. I love you deeply, mademoiselle. To me you are holy innocence. I know it is the hour at which your household have retired to rest, but I had no choice of any other moment. Do you remember that passage of the Bible which some one read before us; it was the twenty-fifth chapter of Genesis. I have thought of it often since. M. Hérode said to me, you must have a rich wife. I replied no, I must have a poor wife. I speak to you, mademoiselle, without venturing to approach you; I would step even further back if it was your wish that my shadow should not touch your feet. You alone are supreme. You will come to me if such is your will. I love and wait. You are the living form of a benediction."

"I did not know, sir," stammered Déruchette, "that any one remarked me on Sundays and Thursdays."

The voice continued:

"We are powerless against celestial things. The whole Law is love. Marriage is Canaan; you are to me the promised land of beauty."

Déruchette replied, "I did not think I did wrong any more than other persons who are strict."

The voice continued:

"God manifests his will in the flowers, in the light of dawn, in the spring; and love is of his ordaining. You are beautiful in this holy shadow of night. This garden has been tended by you; in its perfumes there is something of your breath. The affinities of our souls do not depend on us. They cannot be counted with our sins. You were there, that was all. I was there, that was all. I did nothing but feel that I loved you. Sometimes my eyes rested upon you. I was wrong, but what could I do. It was through looking at you that all happened. I could not restrain my gaze. There are mysterious impulses which are above our search. The heart is the chief of all temples. To have your spirit in my house—this is the terrestrial paradise for which I hope. Say, will you be mine. As long as I was poor, I spoke not. I know your age. You are twenty-one; I am twenty-six. I go to-morrow; if you refuse me I return no more. Oh, be my betrothed; will you not? More than once have my eyes, in spite of myself, addressed to you that question. I love you; answer me. I will speak to your uncle as soon as he is able to receive me; but I turn first to you. To Rebecca I plead for Rebecca; unless you love me not."

Déruchette hung her head, and murmured:

"Oh! I worship him."

The words were spoken in a voice so low, that only Gilliatt heard them.

She remained with her head lowered as if by shading her face she hoped to conceal her thoughts.

There was a pause. No leaf among the trees was stirred. It was that solemn and peaceful moment when the slumber of external things mingles with the sleep of living creatures; and night seems to listen to the beating of Nature's heart. In the midst of that retirement, like a harmony making the silence more complete, rose the wide murmur of the sea.

The voice was heard again.

"Mademoiselle!"

Déruchette started.

Again the voice spoke.

"You are silent."

"What would you have me say?"

"I wait for your reply."

"God has heard it," said Déruchette.

Then the voice became almost sonorous, and at the same time softer than before, and these words issued from the leaves as from a burning bush:

"You are my betrothed. Come then to me. Let the blue sky, with all its stars, be witness of this taking of my soul to thine; and let our first embrace be mingled with that firmament."

Déruchette arose, and remained an instant motionless, looking straight before her, doubtless in another's eyes. Then, with slow steps, with head erect, her arms drooping, but with the fingers of her hands wide apart, like one who leans on some unseen support, she advanced towards the trees, and was out of sight.

A moment afterwards, instead of the one shadow upon the gravelled walk, there were two. They mingled together. Gilliatt saw at his feet the embrace of those two shadows.

In certain moments of crisis, time flows from us as his sands from the hour-glass, and we have no feeling of his flight. That pair on the one hand, who were ignorant of the presence of a witness, and saw him not; on the other, that witness of their joy who could not see them, but who knew of their presence—how many minutes did they remain thus in that mysterious suspension of themselves? It would be impossible to say. Suddenly a noise burst forth at a distance. A voice was heard crying "Help!" and the harbour bell began to sound. It is probable that in those celestial transports of delight they heard no echo of that tumult.

The bell continued to ring. Any one who had sought Gilliatt then in the angle of the wall would have found him no longer there.

Book II
Gratitude and Despotism

❋

I
JOY SURROUNDED BY TORTURES

MESS LETHIERRY pulled the bell furiously, then stopped abruptly. A man had just turned the corner of the quay. It was Gilliatt.

Lethierry ran towards him, or rather flung himself upon him; seized his hand between his own, and looked him in the face for a moment, silent. It was the silence of an explosion struggling to find an issue.

Then pulling and shaking him with violence, and squeezing him in his arms, he compelled him to enter the lower room of the Bravées, pushed back with his heel the door which had remained half opened, sat down, or sank into a chair beside a great table lighted by the moon, the reflection of which gave a vague pallor to Gilliatt's face, and with a voice of intermingled laughter and tears, cried:

"Ah! my son; my player of the bagpipe! I knew well that it was you. The sloop, *parbleu*! Tell me the story. You went there, then. Why, they would have burnt you a hundred years ago! It is magic! There isn't a screw missing. I have looked at everything already, recognised everything, handled everything. I guessed that the paddles were in the two cases. And here you are once more! I have been looking for you in the little cabin. I rang the bell. I was seeking for you. I said to myself, 'Where is he, that I may devour him?' You must admit that wonderful things do come to pass. He has brought back life to me. *Tonnerre!* you are an angel! Yes, yes; it is my engine. Nobody will believe it; people will see it, and say, 'It can't be true.' Not a tap, not a pin missing. The feed-pipe has never budged an inch. It is incredible that there should have been no more damage. We have only to put a little oil. But how did you accomplish it? To think that the Durande will be moving again. The axle of the wheels must have been taken to pieces by some watchmaker. Give me your word that I am not crazy."

He sprang to his feet, breathed a moment, and continued:

"Assure me of that. What a revolution! I pinched myself to be certain I was not dreaming. You are my child, you are my son, you are my Providence. Brave lad! To go and fetch my good old engine. In the open sea, among those cut-throat rocks. I have seen some strange things in my life; nothing like that. I have known Parisians, who were veritable demons, but I'll defy them to have done that. It beats the Bastille. I have seen the *gauchos* labouring in the *Pampas*, with a crooked branch of a tree for a plough and a bundle of thorn-bushes for a harrow, dragged by a leathern strap; they get harvests of wheat that way, with grains as big as hedgenuts. But that is a trifle compared with your feats. You have performed a miracle—a real one. Ah! *gredin!* let me hug you. How they will gossip in St. Sampson. I shall set to work at once to build the boat. It is astonishing that the crank is all right. Gentlemen, he has been to the Douvres; I say to the Douvres. He went alone. The Douvres! I defy you to find a worse spot. Do you know, have they told you, that it's proved that Clubin sent the Durande to the bottom to swindle me out of money which he had to bring me? He made Tangrouille drunk. It's a long story. I'll tell you another day of his piratical tricks. I, stupid idiot, had confidence in Clubin. But he trapped himself, the villain, for he couldn't have got away. There is a God above, scoundrel! Do you see, Gilliatt, bang! bang! the irons in the fire; we'll begin at once to rebuild the Durande. We'll have her twenty feet longer. They build them longer now than they did. I'll buy the wood from Dantzic and Brême. Now I have got the machinery they will give me credit again. They'll have confidence now."

Mess Lethierry stopped, lifted his eyes with that look which sees the heavens through the roof, and muttered, "Yes, there is a power on high!"

Then he placed the middle finger of his right hand between his two eyebrows, and tapped with his nail there, an action which indicates a project passing through the mind, and he continued:

"Nevertheless, to begin again, on a grand scale, a little ready money would have been useful. Ah! if I only had my three bank-notes, the seventy-five thousand francs that that robber Rantaine returned, and that vagabond Clubin stole."

Gilliatt silently felt in his pocket, and drew out something which he placed before him. It was the leathern belt that he had brought back. He opened, and spread it out upon the table; in the inside the word "Clubin" could be deciphered in the light of the moon. He then took out of the pocket of the belt a box, and out of the box three pieces of paper, which he unfolded and offered to Lethierry.

Lethierry examined them. It was light enough to read the figures "1000," and the word "thousand" was also perfectly visible. Mess Lethierry took the three notes, placed them on the table one beside the other, looked at them, looked at Gilliatt, stood for a moment dumb; and then began again, like an eruption after an explosion:

"These too! You are a marvel. My bank-notes! all three. A thousand pounds each. My seventy-five thousand francs. Why, you must have gone down to the infernal regions. It is Clubin's belt. Pardieu! I can read his vile name. Gilliatt has brought back engine and money too. There will be something to put in the papers. I will buy some timber of the finest quality. I guess how it was; you found his carcase; Clubin mouldering away in some corner. We'll have some Dantzic pine and Brême oak; we'll have a first-rate planking—oak within and pine without. In old times they didn't build so well, but their work lasted longer; the wood was better seasoned, because they did not build so much. We'll build the hull perhaps of elm. Elm is good for the parts in the water. To be dry sometimes, and sometimes wet, rots the timbers; the elm requires to be always wet; it's a wood that feeds upon water. What a splendid Durande we'll build. The lawyers will not trouble me again. I shall want no more credit. I have some money of my own. Did ever any one see a man like Gilliatt. I was struck down to the ground, I was a dead man. He comes and sets me up again as firm as ever. And all the while I was never thinking about him. He had gone clean out of my mind; but I recollect everything now. Poor lad! Ah! by the way, you know you are to marry Déruchette."

Gilliatt leaned with his back against the wall, like one who staggers, and said in a tone very low, but distinct:

"No."

Mess Lethierry started.

"How, no!"

Gilliatt replied:

"I do not love her."

Mess Lethierry went to the window, opened and reclosed it, took the three bank-notes, folded them, placed the iron box on top, scratched his head, seized Clubin's belt, flung it violently against the wall, and exclaimed:

"You must be mad."

He thrust his fists into his pockets, and exclaimed:

"You don't love Déruchette? What! was it at me, then, that you used to play the bagpipe?"

Gilliatt, still supporting himself by the wall, turned pale, as a man near his end. As he became pale, Lethierry became redder.

"There's an idiot for you! He doesn't love Déruchette. Very good; make up your mind to love her, for she shall never marry any but you. A devilish pretty story that; and you think that I believe you. If there is anything really the matter with you, send for a doctor; but don't talk nonsense. You can't have had time to quarrel, or get out of temper with her. It is true that lovers are great fools sometimes. Come now, what are your reasons? If you have any, say. People don't make geese of themselves without reasons. But, I have wool in my ears; perhaps I didn't understand. Repeat to me what you said."

Gilliatt replied:

"I said, No!"

"You said, No. He holds to it, the lunatic! You must be crazy. You said, No. Here's a stupidity beyond anything ever heard of. Why, people have had their heads shaved for much less than that. What! you don't like Déruchette? Oh, then, it was out of affection for the old man that you did all these things? It was for the sake of papa that you went to the Douvres, that you endured cold and heat, and was half dead with hunger and thirst, and ate the limpets off the rocks, and had the fog, the rain, and the wind for your bedroom, and brought me back my machine, just as you might bring a pretty woman her little canary that had escaped from its cage. And the tempest that we had three days ago. Do you think I don't bear it in mind? You must have had a time of it! It was in the midst of all this misery, alongside of my old craft, that you shaped, and cut, and turned, and twisted, and dragged about, and filed, and sawed, and carpentered, and schemed, and performed more miracles there by yourself than all the saints in paradise. Ah! you annoyed me enough once with your bagpipe. They call it a *biniou* in Brittany. Always the same tune too, silly fellow. And yet you don't love Déruchette? I don't know what is the matter with you. I recollect it all now. I was there in the corner; Déruchette said, 'He shall be my husband;' and so you shall. You don't love her! Either you must be mad, or else I am mad. And you stand there, and speak not a word. I tell you you are not at liberty to do all the things you have done, and then say, after all, 'I don't love Déruchette.' People don't do others services in order to put them in a passion. Well; if you don't marry her, she shall be single all her life. In the first place, I shall want you. You must be the pilot of the Durande. Do you imagine I mean to part with you like that? No, no, my brave boy; I don't let you go. I have got you now; I'll not even listen to you. Where will they find a sailor like you? You are the man I want. But why don't you speak?"

Meanwhile the harbour bell had aroused the household and the neighbourhood. Douce and Grace had risen, and had just entered the lower room, silent and astonished. Grace had a candle in her hand. A group of neighbours, townspeople, sailors, and peasants, who had rushed out of their houses, were outside on the quay, gazing in wonderment at the funnel of the Durande in the sloop. Some, hearing Lethierry's voice in the lower room, began to glide in by the half-opened door. Between the faces of two worthy old women appeared that of Sieur Landoys, who had the good fortune always to find himself where he would have regretted to have been absent.

Men feel a satisfaction in having witnesses of their joys. The sort of scattered support which a crowd presents pleases them at such times; their delight draws new life from it. Mess Lethierry suddenly perceived that there were persons about him; and he welcomed the audience at once.

"Ah! you are here, my friends? I am very glad to see you. You know the news? That man has been there, and brought it back. How d'ye do, Sieur Landoys? When I woke up just now, the first thing I spied was the funnel. It was under my window. There's not a nail missing. They make pictures of Napoleon's deeds; but I think more of that than of the battle of Austerlitz. You have just left your beds, my good friends. The Durande has found you sleeping. While you are putting on your night-caps and blowing out your candles there are others working like heroes. We are a set of cowards and do-nothings; we sit at home rubbing our rheumatisms; but happily that does not prevent there being some of another stamp. The man of the Bû de la Rue has arrived from the Douvres rocks. He has fished up the Durande from the bottom of the sea; and fished up my money out of Clubin's pocket, from a greater depth still. But how did you contrive to do it? All the powers of darkness were against you—the wind and the sea—the sea and the wind. It's true enough that you are a magician. Those who say that are not so stupid after all. The Durande is back again. The tempests may rage now; that cuts the ground from under them. My friends, I can inform you that there was no shipwreck after all. I have examined all the machinery. It is like new, perfect. The valves go as easily as rollers. You would think them made yesterday. You know that the waste water is carried away by a tube inside another tube, through which come the waters from the boilers; this was to economise the heat. Well; the two tubes are there as good as ever. The complete engine, in fact. She is all there, her wheels and all. Ah! you shall marry her."

"Marry the complete engine?" asked Sieur Landoys.

"No; Déruchette; yes; the engine. Both of them. He shall be my double son-in-law. He shall be her captain. Good day, Captain Gilliatt; for there will soon be a captain of the Durande. We are going to do a world of business again. There will be trade, circulation, cargoes of oxen and sheep. I wouldn't give St. Sampson for London now. And there stands the author of all this. It was a curious adventure, I can tell you. You will read about it on Saturday in old Mauger's *Gazette*. Malicious Gilliatt is very malicious. What's the meaning of these Louis-d'ors here?"

Mess Lethierry had just observed, through the opening of the lid, that there was some gold in the box upon the notes. He seized it, opened and emptied it into the palm of his hand, and put the handful of guineas on the table.

"For the poor, Sieur Landoys. Give those sovereigns from me to the constable of St. Sampson. You recollect Rantaine's letter. I showed it to you. Very well; I've got the bank-notes. Now we can buy some oak and fir, and go to work at carpentering. Look you! Do you remember the weather of three days ago? What a hurricane of wind and rain! Gilliatt endured all that upon the Douvres. That didn't prevent his taking the wreck to pieces, as I might take my watch. Thanks to him, I am on my legs again. Old 'Lethi-

erry's galley' is going to run again, ladies and gentlemen. A nut-shell with
a couple of wheels and a funnel. I always had that idea. I used to say to
myself, one day I will do it. That was a good long time back. It was an idea
that came in my head at Paris, at the coffee-house at the corner of the Rue
Christine and the Rue Dauphine, when I was reading a paper which had an
account of it. Do you know that Gilliatt would think nothing of putting the
machine at Marly in his pocket, and walking about with it? He is wrought-
iron, that man; tempered steel, a mariner of invaluable qualities, an excellent
smith, an extraordinary fellow, more astonishing than the Prince of Hohen-
lohe. That is what I call a man with brains. We are children by the side of
him. Sea-wolves we may think ourselves; but the sea-lion is there. Hurrah
for Gilliatt! I do not know how he has done it; but certainly he must have
been the devil. And how can I do other than give him Déruchette."

For some minutes Déruchette had been in the room. She had not spoken
or moved since she entered. She had glided in like a shadow, had sat down
almost unperceived behind Mess Lethierry, who stood before her, loqua-
cious, stormy, joyful, abounding in gestures, and talking in a loud voice. A
little while after her another silent apparition had appeared. A man attired
in black, with a white cravat, holding his hat in his hand, stood in the doorway. There were now several candles among the group, which had gradually
increased in number. These lights were near the man attired in black. His
profile and youthful and pleasing complexion showed itself against the dark
background with the clearness of an engraving on a medal. He leaned with
his shoulder against the framework of the door, and held his left hand to his
forehead, an attitude of unconscious grace, which contrasted the breadth
of his forehead with the smallness of his hand. There was an expression of
anguish in his contracted lips, as he looked on and listened with profound
attention. The standers-by having recognised M. Caudray, the rector of the
parish, had fallen back to allow him to pass; but he remained upon the
threshold. There was hesitation in his posture, but decision in his looks,
which now and then met those of Déruchette. With regard to Gilliatt,
whether by chance or design, he was in shadow, and was only perceived
indistinctly.

At first Mess Lethierry did not observe Caudray, but he saw Déruchette.
He went to her and kissed her fervently upon the forehead; stretching

forth his hand at the same time towards the dark corner where Gilliatt was standing.

"Déruchette," he said, "we are rich again; and there is your future husband."

Déruchette raised her head, and looked into the dusky corner bewildered.

Mess Lethierry continued:

"The marriage shall take place immediately, if it can; they shall have a licence; the formalities here are not very troublesome; the dean can do what he pleases; people are married before they have time to turn round. It is not as in France, where you must have bans, and publications, and delays, and all that fuss. You will be able to boast of being the wife of a brave man. No one can say he is not. I thought so from the day when I saw him come back from Herm with the little cannon. But now he comes back from the Douvres with his fortune and mine, and the fortune of this country. A man of whom the world will talk a great deal more one day. You said once, 'I will marry him;' and you shall marry him, and you shall have little children, and I will be grandpapa; and you will have the good fortune to be the wife of a noble fellow, who can work, who can be useful to his fellow-men; a surprising fellow, worth a hundred others; a man who can rescue other people's inventions, a providence! At all events, you will not have married, like so many other silly girls about here, a soldier or a priest, that is, a man who kills or a man who lies. But what are you doing there, Gilliatt? Nobody can see you. Douce, Grace, everybody there! Bring a light, I say. Light up my son-in-law for me. I betroth you to each other, my children: here stands your husband, here my son, Gilliatt of the Bû de la Rue, that noble fellow, that great seaman; I will have no other son-in-law, and you no other husband. I pledge my word to that once more in God's name. Ah! you are there, Monsieur the Curé. You will marry these young people for us."

Lethierry's eye had just fallen upon Caudray.

Douce and Grace had done as they were directed. Two candles placed upon the table cast a light upon Gilliatt from head to foot.

"There's a fine fellow," said Mess Lethierry.

Gilliatt's appearance was hideous.

He was in the condition in which he had that morning set sail from the rocks; in rags, his bare elbows showing through his sleeves; his beard long, his hair rough and wild; his eyes bloodshot, his skin peeling, his hands covered with wounds; his feet naked. Some of the blisters left by the devil-fish were still visible upon his arms.

Lethierry gazed at him.

"This is my son-in-law," he said. "How he has struggled with the sea. He is all in rags. What shoulders; what hands. There's a splendid fellow!"

Grace ran to Déruchette and supported her head. She had fainted.

II
THE LEATHERN TRUNK

AT BREAK OF DAY St. Sampson was on foot, and all the people of St. Peter's Port began to flock there. The resurrection of the Durande caused a commotion in the island not unlike what was caused by the *Salette* in the south of France. There was a crowd on the quay staring at the funnel standing erect in the sloop. They were anxious to see and handle the machinery; but Lethierry, after making a new and triumphant survey of the whole by daylight, had placed two sailors aboard with instructions to prevent any one approaching it. The funnel, however, furnished food enough for contemplation. The crowd gaped with astonishment. They talked of nothing but Gilliatt. They remarked on his surname of "malicious Gilliatt;" and their admiration wound up with the remark, "It is not pleasant to have people in the island who can do things like that."

Mess Lethierry was seen from outside the house, seated at a table before the window, writing, with one eye on the paper and another on the sloop. He was so completely absorbed that he had only once stopped to call Douce and ask after Déruchette. Douce replied, "Mademoiselle has risen and is gone out." Mess Lethierry replied, "She is right to take the air. She was a little unwell last night, owing to the heat. There was a crowd in the room. This and her surprise and joy, and the windows being all closed, overcame her. She will have a husband to be proud of." And he had gone on with his writing. He had already finished and sealed two letters, addressed to the most important shipbuilders at Brême. He now finished the sealing of a third.

The noise of a wheel upon the quay induced him to look up. He leaned out of the window, and observed coming from the path which led to the Bû de la Rue a boy pushing a wheelbarrow. The boy was going towards St. Peter's Port. In the barrow was a portmanteau of brown leather, studded with nails of brass and white metal.

Mess Lethierry called to the boy:

"Where are you going, my lad?"

The boy stopped, and replied:

"To the *Cashmere*."

"What for?"

"To take this trunk aboard."

"Very good; you shall take these three letters too."

Mess Lethierry opened the drawer of his table, took a piece of string, tied the three letters which he had just written across and across, and threw the packet to the boy, who caught it between his hands.

"Tell the captain of the *Cashmere* they are my letters, and to take care of them. They are for Germany—Brême *viâ* London."

"I can't speak to the captain, Mess Lethierry."

"Why not?"

"The *Cashmere* is not at the quay."

"Ah!"

"She is in the roads."

"Ay, true; on account of the sea."

"I can only speak to the man who takes the things aboard."

"You will tell him, then, to look to the letters."

"Very well, Mess Lethierry."

"At what time does the *Cashmere* sail?"

"At twelve."

"The tide will flow at noon; she will have it against her."

"But she will have the wind," answered the lad.

"Boy," said Mess Lethierry, pointing with his forefinger at the engine in the sloop, "do you see that? There is something which laughs at winds and tides."

The boy put the letters in his pocket, took up the handles of the barrow again, and went on his way towards the town. Mess Lethierry called "Douce! Grace!"

Grace opened the door a little way.

"What is it, Mess?"

"Come in and wait a moment."

Mess Lethierry took a sheet of paper, and began to write. If Grace, standing behind him, had been curious, and had leaned forward while he was writing, she might have read as follows:—

"I have written to Brême for the timber. I have appointments all the morning with carpenters for the estimate. The rebuilding will go on fast. You must go yourself to the Deanery for a licence. It is my wish that the marriage should take place as soon as possible; immediately would be better. I am busy about the Durande. Do you be busy about Déruchette."

He dated it and signed "Lethierry." He did not take the trouble to seal it, but merely folded it in four, and handed it to Grace, saying:

"Take that to Gilliatt."

"To the Bû de la Rue?"

"To the Bû de la Rue."

Book III
The Departure of the Cashmere

✳

I
THE HAVELET NEAR THE CHURCH

WHEN THERE IS a crowd at St. Sampson, St. Peter's Port is soon deserted. A point of curiosity at a given place is like an air-pump. News travel fast in small places. Going to see the funnel of the Durande under Mess Lethierry's window had been, since sunrise, the business of the Guernsey folks. Every other event was eclipsed by this. The death of the Dean of St. Asaph was forgotten, together with the question of the Rev. Mr. Caudray, his sudden riches, and the departure of the *Cashmere*. The machinery of the Durande brought back from the Douvres rocks was the order of the day. People were incredulous. The shipwreck had appeared extraordinary, the salvage seemed impossible. Everybody hastened to assure himself of the truth by the help of his own eyes. Business of every kind was suspended. Long strings of towns-folk with their families, from the "Vesin" up to the "Mess," men and women, gentlemen, mothers with children, infants with dolls, were coming by every road or pathway to see "the thing to be seen" at the Bravées, turning their backs upon St. Peter's Port. Many shops at St. Peter's Port were closed. In the Commercial Arcade there was an absolute stagnation in buying and selling. The Durande alone obtained attention. Not a single shopkeeper had had a "handsell" that morning, except a jeweller, who was surprised at having sold a wedding-ring to "a sort of man who appeared in a great hurry, and who asked for the house of the Dean." The shops which remained open were centres of gossip, where loiterers discussed the miraculous salvage. There was not a foot-passenger at the "Hyvreuse," which is known in these days, nobody knows why, as Cambridge Park; no one was in the High Street, then called the Grande Rue; nor in Smith Street, known then only as the Rue des Forges; nobody in Hauteville. The Esplanade itself was deserted. One might have guessed it to be Sunday. A visit from a Royal personage to review the militia at the Ancresse could not have emptied the town more completely. All this hubbub about "a nobody" like Gilliatt, caused a good deal of shrugging of the shoulders among persons of grave and correct habits.

The church of St. Peter's Port, with its three gable-ends placed side by side, its transept and its steeple, stands at the water's side at the end of the harbour, and nearly on the landing place itself, where it welcomes those who arrive, and gives the departing "God speed." It represents the capital letter at the beginning of that long line which forms the front of the town towards the sea.

It is both the parish church of St. Peter's Port and the chief place of the Deanery of the whole island. Its officiating minister is the surrogate of the bishop, a clergyman in full orders.

The harbour of St. Peter's Port, a very fine and large port at the present day, was at that epoch, and even up to ten years ago, less considerable than the harbour of St. Sampson. It was enclosed by two enormous thick walls, beginning at the water's edge on both sides, and curving till they almost joined again at the extremities, where there stood a little white lighthouse. Under this lighthouse, a narrow gullet, bearing still the two rings of the chain with which it was the custom to bar the passage in ancient times, formed the entrance for vessels. The harbour of St. Peter's Port might be well compared with the claws of a huge lobster opened a little way. This kind of pincers took from the ocean a portion of the sea, which it compelled to remain calm. But during the easterly winds the waves rolled heavily against the narrow entrance, the port was agitated, and it was better not to enter. This is what had happened with the *Cashmere* that day, which had accordingly anchored in the roads.

The vessels, during the easterly winds, preferred this course, which besides saved them the port dues. On these occasions the boatmen of the town, a hardy race of mariners whom the new port has thrown out of employment, came in their boats to fetch passengers at the landing-place or at stations on the shore, and carried them with their luggage, often in heavy seas, but always without accident, to the vessels about to sail. The east wind blows off the shore, and is very favourable for the passage to England; the vessel at such times rolls, but does not pitch.

When a vessel happened to be in the port, everybody embarked from the quay. When it was in the roads they took their choice, and embarked from any point of the coast near the moorings. The "Havelet" was one of these creeks. This little harbour (which is the signification of the word) was near the town, but was so solitary that it seemed far off. This solitude was owing to the shelter of the high cliffs of Fort St. George, which overlooked this retired inlet. The Havelet was accessible by several paths. The most direct was along the water's side. It had the advantage of leading to the town and to the church in five minutes' walk, and the disadvantage of being covered by the sea twice a day. The other paths were more or less abrupt, and led down to the creek through gaps in the steep rocks. Even in broad daylight, it was dusk in the Havelet. Huge blocks overhanging it on all sides, and thick bushes and brambles cast a sort of soft twilight upon the rocks and waves below. Nothing could be more peaceful than this spot in calm weather; nothing more tumultuous during heavy seas. There were ends of branches there which were always wet with the foam. In the spring time, the place was full of flowers, of nests, of perfumes, of birds, of butterflies, and bees. Thanks to recent improvements, this wild nook no longer exists. Fine, straight lines have taken the place of these wild features; masonry, quays, and little gardens, have made their appearance; earthwork has been the rage, and taste has finally subdued the eccentricities of the cliff, and the irregularities of the rocks below.

II
DESPAIR CONFRONTS DESPAIR

IT WAS A LITTLE before ten o'clock in the morning. The crowd at St. Sampson, according to all appearance, was increasing. The multitude, feverish with curiosity, was moving towards the north; and the Havelet, which is in the south, was more deserted than ever.

Notwithstanding this, there was a boat there and a boatman. In the boat was a travelling bag. The boatman seemed to be waiting for some one.

The *Cashmere* was visible at anchor in roads, as she did not start till midday; there was as yet no sign of moving aboard.

A passer-by, who had listened from one of the ladder-paths up the cliffs overhead, would have heard a murmur of words in the Havelet, and if he had leaned over the overhanging cliff might have seen, at some distance from the boat, in a corner among the rocks and branches, where the eye of the boatman could not reach them, a man and a woman. It was Caudray and Déruchette.

These obscure nooks on the seashore, the chosen places of lady bathers, are not always so solitary as is believed. Persons are sometimes observed and heard there. Those who seek shelter and solitude in them may easily be followed through the thick bushes, and, thanks to the multiplicity and entanglement of the paths, the granite and the shrubs which favour the stolen interview may also favour the witness.

Caudray and Déruchette stood face to face, looking into each other's eyes, and holding each other by the hand. Déruchette was speaking. Caudray was silent. A tear that had gathered upon his eyelash hung there and did not fall.

Grief and strong passion were imprinted in his calm, religious countenance. A painful resignation was there too—a resignation hostile to faith, though springing from it. Upon that face, simply devout until then, there was the commencement of a fatal expression. He who had hitherto meditated only on doctrine, had begun to meditate on Fate, an unhealthy meditation for a priest. Faith dissolves under its action. Nothing disturbs the religious mind more than that bending under the weight of the unknown. Life seems a perpetual succession of events, to which man submits. We never know from which direction the sudden blow will come. Misery and happiness enter or make their exit, like unexpected guests. Their laws, their orbit, their principle of gravitation, are beyond man's grasp. Virtue conducts not to happiness, nor crime to retribution: conscience has one logic, fate another; and neither coincide. Nothing is foreseen. We live confusedly, and from hand to mouth. Conscience is the straight line, life is the whirlwind, which creates above man's head either black chaos or the blue sky. Fate does not practise the art of gradations. Her wheel turns sometimes so fast that we can scarcely distinguish the interval between one revolution and another, or the link between yesterday and to-day. Caudray was a believer whose faith did not exclude reason, and whose priestly training did not shut him out from passion. Those religious systems which impose celibacy on the priesthood are not without reason for it. Nothing really destroys the individuality of the priest more than love. All sorts of clouds seemed to darken Caudray's soul. He looked too long into Déruchette's eyes. These two beings worshipped each other.

There was in Caudray's eye the mute adoration of despair.

Déruchette spoke.

"You must not leave me. I shall not have strength. I thought I could bid you farewell. I cannot. Why did you come yesterday? You should not have come if you were going so soon. I never spoke to you. I loved you; but knew it not. Only that day, when M. Hérode read to us the story of Rebecca, and when your eyes met mine, my cheeks were like fire, and I thought only of how Rebecca's face must have burnt like mine; and yet, if any one had told me yesterday that I loved you, I might have laughed at it. This is what is so terrible. It has been like a treason. I did not take heed. I went to the church, I saw you, I thought everybody there was like myself. I do not reproach you; you did nothing to make me love you; you did nothing but look at me; it is not your fault if you look at people; and yet that made me love you so much. I did not even suspect it. When you took up the book it was a flood of light; when others took it, it was but a book. You raised your eyes sometimes; you spoke of archangels; oh! you were my archangel. What you said penetrated my thoughts at once. Before then, I know not even whether I believed in God. Since I have known you, I have learnt to pray. I used to say to Douce, dress me quickly, lest I should be late at the service; and I hastened to the church. Such it was with me to love some one. I did not know the cause. I said to myself, how devout I am becoming. It is from you that I have learnt that I do not go to church for God's service. It is true; I went for your sake. You spoke so well, and when you raised your arms to heaven, you seemed to hold my heart within your two white hands. I was foolish; but I did not know it. Shall I tell you your fault? It was your coming to me in the garden; it was your speaking to me. If you had said nothing, I should have known nothing. If you had gone, I should, perhaps, have been sad, but now I should die. Since I know that I love you, you cannot leave me. Of what are you thinking? You do not seem to listen to me."

Caudray replied:

"You heard what was said last night?"

"Ah, me!"

"What can I do against that?"

They were silent for a moment. Caudray continued:

"There is but one duty left to me. It is to depart."

"And mine to die. Oh! how I wish there was no sea, but only sky. It seems to me as if that would settle all, and that our departure would be the same. It was wrong to speak to me; why did you speak to me? Do not go. What will become of me? I tell you I shall die. You will be far off when I shall be in my grave. Oh! my heart will break. I am very wretched; yet my uncle is not unkind."

It was the first time in her life that Déruchette had ever said "my uncle." Until then she had always said "my father."

Caudray stepped back, and made a sign to the boatman. Déruchette heard the sound of the boat-hook among the shingle, and the step of the man on the gunwale of the boat.

"No! no!" cried Déruchette.

"It must be, Déruchette," replied Caudray.

"No! never! For the sake of an engine—impossible. Did you see that horrible man last night? You cannot abandon me thus. You are wise; you can find a means. It is impossible that you bade me come here this morning with the idea of leaving me. I have never done anything to deserve this; you can have no reproach to make me. Is it by that vessel that you intended to sail? I will not let you go. You shall not leave me. Heaven does not open thus to close so soon. I know you will remain. Besides, it is not yet time. Oh! how I love you."

And pressing closely to him, she interlaced the fingers of each hand behind his neck, as if partly to make a bond of her two arms for detaining him, and partly with her joined hands to pray. He moved away this gentle restraint, while Déruchette resisted as long as she could.

Déruchette sank upon a projection of the rock covered with ivy, lifting by an unconscious movement the sleeve of her dress up to the elbow, and exhibiting her graceful arm. A pale suffused light was in her eyes. The boat was approaching.

Caudray held her head between his hands. He touched her hair with a sort of religious care, fixed his eyes upon her for some moments, then kissed her on the forehead fervently, and in an accent trembling with anguish, and in which might have been traced the uprooting of his soul, he uttered the word which has so often resounded in the depths of the human heart, "Farewell!"

Déruchette burst into loud sobs.

At this moment they heard a voice near them, which said solemnly and deliberately:

"Why should you not be man and wife?"

Caudray raised his head. Déruchette looked up.

Gilliatt stood before them.

He had approached by a bye-path.

He was no longer the same man that he had appeared on the previous night. He had arranged his hair, shaved his beard, put on shoes, and a white shirt, with a large collar turned over, sailor fashion. He wore a sailor's costume, but all was new. A gold ring was on his little finger. He seemed profoundly calm. His sunburnt skin had become pale: a hue of sickly bronze overspread it.

They looked at him astonished. Though so changed, Déruchette recognised him. But the words which he had spoken were so far from what was passing in their minds at that moment, that they had left no distinct impression.

Gilliatt spoke again:

"Why should you say farewell? Be man and wife, and go together."

Déruchette started. A trembling seized her from head to foot.

Gilliatt continued:

"Miss Lethierry is a woman. She is of age. It depends only on herself. Her uncle is but her uncle. You love each other——"

Déruchette interrupted in a gentle voice, and asked, "How came you here?"

"Make yourselves one," repeated Gilliatt.

Déruchette began to have a sense of the meaning of his words. She stammered out:

"My poor uncle!"

"If the marriage was yet to be," said Gilliatt, "he would refuse. When it is over he will consent. Besides, you are going to leave here. When you return he will forgive."

Gilliatt added, with a slight touch of bitterness, "And then he is think-ing of nothing just now but the rebuilding of his boat. This will occupy his mind during your absence. The Durande will console him."

"I cannot," said Déruchette, in a state of stupor which was not without its gleam of joy. "I must not leave him unhappy."

"It will be but for a short time," answered Gilliatt.

Caudray and Déruchette had been, as it were, bewildered. They recovered themselves now. The meaning of Gilliatt's words became plainer as their surprise diminished. There was a slight cloud still before them; but their part was not to resist. We yield easily to those who come to save. Objections to a return into Paradise are weak. There was something in the attitude of Déruchette, as she leaned imperceptibly upon her lover, which seemed to make common cause with Gilliatt's words. The enigma of the presence of this man, and of his utterances, which, in the mind of Déruchette in partic-ular, produced various kinds of astonishment, was a thing apart. He said to them, "Be man and wife!" This was clear; if there was responsibility, it was his. Déruchette had a confused feeling that, for many reasons, he had the right to decide upon her fate. Caudray murmured, as if plunged in thought, "An uncle is not a father."

His resolution was corrupted by the sudden and happy turn in his ideas. The probable scruples of the clergyman melted, and dissolved in his heart's love for Déruchette.

Gilliatt's tone became abrupt and harsh, and like the pulsations of fever.

"There must be no delay," he said. "You have time, but that is all. Come."

Caudray observed him attentively; and suddenly exclaimed:

"I recognise you. It was you who saved my life."

Gilliatt replied:

"I think not."

"Yonder," said Caudray, "at the extremity of the Banques."

"I do not know the place," said Gilliatt.

"It was on the very day that I arrived here."

"Let us lose no time," interrupted Gilliatt.

"And if I am not deceived, you are the man whom we met last night."

"Perhaps."

"What is your name?"

Gilliatt raised his voice:

"Boatman! wait there for us. We shall return soon. You asked me, Miss Lethierry, how I came to be here. The answer is very simple. I walked behind you. You are twenty-one. In this country, when persons are of age, and depend only on themselves, they may be married immediately. Let us take the path along the water-side. It is passable; the tide will not rise here till noon. But lose no time. Come with me."

Déruchette and Caudray seemed to consult each other by a glance. They were standing close together motionless. They were intoxicated with joy. There are strange hesitations sometimes on the edge of the abyss of happiness. They understood, as it were, without understanding.

"His name is Gilliatt," whispered Déruchette.

Gilliatt interrupted them with a sort of tone of authority.

"What do you linger for?" he asked. "I tell you to follow me."

"Whither?" asked Caudray.

"There!"

And Gilliatt pointed with his finger towards the spire of the church.

Gilliatt walked on before, and they followed him. His step was firm; but they walked unsteadily.

As they approached the church, an expression dawned upon those two pure and beautiful countenances, which was soon to become a smile. The approach to the church lighted them up. In the hollow eyes of Gilliatt there was the darkness of night. The beholder might have imagined that he saw a spectre leading two souls to Paradise.

Caudray and Déruchette scarcely took count of what had happened. The interposition of this man was like the branch clutched at by the drowning. They followed their guide with the docility of despair, leaning on the first comer. Those who feel themselves near death easily accept the accident which seems to save. Déruchette, more ignorant of life, was more confident. Caudray was thoughtful. Déruchette was of age, it was true. The English formalities of marriage are simple, especially in primitive parts, where the clergyman has almost a discretionary power; but would the Dean consent to celebrate the marriage without even inquiring whether the uncle consented? This was the question. Nevertheless, they could learn. In any case there would be but a delay.

But what was this man? and if it was really he whom Lethierry the night before had declared should be his son-in-law, what could be the meaning of his actions? The very obstacle itself had become a providence. Caudray yielded; but his yielding was only the rapid and tacit assent of a man who feels himself saved from despair.

The pathway was uneven, and sometimes wet and difficult to pass. Caudray, absorbed in thought, did not observe the occasional pools of water or the heaps of shingle. But from time to time Gilliatt turned and said to him, "Take heed of those stones. Give her your hand."

III
THE FORETHOUGHT OF SELF-SACRIFICE

IT STRUCK TEN as they entered the church.

By reason of the early hour, and also on account of the desertion of the town that day, the church was empty.

At the farther end, however, near the table which in the reformed church fulfils the place of the altar, there were three persons. They were the Dean, his evangelist, and the registrar. The Dean, who was the Reverend Jaquemin Hérode, was seated; the evangelist and the registrar stood beside him.

A book was open upon the table.

Beside him, upon a credence-table, was another book. It was the parish register, and also open; and an attentive eye might have remarked a page on which was some writing, of which the ink was not yet dry. By the side of the register were a pen and a writing-desk.

The Reverend Jaquemin Hérode rose on perceiving Caudray.

"I have been expecting you," he said. "All is ready."

The Dean, in fact, wore his officiating robes.

Caudray looked towards Gilliatt.

The Reverend Doctor added, "I am at your service, brother;" and he bowed.

It was a bow which neither turned to right or left. It was evident from the direction of the Dean's gaze that he did not recognise the existence of any one but Caudray, for Caudray was a clergyman and a gentleman. Neither Déruchette, who stood aside, nor Gilliatt, who was in the rear, were included in the salutation. His look was a sort of parenthesis in which none but Caudray were admitted. The observance of these little niceties constitutes an important feature in the maintenance of order and the preservation of society.

The Dean continued, with a graceful and dignified urbanity:

"I congratulate you, my colleague, from a double point of view. You have lost your uncle, and are about to take a wife; you are blessed with riches on the one hand, and happiness on the other. Moreover, thanks to the boat which they are about to rebuild, Mess Lethierry will also be rich; which is as it should be. Miss Lethierry was born in this parish; I have verified the date of her birth in the register. She is of age, and at her own disposal. Her uncle, too, who is her only relative, consents. You are anxious to be united immediately on account of your approaching departure. This I can understand; but this being the marriage of the rector of the parish, I should have been gratified to have seen it associated with a little more solemnity. I will consult your wishes by not detaining you longer than necessary. The essentials will be soon complied with. The form is already drawn up in the register, and it requires only the names to be filled in. By the terms of the law and custom, the marriage may be celebrated immediately after the inscription. The declaration necessary for the licence has been duly made. I take upon myself a slight irregularity; for the application for the licence ought to have been registered seven days in advance; but I yield to necessity and the urgency of your departure. Be it so, then. I will proceed with the ceremony. My evangelist will be the witness for the bridegroom; as regards the witness for the bride——"

The Dean turned towards Gilliatt. Gilliatt made a movement of his head.

"That is sufficient," said the Dean.

Caudray remained motionless; Déruchette was happy, but no less powerless to move.

"Nevertheless," continued the Dean, "there is still an obstacle."

Déruchette started.

The Dean continued:

"The representative here present of Mess Lethierry applied for the licence for you, and has signed the declaration on the register." And with the thumb of his left hand the Dean pointed to Gilliatt, which prevented the necessity of his remembering his name. "The messenger from Mess Lethierry," he added, "has informed me this morning that being too much occupied to come in person, Mess Lethierry desired that the marriage should take place immediately. This desire, expressed verbally, is not sufficient. In consequence of having to grant the licence, and of the irregularity which I take upon myself, I cannot proceed so rapidly without informing myself from Mess Lethierry personally, unless some one can produce his signature. Whatever might be my desire to serve you, I cannot be satisfied with a mere message. I must have some written document."

"That need not delay us," said Gilliatt. And he presented a paper to the Dean. The Dean took it, perused it by a glance, seemed to pass over some lines as unimportant, and read aloud: "Go to the Dean for the licence. I wish the marriage to take place as soon as possible. Immediately would be better."

He placed the paper on the table, and proceeded:

"It is signed, Lethierry. It would have been more respectful to have addressed himself to me. But since I am called on to serve a colleague, I ask no more."

Caudray glanced again at Gilliatt. There are moments when mind and mind comprehend each other. Caudray felt that there was some deception; he had not the strength of purpose, perhaps he had not the idea of revealing it. Whether in obedience to a latent heroism, of which he had begun to obtain a glimpse; or whether from a deadening of the conscience, arising from the suddenness of the happiness placed within his reach, he uttered no word.

The Dean took the pen, and aided by the clerk, filled up the spaces in the page of the register; then he rose, and by a gesture invited Caudray and Déruchette to approach the table.

The ceremony commenced. It was a strange moment. Caudray and Déruchette stood beside each other before the minister. He who has ever dreamed of a marriage in which he himself was chief actor, may conceive something of the feeling which they experienced.

Gilliatt stood at a little distance in the shadow of the pillars.

Déruchette, on rising in the morning, desperate, thinking only of death and its associations, had dressed herself in white. Her attire, which had been associated in her mind with mourning, was suited to her nuptials. A white dress is all that is necessary for the bride.

A ray of happiness was visible upon her face. Never had she appeared more beautiful. Her features were remarkable for prettiness rather than what is called beauty. Their fault, if fault it be, lay in a certain excess of grace. Déruchette in repose, that is, neither disturbed by passion or grief, was graceful above all. The ideal virgin is the transfiguration of a face like this. Déruchette, touched by her sorrow and her love, seemed to have caught that higher and more holy expression. It was the difference between the field daisy and the lily.

The tears had scarcely dried upon her cheeks; one perhaps still lingered in the midst of her smiles. Traces of tears indistinctly visible form a pleasing but sombre accompaniment of joy.

The Dean, standing near the table, placed his finger upon the open book, and asked in a distinct voice whether they knew of any impediment to their union.

There was no reply.

"Amen!" said the Dean.

Caudray and Déruchette advanced a step or two towards the table.

"Joseph Ebenezer Caudray, wilt thou have this woman to be thy wedded wife?"

Caudray replied "I will."

The Dean continued:

"Durande Déruchette Lethierry, wilt thou have this man to be thy wedded husband?"

Déruchette, in an agony of soul, springing from her excess of happiness, murmured rather than uttered—

"I will."

Then followed the beautiful form of the Anglican marriage service. The Dean looked around, and in the twilight of the church uttered the solemn words:

"Who giveth this woman to be married to this man?"

Gilliatt answered, "I do!"

There was an interval of silence. Caudray and Déruchette felt a vague sense of oppression in spite of their joy.

The Dean placed Déruchette's right hand in Caudray's; and Caudray repeated after him:

"I take thee, Durande Déruchette to be my wedded wife, for better for worse, for richer for poorer, in sickness and in health, to love and to cherish till death do us part; and thereto I plight thee my troth."

The Dean then placed Caudray's right hand in that of Déruchette, and Déruchette said after him:

"I take thee to be my wedded husband for better for worse, for richer for poorer, in sickness or in health, to love and to cherish till death do us part; and thereto I plight thee my troth."

The Dean asked, "Where is the ring?" The question took them by surprise. Caudray had no ring; but Gilliatt took off the gold ring which he wore upon his little finger. It was probably the wedding-ring which had been sold that morning by the jeweller in the Commercial Arcade.

The Dean placed the ring upon the book; then handed it to Caudray, who took Déruchette's little trembling left hand, passed the ring over her fourth finger, and said:

"With this ring I thee wed!"

"In the name of the Father, and of the Son, and of the Holy Ghost," continued the Dean.

"Amen," said his evangelist.

Then the Dean said, "Let us pray."

Caudray and Déruchette turned towards the table, and knelt down.

Gilliatt, standing by, inclined his head.

So they knelt before God; while he seemed to bend under the burden of his fate.

IV
FOR YOUR WIFE: WHEN YOU MARRY

AS THEY LEFT THE CHURCH they could see the *Cashmere* making preparations for her departure.

"You are in time," said Gilliatt.

They chose again the path leading to the Havelet.

Caudray and Déruchette went before, Gilliatt this time walking behind them. They were two somnambulists. Their bewilderment had not passed away, but only changed in form. They took no heed of whither they were going, or of what they did. They hurried on mechanically, scarcely remembering the existence of anything, feeling that they were united for ever, but scarcely able to connect two ideas in their minds. In ecstasy like theirs it is as impossible to think as it is to swim in a torrent. In the midst of their trouble and darkness they had been plunged in a whirlpool of delight; they bore a paradise within themselves. They did not speak, but conversed with each other by the mysterious sympathy of their souls. Déruchette pressed Caudray's arm to her side.

The footsteps of Gilliatt behind them reminded them now and then that he was there. They were deeply moved, but could find no words. The excess of emotion results in stupor. Theirs was delightful, but overwhelming. They were man and wife: every other idea was postponed to that. What Gilliatt had done was well; that was all that they could grasp. They experienced towards their guide a deep but vague gratitude in their hearts. Déruchette felt that there was some mystery to be explained, but not now. Meanwhile they accepted their unexpected happiness. They felt themselves controlled by the abruptness and decision of this man who conferred on them so much happiness with a kind of authority. To question him, to talk with him seemed impossible. Too many impressions rushed into their minds at once for that. Their absorption was pardonable.

Events succeed each other sometimes with the rapidity of hailstones. Their effect is overpowering; they deaden the senses. Falling upon existences habitually calm, they render incidents rapidly unintelligible even to those whom they chiefly concern; we become scarcely conscious of our own adventures; we are overwhelmed without guessing the cause, or crowned with happiness without comprehending it. For some hours Déruchette had been subjected to every kind of emotion: at first, surprise and delight at meeting Caudray in the garden; then horror at the monster whom her uncle had presented as her husband; then her anguish when the angel of her dreams spread his wings and seemed about to depart; and now her joy, a joy such as she had never known before, founded on an inexplicable enigma; the monster of last night himself restoring her lover; marriage arising out of her torture; this Gilliatt, the evil destiny of last night, become to-day her saviour! She could explain nothing to her own mind. It was evident that all the morning Gilliatt had had no other occupation than that of preparing the way for their marriage: he had done all: he had answered for Mess Lethierry, seen the Dean, obtained the licence, signed the necessary declaration; and thus the marriage had been rendered possible. But Déruchette understood it not. If she had, she could not have comprehended the reasons. They did nothing but close their eyes to the world, and—grateful in their hearts— yield themselves up to the guidance of this good demon. There was no time for explanations, and expressions of gratitude seemed too insignificant. They were silent in their trance of love.

The little power of thought which they retained was scarcely more than sufficient to guide them on their way—to enable them to distinguish the sea from the land, and the *Cashmere* from every other vessel.

In a few minutes they were at the little creek.

Caudray entered the boat first. At the moment when Déruchette was about to follow, she felt her sleeve held gently. It was Gilliatt, who had placed his finger upon a fold of her dress.

"Madam," he said, "you are going on a journey unexpectedly. It has struck me that you would have need of dresses and clothes. You will find a trunk aboard the *Cashmere*, containing a lady's clothing. It came to me from my mother. It was intended for my wife if I should marry. Permit me to ask your acceptance of it."

Déruchette, partially aroused from her dream, turned towards him. Gilliatt continued, in a voice which was scarcely audible:

"I do not wish to detain you, madam, but I feel that I ought to give you some explanation. On the day of your misfortune, you were sitting in the lower room; you uttered certain words; it is easy to understand that you have forgotten them. We are not compelled to remember every word we speak. Mess Lethierry was in great sorrow. It was certainly a noble vessel, and one that did good service. The misfortune was recent; there was a great commotion. Those are things which one naturally forgets. It was only a vessel wrecked among the rocks; one cannot be always thinking of an accident. But what I wished to tell you was, that as it was said that no one would go,

I went. They said it was impossible; but it was not. I thank you for listening to me a moment. You can understand, madam, that if I went there, it was not with the thought of displeasing you. This is a thing, besides, of old date. I know that you are in haste. If there was time, if we could talk about this, you might perhaps remember. But this is all useless now. The history of it goes back to a day when there was snow upon the ground. And then on one occasion that I passed you, I thought that you looked kindly on me. This is how it was. With regard to last night, I had not had time to go to my home. I came from my labour; I was all torn and ragged; I startled you, and you fainted. I was to blame; people do not come like that to strangers' houses; I ask your forgiveness. This is nearly all I had to say. You are about to sail. You will have fine weather; the wind is in the east. Farewell. You will not blame me for troubling you with these things. This is the last minute."

"I am thinking of the trunk you spoke of," replied Déruchette. "Why do you not keep it for your wife, when you marry?"

"It is most likely, madam," replied Gilliatt, "that I shall never marry."

"That would be a pity," said Déruchette; "you are so good."

And Déruchette smiled. Gilliatt returned her smile.

Then he assisted her to step into the boat.

In less than a quarter of an hour afterwards Caudray and Déruchette were aboard the *Cashmere* in the roads.

V
THE GREAT TOMB

GILLIATT WALKED along the water-side, passed rapidly through St. Peter's Port, and then turned towards St. Sampson by the seashore. In his anxiety to meet no one whom he knew, he avoided the highways now filled with foot-passengers by his great achievement.

For a long time, as the reader knows, he had had a peculiar manner of traversing the country in all parts without being observed. He knew the bye-paths, and favoured solitary and winding routes; he had the shy habits of a wild beast who knows that he is disliked, and keeps at a distance. When quite a child, he had been quick to feel how little welcome men showed in their faces at his approach, and he had gradually contracted that habit of being alone which had since become an instinct.

He passed through the Esplanade, then by the Salerie. Now and then he turned and looked behind him at the *Cashmere* in the roads, which was beginning to set her sails. There was little wind; Gilliatt went faster than the *Cashmere*. He walked with downcast eyes among the lower rocks at the water's edge. The tide was beginning to rise.

Suddenly he stopped, and, turning his back, contemplated for some minutes a group of oaks beyond the rocks which concealed the road to Vale. They were the oaks at the spot called the Basses Maisons. It was there that Déruchette once wrote with her finger the name of Gilliatt in the snow. Many a day had passed since that snow had melted away.

Then he pursued his way.

The day was beautiful; more beautiful than any that had yet been seen that year. It was one of those spring days when May suddenly pours forth all its beauty, and when nature seems to have no thought but to rejoice and be happy. Amidst the many murmurs from forest and village, from the sea and the air, a sound of cooing could be distinguished. The first butterflies of the year were resting on the early roses. Everything in nature seemed new—the grass, the mosses, the leaves, the perfumes, the rays of light. The sun shone as if it had never shone before. The pebbles seemed bathed in coolness. Birds but lately fledged sang out their deep notes from the trees, or fluttered among the boughs in their attempts to use their new-found wings. There was a chattering all together of goldfinches, pewits, tomtits, woodpeckers, bullfinches, and thrushes. The blossoms of lilacs, May lilies, daphnes, and melilots mingled their various hues in the thickets. A beautiful kind of water-weed peculiar to Guernsey covered the pools with an emerald green; where the kingfishers and the water-wagtails, which make such graceful little nests, came down to bathe their wings. Through every opening in the branches appeared the deep blue sky. A few lazy clouds followed each other in the azure depths. The ear seemed to catch the sound of kisses sent from invisible lips. Every old wall had its tufts of wallflowers. The plum-trees and laburnums were in blossom; their white and yellow masses gleamed through the interlacing boughs. The spring showered all her gold and silver on the woods. The new shoots and leaves were green and fresh. Calls of welcome were in the air; the approaching summer opened her hospitable doors for birds coming from afar. It was the time of the arrival of the swallows. The clusters of furze-bushes bordered the steep sides of hollow roads in anticipation of the clusters of the hawthorn. The pretty and the beautiful reigned side by side; the magnificent and the graceful, the great and the little, had each their place. No note in the great concert of nature was lost. Green microscopic beauties took their place in the vast universal plan in which all seemed distinguishable as in limpid water. Everywhere a divine fulness, a mysterious sense of expansion, suggested the unseen effort of the sap in movement. Guttering things glittered more than ever; loving natures became more tender. There was a hymn in the flowers, and a radiance in the sounds of the air. The wide-diffused harmony of nature burst forth on every side. All things which felt the dawn of life invited others to put forth shoots. A movement coming from below, and also from above, stirred vaguely all hearts susceptible to the scattered and subterranean influence of germination. The flower shadowed forth the fruit; young maidens dreamed of love. It was nature's universal bridal. It was fine, bright, and warm; through the hedges in the meadows children were seen laughing and playing at their games. The fruit-trees filled the orchards with their heaps of white and pink blossom. In the fields were primroses, cowslips, milfoil, daffodils, daisies, speedwell, jacinths, and violets. Blue borage and yellow irises swarmed with those beautiful little pink stars which flower always in groups, and are hence called "companions." Creatures with golden scales glided between the stones. The flowering houseleek covered the thatched roofs with purple patches. Women were plaiting hives in the open air; and the bees were abroad, mingling their humming with the murmurs from the sea. Nature, sensitive to the touch of spring, exhaled delight.

When Gilliatt arrived at St. Sampson, the water had not yet risen at the further end of the harbour, and he was able to cross it dry-footed unperceived behind the hulls of vessels fixed for repair. A number of flat stones were placed there at regular distances to make a causeway.

He was not observed. The crowd was at the other end of the port, near the narrow entrance, by the Bravées. There his name was in every mouth. They were, in fact, speaking about him so much that none paid attention to him. He passed, sheltered in some degree by the very commotion that he had caused.

He saw from afar the sloop in the place where he had moored it, with the funnel standing between its four chains; observed a movement of carpenters at their work, and confused outlines of figures passing to and fro; and he could distinguish the loud and cheery voice of Mess Lethierry giving orders.

He threaded the narrow alleys behind the Bravées. There was no one there beside him. All curiosity was concentrated on the front of the house. He chose the footpath alongside the low wall of the garden, but stopped at the angle where the wild mallow grew. He saw once more the stone where he used to pass his time; saw once more the wooden garden seat where Déruchette was accustomed to sit, and glanced again at the pathway of the alley where he had seen the embrace of two shadows which had vanished.

He soon went on his way, climbed the hill of Vale Castle, descended again, and directed his steps towards the Bû de la Rue.

The Houmet-Paradis was a solitude.

His house was in the same state in which he had left it in the morning, after dressing himself to go to St. Peter's Port.

A window was open, through which his bagpipe might have been seen hanging to a nail upon the wall.

Upon the table was the little Bible given to him in token of gratitude by the stranger whom he now knew as Caudray.

The key was in the door. He approached; placed his hand upon it; turned it twice in the lock, put the key in his pocket, and departed.

He walked not in the direction of the town, but towards the sea.

He traversed his garden diagonally, taking the shortest way without regard to the beds, but taking care not to tread upon the plants which he placed there, because he had heard that they were favourites with Déruchette.

He crossed the parapet wall, and let himself down upon the rocks.

Going straight on, he began to follow the long ridge of rocks which connected the Bû de la Rue with the great natural obelisk of granite rising erect from the sea, which was known as the Beast's Horn. This was the place of the Gild-Holm-'Ur seat.

He strode on from block to block like a giant among mountains. To make long strides upon a row of breakers is like walking upon the ridge of a roof.

A fisherwoman with dredge-nets, who had been walking naked-footed among the pools of sea-water at some distance, and had just regained the shore, called to him, "Take care; the tide is coming." But he held on his way.

Having arrived at the great rock of the point, the Horn, which rises like a pinnacle from the sea, he stopped. It was the extremity of the promontory.

He looked around.

Out at sea a few sailing boats at anchor were fishing. Now and then rivulets of silver glittered among them in the sun: it was the water running from the nets. The *Cashmere* was not yet off St. Sampson. She had set her main-topsail, and was between Herm and Jethou.

Gilliatt rounded the rock, and came under the Gild-Holm-'Ur seat, at the foot of that kind of abrupt stairs where, less than three months before, he had assisted Caudray to come down. He ascended.

The greater number of the steps were already under water. Two or three only were still dry, by which he climbed.

The steps led up to the Gild-Holm-'Ur seat. He reached the niche, contemplated it for a moment, pressed his hand upon his eyes, and let it glide gently from one eyelid to the other—a gesture by which he seemed to obliterate the memory of the past—then sat down in the hollow, with the perpendicular wall behind him, and the ocean at his feet.

The *Cashmere* at that moment was passing the great round half-submerged tower, defended by one sergeant and a cannon, which marks the half way in the roads between Herm and St. Peter's Port.

A few flowers stirred among the crevices in the rock about Gilliatt's head. The sea was blue as far as eye could reach. The wind came from the east; there was a little surf in the direction of the island of Sark, of which only the western side is visible from Guernsey. In the distance appeared the coast of France like a mist, with the long yellow strips of sand about Carteret. Now and then a white butterfly fluttered by. The butterflies frequently fly out to sea.

The breeze was very slight. The blue expanse, both above and below, was tranquil. Not a ripple agitated those species of serpents, of an azure more or less dark, which indicate on the surface of the sea the lines of sunken rocks.

The *Cashmere*, little moved by the wind, had set her topsail and studding- sails to catch the breeze. All her canvas was spread, but the wind being a side one, her studding-sails only compelled her to hug the Guernsey coast more closely. She had passed the beacon of St. Sampson, and was off the hill of Vale Castle. The moment was approaching when she would double the point of the Bû de la Rue.

Gilliatt watched her approach.

The air and sea were still. The tide rose not by waves, but by an imperceptible swell. The level of the water crept upward without a palpitation. The subdued murmur from the open sea was soft as the breathing of a child.

In the direction of the harbour of St. Sampson, faint echoes could be heard of carpenters' hammers. The carpenters were probably the workmen constructing the tackle, gear, and apparatus for removing the engine from the sloop. The sounds, however, scarcely reached Gilliatt by reason of the mass of granite at his back.

The *Cashmere* approached with the slowness of a phantom.

Gilliatt watched it still.

Suddenly a touch and a sensation of cold caused him to look down. The sea had reached his feet.

He lowered his eyes, then raised them again.

The *Cashmere* was quite near.

The rock in which the rains had hollowed out the Gild-Holm-'Ur seat was so completely vertical, and there was so much water at its base, that in calm weather vessels were able to pass without danger within a few cables' lengths.

The *Cashmere* was abreast of the rock. It rose straight upwards as if it had grown out of the water; or like the lengthening out of a shadow. The rigging showed black against the heavens and in the magnificent expanse of the sea. The long sails, passing for a moment over the sun, became lighted up with a singular glory and transparence. The water murmured indistinctly; but no other noise marked the majestic gliding of that outline. The deck was as visible as if he had stood upon it.

The steersman was at the helm; a cabin-boy was climbing the shrouds; a few passengers leaning on the bulwarks were contemplating the beauty of the scene. The captain was smoking; but nothing of all this was seen by Gilliatt.

There was a spot on the deck on which the broad sunlight fell. It was on this corner that his eyes were fixed. In this sunlight were Déruchette and Caudray. They were sitting together side by side, like two birds, warming themselves in the noonday sun, upon one of those covered seats with a little awning which well-ordered packet-boats provided for passengers, and upon which was the inscription, when it happened to be an English vessel, "For ladies only." Déruchette's head was leaning upon Caudray's shoulder; his arm was around her waist; they held each other's hands with their fingers interwoven. A celestial light was discernible in those two faces formed by innocence. Their chaste embrace was expressive of their earthly union and their purity of soul. The seat was a sort of alcove, almost a nest; it was at the same time a glory round them; the tender aureola of love passing into a cloud.

The silence was like the calm of heaven.

Caudray's gaze was fixed in contemplation. Déruchette's lips moved; and, amidst that perfect silence, as the wind carried the vessel near shore, and it glided within a few fathoms of the Gild-Holm-'Ur seat, Gilliatt heard the tender and musical voice of Déruchette exclaiming:

"Look yonder. It seems as if there were a man upon the rock."

The vessel passed.

Leaving the promontory of the Bû de la Rue behind, the *Cashmere* glided on upon the waters. In less than a quarter of an hour, her masts and sails formed only a white obelisk, gradually decreasing against the horizon. Gilliatt felt that the water had reached his knees.

He contemplated the vessel speeding on her way.

The breeze freshened out at sea. He could see the *Cashmere* run out her lower studding-sails and her staysails, to take advantage of the rising wind. She was already clear of the waters of Guernsey. Gilliatt followed the vessel with his eyes.

The waves had reached his waist.

The tide was rising: time was passing away.

The seamews and cormorants flew about him restlessly, as if anxious to warn him of his danger. It seemed as if some of his old companions of the Douvres rocks flying there had recognised him.

An hour had passed.

The wind from the sea was scarcely felt in the roads; but the form of the *Cashmere* was rapidly growing less. The sloop, according to all appearance, was sailing fast. It was already nearly off the Casquets.

There was no foam around the Gild-Holm-'Ur; no wave beat against its granite sides. The water rose peacefully. It was nearly level with Gilliatt's shoulders.

Another hour had passed.

The *Cashmere* was beyond the waters of Aurigny. The Ortach rock concealed it for a moment; it passed behind it, and came forth again as from an eclipse. The sloop was veering to the north upon the open sea. It was now only a point glittering in the sun.

The birds were hovering about Gilliatt, uttering short cries. Only his head was now visible. The tide was nearly at the full. Evening was approaching. Behind him, in the roads, a few fishing-boats were making for the harbour.

Gilliatt's eyes continued fixed upon the vessel in the horizon. Their expression resembled nothing earthly. A strange lustre shone in their calm and tragic depths. There was in them the peace of vanished hopes, the calm but sorrowful acceptance of an end far different from his dreams. By degrees the dusk of heaven began to darken in them, though gazing still upon the point in space. At the same moment the wide waters round the Gild-Holm-'Ur and the vast gathering twilight closed upon them.

The *Cashmere*, now scarcely perceptible, had become a mere spot in the thin haze.

Gradually, the spot, which was but a shape, grew paler.

Then it dwindled, and finally disappeared.

At the moment when the vessel vanished on the line of the horizon, the head of Gilliatt disappeared. Nothing was visible now but the sea.

Ink, Steam, and Infinite Wind

A Conversation with Andrew Chater *and* Maya Weeks

Andrew Chater: This is Hugo's great novel of the sea, and, Maya, you are a geographer and spend a lot of time in the ocean. I'm excited to hear your take on that particular aspect of the book, because this is unlike any other Hugo I've ever read.

Maya Weeks: Really? Is his other work much more terrestrial?

AC: It is. The other Victor Hugo novels that I've read are predominantly and historically much more concerned with the human experience within cities—think of *Les Misérables* and *Notre-Dame de Paris*—but now we have Hugo encountering the natural world. It's very indicative of where Hugo is at this particular moment in his life. He is exiled on the isle of Guernsey, and so he becomes fascinated by the ocean. He writes this novel set almost exclusively on the seashore, about a man who has to rescue a wrecked steam ferry on a remote rock in the wild and elemental seas. Instead of human and societal antagonists, we have wind and tide and storm and the creatures of the deep. It's a different kind of book entirely.

MW: I grew up on the coast in a small beach town. My family really had no money, but being at the beach was free. It was easy to get a secondhand wetsuit and a secondhand surfboard and go play in the ocean, but also because of the culture of my town, a lot of the socializing just *happened* at the beach. If it was somebody's birthday, you'd always have a bonfire. It feels like home to me, and it feels like comfort. If I'm walking on the beach and

I'm picking up shells and rocks and seaweed and taking photos of seaweed, that feels like home to me. I enter a state where I don't have to think about being, and I just let go and sink into myself.

For my current job, I've turned inland, so I'm learning a lot about the foothills of the Sierra Nevada in California and thinking a lot about the watershed, the water flows, and the rivers. It's amazing to feel how deeply all of those ecosystems are connected. That is something that I really felt throughout this novel. The limpets in *Toilers* are my favorite example, because they're so particular and mundane at the same time. They're kind of boring, not ostentatiously beautiful, but Hugo fixates on them nonetheless.

AC: I find it fascinating that for you, the seashore feels like home, because for me, it has always felt like the "other." It's always been a sort of introduction to a world of drama and mystery. Especially the subaquatic world. Even just looking into a rock pool is this world of absolute mystery and wonder: limpets, urchins, anemones, starfish . . . I can spend hours staring into those rock pools, and I absolutely have a sense that Victor Hugo spent a lot of time wandering around the seashore, being entranced by this world that at that point we barely understood. There was no diving to speak of as we conceive of it now. One of the great joys that has been given to us human beings in the latter part of the twentieth century is not just scuba but snorkeling. You know, just being able to swim down deep and look up to see the iridescent way that light plays in the water—these shafts of cathedral light cutting through and the shoals of fish and the sheer majesty and colors of life under the water.

And for Victor Hugo, this book is an invitation to step into the unknown. Darwin is working seven years earlier, 1859. We're at that cusp where naturalism is becoming a discipline, which is shaking up the world because it is questioning the nature of God. It's explaining human existence as being part of natural phenomenon rather than being superior to it, and Hugo is in that questing mindset. *Who am I in relation to this enormity, in relation to this infinite?*

MW: I loved the little chapter about the infinite wind. I spent most of the book being patient as a reader, but I could zip through this condensed elemental window of a chapter. There's this amazing book called *Waves of Knowing* by a social scientist and surfer named Karin Amimoto Ingersoll. It's all about Kānaka Maoli oceanic knowledges. She talks about how, in this Indigenous knowledge tradition that she comes from and that her community members use, people can read the wind by the surface of the water: the direction of the ripple, the velocity, and the color of the water. When I read her book, I got chills, because I learned so much of that from surfing and growing up in the ocean. But her knowledge is so comprehensive. It's so deeply cultural. I am left too with this image in my head of the octopus being absolutely larger than life. As if it's a giant squid, and I, in Gilliatt's shoes, am catching myself doubting my impression of it. What did you think?

AC: I love the octopus sequence, because sometimes Hugo is just preposterously over-the-top. He has taken Gilliatt to the edge in terms of his experience trying to combat the elements in this environment, and then— good Lord!—he's trapped by an octopus in the water. It's sublime. I was fascinated by the fact that we don't exactly know what creature it is. It's in Hugo's imagination as an octopus, but just a few years later, Jules Verne comes along and uses exactly the phrase "the devil fish" to describe the squid that attacked the *Nautilus*.

MW: We know it's some big cephalopod, but we don't know which one.

AC: The other thing which is so exciting about the subaquatic world is that it is beautiful like a dreamscape, but there is always the possibility of nightmares existing in the recesses of the deep. Somewhere there is a marine biologist in the 1850s who has written this account of a cephalopod and who is saying, *Can I sue this guy for plagiarism?* because clearly Victor Hugo is just riffing on something he read somewhere: "There, at a depth to which divers would find it difficult to descend, are caverns, haunts, and dusky mazes, where monstrous creatures multiply and destroy each other." Apparently "The Abyss" was one of Victor Hugo's working titles for this book, describing sequences that are existentially on the edge of dream life.

MW: And those existential questions parallel Hugo's exile! I loved that the oceanic elements were there, but it's not really a book *about* the ocean. It's really a book about living through a huge historical moment, isn't it? I'm reading, thinking about how rapidly *our* world is changing as well: interconnected political and ecological crisis after crisis; how we're able to sit over Zoom and talk across an ocean, but we don't know how anything is going to affect our lives a hundred years, even ten years from now. I feel like this book hinges around a similar anxiety over retrospect.

AC: Oh yes, Hugo's writing in times of great uncertainty. I think that juxtaposition between the natural world and the industrial force of man is constantly in opposition here. To me, Hugo wants to ask big questions like, *Where are we going? What is the dawn of this new age? Where is it going to take us?* There's the section where he describes so many big fish eating little fish— the sea as a metaphor for existential angst: "To gaze into the depths of the sea is, in the imagination, like beholding the vast unknown, and from its most terrible point of view. The submarine gulf is analogous to the realm of night and dreams."

There *is* another sort of reading of the novel. What is the wreck, and who is this man on this rock? Hugo's more than just a writer; he is absolutely the hero and the idol of the democratic imperative in France through these years of revolution. He has earned that stature, even before he wrote *Les Misérables*. In the midst of the upheavals that followed 1848, he might have become president of France, placed there by the Left as a sort of nominal symbolic figurehead. Instead, what happens is that Louis-Napoléon comes in and stages this coup, and Victor Hugo runs for his life. There are massacres, and many of the people in the assembly on the Left are butchered at this point. Eventually, he makes his way to relative safety in Guernsey. In an allegorical interpretation, Hugo is the man on the rock, and the wreck is France under Napoléon III.

MW: It doesn't seem like a stretch then to imagine the steam engine rescue represents Hugo observing some of the early contradictions of capitalism too. The big fish and little fish. Capitalism making life easier in certain ways, while making it harder in others. Why else would the book hinge around *rescuing* the engine and not the more dramatic crash event? It makes me so curious about what the fishmongers were talking about in the market, selling their local fish. What local history and ancient cultural understanding or lore didn't make it into the novel that may have either got wiped out by Christianity or industrialization?

AC: I think Hugo's full of contradictions, and he can see the ills of this new age and the peril that is ahead in this new age, but he also extols the glories of it because he believes in the indomitable will of mankind, overcoming the elements. Gilliatt is like a pre-Nietzschean superman. We have this society on an island in the middle of the English Channel that has been dependent upon agriculture and fishing, but it's so interesting that the toilers of the sea are not the fishermen. We barely have any fishermen. They're not there. The toilers of the sea, if anything, are the representatives of this new industrial age.

We have this steam ferry introduced, which the people of Guernsey initially consider to be a terrible threat, but then they see that their livelihoods will be transformed by it. The other toilers of the sea that are represented are the sea captains that we meet in various inns in Normandy and Saint-Malo, who are trading in sugar from the West Indies and indigo and cocoa from Guatemala . . .

And all of a sudden, we're seeing an entirely different kind of world. But then we have this *wreck*. Not necessarily in the sense that Hugo is metaphorically showing industry as the wreck because it deserves to be wrecked, but rather this precious object has been ruined and our hero's quest is to bring it back. It is so important to the story, effectively extolling the wonders of this intricate device, this steam engine.

MW: I'm interested that you see Gilliatt as a superman. I'm not sure I see that. He's this guy who goes on this mission, a guy in love with a local woman—tale as old as time. He accomplishes his mission but sees the woman, the literal object of his desire, engaged to another man, so he lets his masculinity deflate and "cedes" her to her chosen fiancé. I put this in quotes because of course no one has ownership over anyone. I think there's a reading here that critiques masculinity, that mocks it. Déruchette as a character, really the only woman in the book, is totally flat. Hard for me to say if this is Hugo being just kind of sexist or another critique of masculinity, but she reads as a noncharacter.

AC: Hugo can write complex female characters, like Fantine and Esmeralda, and others I totally agree are flat, like Cosette in *Les Misérables* and Déruchette in *Toilers*. I guess for many (male) writers in that century of turbulence and revolution, that type of domestic ideal seemed a kind of goal to aspire to. For us looking back it seems so anodyne, but for Dickens and Hugo, achieving passive domesticity is the goal of all that struggle. It's the utopian future they want to believe in.

But as I said, Hugo's full of contradictions. He's riffing, wrestling with ideas, endlessly responding to circumstance. For me, the flaws are what make his writing so human.

MW: What do you think enables Hugo as a writer to be so responsive to his circumstances? I feel like a lot of authors have their topic and that's what they engage with, the lens they look through, but he really seems to have been engaged with where he was *physically*. What tools do you think let him do that?

AC: That's a great question—and yes, I think the physical is the key here. Victor Hugo walking the streets, endlessly inquisitive. When I'm with my students in Paris, we go "bookpacking" with *Les Misérables*. We visit the sewers, the backstreets, the old "passages." We trace the physical inspiration for all those digressions that make Hugo's novels so exciting.

I think of him as a bit like a jackdaw, spending the whole of his life picking up shiny things that he then stuffs into his books. Whatever is around him at that moment is his particular cause of fascination. His stories are like walking into a junk shop and looking around at the strange ephemera of the past, a skeleton upon which he hangs a whole load of glorious detail. In the case of *Notre-Dame*, it's a fantastical piece of medieval nonsense, but the fundamental thread is Victor Hugo wanting to tell you fascinating things about France, the progress of humanity from a hierarchical to a democratic age, architecture and the way that architecture is a way of reading human history. It's amazing stuff.

MW: I'm completely convinced that I have to read that book next. I grew up really working class, shopping exclusively at thrift stores and swap meets. A salvage approach to life, scavenging and using whatever you *have* to make whatever you *can*, really informed my art practice and scholarship. Your metaphor absolutely highlights all of the dimensionality and the layers of surprises that one gets reading a Hugo novel like a secondhand shop. I loved his practical descriptions of textiles in the book too. Like Lethierry, who preferred his tarpaulin overcoat to everything else, so he'd go into town wearing his sailing jacket. I love thinking about this pitch pine–coated canvas jacket two hundred years after it was first conceived.

AC: When you started to read *Toilers*, what did you think of Hugo's voice and his tone? How did he read to you?

MW: I really got the sense of the skeleton in *Toilers* with the limpets, the direction of winds information, the box he uses to keep money dry. But I had a really hard time with the style of writing, the grammar, the diction, the syntax. A lot of what I was thinking about, especially when I first started reading this book, was: *I wish I could read French*. It feels like doing a little bit of translation in the way that reading an ecotoxicology paper can feel like doing a type of translation, where it's obviously not a completely different language, but it requires a couple of steps of processing.

I was finding myself at first *really* trying to pay close attention and comprehend each sentence before I comprehended the next, but that's not usually how I read. Usually, I read for energy and feel and dynamic, so I started letting myself read the way I would read poetry. It's okay to just *zip* through a novel to see how it feels and see what sticks to you. I read Hugo the way I would read Inger Christensen, who is one of my favorite poets. She builds these comprehensive worlds that have layers and layers and layers of cosmic analysis stacked on them, but with such concrete images. I think *Toilers* lends itself to that.

AC: That nails it. Exactly.

MW: So I started letting myself zip through, and then there were moments where I would have to double back and figure it out. It felt like being on a road trip, but what you said about his writing style makes so much sense. I would have these moments where, every fifteen minutes or so, I'd be taking another screenshot of a passage that, like reading poetry, I would think, *This line is it*. It was absolutely delightful having this categorical fiction experience of the story unfolding and getting hit by the absolute precision of some of Hugo's sentences.

AC: As he builds to a climax his style does change too, and I'm getting a sense that you found it easier to read as you adjusted. The length of a paragraph reduces, and he gets to these marvelous moments when a paragraph is just a line, and sometimes a paragraph is just a phrase, and all of a sudden, he's writing a form of free verse. You can feel his hand flying across the page, the ink splattering. At those moments, you can really just glide through his thoughts.

MW: I love thinking about what it was like for him drafting and revising this novel, because like you're saying, there are these moments of feverishness and fine-grained detail. It seemed like I was feeling his thoughts as I was reading it, whereas the intro to the story and the background all felt much more meted out and conscientious.

AC: It is admittedly a very strange novel! The middle section is just Gilliatt on his rock—sixty thousand words without dialogue or any other characters. That section reminded me of Hemingway, *The Old Man and the Sea*. It's wonderful and transcendent, but before you get to that bit there's a whole chunk of exposition. All these characters needing to be introduced and a ferry that needs wrecking, interspersed with digression after digression. Within the very first page of the book he's telling us about Gilliatt's house being haunted, and then he's off on a whole load of stuff about the superstitions of Guernsey. I have to just relax into it. *Oh yeah, Victor, here we go. Take me on your journey. Tell me about it.* I have to go with him as you would go with a slightly eccentric uncle who wants to take you on a walk through the woods and tell you about mushrooms, sharing all the marvelous thoughts bursting out of his brain.

MW: I absolutely loved going down that rabbit hole. I've been thinking a lot about patience and just being absorbed in this story. Getting absorbed in

Toilers is obviously not the same as not having cell service for a week, but it did force my attention in a way that required a real commitment from me.

AC: I feel, as I give myself up to some of these forgotten classics, that it's like visiting a foreign country. It's like the privilege of stepping into another culture and exploring all that is different than one's own. There's the moment on the island where Gilliatt steps down into a subaquatic cave, and it's one of the most electrifyingly beautiful descriptions of essentially an extraordinary subterranean temple. Hugo describes the workings of the vegetation on the rock as if it were a Saracen buckler or engraved vase. You're able to envision these wonders *with* him and be taken by surprise.

MW: I really appreciate that you brought up wonder. I feel like that's such an important point and often so hard to access in so much of working life, right? So much of life is the grind and toil to get stuff done.

AC: Absolutely. The sadness is that we so often consider this classic stuff to be work. My poor students who've been *forced* to read classics. I mean, way to kill the reading experience by giving them books under duress. I think there is a joy in coming back to these reading experiences out of a sense of curiosity, letting go, and releasing oneself into them. Not through a sense of obligation or responsibility or need—simply because they exist, and you can be taken to extraordinary places.